THE
SELDOM
WINGS

ALSO BY BEKA WESTRUP

WINGED SPIRITS TRILOGY

The Seldom Wings

Book #2 (TBA)

Book #3 (TBA)

THE ETERNAL BRIDES SERIES

Demons and Roses (4.2.24)

SALT AND EARTH DUOLOGY

Blood in the Tea Leaves (Prequel Novella)

Beneath the Bloody Aurora

Book # 2 (TBA)

STANDALONES

Song of Dark Tides (11.28.2023)

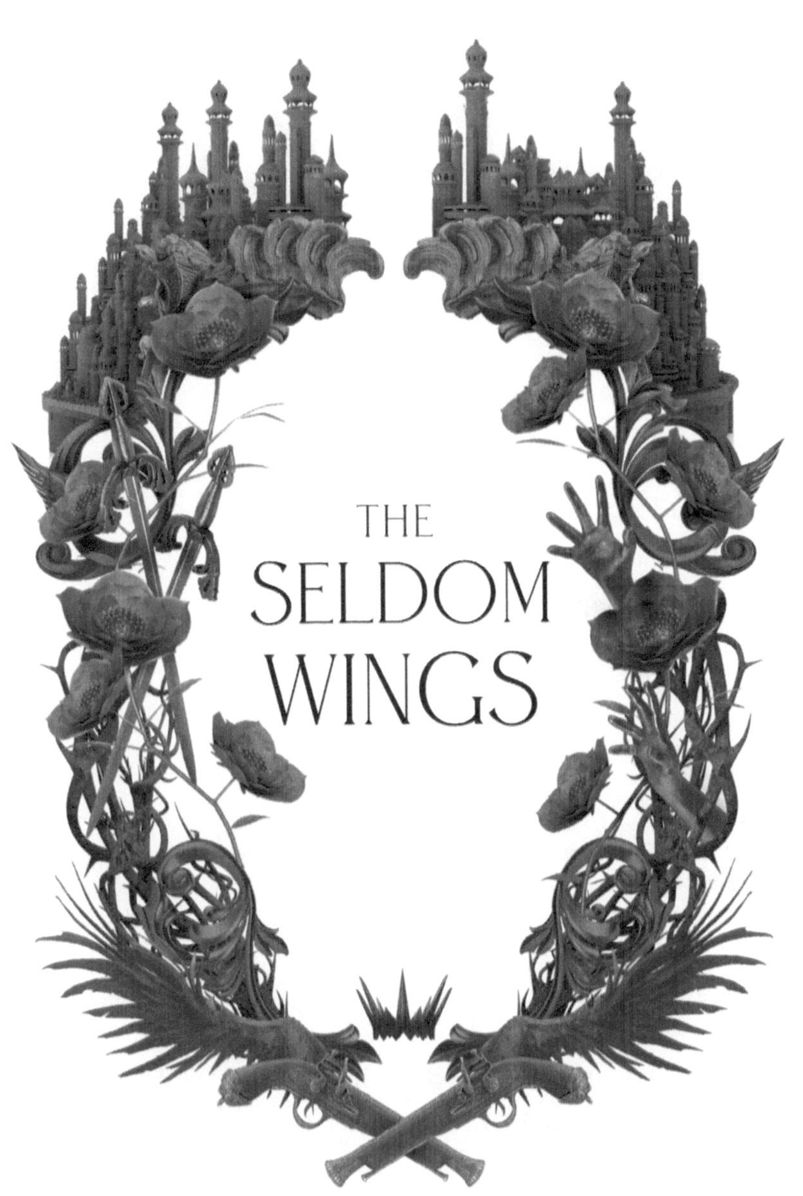

THE
SELDOM
WINGS

BY BEKA WESTRUP

First published in the United States of America August 2023 by Beka Westrup

Cataloging-in-Publication Data is on file with the Library of Congress.

ISBN: 979-8-9863087-3-9 (paperback), 979-8-9863087-2-2 (e-book)

Author website: https://www.bekawestrup.com

Cover Design: Fay Lane

Internal Art (character art): MsMorbid (@msmorbid on Twitter, @msmorbid.art on Instagram)

AUTHOR'S NOTE

This dark fantasy trilogy features a morally gray FMC who doesn't always do the right thing, or even the wrong thing for good reasons. She's complicated and has a lot of growing to do. If you aren't one for "difficult to love" women, then this probably isn't the book for you.

Also, please note that this book does end on a cliffhanger.

Content Warnings:

- Explicit Sexual Content
- Blood and Gore
- Violence
- Death
- Mention of Dead Parents
- Mention of Child Abuse and Neglect
- Animal Death (horse)
- Manipulation Using Sex
- Trauma/Grief Bonds
- Alcohol Consumption
- Mention of Drug Use

PLAYLIST

1. marjorie by Taylor Swift
2. Pierre by Ryn Weaver
3. Honeysuckle by Greyson Chance
4. Break It Right by Emelie Hollow & Ruben
5. Drifting by NF
6. I am not a woman, I'm a god by Halsey
7. Close My Eyes by Hey Violet
8. Arcade (feat FLETCHER) by Duncan Laurence
9. Start a Riot by BANNERS
10. DARKSIDE by Neoni
11. Bad Bitch by Bebe Rexha
12. I Did Something Bad by Taylor Swift
13. The Greatest by Sia
14. Heavy Heart by MOTHICA
15. Trust Issues by Olivia O'Brien
16. Flowers Turn to Fire by O+S
17. Eyes Open by Taylor Swift (Taylor's Version)
18. Back To Me by Daya
19. Wolves by Selena Gomez & Marshmello
20. Angels Like You by Miley Cyrus
21. Just Pretend by Bad Omens
22. Anti-Hero by Taylor Swift

To those who showed up in my life right on time

OTHANA
IMPUNDULU
STYMPHALIAN
HARPIES

SPHINX

FENIX

MALFORIAN
HALCYON
QUINTESSENTIALS
COCKATRIZ

PROLOGUE

Marjorie

THE END OF THE GREAT INVASION

A song of death filled the island – a keening, clicking abyss that took soul after soul, never hesitating, never ending. It even had a smell, like rusted metal and rotten flesh caught in the teeth of whoever it touched, and it certainly touched *them:* the four sisters of Fenix royalty currently tucked into a gnarled bit of forest, hidden from the war waging around them.

"You have to let him go, Joan." Marjorie placed a hand on her twin's shoulder.

Joan shook her off, a low snarl rolling in the back of her throat. The other sisters threw stares of concern in their direction, but Marjorie knew it was only fear. It was the tension and gravity of this night that made her twin so cross, so skittish. War had brought out the most unexpected things in all of them.

Of the four sisters, Joan had always been the gentlest,

warm and nurturing, a gift from the Motherly Goddess herself. She had blood on her hands now – putrid, blackish blood.

Joan rocked their youngest sibling in those stained arms. Her fine dress was ripped in several places, and Marjorie could see the bleeding wound on her leg making her limp. Still, her sister paced. She hadn't put their brother down for longer than a few hours since their mother died, and Marjorie could only imagine how painful this separation must seem to Joan after what they'd seen.

Marjorie grimaced, her body vibrating with impatience. She clenched her hands into fists to keep from forcefully yanking the infant from Joan's arms. They didn't have time for this, for *grief*. Their people didn't have time.

Joan lifted her gilded eyes to meet Marjorie's. "How can we even be sure this will work?" she demanded. The golden wings peeking over her shoulders ruffled in irritation. Her auburn hair was displaced by the rippling feathers, red flyaways clinging to her tear-stained cheeks.

"We must *make* this work," Marjorie replied softly. "There's no other option."

Ellie stood from where she'd been crouched in the center of the room, tracing runes into the floorboards of the abandoned hut. "The Fenix wouldn't let all of us die." She looked between the twins, then to their youngest sister, Helvi, who stared out at the whistling palms and the ship waiting in the harbor. "Would it?"

Helvi hadn't said anything since the war started, since their father died, for days now. Marjorie was beginning to worry she'd never speak again. What a tragedy that would be, considering she had the voice of a lark, every word practically a song.

She wasn't even of age, and here she was, preparing to die.

Joan scoffed, wiping angrily at her tears. "Since when have the mighty spirits ever cared for us past conception?"

"They cursed our wings after giving them to us," Ellie murmured, more to herself than the others as she bent to thicken the lines of another rune. "That's not really encouraging, is it?"

"Now isn't the time to indulge doubt or fear," Marjorie declared, turning to the corner of the room. "Spiro, it's time."

A figure peeled itself from the shadows: a male who pledged his allegiance to their family generations ago, who remained with them throughout the long centuries, war, and unspeakable loss. He strode up to Marjorie, his black wings splayed, his full height reaching to about her waist. His inky hair fell in a limp curtain around his pale face, but his onyx eyes glistened. He was old for their kind, clever and conditioned for moments such as these – moments of tremendous responsibility.

Spiro pulled his leather satchel forward, revealing the charmed interior like a soldier might present a sword.

Joan hesitated only a moment longer, then nodded sharply. Whispering a goodbye, she pressed a kiss to their brother's slumbering head and laid him inside, the child's four golden wings and the weight of the world curled around his tiny shoulders.

Spiro closed the satchel loosely enough to allow air in, then cradled the bag to his stomach and turned to each of the sisters in turn, bowing low. It was the only goodbye he allowed himself before he slipped out of the shack through the broken door frame.

In the distance, the volcano in the center of the island spewed rivulets of steam. Marjorie could feel the fury building, the anger of the disturbed Spirit hidden deep beneath.

The Fenix *would* come.

All four sisters gathered around the window and watched

Spiro dart across the valley between the dilapidated hut and the island's beach dunes, weaving around the ruins scattering the grassy expanse, the forgotten relics and statues. About halfway across, the infant began mewling like a lamb, and the sisters weren't the only ones to hear it.

Across the valley, where palms and grass met sand, a figure emerged from the darkness. The way it walked was lanky and wild, its limbs not quite symmetrical, and the sound it made… the *clicking*.

It was the enemy.

Helvi saw it first and gasped. Joan lurched for the window, a thread of orange flame already curling around her hand as she stretched toward the threat.

"Don't," Marjorie snarled, gripping her sister's arm and pulling her back. "Our position can't be given away, not yet."

"But—"

"They'll be fine. Watch."

Spiro was more than capable. One of the crumbling statues of The Great Mother came to life behind the enemy soldier. Rocky arms seized the clicking creature and ripped it open along the seams of its body, tearing through stitches and sinew and rot. Spiro hurtled past the corpse hanging from the now-still statue and disappeared into the foothills of sand. To safety. To the departing ship.

The sisters released a collective breath.

Joan turned to Marjorie, tears of acceptance glimmering in her eyes. "How soon?"

"Any minute now." Marjorie surveyed the floor. "Is it finished?"

Ellie nodded.

"And you made sure it's correct?"

"I'm as sure as I can be without the confirmation of a witch," Ellie replied dryly. "If you haven't noticed, none of them were eager to stick around and help us."

A brutal wind swept into the hut. As one, the four sisters turned to face it, watching blue-white frost creep over the edges of the busted door.

Marjorie ran to the doorway, leaning out to stare into the star-speckled sky. The air was thick with distant screams, but when her eyes landed on the troupe of seraphim flying in wide circles above the hut, she smiled.

She'd discovered something infinitely lovely in the midst of this agony: a place in herself that loved without reason or hesitation, foolish and wonderful in equal measure.

The figure at the head of the flock, the crowned male with three sets of white wings, didn't look down at her. None of the lesser soldiers did, either. The male flying on his left, though, a speckling of silver threaded through his feathers, returned her smile with a flash of teeth. She could have picked him out of any crowd, any army, because he was *hers*.

Marjorie's hand drifted to the tender flesh above her left breast, to the promise they'd made in blood and secret. His heart beat with hers now, finally and forever in the same rhythm.

He could have still been standing beside her, whispering in her ear, *"I will love you until I can love no longer."* Never alone... not ever again.

They would pass through the veil together.

"The Halcyon are here." She retreated from the threshold and walked to the circle of runes, beckoning her sisters to join her. "Come. Let's finish this."

They linked hands, Marjorie to Helvi to Ellie to Joan.

"We'll see each other soon," Marjorie said, meeting each of her sisters' eyes. "On the other side."

It was a wretched lie – but the less her sisters knew, the better.

Ellie hummed in agreement, the vibration radiating from the back of her throat. Then she spit out a dusting of sparks, just a little magic to trigger the rest. Flames fell from her tongue and skittered over the runes, waking their power. Her fire filled the circle, yellow and as bright as the sun. The runes glowed a soft blue in return.

Joan joined the song, then Marjorie.

The black markings on their collarbones gleamed with an orange luminescence. One by one, they summoned all the fire in their veins, and hoops of light flickered to life above them, spinning threads of molten gold around their heads.

Only flashes of the world were visible to Marjorie beyond her halo – her sisters, her last moments, the passionate love she'd had so briefly and the family she'd lost. Her heart fissured for her little brother, who would not experience such joy, such enormous, unending love. Goddess willing, he would be the one to return, to revive the others, and he would have it then.

Helvi looked around at her sisters, staring blankly until it seemed the reality of everything hit her at once. Her body began trembling, and she opened her mouth, straining to form one syllable, then another. She kept trying, until at last the music returned to her.

Her halo woke above her, brightest of them all.

Marjorie thought it might have been the loveliest thing she'd ever heard, ever seen. Until she saw what became of them next.

They burst into violent flames, coalescing into heat and light and spiraling life: pure *spirit*. Together, they speared through the crumbling roof and into the night sky. They saw everything from there, *felt everything*. Their magic spread open over the land like a set of magnified wings. They burned and burned, submitting to something more than themselves, a greater immortality.

Ice tickled the outer edge, a reminder of love that would soon be forgotten.

As they fell upon the island, turning what remained of their home to ash and ice, they felt the rip in time and space – its form, its curves, the utter greatness of it, miles long where it should have only been yards.

Whatever creature tore into this world was more powerful than they were prepared for, and it carried a bleak magic that would not be overcome.

CHAPTER 1

PRESENT DAY

Rolling onto my back, my gaze locked onto the immense green canopy above me. The leaves fluttered. Streaks of coral and rouge penetrated the branches, the sunset washing the forest in a dreamy glow. The most dangerous creatures in the gnashing forest were just starting to wake.

Our heavy breathing sighed through the glen.

Warmth closed in on either side of me as a rough hand caressed my stomach and hooked onto the dip of my waist. Lips found my hairline, kissing and snuffling my hair.

Lycanthropes could be sickeningly affectionate, particularly after sex, and I had two panting in my lap. My body was tacky and damp, and the last thing I desired was to feel their skin clinging to mine – but I closed my eyes and ran my fingers through the dark head of hair lying on my belly. I indulged their natures, not because I particularly wanted it, but because they needed it. Grief was a wearisome creature, and if I could ease any of its discomfort today, I would.

I'd spent the last few days helping them track down a Vargwolf that had split off from their pack. They had hoped to treat their brother when we found him, but I knew how it was going to end the moment I stumbled across their hunt. Every Vargwolf I'd ever met was too far gone to help – their eyes wholly black and their fur burned away, their *humanity* burned away, from the viral fever they'd spiked.

It was a hard realization for his brothers once we finally caught up with him.

After struggling for hours with the wild creature he had become, after their bones and spirits were broken and their supernatural bodies grew weary, they finally ended his misery. I stood there with them. I watched the life leave their brother's eyes and his body shift back to a limp, mortal form at the very last second. I watched them grieve.

I just stood there.

This – sharing my body, letting them chase a bit of pleasure – had been the only way I could think of to express my sadness for them. Sex was a great distraction. There was no shortage of opportunities for it in these woods, but I wondered if I had made a mistake this time.

We'd been tangled up in this glen for hours now. They touched me like they wanted to keep me forever, but I wasn't a thing to be kept.

When the male kissing my hair started licking me, I mustered the energy to sit up. It was getting dark, and I didn't feel inclined to traverse the gnarled wood without light to guide me home. For all the years I'd resided in this place, it still had ways of disorienting me. This area of the forest in particular carried several trickster spirits.

The wolf who was nuzzling my belly – a Beta with brown skin and yellow eyes – whimpered as I disentangled myself. On my other side, the red-eyed Alpha grunted and leaned up on his forearms, but otherwise didn't express his unhappiness.

His golden hair was mangy from months of migration, but he was still beautiful.

"You could stay," he said quietly, his voice still rough from his grief-stricken howling earlier. "When our pack moves on, you are welcome to come with us."

The looks they had exchanged since we'd found their brother had warned me this was coming. I could admit, the dynamic of their pack was rather unusual. Interesting, even. By all better-known customs in the world of lycanthropy, the Alpha in front of me should not have been allowed to lead their pack. He was turned, not born – I could tell that from the bite scar on his thigh and the color of his eyes.

This pack valued ability and loyalty over breeding.

That must be why they were so open, so willing, to accept me. I admired that, just not enough to pretend I was one of them.

Glancing over my shoulder, I smiled sadly and shook my head.

The Beta frowned, nuzzling into his Alpha as I faced forward again. I dressed quickly in my dress, front-tie corset, and tights, and then plucked a dark swathe of fabric from their clothing. Shaking out the cloak, I admired the deceptive softness of it. It was thick, the kind of material meant to replace a full coat of fur.

It matched the color of my skin almost perfectly – a dusky, dark auburn.

My complexion, like my eyes, maintained a subtle undertone of amber throughout every season. At the best of times, though, it was a rich, brassy brown, like right now. While I lived under the thick canopy of the gnashing forest, I climbed the highest branches when the season turned hottest – braving exposure to the open skies and the eyes above – just to feel the last threads of day on my skin. I managed to get a nice tan that way.

"I'll take this cloak, though, if you can spare it," I murmured. "Mine was shredded." Torn up by the Valg when I'd tried to grapple him, I was lucky my cloak was the only thing he shredded.

The Alpha nodded. "Of course. May it keep you warm in the coming winter."

Unlikely. Winters here were too brutal to stay warm without a real shelter, even with the best supplies. All I had was a hollow tree, a makeshift bed of animal skins from creatures who had died naturally in the forest, and a rickety door with dried flowers hanging from both sides. This cloak would at least help delay the need to use my magic on a regular basis for a couple months longer.

Even that simple reminder of my power made it rumble threateningly under my skin.

I'd used some of it today to burn the Valg's body, but that wasn't enough to quell the call, not enough to ease the incessant pressure built up beneath my ribs. It was unbearable, but with a couple weeks since my last full expenditure, what did I expect?

I shrugged on the fabric and turned back to face the wolves. "Now, about my payment."

The Alpha's blond brows furrowed. "What of the cloak?"

With a faint smirk, I replied, "The cloak was a generous gift, one I shall cherish dearly. I'm afraid my professional wage is far higher than a single item of clothing, magical or otherwise."

They exchanged a concerned look.

"We don't have much in the way of coin," the Alpha finally admitted.

"Lucky for you, I desire something far less physical." I rolled my shoulders back, standing a bit taller. "When we were tracking your brother, you mentioned transporting him to someone after capture, an alchemist. He must be rather experienced in the arcane if you believe he could have helped with the Valgen virus."

There was a long silence, but I'd anticipated the secrecy. When they spoke of the alchemist during our hunt, they had done so quietly, and they hadn't realized I could hear their whispers.

Eventually, the Alpha hooked an arm around his knees and muttered, "He's the oldest practitioner I've ever met, but he doesn't exactly like strangers. He dislikes unannounced visitors even more."

"Are you going to call me a stranger after the time we've shared?" I pout. "The things we've done? I'm feeling so used right now, pup."

The Alpha growled at the pet name, but the threat was mild.

I had been used by them both, in the most delicious ways. A pleasant soreness swirled in my belly, and that lingering sensation served to shed the tension from my body like a reptilian would an old skin. I didn't know how long it would last, but I was grateful for any time free from taut muscles and a clenched jaw. *I might even get a decent night's sleep tonight.*

The Alpha said through gritted teeth, "I didn't mean it like that."

"Sure, you did," I sighed. "You don't trust me."

Who in their right mind would *trust me, after seeing even a fraction of what I am?*

The Beta leaned forward and interjected, "We feel protective of him, that's all. He's a cranky old male who takes good care of those in the forest without a family. Our pack wouldn't have found each other if it wasn't for him."

"I have no intention of hurting him, I promise you. I just need a little help myself."

The Alpha chuckled softly, tilting his head. "This wouldn't

have anything to do with your little display earlier, would it? Those charred embers—"

"Please," I pressed. "I just need a name."

I needed a break. I'd been searching for someone who could provide me with answers in this forest since day one. I sought answers about my magic, and I knew this would be the best place to find them. Unfortunately, I learned quickly that most ancient beings are very good at staying hidden. That was when I started helping strangers, garnering a reputation, earning favors. I knew, eventually, I would find the right person with the right knowledge. These lycanthropes were exactly that; I felt it down in my bones.

"His name is Ehlark Qinan."

The Alpha twisted to glare at his Beta, who had been the one to give up the name. A low growl of warning rolled through the glen.

I ignored the Alpha's protest and took a step closer, turning my full attention to the yellow-eyed wolf. "That sounds elvish."

The Beta nodded, unbothered by his Alpha's agitation. "He is elven, in part. He's got enough human in his blood to make him prickly, rather than a full-blown nightmare. Search for him at your own peril."

I could tell I wouldn't get anything more.

It wasn't enough information to find him on my own, but I wouldn't push my luck. Goddess forbid I *anger* these wolves. I had seen exactly how wicked and rough they could be. Hiding a pleased smile, I plucked the leather strap from my wrist and ran my fingers through my knotted hair so I could braid the length back. The weather was still warm and humid, and I didn't want it weighing on my shoulders. I should just cut it. That would be easier, but I could never bring myself to follow through, despite how often I thought about it.

This was my mother's hair first.

"You shouldn't have told her all that," the Alpha grumbled as they rose from the ground, their bodies shimmering with sweat. It was such a glorious sight, I couldn't force myself to look away yet, to depart like I knew I should.

A smug grin spread over the Beta's face. "Even if she does manage to find him, she won't hurt him. She can't. She's already promised us she wouldn't, and I don't think *anything* makes her special enough to be able to break an oath like that." He turned his smirk on me. "Right?"

Hardening under their scrutiny, I simply agreed. "You're right."

Then, I turned and disappeared into the bramble before they could demand anything more from me. As I navigated the path home, I heard their howls farewell. I felt the woods grow cold and dim. This piece of the world was as familiar with me as I was with it, so any danger lurking nearby did not rise to meet me – it knew better.

Still, I heard the forest's laughter.

I drew the sides of my new cloak closed and hurried along, letting the warmth shield me as I climbed the last few thickets separating me from my bed.

Something was waiting for me, nestled between the dried flower stalks on the door to my tree hollow. The magic that brought it here still lingered in the air, tangy like citrus with the faint scent of smoke. My heart jerked and twisted in my chest, as if awakening from a deep sleep.

It was a letter.

The letter led me back home. From above, this toxic coast always appeared like a dream.

Lights of civilization shone in soft bursts of gold throughout the smog, piercing the tapestry of thick, white brushstrokes that coated the forest. At twilight, this place became an ocean of periwinkle-tinted clouds, a beautiful poison.

I had traveled the last few miles on foot, through the quiet wild of the woods.

Sandstone brick spires emerged from the smog first on my approach. Then came blooming rose bushes. Moonlight reflected off the windows of the brick house, and the scent of rain-soaked mulch curled around me, kicked up from beneath my cloak to twine with the smoky air.

Mercy wasn't descending upon Gwaith House this night, as its Lady teetered on the brink of oblivion, because, to put it plainly, the human lands didn't know mercy as a friend.

To this coast, it was ever a reaper.

A gray veil choked everything within a ten-mile radius of the capitol city. Factories ran at all hours of day and night.

Newspapers hit the mucked streets to spread dread like a viral disease. Nothing cleansed this air, not the trees nor the frequent rain. Even the clearer skies of the beach were rarely braved, for fear of the creatures that crawled up onto the black sand to consume anything within reach of the tide. Around here, the human dilemma could be summed up in one question: *how would you most like to die?*

Mercy wouldn't arrive tonight, searching for the Lady of Gwaith House, but *I* did.

Her old window was dark, so I knew she must have switched bedrooms when she married. She never slept without a nub of candle flickering on her nightstand, and it had always broken my heart a little – her fear of the dark.

Her awareness of the world wasn't something she outgrew, like some children might outgrow fearing the shadows in their room. No, she feared monsters all too real.

Mud caked my boots and sweat drenched my skin beneath my corset, my hair a greasy mess. I wasn't at all what my family expected of me, not a vision of refinement or grace. Nor was I what I expected of myself, which happened to be the bare minimum as of late. I would have to be enough. *Enough to save her.*

Rounding the house to the servant's entrance, I found the door locked. After a few moments of pounding with my dirty fist, I sensed the room stir. Footsteps sounded, metal clicked, and the door creaked open, though only an inch.

A servant peeked through. The butler, judging from his uniform. It was late, I supposed, though time had recently lost any meaning to me. Candlelight silhouetted his tall, slender figure. He opened his mouth, but I was already shoving my way through the door. The butler tried to close the passage on my arm, but I easily overpowered him, gripping the door and wrenching on it so hard, it smacked him in the forehead.

He stumbled back, colliding with the kitchen counter

behind him. His eyes were wide, trained on my cowled face as he blinked away his shock. The edge of the door had cut into his brow, and I swallowed inky guilt as blood seeped over his eyelid.

One of his hands drifted back while the other rose to ward me off, as if it would keep me from seeing him grapple with a butcher knife on the counter. "Away, fiend."

"Where is she?" I demanded, kicking the door closed behind me.

His fingers stilled on the handle of the knife, unsettled by my feminine voice. "Who?"

I exhaled sharply. "The lady of this house."

"The lady will not have visitors. You need to leave. Now."

"She will have *me*."

He shook his head. "The lady is sick and his Lordship has prohibited any visitors. If you leave your name, I will let her know you stopped by."

Yes, she's very sick. Too sick. Why else would I be here, after I swore I would never return?

The butler stepped around me to open the back door, his hand gripping the handle of the knife so tightly, his knuckles were white. Afraid, as he should be.

"If you won't take me to her room, I'll find it myself." Before the words even registered with him, I was halfway across the threshold into the rest of the house. I entered the foyer and turned to ascend the staircase to the second level when a hand clamped down on my shoulder.

"You will not." The dull edge of his butcher knife pressed against my side.

I turned, grabbing his wrist. With one twist, the nerves in his fingers seized, and he dropped the blade. His other hand tore the hood off my head as I spun to face him, but I'd already hooked a leg behind his knee and grabbed him by the throat.

His legs buckled as he fell against the banister.

I towered over him, my teeth bared. My amber eyes glowed. Faint illumination kissed his cheeks, the twin rings of tawny light reflecting off his pupils. I had let a little power loose.

In my current state, I'm sure I looked like a threat, like a monster. I took ownership of it, of his fears and judgments, giving life to them even when doing so caused an ache in the pit of my stomach. It was easier this way – to let a stranger tell me who I was for a moment or two. It never failed to give them exactly what they wanted, what they expected, and it protected me. It kept them from seeing too much.

My father taught me well.

"I will only say this once," I snarled. "I do what I wish, whenever I wish it. I will see the Lady of Gwaith tonight, and if you get in my way, you will learn your lesson. If you touch me again, I will cut your hands off at the wrists. If you stand between us, it will be the last stand you ever make. The only life of any consequence to me is *hers*."

All the blood drained from the butler's face.

I didn't even notice the woman on the top landing until she bellowed, "What's going on down there?"

My head whipped in the voice's direction. When my eyes landed on a familiar face, my fingers loosened on the butler's throat.

"Sia, is that you?" The old maid's hand flew to her chest.

"Obviously," I grumbled. "Would you mind informing this fool of who exactly he's dealing with, so he'll leave me alone?"

Her dark eyes flicked over our bodies. "I think you're managing just fine."

I smiled faintly. I fully released the butler's throat and tugged him up by the lapels of his jacket, smoothing the mate-rial once his feet were beneath him. He remained stiff as a board. "I'm so glad we had this talk, aren't you?"

I met Lila at the top of the stairs, chuckling to myself as the butler scrambled out of the foyer.

Lila waved me down a long corridor, grimacing. "Was that necessary?"

I fell into step with her wobbly gait. She'd wrinkled further since I last saw her, the skin of her chin now drooping like a rooster's. "He shouldn't have grabbed me from behind. I have instincts."

A shadow passed over her face. "Yes. I do forget that sometimes, especially when you look like this." That was the point.

Lila led me to the master bedchambers – the same quarters the woman I'd come for swore she'd never occupy. They were once her parents' chambers. It shouldn't surprise me that she overcame her reservations; she'd been little more than a child when we spoke about it.

We had both been too young to make promises of forever.

I paused on the threshold of the room, on the edge of the solitary candle's glow. She looked different. I figured she would, but the shock of it still struck me like an arrow, sharp and piercing from a distance. Her blonde hair had lost its sheen, the curves of her face sharpened. Her skin was a sickly, bluish shade.

Her beautiful body...it had withered away to nearly nothing.

In the crook of her arm, a child slept, a child who looked like her, but full of life where she now had none.

"Tova," I whispered.

Our eyes met. Her gaze wasn't bright, wasn't warm, wasn't familiar.

A sob shook her chest. I think she attempted to say my name, but her voice was so weak, it came out strangled.

Rage swept through my spine with no destination. She had been suffering, and I was furious I couldn't exact punishment *somewhere* for such an evil. I unbuttoned my cloak and let it slip to the floor. In this moment, all I wanted to do was *hold* her. I unloaded my weapons onto her dresser—first, the belt at my waist, loaded with daggers and aerial stars, then the straps across my torso, my bow and quiver. By the time I hitched my dress to remove the sheathes from my legs, Tova was wheezing.

When I looked up, her eyes were dancing with light. She was laughing, or trying to at least. "Goddess, do you have a cannon hidden under there, too?"

My heart filled with crackling heat. This was still the Tova I loved, beyond the illness and that golden band on her finger.

I caressed the bodice of my gown and raised a brow. "In this old thing? It's hardly fluffy enough." I undid the buttons down the front of the dress and removed the dagger hidden along a bone in my corset.

"You might as well have. You've got an arsenal strapped to your body."

"Sweetheart, you know I wouldn't be able to fit a cannon between my legs. You can inspect my skirts yourself, if you want." I winked at her.

Her bony shoulders shook again with laughter, and that drew out a cough. "I forgot how naughty you could be," she rasped around the fit.

Lila grunted, but I didn't spare her a look.

She'd always been disapproving of our relationship, always a barrier trying to keep us apart because of Tova's title and her responsibilities to Gwaith. I might have slit her throat for her meddling if I didn't admire her fearlessness. She'd never backed down from me, even after discovering what I was capable of.

Tova looked over at Lila, gesturing to the child on her lap. Lila lifted the little one from the bed, and as she walked past me, I saw the candlelight travel across a swathe of long, golden hair. A *daughter* – Tova had a daughter.

The governess retreated into the hallway, leaving the Lady of Gwaith and me alone.

My humor gave way to something more tender as I placed my last blade on the dresser. I approached her bed slowly, feeling less secure than I had in years. There was only my body, my thoughts and heart, stripped bare for her the way they always were.

Every step brought me closer to her frailty.

When she sent me that letter, I knew it had to be bad, as she'd clearly been sick for a long time. I paused at the foot of the bed, crushing my fingers together in front of my stomach.

Her eyes pinched. "Please, don't be afraid of me, Sia."

She didn't mean herself in the way predators did. There had never been anything about Tova that could maim or kill – not in a physical sense, anyway. She meant the death rising in her. *Don't be afraid of death.*

"I'm not afraid." I lifted my chin.

"Of course, you are."

Yes. It seemed, lately, I was always afraid, but only of myself. I swallowed around the sudden lump in my throat, my eyes prickling as I edged around to her side of the bed. "I'm not afraid, because you're going to be okay."

"I'm not. That's why I asked you to come. To say goodbye."

I shook my head. "Don't speak like that."

"See for yourself," she whispered. Her arms opened, beckoning me into an embrace.

When I hesitated, she tapped the center of her chest. *Right here*, the motion said. *Listen.*

I perched on the mattress, and my hands pressed down on either side of her waist. Gingerly, I rested an ear against her chest. Between the folds of her nightgown, her skin burned. Though I'd been in this position before, it didn't feel the same as when we used to lay together with nothing between us. When her breath caught, it wasn't in desire. I heard the rattling.

The smog had taken her lungs away.

My ribs tightened painfully, and my voice shook as I murmured, "Oh, Tova." I met her eyes, and they were stagnant, hard – stone where there had once been flesh.

"I need you to promise me something," she said somberly.

The skin along the nape of my neck prickled. My body wanted to run from that request –

Tova knew what promises meant to me. "Why?"

"Because I'm dying, and you are the only one I can trust."

She reached for my cheek, but I swiftly pulled away. "I won't promise you anything," I replied fiercely. "This isn't your death. I won't allow it."

She narrowed her eyes at me and braced her hands beneath her, attempting to sit up. Her body trembled with the effort.

"Stop." I gripped her shoulders and pushed her back into the pillows. "You're going to hurt yourself."

Tova's hands tightened on my forearms, her nails digging into my skin. "I need you to listen to me."

I cradled her clammy face in my hands. "I *am* listening, but you're speaking nonsense."

"It's about my daughter, Sia. I need you to ensure she's not left alone. She has no one. I'm afraid of what will happen once I'm gone."

"Tova," I choked. "Don't ask this of me."

Tears pooled in her eyes. "She needs to be cared for the way *I* would care for her, the way she deserves. She needs to be told how much her mother loved her. Don't let her forget."

I understood the deeper implications of her request – it called to the depths of my heart. I knew what it was like to live without a mother, to wonder what that kind of love felt like, to covet those who had it. I would never be able to break this promise, even if my nature allowed me to.

"Promise me," she insisted.

My vision swam, blinding me briefly before the tears brimmed over. The inky droplets fell, staining her bedspread. Bracing my arms on either side of her, those tears flowed in a trail across Tova's chest and neck as my dark red hair spilled around her face.

Her sunken eyes widened at my sudden proximity, but she didn't push me away.

"I promise you," I said roughly. "She will be loved and cared for. I promise to ensure her safety, but that will be done by *you*. You are not going to die."

"How could I survive this?"

"Take my tears. Taste them."

"I can't do that." Tova shook her head sharply. She lifted a hand to my shoulder and tried to push me away, but I quickly caught her wrist. Her bones ground together like dry stones under my fingers, and her rejection brought a fresh wave of grief to the surface.

I knew it was an intimate thing to ask of her, and I knew she wasn't mine anymore. She'd moved on, but she sure as hell wasn't going to die, not if I could prevent it.

"For once, don't argue with me. You said you trusted me, so trust me now and do as I say." I shifted above her so that my tears fell onto her lips.

Her tongue darted out instinctively, dragging one into her mouth.

Once that initial tear dissolved on Tova's tongue, she reached up and took hold of me with a desperation I knew my magic had sparked. She licked my tears away, and as she did, I wept for the future we could not have.

Some minutes or hours later, I sat back, and Tova's hands found mine again, her grip a little stronger. Her coughing and trembling had finally stopped. She stared up at me with soft eyes, confusion wrinkling her forehead.

"How do you feel?" I asked.

She blinked slowly, as if navigating a maze in her mind. "I-I'm not in pain. Sia, how am I not in pain anymore?"

I knew Tova wasn't mine, that she never would be mine again, but I put that knowledge aside to lay beside her, wrapping my arms around her thin body. Though her lungs expanded easily, her airways still wheezed. I'd have to stick around a while longer, until her organs were fully healed, and that could take weeks.

I tried to be upset about it, upset about being here, in this land I wanted desperately to escape, but I wasn't. Because I was with her.

I pressed a chaste kiss to Tova's forehead before tucking her into my side, ignoring the way her body went rigid. My affection had become foreign to her; I'd become a stranger. After a minute or two, Tova's body finally melted into mine. When she finally drifted to sleep, I was left in the silence of her marriage bed, burdened with so many worries, I didn't know how much longer I would be able to breathe beneath them. Stone upon stone, weight upon weight.

It was a heaviness I carried alone.

A twinge struck my heart, and I bit down on a wince. The pain quickly ebbed, the hurt so brief that I very well could have imagined it. My hand swept up to press against the ridges of the scar over my heart, the promise hanging above my head like an executioner's sword. That was how I knew I didn't imagine it, that it was real – touching the evidence as if I could read the scar's thoughts, as if I could *change* them.

The pain was happening more and more often, a bone-deep ache that spread in a wave through my body, grinding like salt in my joints. It was a warning, but one I already resolved not to listen to. This pain would only get worse, and I just had to deal with it.

I pulled my dress up to cover the swell of my breast, hiding the scar away. I hid from it, because that was the only thing I could do.

I was tempting a spirit of destiny by being here, returning to the coast of my youth, close enough to my father that I could almost taste his bitter disappointment. It was only a matter of time before he acknowledged my presence.

It was only a matter of time before the vultures swarmed.

CHAPTER 3

A dismembered body had washed up on shore.

I reread the article, scanning every uneven line. Against my will, my eyes drifted to the gritty photo on the right. The victim was a human woman, and now, she'd be buried or burned without her legs. This killer was cutting people into pieces and taking whatever they wanted.

The newspaper transferred ink to my skin as I rubbed the thin paper between my fingers.

This was the fifth murder I'd seen since my return. The missing persons page at the back of the newspaper was full, alarmingly so. Granted, I hadn't lingered in this area in a long while, and drownings weren't exactly rare on this side of the country, but *still*.

The city also had iron barriers erected in the sea to keep the serpents from getting too close to the general population. Serpents couldn't get within a few feet of the iron without becoming violently ill, much less manipulate chain mail in order to slip through. Unlike these journalists, I knew how the serpents fed. They ate every part of their prey, until nothing was left to wash up—not even a skeleton. I'd been cautioned against the dangers of the sea since I was a child, warned to keep my distance lest I become one of them myself. If these murders belonged to the serpents, they were doing it to make a statement, and the human lands had more to fear than a growing list of missing persons.

War.

A tug on my elbow brought me back to the garden. Tova and I were ambling arm-in-arm along the rose hedges. This early in the morning, the smog was at its thinnest.

"You're ignoring me." She pushed her lower lip out, revealing a tempting pink stripe of flesh. A pang of shame curled in my stomach. It was true – she'd been prattling on about an exotic species of rose she had imported a couple years ago, and I couldn't help but tune her out.

Tova *loved* her roses. They were one of the only flowers that bloomed in this smog.

She was doing better, finally showing some color in her cheeks. I should be treasuring these moments, soaking up every glimpse and touch, because our time together wouldn't last.

I dosed her every night with my tears, weeping into vials rather than letting her lick them from my face. She didn't want that closeness. I could tell she felt guilty for letting me sleep in her bed, even that first night, though I wasn't sure why, considering her husband was nowhere to be found. When she asked me to sleep in the den downstairs, I pretended it didn't bother me, but I would do anything to get back to her bed, between her legs, and into her heart.

Maybe that was why I was still here, why I hadn't taken off in the night, left the smog and the memories of us behind. I still wondered, still hoped.

My tears had repaired the worst damage to her organs, but her deteriorated muscles were a different battle. It took several days for Tova's legs to steady enough for a walk in the gardens, so I kept my arm linked with hers, just in case.

As I lowered the newspaper, I offered up a contrite grin. "Yes, I was ignoring you. I'm sorry."

"It's okay." Her eyes flicked to the newspaper as I rolled it up like a scroll. "I know my domestic life isn't exciting – not anything compared to the adventures you must have." Her voice was loaded, clearly prying.

I pressed in closer to her, smiling warmly. "You are better than all the wonders of the world. I said I was sorry, sweetheart." I tucked her into my side, cherishing every inch of her that touched me. She was so good at making me feel needed with nothing but a forlorn glance.

I redirected the conversation before my guilt could settle in again. "I got distracted by an article about the dismembered bodies washing up on shore. How long has this been happening?"

She frowned. "Since before I got sick, when I was pregnant with Erlene – so it's been a few years now. They weren't nearly as frequent then; maybe one body every few months."

"What are the Houses doing about it?"

Gwaith House was one of several seats of authority along the western coast. Each fortune oversaw a certain stretch of land, ensuring laws were kept, the economy flowed, and that properties were taken care of. The more the land was divided, the better, especially now that taxes didn't rake in nearly enough profit for the Houses of the countryside. Human families who were smart, who had no roots in the land, fled the smog before it killed them.

"I don't know," Tova admitted, pulling her bottom lip between her teeth. "I hope they're doing *something*. It's been a long time since I've met or talked with anyone of importance. When I got sick, Destin took on my responsibilities, in addition to my father's. He's been incredible."

A surge of heat rolled through my veins at the mention of her husband. Every time she spoke of him, it was with a gentleness and affection he didn't deserve—she loved him too much, even after he abandoned her. "And the Baron?" I prompted.

Tova huffed a laugh, reaching out to tap roses as we passed them. "As if he cares for our little cities."

The Baron had enough money to tackle any issue the Houses couldn't, as long as he *wanted* to. One man lording over the rest – it was all very old-fashioned, but that was how they'd functioned ever since seraphim landed on their coast decades ago, those golden-feathered beings driven from a cluster of islands south-east of here.

Seraphim lived as separately from humans as dawn was to dusk, forming tight-knit colonies on the mainland as well as the islands, sticking close to landmarks like mountains, caves, coasts, and waterfalls, human settlements filling out everywhere else.

When those golden seraphim formed their civilization here, in the floating city above the smog, the coast's economy suffered the loss of tradesmen who couldn't stomach co-existence.

Then, the rebels appeared, eager to destroy the fragile peace struck between humans and the seraphim newcomers. That hovering city was a constant reminder to angry mortals that seraphim lived above them in *all* ways. There was nothing seraphim couldn't do, couldn't take, if they wanted it. I imagined the city made humans feel a lot like ants, and, like ants, they had formed a skeleton over their skin to keep seraphim out of their hearts.

That was one of the reasons I left this coast. Not the most important reason, but a close second.

"He'd better start caring," I grumbled, crushing the newspaper in my fist. "Before the murders spread his direction."

Tova's gait slowed. "I didn't know it had gotten this bad," she whispered. "Destin kept the newspapers from me once I was prescribed bed rest."

I ignored the mention of him once again. "You should have sent for me sooner."

Tova looked forward to where Lila and Erlene were clipping fresh roses. "I'd hoped I wouldn't have to," she murmured.

In other words, she hoped she wouldn't need me. My grip loosened on her arm. I couldn't keep the edge from my voice as I said, "Well, your stubbornness and pride nearly killed you. I gave you that quill for a reason. For emergencies. I told you not to hesitate."

Tova blinked. "It wasn't pride that kept me from writing to you, Sia." I only stared at her, and she sighed, shaking her head. "*You* left *me*, or have you forgotten?"

I wished I could. That summer was a mark on my bones, the taste of her an incandescence on my tongue. I'd wanted her to be mine more than anything, and I had been willing to do anything to make that possible. Then, she turned around and pledged herself to someone else. She had said nothing needed to change between us, but I'd known better.

Tova squeezed my hand. "I was so proud of you. You escaped the smog and everything above it. How could I bring you back here when you were living a better life? A *free* one?"

My eyebrows stitched together. "My life is not more precious than yours."

"It is." I opened my mouth to object, but she continued. "If it were only about me, I wouldn't have written at all, but for Erlene, I did. After seeing you, I'm glad I did. You look like hell, Sia. Whatever life you've been living...it's not the one you hoped for, is it?"

She was doing it again – laying my everything bare, telling me what I least wanted to hear. I could hide from bounties and predators and my father, but I couldn't hide from her.

I smirked. "I look like hell?"

"The clothes you showed up in hadn't been washed in months. You've lost some of your curves, and your *hair—*"

"What about my hair?" I demanded, self-consciously running a hand over the dark red locks cascading down my shoulder.

Her lips pursed. "You used to wear such lovely ribbons in your hair."

Yes...and she'd loved playing with them. I'd forgotten about that. I couldn't remember the last time I'd bothered making any part of me more beautiful, more appealing, just for the sake of it. "Living as a creature of the wild does not lend me such luxuries." I turned to continue our walk back to the House.

The morning smog was thickening now, and she needed to get back inside, where the air could be better controlled, but Tova stopped me.

She reached behind her dress, pulling the blue ribbon around her waist loose. Then she stepped behind me, and her hands found my shoulders, pressing down in a silent command.

When I crouched, her delicate fingers threaded through my hair. I stopped thinking, stopped breathing. She couldn't see my face, so I allowed my eyes to flutter shut as I bit my lip to stop it from trembling. Tova meticulously worked through a few knots, gathering the hair around my ears to the back of my head. She was silent as she weaved the ribbon and secured it in a bow, but her fingers lingered, gentle and warm, perhaps the only affection she had left to offer me.

When she finished, she tapped my shoulders, and I rose.

She remained a warm presence at my back. "You weren't

meant to live that way, Sia." Her voice was barely audible over the squealing of her daughter a few yards away.

I met her gaze over my shoulder.

Tova smiled. "There's a wild inside you that you carry wherever you go." She shook her head, chuckling softly. "You're not a single creature. You're the whole damn forest."

She might have been right.

I was wild, dangerous, and my head swirled with a thousand thoughts that could easily pass as monsters. She was wrong about one thing, though – it didn't matter where I ended up, because I didn't fit in *anywhere*.

CHAPTER 4

"I have a favor to ask of you."

I looked up from the piano, even as my fingers continued to flit across the keys, a soft melody filtering through the den.

Tova sat on the couch adjacent to me, Erlene dozing in her lap, and a book cradled in one hand. Her eyes pinched in hesitation. "You have done so much for me already. I know I shouldn't expect anything more, but—"

"What do you need?" I asked, letting my hands fall into my lap.

She shifted, holding Erlene a little tighter. The girl stirred, clutching the collar of her mother's dress before quickly drifting off again. "I need you to find my husband."

My heart stopped. I stared at the keys, battling the urge to smash them to pieces. I wouldn't be able to ignore the mention of him this time.

"He doesn't know," Tova continued, "that I'm getting better, and I don't know how to reach him. When Destin left, he wasn't himself. He was distant, distraught by my diagnosis.

I know if anyone can figure out where he went and bring him home, it's you."

My vision blurred, and I quickly blinked the tears away. I swallowed the hot bile creeping up my throat. I hadn't even met this man, but I already despised him for leaving her like this. For making her fear for her daughter's future. For stealing her heart and making me doubt she ever loved me at all.

I couldn't let Tova see any of that. If he was what she needed, I would do my part.

Slowly, I lifted my hands back to the piano and started a new piece, something that echoed how lost I felt. "I'll leave at dawn."

When I glanced up, Tova's cheeks gleamed with tears, and I had to look away before my heart shattered entirely. "Thank you, Sia."

"It's nothing."

"It's everything."

I frowned, playing louder. I stomped on one of the pedals beneath me, hoping to drown out her weeping – I didn't even care if the child woke.

As I watched my hands dance over the ivory keys, the door to the den swung open.

Lila stood on the threshold, her chest heaving. "My lady." She hobbled into the room, nearly tripping over the fine, red-and-umber rug. She extended the envelope in her hand. "A letter arrived for you. I think it's from his Lordship."

Ice trickled up my spine. *Speak of the evil and it appears.*

Tova slid Erlene from her lap and stood with a bright smile, seeming more recovered now than ever. She took the letter from Lila, and they swept out of the room together.

As their footsteps disappeared up the stairs, I stopped playing. The last note lingered in the air. It was time for me to leave. Hopefully, that letter meant I was free from Tova's favor, that her husband would be home soon and she would be happy, and I—

I would be alone again.

I let my face drop into my hands, the lines of my palms radiating heat as I tried to slow my breathing. It was silly to stay when I knew there was no place for me. *No one* for me.

A spasm of ice spread over the nape of my neck, and the air in my lungs seemed to freeze as a light breeze hit my cheek. I looked up. The hearth in the den was ablaze, and the windows were shut against the smog. Where had the breeze come from?

A torn section of paper materialized in mid-air. It oscillated, descending toward my lap. I snatched the paper out of the air and scanned both sides, my muscles easing when I spotted the familiar writing crowding one edge.

Are you ignoring me again?

These notes had followed me around for months now. When they first started, I assumed my family was behind them. Notes like this, made with charmed parchment and ink, could be sent to anyone, as long the sender knew the name of the recipient, could visualize them in their mind. I didn't write back for a long time, but as they piled up, the voice developed a tone I didn't recognize – one of sarcasm and wondering humor. It asked about jobs I took on whenever I stepped into a stranger's business, which was often, considering how much trouble forest-dwellers so easily got themselves into. Messages would appear in my hand within days of each excursion, as if they were tracking me.

If the notes were from my father, he would have come for me as soon as he figured out exactly where I'd gone.

Then, one night, a note fell into my lap asking how long I'd be hissing at the broken ankle I sustained from a feral water nymph. A small tin of healing balm had accompanied it. I'd been in a foul mood, so I scrawled a response, complete with a crude drawing on the back that would have provoked even the most peaceful of forest spirits. I let myself simmer with equal parts anger and satisfaction, even as I opened the balm and rubbed it generously into my skin.

The bones cracked back into place instantly, and so my anger towards this mysterious being began to fade, curiosity rising in its place.

When the parchment reappeared, the response was…interesting.

I hear you're looking for information, and I'd like to help.

At the time, I'd been searching for the home the water nymphs had abandoned in favor of terrorizing the nearby rivers. It was a well-kept secret, as most homes were for those who live in the gnashing forest.

I had snarled at the parchment, yet wrote back all the same.

Unless you have access to ancient cryptid archives so you can tell me what land these water nymphs originally claimed, you can't be of any help to me. Now, fuck off.

Surprisingly, the parchment returned to me.

Consider it done, darling. I only have one condition.

I remembered rolling my eyes in irritation. *What might that be?*

Don't ignore me anymore.

The next day, a map had appeared with the next note, the nymph's land circled, and that was that. The mysterious note sender came through for me, and I stopped ignoring them.

I knew then that whoever it was had to be unbelievably brave, looking into archives near impossible to get ahold of, ones kept under lock and key. I tried my best to figure out who it was, but they kept each conversation limited to the space on a sheet of parchment, never a word more.

With each new page, I found myself writing smaller and smaller, so that the paper lasted longer between us. I came to treasure these notes and the person behind them.

I read the second sentence written on the note in my hand now.

I can't live in these conditions.

Smiling, I walked to where my possessions sat behind the couch. I withdrew an enchanted quill from my quiver, twin to the one I'd gifted Tova years ago, and leaned against the brass mantle.

Then die, I wrote, giggling as the parchment evaporated above my hand.

I twirled the quill between my fingers as I waited. My eyes locked on the fire, on the swelling, curling blaze of it. Less than a minute passed before the paper reappeared.

How absolutely ruthless of you, but I'll suffer it because you finally replied. Where have you been?

I'd wake up littered in parchment if I purposefully ignored you. You think I don't know your tricks? I smiled again, thinking of the morning I woke with several paper cuts on my face and my hollow filled to the brim. *Stop working yourself up – I misplaced your last message on my trek out west.*

A longer pause stretched before the response came, only two words.

New job?

I chewed my lip. They weren't watching me right now, it seemed. I wondered how much I should tell them about Gwaith, and I eventually settled on nothing. *No. This is personal.*

Well, you've piqued my interest.

Pique it up your ass.

You're horrible. One of these days, you're going to make me cry, and then what?

Then, I scribbled back, *you'll finally take the hint and stop bothering me.*

As the paper disintegrated, I realized my free hand was reaching toward the fire. Absentminded heat trickled from my fingertips, a deluge of black sparks that kissed and licked at the orange flames. I gasped and stepped back, shaking my hand, wicking away the warmth and the darkness forming between my fingers.

My eyes darted to the little girl sleeping beside me, and my stomach rolled. I could have hurt her – I needed to be more careful, more present. This wasn't like the great expanse of the gnashing forest, where I could lose control without facing the consequences.

I was still swallowing against the burn in my throat when the note slipped back into the room.

*Never, darling. You love it when I bother you. Just wait until
I can do it in person.*

I stared at the words, sorting out the sensations of want and hope that instantly sieved through me. They'd made the promise to meet me before – so many times this past year, I'd wished these notes would stop. This wasn't real. If it was real, the person on the other side would have faced me already.

I considered tossing the note into the fire.

Then, a scream tore through the House.

I jolted from my thoughts and followed the crying, across the foyer and up the stairs, down the hall. When I reached Tova's room, she was kneeling by the edge of the bed, her face buried in the blankets. Lila stood near the door, clutching something to her chest.

"What happened?" I demanded.

Lila passed me the crumpled letter. I scanned it, and my stomach fell through the floor.

"I'm going to kill him," I growled.

Tova lifted her red face from the covers. "No, you won't. Don't you *dare.*"

"Why are you still defending him? He has just disgraced you in the vilest manner possible."

Lila interjected, "He's only doing his duty, Sia."

I turned to her, my eyes bulging out of my skull, my pulse hissing in my ears. "What are you talking about?"

"The current Lordship of this house cannot be maintained without a woman. He's found a wife because he believed Tova would be passing soon."

I balked. "That's horrific."

"It is the law," Tova rasped, rubbing the tears from her eyes. "He did it to protect our daughter's inheritance. He must marry; otherwise, everything would have been given to one of my cousins."

"You aren't dead," I snapped.

Tova leveled an empty stare at me. "I was dying."

"He's a pig. When he finally shows his face again, I'm going to—"

"You will do nothing," Tova snapped. "He's my husband. He is the Lord of this House and the father of my child. He is all the family Erlene has left."

I glared at her. "Open your eyes, Tova. He abandoned you both."

"You will not hurt him," she declared. "*Ever.*"

"What will you do, then? Wait until he arrives with his new bride and welcome her with open arms? Make room for her? I thought you didn't want anyone else in your bed." It was a low blow, but I couldn't help myself. I couldn't believe she was so willing to overlook what he'd done – how he'd betrayed her and then informed her by letter after the fact.

Tova stared at the covers clutched in her hands. "I want to sleep now."

I took a deep breath and grabbed one of the inky tonics left on her dresser. "After you drink this. Here; it'll help with your nerves."

"I don't want it."

A spike of fury ripped through my chest. She wasn't healthy enough to skip a dosage yet. "Don't be stubborn. Take the tonic." I stalked toward her, but she stood abruptly, and I staggered to a stop as she ripped the vial out of my hand.

"*I don't want any part of you.*" Tova flung the vial across the room, and it shattered against the wall. She collapsed onto the bed, twisting away from me as she whispered, "I want my daughter, and I want to sleep."

I stood there, not moving, not breathing. Lila turned on her heel and left the room.

I should have left right then, but the pieces of my heart were scattered on the floor between us. She was the one my heart belonged to, and as long as she lived, I would love her like this, lost and ever-hoping, even when there was none.

Lila returned with Erlene and deposited her in Tova's arms. The child reached up to cradle her mother's head, and her sweet voice garbled, "Is okay, Mama."

Numbness spread down my throat and into my chest.

Lila backed away and fell into place beside me, resting a hand on my arm, but I couldn't find the strength to shake her off. If I hated myself any more, I would have crossed the room and kissed Tova to make her see the error of her heart. I would have forced her to love me again.

If I hated *her* any more, I would have walked away.

"Sia." Tova's stern voice made me jump. "Will you come here?"

I approached the bed, rounding to the opposite side, and sat down on the mattress facing her. Erlene had already fallen back to sleep in her arms.

Tova's lips trembled. "I'm sorry. I really didn't mean that."

"You did," I croaked. "But it's okay. You don't owe me an apology."

She released another rattling breath. "I shouldn't have said it, Sia. I love you. You know that, right?"

I swallowed the spark of relief in my throat. "Yes."

"You are the only one I can trust. I meant that. Lila, are you still there?"

"I am."

"Good," Tova rasped. "Then you are witness to this. From here on out, I want Sia to be Erlene's guardian. All decisions concerning my daughter's well-being will be made by her."

A frisson of terror rushed through my veins, turning my stomach with brutal hands. "That won't be necessary. I don't—"

Tova's eyes flashed open, burning brightly…so, *so* brightly. "Don't break your promise to me."

I bit my cheek. "I won't."

"Good," she repeated.

I wanted to argue. I wanted to know her mind. There was a reason she put Erlene in my guardianship. Maybe she intended to hurt herself, to finish what the sickness had started, but she was tired and holding her daughter, and there wasn't anything nearby she could harm herself with. I knew she'd felt and seen and heard enough, so I kept my mouth shut.

I reached over and took her hand in mine. To my surprise, she let me. There was so much I wanted her to allow, but I was content to suffer in silence with whatever she gave me.

Lila eventually left, and I remained in the bed beside Tova, even though I hadn't been allowed to sleep here since the first night. Tova didn't seem to care tonight, though. I watched sleep consume her, then stared blankly at the ceiling until the darkness consumed me, too.

What felt like moments later, I woke to a high-pitched cry.

A silky voice brought me to consciousness. It was Erlene. She sat beside Tova, shaking one of her thin shoulders, but Tova wasn't waking up.

I noticed her blue lips and shot upright. I shook her shoulder myself. I called her name. Tova didn't answer, didn't breathe. Screams filled the room, and I realized after Lila burst through in her robe that it was me. *I* was screaming.

Erlene touched her mother's face. *"Mama. Mama."*

A rumble sounded then from the back of Tova's throat, raising the hairs on my neck. One of her lifeless fingers twitched.

I surged forward and scooped Erlene into my arms. I tried not to think about how those little hands grasped at the empty air – how I ripped the child from her mother so easily.

Erlene began kicking and thrashing as I backed away from the bed.

Another one of Tova's fingers twitched. A muscle in her neck ticked.

I reached for the dagger on my thigh, the one I didn't have the energy to remove before I fell asleep.

Lila looked between the dagger and Tova's body. She nodded, turned to set the candelabra in her hand on the dresser, and reached for Erlene. The old maid's eyes were dark and knowing.

I shied back. "I can't." My admission was barely a whisper.

Lila grimaced. Her eyes hardened as she took another step forward. "I can."

She wrapped her leathery fingers around mine and removed the dagger from my hand. Guilt plummeted through me, but I didn't give it a chance to change my mind. I fled the room, the child fighting against my arms with every step. I walked until I couldn't anymore, but we only made it to the corridor.

From the end of the hall, I heard a moan as Tova re-woke. Lila muttered a choked apology, and then there was a squelch as I listened to my blade sink into Tova's stomach—her sacral chakra, where her human spirit resided.

There was no mercy for the human race, even in death. Mortal souls lingered, and the world could only speculate why.

I knew, or I liked to think I did.

The mortal second life lasted three days, and that was if a remnant soul could not reap another before then. Whatever rose in death stopped at nothing until it latched onto another human soul, someone to accompany them to the beyond. They lost all feeling, all sense, all...*self*. The human spirit didn't want to be alone when they passed. They were not designed for it. That was why so many mortal couples died together. If one passed silently in the night, they would both be gone by morning. I've heard of many who willingly laid themselves at their dead lover's mercy, ready to brave anything that came after, as long as they braved it together.

It was beautiful, if a little tragic.

He should have been here. Her husband. Destin should have loved her like that, loved her beyond life, loved her recklessly and endlessly, loved her so much it hurt. She shouldn't have died *alone*.

Erlene wailed in my ear. Even as a child, I knew she felt it, that she was experiencing the loss as I once had. We were the same – two daughters left behind. Two daughters, abandoned by the ones who had fiercely loved us into existence. I clutched Erlene tight enough that I imagined I could absorb the pain she radiated. I imagined I might steal her agony.

She shook in my arms, her nails digging into my back.

"I'm here," I cried. "I won't leave you alone."

She screamed louder, as if to say I was the last person she wanted. I knew it was true.

My legs gave out and we sank to the floor together. My veins simmered, they *burned*. I pressed a hand to the floorboards beneath us and shoved that heat away, into the destiny lines of my right palm. Better that I burned there than burn the child in my arms. The scent of wood and polish and char drifted through the hall as my hand left a brand on the floor.

My ears rang, my head aching with every shriek. So, I did the merciful thing. I lied.

"It will be okay," I whispered. I said it over and over, until Erlene quieted enough to hear the rest. "Someday," I told her, "this won't hurt so much."

Tova had no intention of living after that letter came. She'd given up her will to keep fighting. As Erlene, worn out and sniffling, fell asleep against my shoulder, I realized something else that cleaved my heart completely.

All her life, Tova chose her House, her duty, over everything else. Over freedom. Over herself. Over me. Tonight, though, her heart chose love – love for her husband. Tova had not truly loved me at all, not enough, not like *this*. She loved Destin, and every inch of my soul *loathed* him for it.

I'd be forced to look him in the eyes. I'd be forced to coexist with him. The promise I made to Tova still stood: ensure Erlene would be cared for, that she would get the love and attention she needed from a father who couldn't be bothered to watch his own wife die. With his new bride coming home with him, I would have to ensure that *she* cared for Erlene properly too.

I was shackled once more to this goddess-forsaken coast, this time by a promise I'd made to a dead woman.

Deep down, I knew that no amount of my tears could have saved Tova from succumbing to her broken heart. Still, that didn't stop me from wishing I had done something—*anything*—to protect her.

CHAPTER 5

I stood expectantly on the front steps. In the distance, through the swirling smog, a train of carriages passed through the gates. The instant they appeared on the horizon, Lila ran through Gwaith House, summoning staff away from their tasks.

His Lordship was finally home.

When I heard, I'd been tempted to duck out from under Lila's scrutiny and take Erlene on a walk through the gardens, but I knew from the look in the governess' eyes that she might very well strangle me if we disappeared. I supposed it was a good idea, to let Erlene greet her father.

In just a few weeks, this girl had wrapped me around her finger. Every time I looked at her, I found new similarities to Tova—the way she wrinkled her nose when the smog was at its thickest, or how her laugh brightened the entire room and echoed in my head for hours. I don't know when exactly it happened, but she became precious to me. My time and attention, what little love I found my heart still capable of, were trained on her, exactly the way Tova had desired.

I knew someday, I would regret caring so deeply. Someday, I'd resent Tova for finding this final way to strip me to the bone. For now, though, I cherished these moments, these treasures that lasted just long enough to stitch me back together.

Erlene's little hand tightened in mine.

She hid behind my skirt as the carriages drew closer, and I squeezed her fingers. She peeked around me to stare at the carriage as it stopped directly in front of the steps. The carriage that carried Erlene's father and Tova's widower.

He hadn't bothered coming home in time for the funeral. It was just me and Lila, standing at the edge of the forest as my flames consumed Tova's body. Me and Lila, burying the ashes. If I hadn't already wanted to, that alone would have made me want to kill him – but I also knew, sooner or later, my past would come for me. When that time came, Erlene couldn't come with me, nor could she be left alone here with humans I didn't trust to care for her. Sorting out this mortal was my only option.

I was flirting with the impossible.

As the carriage rolled to a stop, I brushed my fingertips over the thick, bronze necklace on my collar, ensuring it laid flat. The dress I wore strained over my breasts, inhibiting my breath. The skirt was short enough that the breeze tickled my ankles.

It made me a little sick to wear Tova's clothes, but she'd insisted on disposing of my only dress when I'd arrived. I resisted the urge to run a hand through my hair and dislodge the ribbon I'd tied it back with. I couldn't shake Tova's words. I couldn't stop wearing the ribbon she gave me – her reminder of the woman I was, beyond my survival, my instincts.

Searching for her felt like grappling with a needle in the dark. I just kept bleeding.

The carriage door swung open, and a man ducked

through the threshold. His mop of dark hair spilled over his forehead. The hand that wrapped around the handrail was delicate and long. Once his frame cleared the door, he straightened and lifted his chin to scan the stairs. His body wasn't spectacular by any means, even by human standards, but it was lean. He wore simple clothing, black and finely sewn. His slate eyes seemed to simmer as they slid over me, his hands dropping to shake out the sides of his tailored jacket.

Those slender fingers brushed over the bronze gun on his hip, its flared barrel pressing into the top of his thigh. That, at least, was rather intriguing. There weren't many weapons like that on the market, here or anywhere else. I wondered where he managed to get his hands on one.

I understood Tova's attraction.

The symmetry of his face was pleasant, with cheeks that hollowed in ever so slightly, more marble than man. His jaw and nose struck sharp angles. He looked all at once wicked and gorgeous. There was even a touch of the feminine there. *Pretty bastard.*

A young blonde woman followed him out of the cab, but Destin didn't spare her a glance as he forged ahead, ascending the staircase with his eyes locked on Lila.

The old governess shifted her weight, feigning a smile as he mounted the steps.

Destin's bride followed him silently, hitching up the layers of her pink dress in one hand. As she caught up to him, she hooked her pale soft hand under his elbow. She was lovely, with dark eyes and hair a striking shade of flaxseed. A familiar shade.

I swallowed my revulsion.

He'd replaced her, as if he thought finding Tova's features in a different face would be a good enough fix. I hated him more than I thought myself capable of hating anyone. I hated him more than I hated myself. The creature of nothingness I'd recently become, anyway.

Destin's voice was as tumultuous and dark as a storm cloud. "Where is she?"

Lila's throat bobbed. "Well, sir, we burned her –"

"Not *her*," he snapped. "Where is my *daughter*?"

"With me." I emerged from the line.

Destin and his bride turned. The woman's face pinched as she leaned into Destin's side, and Destin went incredibly stiff. Extricating himself from her arms, he approached the end of the line, looking me up and down.

His gaze caught on Erlene, still clutching to my skirts.

When their eyes met, she ducked back behind my legs, and I twisted to brush my fingers over the crown of her head. "It's okay. I have you," I whispered.

"And who the hell are you?" Destin's voice was louder now, harsher.

I looked up and found he had taken a step toward me. He was trying to impose himself, make me feel smaller, make himself seem more intimidating. I stood my ground. His wife inched back beside him, taking his arm for a second time. Her eyes flicked between the two of us, and I could see the insecurity even from the corner of my eye. I bit back a scoff. As if I would ever view him as anything better than the muck on my shoe.

"I'm Erlene's guardian," I said simply.

Destin's jaw clenched. "You have no right to that title."

"Your wife gave it to me. She was the true heir to this estate, so her request will stand, even if you dislike it." I crossed my arms and forced a chuckle. "Oh, I'm sorry. This must be so very confusing to you. I mean your *late* wife. You know, the one you betrayed."

He blinked.

When his wife tugged on his sleeve, he jerked his arm out

of her grip so sharply, I wanted to wince. The poor woman. It didn't look like this marriage was the product of affection. I wondered, with a twinge of pain in my chest, if she even had a say in it.

"You're lying," Destin muttered. "She would never do that without consulting me."

"She would have consulted you while you were courting a new bride?" I laughed again, humorlessly, as ripe color bloomed in his cheeks. "I have a difficult time imagining that."

His throat bobbed, but when he spoke again, it was even darker than before – black, sheen-less velvet. "I don't need to justify the stipulations of my marriage or my title, especially to a *stranger.*"

"You were a traitor to the only person who mattered," I retorted. "Are you aware your most recent love letter is what finally destroyed her? She died of a broken heart, because of *you.*"

Destin's eyes narrowed to slits.

"Oh dear," his bride murmured, splaying a hand over her bosom. "This is hardly a conversation to have in front of the child." She reached for Erlene, as if to pull her from behind me.

Before I even registered the instinct, a growl erupted from my throat. *"Don't you dare."*

The young woman recoiled. "I only wanted to take a stroll with her," she breathed.

Destin stiffened, his gaze boring a hole through my skull.

I stamped out the heat warming my veins. *Control it.* She was right. I shouldn't be saying these things in front of Erlene. If it was my intention to bring her and her father together, she needs to trust him. She needs to love him.

I cleared my throat and forced myself to consider Destin's bride with a little more gentleness. "I apologize. I shouldn't have snapped at you. Are you quite alright here, with *him*?" I nodded at Destin without bothering to glance his way.

The woman studied me in my entirety, and then something not so helpless broke the surface. Her lips quirked into a mocking smile. "That's an odd question to ask. Of course, I'm alright here. This is my *home*. The only person who doesn't seem to belong here is *you*."

I stifled a sharp inhale. He found a right treat for himself after all. Fantastic.

She gestured to Erlene and asked sweetly, "Now, may I take my new step-daughter for a walk, or would you like to gnash your teeth at me some more first?"

I carefully unclenched my jaw and replied flatly, "Perhaps you should ask Erlene what *she* wants to do."

The woman peered around my body with fresh warmth in her face. "Hello, Erlene. My name is Felicity." She paused, waiting for Erlene to come out. When the little girl didn't respond, she added brightly, "I brought home some lovely gifts for you. Would you like to see them?"

That caught the child's attention. Erlene looked up at Felicity and squeaked, "You did?"

"Oh, yes. Candies and dollies and a whole trove of my old dresses. Can I take you for a walk while they're being unloaded? You could show me around the garden. Doesn't that sound fun?"

After a thoughtful moment, Erlene nodded, and Felicity reached for her. It was the child's choice this time, even if it was a coaxed agreement, so I allowed her to walk Erlene inside.

Once the door closed behind them, Destin dropped all pretense of politeness.

"I won't tolerate incivility and accusations," he snarled, leaning into my personal space. "Your judgment is misplaced. My wife was sick."

I took a step toward him in return, raising a rebellious brow. "You're right. She *was*, but did you know she'd started walking again?" His face fell instantly.

I let rage seep into every word, because if it wasn't in my words, it would be in my eyes, in my skin. If it wasn't rage, it would be grief, and I was sick of crying. "You couldn't have known, because you disappeared. Do you realize what that did to her? How broken she was in your absence? She was prepared to send me out to search for you, but then your letter came, and she died within hours. You won't convince anyone here that was a coincidence."

Destin glanced at the staff, but they averted their eyes, looking at the smog, at the house, at me. "You're lying," he repeated weakly, even as his gray-blue gaze slid back to me.

"Lila?" I urged haughtily.

Lila sighed, disapproving of my mood. "It's true."

Destin didn't, or maybe *couldn't*, accept it. He pointed one long finger into my face, nearly touching my nose. "You're leaving. Now."

"Lila's witness substantiates my claim," I retorted with a violent grin. "I only need one witness to remain here as Erlene's guardian. I'm not going anywhere at *your* willing."

I had no intention of staying long, but he didn't need to know that. I only needed to goad him into taking an active role in his daughter's life, stay long enough to ensure it, and then I could leave.

A vein pulsed in Destin's temple. Before it could explode, he closed his eyes and took a step back, turning away from me as he drew in a steadying breath. When his eyes opened, all the emotion in his body had trickled away.

He asked Lila, "Did you set aside the item as I instructed?"

"Of course."

"Good. Once you've brought it to me, Gwaith House no longer has any need of you. Pack your bags. I'll prepare a

carriage to take you to the city or wherever else you wish
to go."

"What?" the governess balked.

"Don't tell me I need to say it slower for you? Pack. Your.
Room," he said emphatically.

"Sir," she whispered, "I've served this family for three
generations."

"And now I've released you from your service." His eyes
flashed with a burst of anger, and I recognized his intentions
for what they were: retaliation for a perceived betrayal. He
should have known that her loyalties would always lie with
the young woman she had helped raise. "We don't need three
women running around this house, and I refuse to waste
Gwaith's limited fortune. Now that Erlene has a guardian and
there is a wife to run the House, what use could I have for
you?"

Her eyes welled with tears, but she spun on her heel and
retreated into the House before they could fall. I stood frozen
to the step, glaring at Destin with such hatred, I was surprised
he didn't burst into flames right there.

"You didn't deserve her," I spat.

Destin acted as though he didn't hear me, or perhaps he
just didn't care. As he stepped sideways down the stairs,
toward the line of wagons in front of the stables, he said, "You
may take Lila's chambers for yourself. Keep my daughter out
of the den and away from my rooms."

I heard the unspoken command. *Keep my daughter far away
from me.*

I TOOK the stairs to the second floor two at a time, my heart
thumping against my ribs.

Passing the massive window on the middle landing, I briefly scanned the garden. Erlene's little figure spun in the distance, playing with the swirling smog as Felicity walked idly between the trickling fountains and the stone sculptures of estranged deities. She inspected her nails, as though none of the opulence impressed her.

Rickety unease bloomed in my chest. I shouldn't leave Erlene alone in her care for too long, not until I understood what kind of person she was and whether she could be trusted. If she proved up to the task, it would make me more comfortable leaving. At least someone would be taking care of Erlene on a daily basis. Unfortunately, I didn't think I had enough time to determine that. I'd intended to linger only long enough to meet Destin and planned to pass Erlene's care on to Lila if he refused to listen.

With Lila gone, this had become far more complicated.

When I reached her room, the old woman was already pulling the clothes from her dresser. A worn, floral suitcase rested open on the bed.

"He can't send you away," I told her.

Lila ignored me and rolled a nightgown between her hands. I entered the room, pausing just past the threshold when she gave me a sharp look.

"Gwaith needs you," I insisted. "Erlene does too. You're the only consistency she has left."

"She has you now," Lila muttered.

"You know that won't last, that I can't stay. You *can't* go."

She closed the empty drawer. When she turned to me, her expression was carefully composed, filled with all the grace of a good governess. The silver beads threaded through her braid gleamed in the gray daylight, a sign of her wise age and celibacy, her selflessness.

We studied each other for a moment, and I knew she saw the raw panic in my eyes when her expression softened with pity. "I don't have a say in this matter, girl. I must obey Destin's order, regardless of the obligation I feel to Tova's ghost. You're lucky, Sia, that you do not answer to anyone in this way."

She'd never been more wrong. I had an authority, but I chose to run from it. After sitting in one place these past weeks, I didn't realize just how long I'd been running. How hard. How far.

"Where will you go?"

Her eyes shuttered. "I don't know. I-I have some savings, but it's not enough to sustain me longer than a few weeks. When I get to the city, I guess I'll be forced to search for a new House and hope there's a position for me somewhere."

Before I could stop myself, I crossed the room. My fingers flew to the pouch on my hip and grappled with the strings attaching it to my belt. I withdrew a few gold pieces from it and tucked them away into my corset before I lifted her hand and placed the heavy pouch in her palm. "Find a safe place in the city," I commanded quietly. "Stay well, and wait for me to come find you once I've made Destin see reason."

If that's even possible... Goddess spare me, I prayed it was possible.

Lila shook her head. "I can't take this."

"Tova would want you taken care of. She would want me to do this for her, for Erlene. I promise to bring you home. I can't have you swearing service to another family in the meantime."

The entire length of her neck's soft skin quivered. "I hope with my entire heart you can keep that promise."

"I don't really have a choice." I swallowed the bitterness rising in my throat. So far, I'd managed to keep every promise I'd ever made. Well, except for one, but I refused to think of that now...*or ever*. If I pretended it didn't exist, maybe I could trick myself into forgetting it. That was the plan.

"I won't allow you to die in the city," I assured Lila, closing her fingers over the bag.

"Thank you." Her eyes shimmered.

Turning on my heel, I strode to the hall, but I paused when Lila called my name. I glanced over my shoulder, and my blood ran cold when I caught the look in her eyes. Pain and regret.

"After Tova fell ill," she rasped, "I believe Destin did something terrible. I don't know where he ran off to, but I can guarantee it wasn't to find a wife. I overheard him speaking with a man in his office many months ago, someone who arrived here under the cover of night. They had discussed plans to cast a net through the smog. I think the real reason Destin came home is because he finally caught what they were after. I think he's aligned himself with the rebels." She inhaled shakily before adding, "Be careful here."

I couldn't move. I was frozen to the floor as her words sunk in. *A net.*

There was only one creature the rebels could have been searching for in the smog that would be captured that way. *One* creature that mortals – those foolish enough to think they could change the way of the world with acts of civil war – *knew* were worth catching.

Destin must have a goddess-damned death wish.

Lila's complexion bordered on green as she pulled a pouch from her hip. Her wrinkled fingers rooted around in the bag and drew out a ring. Tova's ring. She offered it to me. "Please hand this over to his Lordship for me. It's what he asked for, but I can't – I can't face him right now."

Must be nice to have that choice.

I accepted the golden band and frowned at it. Was this all he felt was worth keeping of Tova, worth saving? A bit of gold to give to his new wife? I lifted my glare to Lila and asked,

"You weren't going to tell me about this, were you? About the rebels and what he'd done. *Before* I gave you the coin?"

She winced. "I—"

"It doesn't matter." I turned away, easing that predatory fear in her. "You changed your mind, and that's all that matters."

As I left the room behind, my palms burned in the fists I made. Destin was not in any place to be trusted with his daughter right now. With Lila gone, if I left, Erlene might very well be brushed aside and ignored, forgotten, and I couldn't allow that to become her reality. I'd treat Destin like a job, no different than playing peacemaker between warring witch-clans or nullifying thieves along the roads of the gnashing forest. I could fix this, because there would be a solution.

There had to be.

CHAPTER 6

This new information about Destin made my task to reconcile father and daughter a million times harder. A common mortal prick I could deal with. I was prepared for that, but I had a feeling he was beyond it. He was *enraged* – at the world, at his position, at life's lack of mercy. He'd decided to fight back.

Now, this entire House could be in danger.

I slipped out of the servant's door and through the outskirts of the garden, behind the hedges leading to the stables. I had to confront Destin about the rebels. I had to explain exactly what he risked by getting involved with them, even in a small way. Making enemies with any of the seraphim hovering above this land was a sure way to have your family killed and your property turned to ashes. The gold-winged beings had plenty of flames to spare.

I heard the men before I saw them, grunts and swearing and gruff voices shouting orders as the wagons were unloaded. Slinking along the side of the stable, I peered around the corner.

The men were dressed in black leather, and they unloaded

the wagons with a sense of purpose and synchronicity. It was clear most of the items being unloaded were Felicity's belongings, but they were set to the side while several other crates were carried into the stables. The horses had been put out to pasture beyond the building, and I caught a glimpse of the stable master unbridling and brushing them down.

He didn't lead them back inside. No, the stables were being used for something else.

I observed for several minutes, until orders were shouted from the stable door and the men turned to the last wagon. A large, black sheet obscured the contents, the material anchored at each corner. Two men vaulted up onto the wagon and tore the sheet away. My stomach plummeted.

There was only one item on the flat, and it reaffirmed every worry I had for the mortals on this property. A black box, so dark and glistening, it seemed made of night.

If I really strained myself, I could hear the muffled screaming coming from it. Yes, Destin had caught something, something large and powerful. Something that required an onyx cage to keep it contained. It took every man on hand to lift the box as it shook and teetered. I watched as the creature within seemed to throw itself against the interior walls, again and again, searching for a way out, a way home.

The men laughed and jeered, and one particular word drifted towards me. *Angel.* A curse. A term of ridicule for the winged immortals. These were definitely rebels...and I was in deep, deep shit.

The rebellion was a plague spreading on this side of the country, men and women doing everything in their power to wreak havoc on the seraphim and their cities.

Seraphim rarely chose to roam the human lands for anything. There were many reasons for it, but the main one around here was the annoyance of flying through the smog. It wasn't because they feared it. Seraphim were immune to the smoke, healing too rapidly to sustain any permanent damage, but that didn't make it appealing to navigate. Where there was smog, there were those who wished to hide and scheme within it, those who thought just because it could hide them, it would keep them from harm.

They were so deeply wrong.

The promise I made to Tova closed in like a storm cloud, daunting and heavy. I wasn't just flirting with the impossible anymore, I was *eye-fucking* it. That dreadful black box.

My stomach turned as I grappled with my thoughts, pulling thread after thread out of the knotted mess. First things first: I had to release what was in that box before other seraphim realized what had happened and tracked it here. I also had to ensure none of them would return to Gwaith House for retribution, for Erlene's sake.

That would be a small miracle in itself; seraphim were not forgiving creatures.

Then, there was the matter of the widower's loyalties. He would never spare his daughter a second glance while his sights were locked on a bloody horizon, would never consider her safety and comfort paramount. With all these rebels swarming the property, I could see now that he was more entrenched in the cause than I'd feared.

The black box rocked again in their hands, and this time, one of the men grumbled to the others. They let the box fall hard enough to jostle what was within it before they laughed and tipped it over. A muffled roar echoed from the confines.

I took a step forward, eyes locked on the bearded rebel who continued to spew profanities at the captured creature.

Then, the smog swirled to my right as Destin appeared.

One of his arms whipped out and gripped the corner of the stable to keep me from taking another step toward the men. He leaned in, his mortal body seeming harder, rougher, now that it was so close, now that he was towering over me.

The fact he snuck up on me, that my instincts had *allowed* him to, stunned me.

I looked up at him, looked and looked. He really was very pretty for a human.

His gray-blue eyes narrowed, a hateful little smirk spreading over his mouth. "I knew at first glance that you were a hedge-creeper."

I blinked. "Pardon?" There was no way he'd *really* just called me a prostitute. Had he?

He pressed in even closer to me, and my back flattened against the stable wall. I was disarmed and disoriented by the cruel loveliness of his face. "Get back to the house and stay away from my men."

My jaw dropped. It was true. He actually thought I was a whore.

"Did you hear me? I said, '*now*.'" He grabbed my elbow, and that snapped me free.

With sharp precision, I twisted the arm he held so my hand gripped the inside of his forearm. I wrenched him toward me, spinning us as I hooked a heel into the back of his knee, and Destin's eyes widened as he took my place against the stable wall.

He gasped as my blade pressed against the base of his throat and nicked his skin. As his blood kissed the edge of my blade, I thought I'd never seen anything more beautiful.

His shock ebbed in the next instant. He lifted a hand to cover mine, shifting his feet, but before he could get his balance, I pressed another blade to his crotch. Destin stilled entirely.

"Consider your next move *very* carefully, my Lord. It might disappoint your bride if her new plaything went missing." I cocked my head, smiling. "Or perhaps she won't mind at all. Your ego is so large, I'm willing to bet it's compensation for some lacking elsewhere."

"Release me," he growled.

I leaned in and let the scent of his blood wash over me. Iron and ash, the earthy hint of mortality. Beneath that, a muskiness emanated overwhelming sorrow. Sometimes – rarely – mortals felt so much, so deeply, that it tainted their blood.

I didn't let myself think about it.

"Do you think I'm going to act as helpless as Tova?" I whispered. "That I will allow you to touch me whenever the whim strikes you, to order me around? Let me make myself perfectly clear: I'd sooner skin you alive."

I felt the bob of his throat against my knife as his hands fell away, his dusty palms turning up at his waist in surrender as his eyes turned a dark, dull gray.

"Go ahead, then," he exhaled. "Do it."

I flinched at the empty command. He *wanted* me to hurt him.

It would bring me no satisfaction to give him anything he wanted, even suffering. I wouldn't dole out a punishment to make him feel better, to make *myself* feel better. Though, the fact he thought it was what he deserved...

Perhaps he had cared for Tova a small fraction of how much I did. A sliver, maybe.

The widower might not be a lost cause, though it was still to be seen. I pushed away from the stable wall, taking measured steps until I could study Destin from a distance.

A flicker of disappointment tugged at his brow, but he quickly tucked his emotion away as he had on the staircase. He braced his slender hands behind him and straightened.

"Tova was a fool in love," I said quietly, spreading the panels I'd cut in Tova's old dress to sheathe my daggers on either thigh. Destin's gaze snapped to the bare skin, as if on instinct, and then swiftly looked away. "She would never forgive me if I hurt you. In case she watches us now from above or below or somewhere between, I won't."

Of all the realms that existed in this universe, I knew there was a pocket where Tova might remain.

There were stories about those who did not complete their passing right away, about those who chose to linger between death and the Goddess' realm, where the Great Mother laid souls to rest. Sometimes, souls hung back, waiting for the ones they left behind so they could make the final journey together. Tova was the sort of woman to do that, to wait dutifully for her husband. If she didn't pass on, if she was watching over her daughter and the man she loved, I wouldn't give her another reason to be ashamed of me.

Destin fiddled with his sleeve cuffs. "Well, now that your temper fit is over, I'm going to have my say."

It took everything in me not to draw my blade again and fling it at his head.

He rolled his shoulders, and I had to admit, he knew how to put on a convincing front. Gone was that fleeting guilt, that vulnerability, that musky tang in the blood trickling down his neck. How often did he look in the mirror and practice that sneer? How often did he allow himself to show the world what was underneath it?

"These stables are off-limits," he said. "You may be Erlene's guardian, but that does not extend you any right to this property. If you cannot respect my boundaries, I will be forced to find you two separate accommodations in the city."

Being at the heart of the smog was the last thing I needed to deal with right now, being somewhere that would seclude us and endanger Erlene's health. I had to remain close enough to Gwaith House to preserve it. Erlene would inherit this place someday, as long as Destin didn't throw it away in his efforts to promote civil unrest. I had to be clever, careful.

"That won't be necessary," I said tersely.

He licked his lips and closed the top buttons of his shirt, covering up the cut on his neck. "Good."

I turned away.

"One more thing," he called. When I glanced back, he'd stuffed his hands into his trouser pockets and tilted his head to study me. "What shall I call you?"

"You mean other than 'hedge-creeper?'" I taunted.

He didn't react, only waited for my answer.

I sighed. "My name is Sia."

All the color drained from his face. "Ah." He swallowed hard. "Well, my wife's actions make more sense now. She spoke of you often."

"All terrible things, I hope."

Of course, she spoke of me, but I doubted she ever referred to me as anything more than a friend. That was what she said to me when we said goodbye the first time, after all. She'd clung to my wrists, trying to stop me from leaving her on the outskirts of this very property. My lips had still been warm and swollen from her kisses. Her cheeks had been flushed from the pleasure I gave to her before telling her I was leaving. Tears had shimmered in her eyes as she pleaded with me. *You're my best friend, Sia. I don't want you to go.*

I had always been a friend to her, and she had been my everything.

I didn't say anything else before disappearing between the hedges. Truthfully, there wasn't anything left in me.

Halfway back to the House, I heard a wailing on the wind. *Erlene.*

I ran through the courtyard and garden, past the petal-strewn fountain and into the maze of boxwoods. Just past the first fork in the greenery, I found them.

Felicity's pale pink skirts were spread around her where she kneeled in front of Erlene, and she was visibly frustrated – her cheeks were almost as red as the child's. Erlene screamed, shrinking away from the woman's outstretched arms. In her little hands, she held a mangled rose, and her fingers were bleeding.

Felicity took notice of me and rolled her eyes before turning back to Erlene. She reached again for the child. I realized then that she was trying to get the rose out of Erlene's hand. "I don't need your help," she shot over her shoulder.

She did need my help, actually. Erlene was cornered by boxwoods, but she wouldn't allow Felicity close enough to touch her. I could tell Felicity was trying her hardest to be gentle, but she was trying to take the rose away, and Erlene didn't trust her.

I stalked forward. "I'm not here to help *you*," I spat.

Felicity saw me coming and sat back on her haunches, glaring as Erlene allowed me to pick her up. "I was just trying to take the rose from her," she grumbled. "But she wouldn't let go of it. She doesn't listen."

The rose bushes had been special to Tova, and therefore, they had become special to Erlene. Whenever Erlene and I took a walk through the garden, I would snip a rose off the bushes for her to hold. It was our routine. I can only assume Erlene had wanted that comfort today, but Felicity was clueless as to why.

Erlene was a strong-willed little girl. It didn't surprise me that she would rip a rose off the bush for herself.

"She doesn't have to listen to you," I retorted, before I started snapping the prickles off the rose stem as Erlene held on tight to it.

"Yes, she does," Felicity insisted, her voice impassioned. "I'm her mother now."

I threw a scowl down at her, where she was still seated on the ground, and I saw that there was nothing unkind in her face. There was frustration still, of course, and worry. I knew she must be worried about her new role in Erlene's life. She had likely been told that it would be a prominent one, by both Destin and the family she came from.

It might be helpful for her to become more involved in Erlene's life. Maybe if she grew attached to the child, Destin would follow suit.

Another smaller part of me didn't want her getting close to Erlene, didn't want the child's memories of Tova tainted by this look-alike. It was selfish of me, but I didn't want to share Erlene's trust in that way, or her love.

Destin rounded the corner of boxwoods at that moment. He took in the situation, his eyes locking on Erlene, on the blood smeared over her hands and my dress.

Felicity's face softened at his arrival, and I wanted to claw the exaggerated concern from her face. "Oh, thank the goddess you heard us, dear. Erlene was *hysterical*. I was so afraid I wouldn't be able to keep hold of her long enough to carry her inside."

Erlene went quiet, absolutely calm as her face burrowed into my neck. Destin noticed. He definitely noticed how tightly she clutched to me and the ruined rose in her hand.

Felicity waved at her husband in a silent command to help her up, and Destin obliged, but his eyes remained on me and Erlene.

"Is she all right?" Destin asked, leaning toward us as if he wanted to approach and check for himself.

"She'll be fine," I replied sharply.

Erlene's arms tightened around my neck. Only a few years old, and she heard my love and devotion for her in those three words. Judging from the shift I saw in Felicity's eyes before leaving the garden behind, she heard it too.

CHAPTER 7

There was only one woman more insufferable than
Felicity, and, unfortunately for me, it happened to be
Felicity's closest friend. The woman traveled in
from a few towns away to help Felicity settle into Gwaith
House, arriving the morning after the Lord and Lady
returned.

It had been a week now, and she was still here. *Hovering.*

The petite brunette spoke of nothing but gossip in an
inane, nasally voice. I was starting to suspect that was simply
because there wasn't anything else for her to talk about. From
what I could gather in my brief interactions with her, the
woman was unmarried, untitled, and past a desirable marital
age. She wasn't helpful in terms of learning how to run a
House or manage the family, but I didn't think that really
mattered to Felicity.

Her friend's presence was simply a joy. Their friendship
was a comfort, and a *weakness.*

Personally, I didn't know how anyone could be around her
for more than a few minutes at a time. The pitch of her voice

alone gave me headaches from rooms away, and I was becoming antsy, waiting for the day when this stranger was finally out of my way.

I couldn't pursue the black box in the stables while she was here. She was too nosy. She and Felicity followed me around when they thought I wasn't paying attention. I could sense them all the time, lingering in hallways and outside of my room, eavesdropping. Not that they heard much. I didn't talk, except to Erlene.

In the rare moments when Felicity's friend allowed her eyes to meet mine, I saw a suspicion there that told me she was cataloging my every move.

Destin was absent from the house more than not, taking day trips to nearby townships, working in the stables on Goddess-knew-what, and holing up in his den when he could manage it. Judging from the scent of cork and spice I caught when passing the room, I knew he spent his time there drinking himself stupid. His schedule had no semblance of order or regularity.

My nerves split whenever I thought of that black box. There was no telling when I would get a chance to empty it.

Beyond the worry of being caught by Destin, as sly and quiet as he was, there were multiple guards standing watch over the building, day and night. It wouldn't be as simple as slipping through a window.

I chewed my lip as I stared in the direction of the stables.

There wasn't much of it to be seen through the window of the sitting room, but I still watched. I registered the movements of the guards traveling back and forth.

Usually, I fled the House with Erlene around this time, mid-afternoon, every day. It gave me a chance to study the stables and interact with the guards from afar, but this morning, Erlene woke with a cough.

The smog billowing outside seemed too malicious to endure, so we settled for a day spent in the sitting room, sewing and reading instead.

Felicity swept into the room unexpectedly, and her gaze slid over us, the needlework, the stack of books at our feet, and eventually locked onto the table crowded with cookie tins. Erlene's mug sat on the table as well, the liquid swirling with dark clouds – my tears disguised as tea. I was being overly cautious, but when it came to Erlene, it was hard not to be.

Her Ladyship rolled her eyes. "Intent on devouring every sweet in the household, Sia? Save some for the rest of us."

The powdered sugar of the cookie I was chewing promptly turned to ash in my mouth, and I had to make every effort not to stand and drive my stitching needle into her pale, thin throat. I didn't do it, but I didn't make any motion to leave the room either.

She wouldn't drive Erlene or me from any room. This was *Erlene's* House.

To spite her, I shoved another cookie into my mouth and reached for the tea, sipping it to cleanse my mouth of the grainy burnt bits between my teeth. Then, I watched over the lip of the cup as Felicity's friend followed her into the room.

The woman's pert freckled nose was buried in the morning newspaper.

The butler trailed after them, carrying a cluttered silver tray. He acknowledged my presence, smiling warmly before he deposited the steeping teapot on the table.

Felicity saw our exchange and scowled, and the butler quickly fled her glare.

As the two women sat at the formal table on the other side of the room, Felicity's friend said, "You should read this whisper piece, Lissy." I winced at the excitement hitching her voice. "It's an article about the hovering city."

My stomach dipped. I forced my face to remain blank, but my fingers curled tightly in the tablecloth Erlene was stitching pretty flowers on.

"There's a story about the hovering city every other week, Kim," Felicity replied flatly, plunking five white sugar cubes into her cup.

"But this one has a picture accompanying it." Kim dragged her chair closer to Felicity's until they were shoulder to shoulder. I saw it—the subtle pull in Kim's body, the way she leaned into Felicity as if she might consume the very breath in her lungs. I was too well-versed in this sort of longing to ignore the signs. Felicity was, unsurprisingly, oblivious. "*A chariot was spotted sailing through the skies earlier this week. Twelve pegasi led the carriage, each beast painted brilliant shades of blue.*" I rolled my eyes. The horses weren't painted blue. That was how they were born, how they were bred. Vibrant colors were cherished amongst the seraphim. "*One can only assume that this extravagance points to a guest of royalty visiting the city.*"

It took a moment for the article's words to sink in. *A royal guest.* I shifted in my seat, every inch of my skin tingling.

As the tingle spread across my scar, it turned into a spear of pain. I gasped quietly, startling in my seat as the pain dragged on a few seconds longer than I was used to. Tears welled in my eyes. Biting the inside of my cheek, I willed the ache to pass before anyone in the room was made aware of my discomfort. Eventually, the pain ebbed, but it was a slow fade.

My attacks had never lasted that long before, but I didn't have the courage to wonder what that might mean for me.

Luckily, the two women across the room were still distracted.

Felicity was leaning over their table, peering at the paper. "They actually caught a picture of the carriage beyond the smog?"

"It would appear so." Kim's eyes flickered up and caught on Felicity's mouth as she continued to study the picture. After a long moment, she shook her head and tore her gaze away, focusing on the article. "It's a little blurry, but you can see an outline of the beasts and chariot. Can you imagine how large the occupants must be? It's twice as large as any cab I've seen."

"Seraphim are boulders of muscle and feathers and hatred. I'd be surprised if that chariot fits even one of them comfortably."

I bit the inside of my cheek. A bit of magic worked wonders for tight spaces like that. Five or more seraphim could sit within an enchanted cab; if it was truly a royal chariot, three times as many.

A small, uncertain smile spread over Kim's face as she slumped back in her chair. "What does a girl have to do to get in with a man like that?" The way she said it made me think she was far more interested in seeing what Felicity had to say about it.

Felicity shot her a hard look. "They aren't men. They're savages."

My stomach churned.

Kim pouted, her eyes prying, and Felicity's expression softened slightly.

"Though," she added slowly, "I suppose seducing a savage might make for an *interesting* night."

I couldn't help it. I snorted.

Felicity's head whipped toward me, her eyes widening at first and then narrowing, as if she'd forgotten I was there. "Do you find something funny?"

Yes – the lunacy of her last statement. Seraphim were practically immortal, living for centuries after hitting full maturity at twenty-five. They lived in that form until their spirit grew too tired to resist oblivion, or until someone ended their existence for them. Mortals survived maybe sixty or seventy years, if they weren't taken first by illness or injury. Immortals forming attachments to a life so fleeting was fool's folly.

I smirked. "It's certainly laughable. You think a seraph would be interested in bedding mortal women? That's absurd. They have no shortage of their own females."

"Yes, that must be why they lurk in our taverns and rape us at will," Felicity snapped. "It's not a mystery that brutes desire a bit of softness in their beds. All men do. I guess you wouldn't know much about that, with those gnashing teeth of yours."

She wasn't wrong. Rebels ran rampant in the human lands for a reason. In addition to the fact that humans felt entitled to this coast, their sense of oppression was worsened by the wingless exiles, the males and females who boasted of their seraphic ancestors while brutalizing the humans they'd been thrown down to equal standing with.

Few mortals ever stepped foot in the hovering city, or any winged settlement for that matter. The few who did were only allowed citizenship through marriage.

Love like that, the kind that crossed chasms of age and power, occurred so rarely, I could count how many times it happened in my lifetime on one hand. Any child born from such a union faced unique scrutiny. If they were born without wings, they had to marry someone within the city or face expulsion when they hit maturity. It was almost guaranteed that any ordinary citizen of the gilded city – those who carried only one set of wings on their back – would produce a flightless child by copulating with a mortal. That was simply how the genes worked.

The noble seraphim – those with two sets of wings – had a better chance of passing their wings on, but nobles found little allure in binding themselves to a human. They preferred to marry and breed carefully, ensuring double blessedness for future generations. Marriage for seraphic nobles was politically arranged, mostly loveless.

Sometimes, though, two ordinary seraphs gave birth to a child without any wings, and those circumstances were the most heart-breaking, *soul-crushing*, when the magic running through their veins simply grew too faint to persevere. Those circumstances produced exiles, males and females who caused pain in human lands simply because they could.

Not all seraphim were like the exiles. Not even all exiles were cruel. Most were decent, remembering that their ancestors had once been human, too.

The hovering city was to blame for the animosity across this coast. Seraphic Law was brutal, unfair, and it would never change, despite how earnestly I wished it would. Because of that, I extended my compassion to places where it could actually make a difference, to people who really needed it. I had deemed the forest, and those creatures within it, worthy of my time.

As I looked into Felicity's eyes, I couldn't find a speck of that goodness to spare her.

"What does Lord Destin think of your worldly wisdom, my Lady?" I asked sweetly. "Is he relieved he doesn't have to educate a virgin on what he likes in bed?"

Shock flashed over her face, and I knew I'd hit my mark. It was easy to guess she was inexperienced and worried about it. She was too wound up. I never saw Destin retreat to their bedchambers in the evening, either. That had to upset her.

She quickly composed herself as she spat, "Who knows, Sia. Maybe *you* should try your luck with an angel. You have no inheritance. You might even survive it, might win one of those savages over with your foul manners. I'm sure *they* wouldn't have an issue throwing your body weight around." Both of them laughed at that.

I wrestled with the heat in my veins; not because Felicity had succeeded in making me feel ashamed of my lush body, but because I was so sick of her constant snobbery. Sick of this house. Sick of the memories that lingered around every corner.

It was killing me slowly, being here, remembering who I used to be.

Felicity was jealous, and I understood why. No one had prepared her for my presence in Erlene's life. I was a strange woman taking up space in her new home. I couldn't react, couldn't lose control. Just a few more days, and the friend would be gone. Then, I could do what was needed to free myself from this coast forevermore.

I averted my gaze, needing to stare at *anything* but Felicity's venomous smile.

It slid to the newspaper in Kim's hands, and I saw the headline. Another dismembered body had been found, but this time, it wasn't on the beach.

I slipped Erlene off my lap and crossed the room in the span of a heartbeat. The two women flinched as I snatched the newspaper out of Kim's hands and read the article. My heart leapt into the base of my throat when I recognized the road the body was discovered on, had stumbled around in its second life without arms or a jaw.

It was found on one of the roads leading to Gwaith House.

"Well, that was rude," Kim finally murmured.

At that volume, her voice wasn't so unbearable. I took a step back and lowered the newspaper to look at her. There it was again: that glimmer of suspicion in her eyes. Something more rose to the surface, simmering and twirling. Her full lips parted, curling up slightly at the corners, and I admitted to myself that she was actually somewhat pretty...for an insipid gossip.

I folded the paper and tucked it under my arm, wiggling my fingers toward Erlene. The child leapt from her seat and joined me as I walked under the arch leading to the rest of the house. "Come along, sweetheart. Your brain will rot if you continue listening to this nonsense."

CHAPTER 8

I'd just finished a cup of tea and was walking down the hall of the second floor that evening when I heard movement beyond the door to my temporary room. I stopped, pressing the open book in my hands to my chest as I re-examined the hallway.

Erlene's door was closed, the room dim. Usually, when she woke after being put to bed, it was in tears, so the silence told me it couldn't be her. Destin was still in the stables. That left two options, and I had to admit, I was curious to see which one of them had mustered the bravery to enter my room.

I tried to slip through the door undetected, but the creaking hinge gave me away.

Kim spun to face me, her hands flying to hide behind her back. She was standing in front of my nightstand. From what little I could see, it was open.

With a smile, I shut the bedroom door behind me.

I couldn't do anything to Felicity. She had her own role to play in Gwaith House, and I would be risking the already delicate trust Destin had placed in me by messing with her. He brought her here as his wife, Goddess knew why. She meant something to him.

But I *could* do something about *this* woman.

"I wasn't expecting you to visit my room so late in the evening, sweetie," I purred. "You must have forgotten to warn me."

"I'm sorry?" She released a breathless laugh, backing up so the nightstand drawer closed behind her knees. *She's clever*, I thought. *But not nearly clever enough.*

"It's rude to show up in my room without giving me time to prepare for you."

Her brows furrowed. "Prepare?"

"Oh yes." I slid my book onto the dresser and carefully removed the ribbon from my hair. "But don't worry. I'm always up for a little *fun*."

She blinked at the warmth in my voice. I think she sensed the intent behind it too, because she took a step forward and brought her hands out from behind her back. She was holding the book of psalms Lila had left behind. "Look. This was an innocent mistake. You see, I was only looking for—"

"Dirt," I interjected. I strolled toward her, my movements as smooth as glass. "You were looking for something to destroy me with. It's okay, you can admit it."

I cocked my head as my body closed in on hers. She inched back, nearly losing her balance as the back of her knees ran into the bed.

"So, did you find anything interesting?" I asked. Judging from the bulge remaining at the foot of my bed, she hadn't found my pack. "Or were you simply waiting for me to find you?"

Kim's head rocked back, her eyes narrowing at the challenge in my smile.

"There's something wrong with you," she spat.

"You have no idea."

"Yes, well, I'm going to figure it out." She pulled her shoulders back, standing taller. Honestly, she should use these low, threatening tones more often. They made her more bearable to be around. "When I do, you'll have to get the hell out of this House. You shouldn't be here, and I'm not going anywhere until you're gone."

Now that wouldn't do at all. I had run out of patience for this little visit, run out of patience for their dance around the House. Maybe her threat would have impressed me, excited me, if I thought she had any power to follow through, but I played games better than anyone.

I pouted, letting my gaze drift over her chest. She wore such a thin gown, I could see everything. "You poor thing. You would do *anything* for Felicity, wouldn't you?"

Kim swallowed. "She's my friend."

"That drives you mad, doesn't it?" I clicked my tongue. "Wishing she would see how much you care for her, knowing she won't because she's married to someone else."

"I have no idea what you're talking about." Kim surged forward, trying to elbow past me, but I reached out and put a firm hand on her waist. She stilled, and I brushed my thumb over her hip.

She looked up at me, her breath hitching.

I took the book from her hand and tossed it onto the bed before I brought my other hand up to trace the white lace strap on her shoulder. "You think I don't see it? You don't think I recognize what this is? Unrequited love can waste your life if you let it. It almost wasted mine."

Her next breath was stunted. "I—"

"I *did* get to taste her, though."

She stopped breathing as I leaned down to kiss the tantalizing hollow at her throat.

I traced my lips over her ear as I whispered, "I tasted her a few times, actually, before she left me for someone more suitable. Would you like me to show you how I did it?"

Kim leaned back, searching my face. "What do you mean?"

I shrugged, reaching up to tuck a lock of chestnut hair behind her ear. "I can see in your eyes you'd have no idea where to start, no idea how to seduce her. I could show you how. You could make her come, and maybe that will win her over."

Her eyes widened, the poison of my words tainting her thoughts. She shook her head. "As if she'd ever let me close enough."

I huffed a laugh. "All those nights you sneak into her bed when her husband doesn't show? She lets you do *that*. What's a little more?" I smiled again, all teeth and temptation. "All it takes is a chance and a trick, and I could show you mine. They're very good tricks, I promise."

She swayed under my touch, and I felt victory kissing my fingers, kissing my tongue. "Felicity can't stand you," she murmured. "I shouldn't—" She cut herself off as I nipped her earlobe. She reached up to clutch my arms, holding me to her.

"That's the funny thing about hatred," I whispered. "It's a disease, spreading as easily as one breath and a word, and the fire it burns in your belly..." I moaned into her ear and her legs trembled against mine. "It can be transmuted into another sort of heat."

I leaned back to look into her eyes, not caring to mark the color. "Do you want me to show you?" I repeated. I needed her consent for what I was going to do.

With a shudder, she nodded.

"Then pay close attention." I smiled. Then, I drew my hand on her shoulder down to her chest and swept my fingers under her nightgown to expose her breast, trussed up by the structured bodice. Without pausing to admire, I took her nipple into my mouth, watching from under my lashes as her face paled in surprise, then reddened as my tongue and teeth worked her delicate flesh. Her nails dug into my arms as I repeated the process on her other breast.

A low whine started in the back of her throat, high-pitched and breathless and loud. I smiled around her breast as she arched into me.

I moved off her nipple and knelt, hitching her silk skirt.

I found that she wasn't wearing undergarments, and I wondered if she touched herself after Felicity fell asleep beside her. I understood that twisted urge like the back of my hand. As I lifted her gown, I could smell the cream she'd applied to her skin, soft and floral.

She gasped as I hooked one of her legs over my shoulder, as I ran my nose up and pressed a kiss to her inner thigh.

Her eyes were hazy, and dark tendrils of hair spilled forward to caress her breasts as she leaned toward me and shook her head. "What are you—"

I used the hand I had beneath her to spread her open and let my tongue slide through her soaked seam. She gyrated, unable to control her instincts as I licked her again. That pitchy voice cried, "Oh…*Goddess*."

"Not quite," I rumbled into her flesh. "But close."

Her hands found my shoulders, found my hair, as I sucked on her swollen flesh.

When her legs finally buckled, I reached up and shoved her onto the bed. She moaned loudly as her legs wrapped around my head and my fingers found her breast, as I tweaked her nipple hard enough to make her beg.

If I shut out the unfamiliar moans, I could almost pretend she was someone else.

When Tova first opened to me like this, I cherished every second of it, of her. Kissing her was a gift. My first love and my first desire. I was hers. I knelt between her legs and forgot everything about my home life. She was a rose blooming for me, fragrant and new, edged in an ecstasy that numbed me to her thorns. I tried to bring myself back to that place, but she wasn't here. She was gone, and this woman under my tongue would never compare.

It didn't take long for Kim once I filled her ache with my fingers. She liked it fast and hard, and that was exactly what I gave her. I gave and gave, until she was screaming at the top of her lungs, at a frequency I imagined every predator in the forest would be able to hear.

There was only one person I wanted to hear, who *needed* to hear, and she barged into the room right on time.

Kim was whimpering through the end of her pleasure as Felicity staggered in. She looked upon us and went rigid, her jaw dropping as she saw my face under her friend's dress, my vicious smile as I turned to her and blew her a kiss with glistening lips.

I wanted Felicity to know there was no line I wouldn't cross, no person she cared for who would be safe from my fury if she continued to tread the line between us. I was here for Erlene, and I wouldn't leave until *I* chose to.

She'd thought nothing of me, and it was a mistake she wouldn't make again.

Kim scrambled to her feet, but Felicity was already gone.

I lifted myself off the floor and strolled to the hall, watching as the master bedroom slammed shut and Felicity's friend pounded on the door, pleading to be let in. Leaning on the door frame, I stifled a chuckle as Kim finally gave up and backed away slowly, fixing the bodice of her nightgown before turning to me.

She glared through the silvery human tears streaming down her cheeks. Her lips parted, but no sound came out of her. Silenced, for once.

Then I saw her suffering, and the mirth died in my chest.

If I was a smarter monster, I would do what this woman suggested and leave, but that required me to leave behind a little girl who wouldn't understand why she was alone, why the people around her died or pushed her away. It was an evil I couldn't breach.

The promise I made to Tova hung over me like a fading star.

There was bitterness attached to my memories of us. She'd been the one for me, and I was only just beginning to understand that I had been used. It wasn't all ecstasy and warmth, forbidden desire and love. Maybe I'd imagined that depth when I fell, and her death had torn a veil. Now, I saw the reality of those hopes I had held onto, the lies that lured me toward this sharp and terrible maw. I didn't notice her teeth until my heart was ground to dust.

I blinked a few times, letting my face and voice soften before I said, "I saved you a lifetime of heartache. It's better this way."

I leaned against the door to my room once I closed it, staring blankly across the chamber. Perhaps I'd taken it too far, taken things out on the wrong person, but I wouldn't feel bad. I swept forward and lifted the end of my mattress, sliding the used slip of paper out of my bag. I didn't think as I wrote on it. Once the ink had dried and the paper finally disappeared above my palm, it hit me.

I'd written, *I didn't save her.*

Like a fool, as if the mysterious person on the other end were a friend I could bare my heart to, a person I could trust. I suddenly felt so fragile, like if anything touched me, I might shatter. Here I was, letting someone in. Hadn't I learned my lesson after my family? After Tova? I fisted my hands in my lap and bit my lip hard enough to chase the taste of sex from my tongue.

The note came back almost instantly, silencing every worry in my head. It said,

Didn't or couldn't?

At that, tears began rolling down my face and I squeezed my eyes shut. Still, they flowed, rushing out of me like the words had on paper, like my magic did in moments I least wanted it to. I had never been able to control myself as a child. Feeling too much was a weakness I couldn't overcome, despite how badly my family wanted me to, how many times my father begged me to. Now that I was back here, I was feeling all of it again, this loss and pain and anger, and I didn't know if I would be able to bottle them back up. They didn't go away, despite how long I ignored them. Perhaps neglected emotions only grew over time. Perhaps I only gave them time to become larger beasts I would still have to fight alone.

That made sense, didn't it? Children grew up, even while being neglected. Trees reached for the sky, even with no one around to watch them. The world had a way of always finding what it needed in order to survive. Even me. Even my grief.

I cried over the note until the ink on it bled.

A chill rippled over my overheated skin, and a new note spiraled in front of me, landing lightly on my lap.

Don't blame yourself for what you can't control.

I wondered in that moment if the person on the other side of this ink had gotten into my head, if they could hear my thoughts as well as read them. Then, another note appeared, settling into place on top of the other. This parchment was different from what I was used to receiving from them, thicker and textured, but it felt familiar too, somehow.

Tell me where you are, and I'll come to you. You shouldn't be alone.

My breath caught. They wanted to meet me *now*? Was it out of pity, or because they thought I was weak and vulnerable enough to get what they wanted? That was a very real fear I carried with each note.

Being alone was safe. I'd never been hurt or misunderstood or disappointed that way.

I forced my weeping to stop, wiped my tears away with the dark material of my dress, and straightened in my chair until I was at last the woman I needed to be: strong and uncaring.

Instead of saying yes and indulging the piece of me that so badly wanted to hold them in my arms, to thank them for holding *me* together all those months in the gnashing forest, I asked them for what I needed most. I gave them Ehlark Qinan's name.

Then, I wrote in farewell, *I like being alone.*

And I swore to myself that I meant it.

CHAPTER 9

The piano keys were frigid, like satin under my fingertips, the melody a whisper drifting through the dark den. I listened to the footsteps as they thudded down the hall, closer and closer. The doorknob rattled, and the bronze lock clinked as a key was slotted into it.

Destin slipped inside but halted on the threshold when he saw me. He glanced down at the doorknob and frowned. "You shouldn't be in here."

"You said not to let *Erlene* in here. She's sleeping upstairs."

"The door was locked."

I didn't stop playing. "The lock is shit."

Destin blinked. "Get out."

"This is the only instrument in the entire house, and I'm tired of evenings without music," I said toward the piano. "The silence is deafening."

He didn't reply to that. After hesitating a moment, he shut the door and walked briskly to the desk. When he reached for the opaque amber bottle there, he gasped. "What did you *do*?"

I smiled at the ivory keys. "Do you think you're the only

one who can guzzle liquor?" My head swirled as I looked at him over my shoulder.

My chest tingled with satisfaction as he returned my gaze, his jaw slackening. "You drank all of it? There was more than a pint left."

I chuckled. "That's nothing. You should see the damage I can do in a tavern."

He shook his head. "I don't ever wish to see that, Goddess help you." He paused. "Were you drinking...because of what happened earlier?"

I sighed, my smile fading. "You've heard of my prowess, I see."

"Yes. The entire staff is talking about what they heard."

"Well, obviously." I rolled my eyes. "She has a horrific wail."

"Are you proud of yourself for what you did? You really upset Felicity."

"I like sex." My lips twisted as I considered the music springing from my fingers, then I added, "Her friend smelled lovely, and that was reason enough for me."

I felt his eyes on me, *all over* me.

"Besides," I shrugged, stumbling over a few notes. "I needed you to have a clear head for what I want to speak with you about." I allowed my hands to fall from the piano.

When I turned on the bench to face Destin, he had his arms crossed as he sat on the edge of the desk. "And what exactly did you want to discuss?"

I nodded at the bottle and the newspaper I'd pinned beneath it. "Did you see the news?"

Slowly, he removed the bottle and tilted the paper toward the fireplace. His eyes scanned the article I'd marked with charcoal before he tossed the paper back onto his desk with a shrug. "What about it?"

"That walker came rather close to the House, don't you think?"

"So?"

"*So*, I'm wondering what precautions you plan to take to prevent any other wanderers from getting onto the property."

His eyes narrowed, the slate blue gleaming in the low light. "I knew about the walker, Sia. I was sent word the moment our authorities responded to it, and I've already doubled the watch along our boundaries."

"Oh." I nodded. "Good."

"Is that why you invaded my office? You want to tell me how to take care of my home?"

"How was I to know you aren't totally incompetent?" Before he could respond, I asked, "Is there any particular reason you sleep here rather than the bedroom upstairs?"

Destin's hard expression slipped as he glanced at the couch, at the mess of blankets and pillows there. "That's none of your concern," he mumbled.

"Normally, I wouldn't care, but Felicity was exceptionally difficult today. If you saw to your marital responsibilities more frequently, maybe she'd pull the stick out of her ass."

His brow furrowed. "What do you mean by difficult?"

"Unpleasant. Bitter. Infantile. I'm dealing with not one but *two* children every day."

His lips twitched. "Sorry to hear that."

"I've decided that when Felicity's friend is taken to the train tomorrow, Erlene and I will travel with her. I have shopping to do."

Destin narrowed his eyes at me, and then ran a hand through his dark hair. "I must be hearing voices of some sort."

"Are you?" I said flatly. "That *is* concerning."

"You just brought the dismembered bodies to my attention out of concern for this property. Now, you plan to travel towards the source of that danger? With my daughter?"

"She'll be safe with me." I turned back to the piano, searching for a song amid my jumbled thoughts. The liquor was topping me. *Whoops.* "I was simply letting you know in advance so you could send along the proper security for us."

His feet thumped against the floor to me. "I don't want you to take Erlene. Leave her here with Felicity." He halted beside the piano bench, close enough that I felt the night air sloughing off him. He'd been in the stables. I could smell it.

I scowled up at him. "Absolutely not."

"Why?"

I didn't want to get into the details of my annoyance with Felicity. My jealousy. After what I did tonight, she was going to be furious with me, and I didn't want to give Erlene a chance to become some sort of pawn in the power struggle between us.

"I don't know her," I muttered, "and neither did Tova. Why would I entrust a stranger with the future of Gwaith House when I can't even trust her father? I'd rather stretch my luck with a handful of trained guards. They're more reliable."

He didn't respond, just continued glaring at me.

"Where did you get all this extra security, anyway?" I wondered aloud, keeping my expression static. "It can't be typical of a House your size. I find it unlikely you're employing them yourself, considering you felt the need to offload a governess for the sake of this House's fortune."

"The Baron sent them." Destin had answered immediately, as if he'd let the truth slip out before he could catch it.

Did the rebels belong to the Baron? Him being aligned with the rebels would mean the cause went higher than underground operations. It meant the animosity towards seraphim was spreading, festering. If Destin was working directly under a man with that kind of power, that kind of influence, my usual tricks weren't going to remedy this.

A hint of that awful realization seeped into my voice. "Why would he do that?"

"I'm helping him patrol our borders." An explanation vague enough that I knew it had been parroted.

"How very convenient for Gwaith House," I mused. I needed to get out of here before I punched him in the face. "Well, you should probably learn to accept that you don't get to make demands concerning your daughter's safety. You don't get to pretend that you care for her when, in reality, you ignore her. That's why Tova didn't trust you, why she sent for me: to do what *you* could not."

Destin slammed the lid of the piano down so hard, I knew my fingers would have been crushed if they were still in the way. I wondered if he wished they were. "What could you possibly need from the city that can't be provided for you here?"

I didn't recoil, even though his nose was only inches from mine.

"I've been wearing Tova's clothing for weeks now," I replied. "I'd like to purchase some items that actually fit me."

His lips parted, his gaze softening as it trailed down my torso. "Oh." He took a step back and ran a palm over his jaw, the faint stubble audibly scraping against his calluses. "I hadn't noticed."

"Now you know. I'm sure you of all people understand how painful it is to be reminded of loss every time you look in the mirror."

He retreated another step. "What do you mean, *me* of all people?"

"That's why you won't look at Erlene, isn't it?"

Destin stared at me like I'd just told him the moon was falling. "You don't know anything," he retorted, gripping the lip of the piano's grand belly.

I stood from the bench, taunting him with a small smile. "I know more about you than you're willing to admit. You're a coward, and when you stop lying to yourself, you'll see that I'm right."

The polished wood squeaked under his fingers.

"What you are is a nuisance," he snarled. "The newest scourge of my life."

"I certainly hope so." I walked past him.

Destin's hand touched my arm, not grabbing, as it had next to the stables, but… pleading. His lifeless eyes were locked on my hair.

His hand drifted up the length of my arm and I tensed, my body surging with heat. To my surprise, his pointer finger only hooked around a lock of my hair. It gleamed maroon in the firelight, and the blue ribbon Tova gave me peeked through. The ribbon I could not go a day without. The one I'd pulled from my hair before kneeling between that woman's legs, because I couldn't bear to let it caress a stranger's thighs. The one I'd drawn to my chest once it was all over, trying to beg forgiveness from a ghost, for both what I'd done and what I'd thought.

Nothing had assuaged the brokenness I'd felt.

"This ribbon," he exhaled. "I *do* remember."

Destin's throat bobbed as his thumb caressed the worn silk.

I stepped away. His eyes met mine, and they were beyond lifeless. They were buried beneath the sorrow I'd once scented on him, and I found I could not hate him as fiercely as I wanted to. "It's the only piece of her I'll keep," I whispered.

I was halfway to the door when he said, "You play beautifully." His tone molded the compliment into a question. It asked *how*. Tova didn't tell him everything, it seemed. She told him the barest details of what we were, perhaps a few smaller truths, but not enough for him to understand who stood before him. *What* stood before him. Thank the Goddess for that.

"Did you think Tova picked me up off the street, or a hedge, as you've suggested?" He didn't reply, didn't so much as blink, so I continued. "We were a good match. Unexpected and unconventional but equals in all the ways that mattered. I loved her from the first moment I saw her, and she reciprocated a fraction of those feelings for me for several reasons, my appearance and sex being the very least of them. My skill with the piano, on the other hand..." I huffed a weak laugh. "Did you know that Gwaith House didn't have a piano before we met? There was no music here, not for all the generations that came before her. She loved music."

Again, he said nothing. His eyes slid over the instrument, then returned to me.

I smiled joylessly. "You know what I find really sad about this whole mess? I think she truly loved you. Then you turned out to be nothing more than a pretty face laid over a rotting soul. What a fucking waste."

Destin's eyes slid shut, his hands loosening to hang limply at his sides. Only the crackle from the fire responded as I slipped out of the den.

CHAPTER 10

Despite the chilly breeze drifting in from the ocean, a layer of sweat drenched my face. I blamed the cowl, which served to mask everything below my eyes as Erlene and I walked purposefully through the foggy streets of the city.

I held tightly to Erlene's hand, walking slow enough that she kept pace but quick enough that her little legs had to jog.

The smog swamped us, the thickest I'd ever seen it as we neared noon, thick enough that the world was reduced to a circumference of ten feet in any direction. I always wondered what these streets would look like without it. Brief glimpses of brick buildings and the wrinkled posters plastered over them peeked through the veil of white to our left. The murky cobblestone flew by beneath our feet, and a line of lamp posts flickered to our right.

The humans on the street saw even less than I did, so I guided us around them as they appeared in our path.

Men in three-piece suits of varying shades passed by, as well as a few women in bright dresses and thick scarves wrapped around their faces every which way. I pointedly looked away from the bloody handkerchiefs when I saw them.

I didn't want to think about the implications, the way those who suffered afflictions here were forced to work through it with little to no treatment, the way flowers were pinned to everyone's clothing in an attempt to ward off the fragrance of death, most of which seeped into the streets from the apartments overhead. I didn't want to think of how many had died last night and were now waiting to be found.

I slowed for a moment to fiddle with Erlene's cowl, ensuring it covered her nose before continuing on.

One man passed by wearing a mask stitched together with dyed hide and thread, the leather extending in front of his face like an elongated beak. I was thankful for my cowl, because there was no restraining my frown. Those masks were a silent mockery of the seraphim, harkening all the way back to their origins, to those sacred winged spirits they were borne of, those deities lurking within the greatest wonders of our world.

Brainless, squawking birds, humans liked to sneer.

It was foolish of humans to wear those masks, to taunt those who would not hesitate to respond with violence if the opportunity arose. This city was lucky that seraphim rarely walked these streets. Almost never. The Fenix did not like to leave their home in the sky. It was beautiful there, innovative, even for the advanced technology and sciences of the seraphim. It was so beautiful that most allies of the Fenix preferred to travel up to visit rather than have the Fenix travel down.

The memory of that place sent tingles up my spine, and I pressed my fingers against the scar over my heart in preparation for the pain coming.

It was a particularly difficult morning for my body. The pain had been a recurring nuisance, hitting me again and again as we rolled into the city. I could no longer ignore the truth. I was certain that the promise hanging over my head was starting to affect me, but I didn't have a solution. There was no fixing this pain. All I could do was grind my teeth together and bear it.

I hated that this would be the rest of my life, living with this...fear. Eventually, either weeks or years from now, the pain would become unmanageable, debilitating.

Footsteps pounded into the cobblestone behind us, and I turned to find the guard Destin sent to escort us finally catching up from where we'd lost him at the train station after dropping Kim off. Erlene and I had slipped out of the carriage while her bags were being unloaded.

I sighed as the guard fell into step with us.

His brown eyes seared into mine, the only visible sign of his frustration. "You were supposed to wait for me," he said, his voice muffled by his own black scarf.

"You were moving too slowly."

"You ditched me on purpose."

I shot him a brief, bored glance. "If I hadn't wanted you to find me afterwards, you wouldn't have. Just try to keep up with us now."

The guard's eyes flashed like he was tempted to reply, but he started coughing. The silver threaded through his dark brows gave away his age. He shouldn't breathe in more of this smog than he needed to; speaking was a luxury he couldn't afford.

He seemed to come to the same conclusion, because he kept his thoughts to himself, continuing to glare at me as he fell into place behind us.

As we turned down one of the main streets, I scanned the brick shopfronts. The air was slightly clearer here, allowing me to see to the end of the street. We were near the bay. I hadn't been in this area for a long time, and even years ago, when I'd been somewhat familiar with the city, I didn't visit many of the shops, only a few taverns and stores that carried specialty wares. Still, it was easy enough to spot the seamstress sign.

The bell over the door rang as we entered.

Once the door shut behind our escort, the smog following us dissipated in long, wispy curls. The entrance was framed on either side by air purifiers, hulky contraptions with spinning wooden blades and mechanical bronze misters.

The smog might have been remedied, but now, the air was suffocatingly wet. I ripped Erlene's cowl down and then my own as we ambled into the shop.

A woman dressed in vibrant purple fabric emerged from behind the counter. "Hello. How can I help you?" Her eyes slid over Erlene and me, but she blinked when she finally spotted the guard. I could understand her reticence. He hadn't pulled his cowl back yet, his body wrapped in black leather, and this was…well, it was a woman's shop.

I waved flippantly in his direction. "Just ignore our shadow. I plan to."

The woman smiled tightly. "Of course. What can I help you with?"

I quickly showed her the dress I was wearing and told her which sizes and styles I would need, ignoring her look of disapproval as she listened, presumably because the sizes I ordered were loose enough to fit weapons beneath them, swamping my generous curves.

Her eyes flicked several times to a small altar set up between racks of clothing, a carved crystal statue erected in the center of it. I saw the direction of her thoughts, the way she compared my body to the naked depiction of our Great Mother. I should have taken it as a compliment, I supposed. My wide hips and supple thighs had always earned me second glances, always garnered special attention, whether I wanted it or not. It was a sign of the Mother's favor.

To any believer, drowning my blessed figure in fabric was a travesty.

As she disappeared into the back room to fetch an order form, I directed Erlene toward the girls' section and walked around the shop, looking at the available materials.

The guard, thankfully, remained with Erlene.

I pulled simple material samples, all in solid jewel tones, avoiding the nauseating shades of red and orange. I couldn't purchase anything extraordinary, not after I'd given most of my coin to Lila, but one gold piece still went a long way in the human lands, so I didn't shy away from the more durable threads.

Despite my resolution to remain practical, I found myself drawn to the front window, where a powder blue swathe of fabric glimmered. I hadn't glanced at the display walking in, but now that I was looking, I couldn't turn away. I tugged my cowl looser around my neck, gasping for air through the humidity spilling from the purifiers as I stepped onto the plat-form. The back of the dress plummeted, exposing the entire back of the mannequin, and connected to the front by two thin, sequined straps. A bow rested in the center of the mannequin's lower back, soft and matte and delicately tied.

As I peeked around the curve of the platform, my jaw dropped.

The bodice was etched like a sheet of fine, frost-coated glass, the material pulling tight at the chest, a lighter lace sewn over and bunched together at the waist. The waistline itself was crusted in a thin speckling of rhinestones that faded as the skirt fell to the floor.

I touched the skirt, lifting it.

The material reflected a lovely sheen as it moved, shifting to a pastel purple when the light fluxed over it. The weight was negligible, no doubt weaved with magic to feel lighter than air. It took me a minute to stop gaping down at it, and then another to shake myself out of my stupor. This was exactly the sort of extravagance I couldn't have, the sort that reminded me of everything I had run from and perhaps emulated all that I had lost since.

Luxury. Beauty. Weightlessness.

A gust of cold air encroached on my back, and the nape of my neck prickled. A twinge speared through my back into my chest, swirling around my heart like a glass case exposed to heat, ballooning, *expanding*.

Someone had their eyes on me.

I glanced up. The seamstress hadn't returned from the back room yet. Erlene was preoccupying the guard, piling dresses into his arms, and there were no other patrons. Turning slightly, I scanned the streets as the smog swirled ominously beyond the window.

A couple passed by, not raising their eyes from the ground. I squinted, trying in earnest to see farther. A few carriages rolled down the road, but none of them lingered. Still, that icy exposure along my spine didn't let up. There was no way they'd found me so quickly. If they *had*…

No, I wouldn't allow myself to consider it.

I staggered off the podium, pulling my cowl up. I returned to Erlene and helped her choose a new dress from her mountain of material. By the time we walked to the back of the shop, the seamstress had emerged and took my order.

When she heard where I wanted the dresses delivered to, she gave her congratulations on my marriage and luck in my role as the new Lady. Because I didn't want to get into the details of who I was, I smiled politely and let her assume what she wanted.

The guard harrumphed as if he might correct her, and I discreetly stomped on his foot.

The seamstress returned and handed me a receipt with the date I could expect the clothes to arrive. "Thank you," I said warmly. "Now tell me, does this shop have a back door?"

The woman's brow creased in surprise. "Yes."

"May we use it? It's just...I think I saw an old friend out front, and I'd really like to avoid them."

The guard shot me a skeptical look, but one shift of my foot had him stepping back and muting his expression. He sighed quietly – a surrender. The shop owner didn't respond right away, nervously fiddling with the cuff of her dress.

I smiled. "Please?" I let my gaze go a bit molten, let it glisten a luminous amber in the shadow of my hood, and she gasped.

The woman's lips twitched, and she beckoned us through the sectioned curtains into the back room. It wasn't magic, my charm. It was a natural gift I'd discovered was always there, ready to be wielded. I'd learned that from my father too. Usually, I relied on other methods of coercion when it came to getting my way, methods that didn't require such exhausting masks. Blades and bribery worked wonders in the forest. Human cities, not so much.

Fleeing the shop through the back door *should* have remedied the chill in my bones, should have appeased the paranoia I felt, but it didn't. That prickle lingered. My back dampened with sweat, despite being relieved of the humidity from the shop. I still felt those invisible eyes.

I should have returned to the carriage, but dresses weren't my only reason for this trip.

As we entered a market street adjacent to the bay, I halted in front of an unmarked shop. "I just need to run in here for a moment." I said, herding Erlene toward the guard. I waved at the flower wagons behind them. "Take Erlene to admire the blooms. She'll love that."

"I was advised to accompany both of you," he replied.

He'd been advised to track my every move.

I shook my head. "I'm afraid I can't let Erlene join me. This is an herbalist's shop, and I need to purchase some tonics for my cycle." His grimace practically pierced through his cowl when he heard that. "I wouldn't want Erlene exposed to any unnecessary hormones. She's too young, and Goddess forbid *you* should absorb too much, either. You may find yourself growing," my gaze flicked to his broad chest, "unwanted assets."

Red crept up his cheeks. He cleared his throat and took Erlene's hand. "Right. We'll wait for you in the flower market." Then, he led the girl toward the colorful stands.

Chuckling to myself, I pushed open the door to the shop.

A dull bell rang above my head as I entered. The air was humid here, but at least the purifiers were stationed farther inside the room. Incense burned throughout the dim shop. The scent of sage and woodsy resin assaulted my senses, their embers gleaming amidst the dusty shelves, spitting white smoke that curled up against the ceiling.

The muscles in my neck instantly uncoiled.

Whatever manner of alchemy the herbalist had used to create this incense, it was effective. The last time I'd been here, the shop was abandoned. Raided. Every trace of life and magic had been destroyed. Being here again should unsettle me, should remind me of how I knew about it in the first place, but it didn't.

I was confident this herbalist would be able to help me.

Candlelight filtered from the back of the shop, illuminating the jars and vials cluttering the room, the dried plants hanging from the ceiling, and the elderly woman standing behind the counter. Her silver hair fell forward heavily, shrouding most of her face. She didn't look up from the steaming mug in front of her, even as I halted on the other side of the counter.

"What can I do for you?" Her voice was rough, splintered. The words were barely out before she started hacking into a stained handkerchief.

Once her fit subsided, I said, "I'm here to trade goods with you."

The elder looked up. Her eyes were narrowed and blood-shot, and beyond the dilated pupils, there was a blue so dark, it was nearly black. She raked a cursory glance over my torso, my shaded face, and replied, "I don't deal in trades."

"Trust me, you'll want this." From the pack attached to my waist, I withdrew a small vial and placed it on the counter between us. The ebony contents swirled.

She coughed into her napkin again, a spittle of blood leaving a fresh stain on the cloth. "And why would I want *that,* pray tell?"

"They're holy tears."

The herbalist jolted, her spine straining against the perma-nent curve in it as she squinted at the vial. "I have seen holy tears before. Those don't look right."

"I harvested these tears myself. I'm sure of their authenticity."

She waved me off. "That may be so, but I have a business to run. I won't be tricked. If you aren't going to purchase something with physical coin, I must request that you leave."

"Try it."

"What?" The woman's brow furrowed.

"You're suffering from an affliction of the lungs. I can smell the tonic in your mug from here, the peppermint. You're masking painkillers, if I'm guessing correctly, which means you're beyond the usual treatment. So, try the vial. Consider it a goodwill offering. If it works, then you will know I'm telling you the truth, and you can trade with me."

She blinked, considering my offer for a long moment. "And if it is poison?"

"Certainly you have every manner of antidote here."

Her eyes flickered. Yes, she carried far more here than what she placed on the shelves.

"On the other hand, if it works," I said quietly, "you'll get better."

After another long stare, the herbalist grasped the vial. She shook the crystal container, holding it up to a flame to study the swirling blackness in the light.

Her frown didn't deepen, but it didn't ease either.

She uncorked the vial, smelled it, and then downed it in one, long swig.

I pushed back my hood then, letting it fall to my shoulders. One full minute was all it took for the tonic to take effect. The herbalist took a deep breath, and instead of the air catching short, her lungs filled.

Her eyes flew to mine. "How is it possible? Where did you get this? From *whom?*"

"That's not important." I withdrew a second vial from my pouch. Her gaze followed it as I set my offering on the counter. "Will you trade with me now?"

"What do you need?"

I ran a hand over the curls resting on my shoulder. "I need red henna, the strongest you have, and a few rarer herbs, if you happen to carry them."

The woman gave me a wily grin. "For you, I have it all."

CHAPTER 11

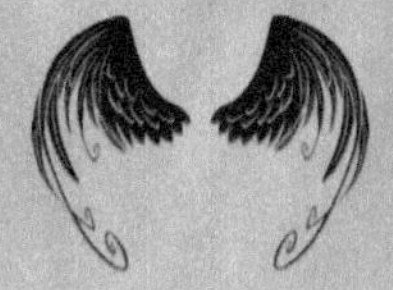

The sensation of being watched returned in full force as I left the herbalist shop.

When I surveyed the street, all I found was stale smog and empty cobblestone. Then, I realized the torches hanging off the buildings had been snuffed out, and the sound of grinding stone was echoing above my head.

I spun toward it.

A gargoyle was perched on the ledge of the building next door, its gray mouth widened in a puff of debris. Pebbles bounced off the front of the building, scattering around my feet. The living statue tilted its head, one way then the other, as if it were stretching a nonexistent spine.

Stone teeth chattered as it said, "What a marvelous disguise you've contrived, Sabrina. For a while, I was sure my eyes had deceived me, but it's true. You've returned."

Those must have been the eyes I felt all morning.

The street was barren around us as the stagnant fog closed in. Whether it was a coincidence or if he'd thrown up some sort of ward to keep the humans away while we conversed, I couldn't be sure. I wouldn't put it past him.

I snarled, "I haven't returned, Spiro, and I'm certainly not staying. Leave me be."

The gargoyle's brow furrowed with a crackle. Before I could anticipate his next move, the creature leapt off the building and landed with a crushing thud in front of me. He stepped forward, pulverized cobblestone shifting under his feet.

"You need to come home." Though his appearance was hard, his voice was gentle. "This has been going on long enough. Your father is riddled with worry now that your birthday of promise approaches, and your brother has snuck out several times in the last several months to search for you. When will this be over?"

I ran a hand along the inside of my cloak.

A spark of regret flickered in my stomach at the knowledge of my brother leaving the floating city to search for me. He was the only one I really missed, my dear Kahem. He had risked capture, injury, or worse by roaming the forest on his own, but as Spiro continued to stare at me with his beady black eyes, that guilty twinge in my gut faded.

Spiro was my father's closest confidante. The spirit possessing this stone belonged to a physical body far away from here, and that was the only reason I hadn't already been snatched up against my will. He technically *couldn't*. He knew I'd smash his statue to rubble before he dragged me a foot. I wouldn't be surprised if my father was sitting in the same room as Spiro's meditating body right now, just waiting for him to wake and divulge my location.

He'd always done this: used others to communicate while he kept me at a distance. This was our entire fucking relationship. Never flesh, always stone.

Once Father knew where I was, he would send someone down here for me. He didn't feel compassion for my position or my desires, and in the end, neither did my brother. Maybe he'd even send my brother to retrieve me. I couldn't deal with facing Kahem. I'd crumble.

"If Father wants me home so badly, then he should fetch me himself, instead of sending messenger after messenger. Your bounty hunters are pathetic."

Rock screeched as the gargoyle swiveled its head. "I don't think you understand how close he is to taking matters into his own hands, Sabrina. Trust me, you will not like how that would end."

I slipped my hand into the inner pocket of my cloak. "I can't come home. I can't be what you all need me to be."

If any stone face could look tender, it was this one as it said, "Of course you can, Sabrina. You were born to your father for a reason, for a purpose. You are exactly what we need."

"Everyone back home knows that's a lie. Our visitors will, too."

"Eventually, perhaps." His stony shoulders rose and fell, more debris tumbling and scattering over the ground. The statue was inches from falling apart. "But they will know nothing until it is too late."

"Until I am bound to one of them for the rest of my existence," I amended through my teeth. Given away like a Goddess-damned present. It wouldn't happen – I'd rather return to the forest, as lonely as it was, to the trees that did not hunt but held me instead.

The statue sat back and stared for a long moment, straight into my soul. "You are bound already. They have arrived and are asking after you, and we can't keep making excuses. You cannot run from your future. It will find you. *No matter what.*"

The scar over my heart twinged.

"Not if I can help it." I quickly withdrew the satin pouch from my cloak.

Spiro's gaze locked on the bag, the careful combination of herbs and flammable resin. "Sia, please—"

I blinked, and the pouch caught flame. Black flames consumed my hand, burning the herbs to smoke in an instant. They licked harmlessly across my skin. My fire did not illuminate, did not emulate the light or goodness of normal flames. They only destroyed.

And that was exactly what I needed right now.

The air darkened in front of Spiro as I uttered a spell of banishment, something I'd learned in the forest many months ago.

The stone went rigid as those black eyes turned porous gray. The gargoyle crumbled before me, and as it did, I dropped the smoldering pouch into the ruins and let my darkness eat the ashes.

The fire searched for a way to endure, but I couldn't let it.

As I turned away and strode toward the flower market, I massaged my tingling hand. My skin crawled. The heat roared in my veins, trying to burrow a way out through the opening I had made for it. I shoved it down, covering my burning palm with the other, suffocating the magic. *Go away. Please, please go away.*

The pressure under my skin eased as I wound my way between the carts overflowing with flowers. I kept my head down, hiding my glow, willing the amber hue in my eyes to fade.

I was insanely lucky.

If I hadn't obtained that spell bag when I did, Spiro would have found a way to keep me contained until someone arrived to deliver me to Father. If he'd learned about Erlene, about the rebel guard, if they knew what I was *really* doing here…there was no telling what Father would do to remedy the situation.

The spell bag had been intended for Gwaith House, to ward off whatever evil was killing innocents on this coast. It was a knapsack I'd asked the herbalist to blend for me, filled with rare herbs that could take the intention of the burner and banish anything that might intend harm. Now, it had been wasted.

At least Spiro couldn't reappear in some other inanimate form here; his spirit was now effectively repelled from the area, from the entire city if the herbs were potent enough.

But others would be coming.

I felt their phantom hands grip my lungs, attempting to drag me back to the person I used to be. Someone contained and obedient. That was the way Father wanted me, the only way I was of value to him.

I had to get out of the city, *now*.

CHAPTER 12

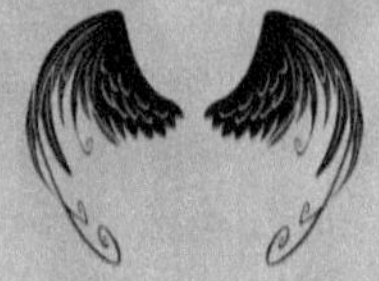

I tracked Erlene and the guard down between two aisles of wildflowers. She was rubbing the velvety petals between her fingers, and the guard did his best to stop her from tearing them all apart completely. She already had a couple small, crumpled bouquets in her hand that he couldn't save.

"Let's walk back," I said as soon as I reached them. "I'm not feeling well."

The guard leaned away from me, and I rolled my eyes. The fool probably thought my feminine woes were contagious.

Erlene pouted, tugging on my fingers. "Can we pick flowers for Mommy before we go?"

I should have guessed she would ask that. Surrounded by all these blooms, in the same market her mother used to visit as religiously as a temple, how could I expect anything less?

I remember the first time I laid eyes on Tova. It was here, in this city, close to this very spot. She'd had her arms full of flowers, a startlingly vibrant smile on her face. I was drawn to her without intending to be, and she'd embraced me so easily.

I'd been bewitched by her beauty and kindness, her

endless energy, as sprightly as a forest nymph on the full moon.

After Tova passed and we'd buried her ashes, Erlene and I placed more flowers than ever would have fit in her arms upon her grave. They'd since wilted with the turn of the season. This might be the last opportunity to give her fresh flowers before the winter frosts began, before I was gone.

"Yes," I conceded, "but we have to be quick. Do you have something special in mind for her?"

She pointed at a cart a few yards away. "The blue pansies."

I smiled gently. "Good choice."

As we headed toward that stand, the guard hung back. "I have to attend to a matter for his Lordship while you two finish shopping." He glanced at the blacksmith hammering away down the block. *Right.* Destin had likely asked him to get Tova's ring resized. "I'll be back to accompany you to the carriage in a moment. No running off."

"I make no promises, old man."

He issued a grunt before stalking away.

Erlene led me to the pansies, and I let her fill my hands with them. I tapped my foot, staring intently at the owner of the stand, trying to catch her eye. The vendor was indulging in mindless drivel with another customer. When Erlene grew tired of counting the petals in my hand, her eye caught on another stand across the aisle, and she darted towards it. I pivoted to follow, her name on the tip of my tongue.

Instead, my body collided with hard muscle.

My vision flooded with black and purple silk, and an arm looped around my waist to keep me from being knocked back on my ass.

My hands, which were still clutching the pansies, hooked instinctually into the stranger's vest. The brush of cool metal kissed my fingertips, the texture totally unexpected, and I glanced down to see a silver watch chain hanging over the purple embossed silk.

Then, I saw the man's abdominal muscles straining beneath his sleek suit.

I blinked and forcefully tore my eyes away from his body. My gaze slid upwards and caught on the red handkerchief tucked into his breast pocket. I couldn't help it. I was so unprepared for that shock of color that I recoiled.

He spoke then, his voice deep and impossibly soft. "Apologies, miss."

I looked up, fully prepared to put a face to that delicious voice. Instead of a face, I was met with a leather beak. A shoot of fear and disgust sheared through my ribs, and I would have pushed him away if he wasn't holding me so closely, so firmly. He wore a black hat, but tufts of dark blond hair peeked out around his temples and ears, overgrown but tamed. His mask concealed almost everything else except his eyes, and I couldn't breathe when I saw them.

His eyes were a pale, piercing blue and incredibly large. I could have sworn the outer corners crinkled in a smile as I studied them.

"You," he breathed.

The ballooning of my heart filled with noxious fumes as a memory flickered there. It took a moment to notice his arm tightening around me. I put aside my fascination and squinted at him, raising my arms between us, damaged flowers and all. "Are you going to let go of me anytime soon, or will I have to make you?"

His eyes fluttered, and he instantly took a step back. "Yes, of course."

Muttering my annoyance, I picked out the worst of the crushed flowers and tossed them on the ground. Then, I fixed my cowl.

When I looked up, I realized the stranger was still there.

He'd taken his mask off and was staring unabashedly at me. Not devouring, as I came to expect from men, but studying me. That gaze searched me like a child turning toward their first shooting star, like a man looking for salvation in the Mother Divine without any understanding of how to pray.

"What are you looking at?" I snarled.

He shook his head, chuckling. The mask swung heavily from the strap around his neck. He'd taken it off his face, and I wanted to tear it off his neck and burn it. "I'm sorry. You knocked the sense right out of me." His lips were plush and pink, and the rest of his features cut sharp, strong angles in comparison. Golden stubble coated his cheeks and jaw.

I bit my lip to stop ogling. This was neither the place nor the time.

"Well, I assure you, it wasn't on purpose. Watch where you're going." I made to step around him, but he moved with me, like a magnet turned to the wrong side, keeping his distance but drawn to me around the edges. He lifted a hand toward me, as if he might try to keep me.

If we weren't surrounded, I would have laid him out on the cobblestone, but as it was, the market was busy, and I didn't need the trouble.

"I was walking in a bit of a daze, I'll admit." He chuckled again, the knot in his throat bobbing as he gestured around us. "I'm not used to all this." He must be a new transplant to the city. The city hired from the outside often. The best paid jobs were here; it was just a pity the smoke killed in exchange for a comfortable wage.

"If you knew what was good for you, you'd never get used to it. Now, if you'll excuse me." I craned my neck, searching the haze for Erlene. She was on her way back to me with a bundle of orange poppies in hand.

The stranger nodded at the pansies between us. "Lovely. Is blue your favorite color?"

He cut off my path again, and I huffed in exasperation. "What?"

"Are these your favorite flowers?"

I balled my hands in my skirt. "They're not for me."

"Pansies!" Erlene exclaimed.

The man started, pivoting toward the small voice. "Oh." His gaze flitted between the two of us as Erlene stepped forward and gripped a handful of my dress. "Hello, little one."

"The flowers are called pansies," Erlene said, taking on a delightful confidence only knowledgeable little girls attained. "You're supposed to hold one and think really, really hard, and then the pansy takes all the thoughts out of your heart so you can give them away."

Pride swelled in my chest. She'd learned that from me. It was wisdom I'd absorbed from my mother's flower journal when I was also young and innocent, when I read it a thousand times to memorize all the herbs and flowers she'd ever encountered and pressed. I obsessed over that journal, touched the places she'd touched over and over again, imagining it was as good as feeling her skin.

No one else had ever seemed willing to listen to my flowery superstitions, but now, here they were in Erlene, being believed in.

The stranger smiled, kneeling to better match her height. "Well, I'm glad I ran into an expert like you to tell me what's what. Are pansies *your* favorite, then?"

"No." She fiddled with the poppies. "They're for my mama. She sleeps in the ground."

"Erlene," I whispered, but it was a warning I knew she wouldn't heed.

The man's eyes briefly met mine. Maybe I imagined the glimmer of sadness there, but my chest caved in like a compromised mine anyway, popping the balloon around my heart. Noxious fumes seeped into my body as that old memory flickered again, like a miner calling out from under the rubble. Buried, muffled. I wasn't sure I wanted to unearth it.

"I'm very sorry to hear that," he murmured, turning back to Erlene. "You are strong, to think often and fondly of her when she's far away. I wish I was strong enough to do that."

"We need to be going," I said. We didn't have time for him, for this. I felt our precious time ticking away with each of my heart's rhythmic taps against my ribs.

My father would not hesitate. My leash was shortening by the second. I stepped forward to take Erlene's hand, but then the man kneeling before us gasped loudly, freezing me in place.

"Hold on." A sudden playfulness seeped into his voice. "What is *that?*"

Erlene's brow scrunched.

The stranger pointed at her left ear. "What is that thing in your ear? My goodness, it's gigantic." He reached out and pinched the air next to her head. When he brought his hand down, it held one of her orange poppies. "Look, you're growing flowers from your ears!"

Her eyes went round as saucers as she reached up and patted the side of her cowl. She realized in the next moment what he'd done, just as I did – that he'd deftly stolen a flower from her bundle. "No, I'm not. You're trying to trick me."

He clicked his tongue. "Ah, you're too clever for me."

The stranger returned her poppy, stood, and turned his gentle smile on me. I smiled back, despite myself. It was sort of lovely, these brief, mortal connections that fizzled into my heart. I had been on my own for so long, any speck of warmth felt like a hearth, but I also knew this pull towards him wasn't so innocent.

I was *addicted*.

Ever since Tova, I'd been hooked on the human race, on

how much they felt and what they were willing to risk so quickly for love and affection. They had so little time, and they rarely wasted it. That was part of why I desired to be around them so badly, even when I knew how these connections ended.

The flower stand owner chose that moment to take notice of us and wave me over. As I grappled with the bag on my belt, the stranger withdrew a couple coppers from his blazer and said, "Don't worry, I've got it."

I frowned. "That's not necessary."

"It's my pleasure," he insisted, "really."

I grabbed his arm. His bicep flexed under my fingers, sending a shock of tingles into my arm, up and between my ribs. "I don't want to owe you anything."

I'd already indebted myself once to a mortal by loving her and look where it got me.

It was starting to sink in, now that Tova was gone, that I may have given her more love than she ever thought to reciprocate. I may have loved her with a love greater than any human could fathom, expecting forever when it was not so, when she'd already committed her heart to honor and a man who could not love her back the way she deserved.

After all, that was what had been expected of her, what was expected of *me*.

"This is a gift, no strings attached." His lips curved with a slow, sensual grace. "Consider it an apology for running into you earlier, if that makes you more comfortable."

When I didn't immediately shut him down, his smile broadened.

I took a large step back. "Very well, your apology is accepted. Come along, Erlene." I held onto her with a vice grip and guided us down the maze of aisles, not bothering to spare him a backward glance.

Less than a minute later, footsteps pounded after us, and he reappeared at my side. "Can I ask you a question?"

I sighed. "I knew your generosity was too good to be true."

"What's your favorite flower?"

"I don't see how that's any of your business."

He let out a strangled chuckle, rubbing his jaw. "You don't indulge in pleasant conversation much, do you?"

"Fine," I conceded with a sigh. "Tulips, but I'm warning you now, if you try to pluck one from my ear, I'll shove it down your throat."

"Duly noted. Speaking of—"

In the distance, sirens began to blare. The city's alarm rumbled through the cobblestone.

Erlene whimpered in confusion, tugging on my skirt, and I swiftly scooped her up into my arms. The market was scattering around us as every stand threw sheets over their wares.

There's no way my father descended on the city so quickly, I tried to assure myself, even as I elbowed past our new acquaintance to search for our missing guard.

To my annoyance, the strange man followed us. "What's going on?"

"You've never heard the alarms before?" I paused to look at him more fully. His ignorance was a shock to me. The alarms were so loud, one could hear them from several miles away. Even Gwaith was within their range, and that was quite near the outskirts of the smog.

He shrugged. "I tried to tell you, I'm not from around here. I traveled in from across the forest."

The crowd jostled the man and I closer, and I felt my brow furrow. "That's not possible." There were monsters in the forest, thieves and predatory magic. Few mortals lived through that journey, unless they were exceptionally clever.

He smirked. "Yes, well, I came to solve a mystery of sorts."

Ah. The city had brought in reinforcements. Thank the

Goddess. "Well, it took you fucking long enough to get here." His eyebrows shot upward. "Would you mind telling your detective friends here to get their shit together before these murders hit the countryside? Houses out there aren't equipped to deal with a serial killer."

The stranger's eyes pinched. He opened his mouth, but his response was cut off by the appearance of our guard.

"There you are," the old man barked as he took my elbow. "Let's go."

I glanced back, but the stranger was already gone, swallowed by the mayhem building around us. The guard led the way toward the train station. Chaos infiltrated every street, slowing our retreat even as our guard barreled people over. Through a break in the crowd, I realized the sea of bodies were piling into the market from the adjacent ports.

The city bells tolled again. Once. Twice. Three and four times.

There was a slight pause before the succession of four chimed again. One for attack by land. Two for sea. Three for sky, which was what I feared most. But *four*…

That meant second-lives were loose in the city.

Judging from the movement of the crowd, the ports were the source of it. I hadn't been able to put Tova out of her misery. She'd meant too much to me, but I felt an obligation to that decency now. The innocents of this city might suffer if I didn't intervene.

I tugged at the guard's cloak to make him turn around, and then handed Erlene over to him. "Take her and keep going. I'll meet you at the carriage later."

He growled in protest and reached for my arm to stop me, but it was too late. I'd already disappeared into the crowd.

CHAPTER 13

Letting my vision burn into the oncoming crowd, those who noticed the amber glow under my hood quickly jumped out of the way. My hands slipped under my dress as I drew my twin blades from their sheathes.

I passed through the rest of the market and turned down one of the winding alleys leading to the ports. Grungy, salt-worn brick, yellowed posters, and gray stone blurred together on either side of me. All the roads and alleys in the city eventually led to the bay. It was the city's heart.

Below the sirens and bells, screams echoed down the alley toward me.

Those cries grew louder and louder until they finally overwhelmed the alarm. I emerged into the open air of the ports, the large space marked with crates and distant sails and a glorious clearing of the air. Dark, dangerous waters glittered up ahead, past the iron gates monitoring the bay. Guards paced the wall, undisturbed by the death unfolding before them.

Outbreaks weren't uncommon, especially in the city,

where the newly dead were always one windowpane away from the rest of civilization. It was rarely enough.

I had expected one or two walkers, maybe a small group. I didn't expect an entire horde. There they were, a dozen or more walkers herding port workers down the pier. They weren't old, either. Most appeared young and healthy – the parts of them still visible and intact, at least. These undead had been ripped apart.

Some of their wounds were still gushing, stumps where there had once been arms or legs. One was headless, walking with hands outstretched, feeling past the others. It didn't stumble off the pier; even in death, its instinct to survive endured.

I weaved through the bloodshed.

Corpses were scattered in front of me, evidence of the violence I'd been too late to stop. One or two of them were port workers whose souls had been taken by the dismembered undead, claimed like precious tickets into the afterlife.

Once my feet hit the creaking planks of the pier, a few of the undead turned to acknowledge me. Their souls latched onto mine as they surged for me. My blades tore through clothing and skin and bone as I pierced the spirits in their stomachs, putting the lost souls out of their misery. They fell, empty corpses shaking the wooden planks under my feet. They weren't from this city. Instead of fine suits and dresses, they wore leather, gold, and billowing blouses.

These were sailors.

A pair of thin, blueish arms wrapped around my neck. The snarling walker – one I had apparently missed while navigating the carnage amidst the ports – dragged me back down the pier. Its jagged nails dug into my collarbone as I struggled to keep my footing.

So, I threw my body backwards.

We hurtled to the ground together, and as we collided

with the wooden planks, I twisted enough to see blonde hair. The woman's eyes had been gouged out, but for a moment, I saw Tova there, staring at me. In my hesitation, the undead flipped me over with unnatural strength. Her elbow dislodged one of my daggers and sent it skittering above my head. Her nails started slashing at my face, so I tightened my grip on my remaining dagger and sliced those fingers off. Thick, gelatinous blood rained down over my chest. Her other hand reached for my throat, and I knocked it away, then drove my dagger up into her stomach.

She choked on her next snarl, the grotesque bloody skin around her eyes relaxing. She slumped forward, and I jerked to the side just quick enough to avoid being pinned by her body.

As I shoved at the corpse laying half on top of me, two more farther up the pier took notice. The first was on me in an instant. I threw the dead body off in time to sweep the legs of it and pin them down, but my dagger was still buried in the first corpse, and the third walker was about to descend.

I lurched to the side, thrusting my hand between the wooden planks of the pier and decaying flesh, trying to feel for the hilt of my blade. The dirty nails of the undead's hand beneath me raked across my chest, and I choked on a cry of frustration as my fingertips brushed metal, still too far away to pull out.

Something whistled past my head, missing me by an inch at most.

I watched, wide-eyed, as the undead about to reach me staggered back and collapsed. My second blade I'd lost was there now, embedded in its gut.

In a flurry of black silk, the stranger from the market appeared beside me as he plunged a silver dagger into the second-life beneath me. The corpse went limp.

The stranger's staggering pale eyes met mine, reflecting a

chilled, death-like stagnancy as he withdrew his dagger and cleaned it off on his pants in two, methodical swipes. From this angle, I could see the entirety of his imposing profile. His long, lithe form. The square jaw. Beneath his ear, stretching over his neck and down under the collar of his tunic, his skin looked like it had been twisted in long, embossed stripes. Scar tissue. There would have been no discerning it while looking at him head-on.

Whatever did that to him, it must have been horrible.

Those unsettling eyes scanned my body. I was still straddling the corpse, and he seemed to find that a little funny. "You good?" he purred with a half-smile.

I managed a nod.

Then I watched, breathless, as he stalked down the pier to the remaining walkers. He executed them swiftly, efficiently. I'd barely retrieved both my blades by the time he was finished with them. Then, he calmly sheathed his weapon and turned to address the port workers.

Perhaps he really did have the skills to help this city. What a relief.

Forcefully tearing my gaze from his broad back, I considered the eyeless woman at my feet. I dragged her onto solid ground, where authorities would be more inclined to bag her rather than try and dispose of her beyond the bay, where the serpents could get rid of her. This area didn't exactly have the best reputation when it came to missing persons, and I didn't want this sailor to become one.

I was turning to leave when I saw it.

The feather.

A single, metallic-silver plume rose from the carnage, seeming to wave at me under the ocean breeze. I walked toward it, all too aware of the precious time slipping away from me with this diversion, but I had to know. I found another feather, then another. They led me into an area of the ports crowded with shipments, presumably from the ship anchored up ahead. Narrow walkways had been constructed between the stacks. Massive, ivory sails loomed over me, and the scent of iron filled my nostrils, leaving a film on the back of my throat.

I emerged on the other side of the shipment and froze.

This was the source of the walkers: the crew of the ship. Those who were lucky enough to have their abdomens cut open were scattered between me and the pier up ahead. Guts were everywhere, and there was so much blood. One of the undead sailors was still lucid, crawling around on the edge of the ship without any legs.

What could have done this?

The undead did not feel the need to rip people apart. They only wanted the soul within, not the body.

A serpent from the ocean was capable of overpowering several mortals, I supposed, but I didn't know what purpose that would serve them here. Besides, some of these bodies had been killed on land, and I couldn't imagine serpents could have done this much damage without the ability to walk. All they had were scaled tails where their legs had once been. Before they devolved.

There were more feathers here.

I was eventually led to the mutilated body they belonged to. When my eyes landed on the seraph, I lurched for the corpse. I knew in my heart they were already dead, but I couldn't stop myself from gripping their shoulders and shaking them. Their hard iron feathers clanged at the motion, their black skin cold to the touch.

What the hell was a Stymphalian doing here?

This species of seraphim typically lived in settlements along the coast just south of here, where forest bled into flourishing ridges and valleys. They were born with wings of metal and brilliant minds, known for their preternatural sense of strategy and innovative weaponry, but they also happened to be an extremely gentle people. They rarely ever participated in battle or bloodshed, and when all those seraphim were driven from the islands, they welcomed one of the displaced species with open arms.

Whatever reason the Stymphalian had for being here, it was their death sentence. A slice across their throat from the looks of it. The cut was clean and deep. When seraphim died, it was permanent. Their souls were not tied to the sacral chakra.

I quickly surveyed the body, trying to determine what I should do, if anything. I didn't want to leave them here. The mortals would not treat them with respect, even in death. If the wrong type of human got ahold of these wings, they would harvest and pin them to some wall. They would make a mockery of it. Even worse, if another supernatural creature got ahold of them, they'd try to steal the wings' magic.

I wanted to drape the Stymphalian over my shoulder and carry them out of this place, but the wings were going to make that difficult; the feathers could cut me to shreds if I wasn't careful. I couldn't exactly carry the corpse back to Erlene, either. I didn't want her to see this.

I looked up and scanned the skies. *I really don't have time for this.*

Maybe I could melt the wings to keep anyone else from taking them. Grasping the Stymphalian's shoulders, I carefully turned them over.

I gasped softly at the damage on their back. It looked like someone had already tried to dig their wings out; there were jagged, deep cuts peppering their shoulder blades. It also looked like whoever had attempted to harvest them wasn't prepared for the sharp feathers, or maybe the Stymphalian had still been alive at that point to fight back.

Red-hot anger flashed through me.

If I ever found out who did this, I was going to rip them apart myself. I didn't care what it took or who they were. A silvery-black flame spat to life in my hand, and I started lowering it to the seraph's wings.

Before my flames could touch them, a silken voice spoke from behind me. "Would you like to tell me what the hell you were thinking?"

I clapped my hands together, snuffing out my flame as I shot to my feet. Spinning, I locked eyes with my friendly, flower market stranger. Well, maybe not so friendly now. He was scowling.

Tucking my hands behind my back, I said, "What?"

"You could have been killed," he growled, eating up the space between us with long, measured steps. "Running in alone like that."

I narrowed my eyes at him. "I had everything well in hand."

"The hell you did. You were just *lying* there, and you didn't even—" His voice cut off, his face dropping the scowl as his eyes fell on the seraph behind me. "Oh my."

"This isn't their fault," I said instantly. "The Stympalian wouldn't have done this."

He grimaced. "I would hope not."

Swallowing hard, I whispered, "You have to send the body back to its family. You can't let the authorities sell them off or display them, I'm begging you."

"Don't worry," he said quietly, his eyes still locked on the seraph as he crouched before it. He traced a finger over one of its feathers. He was wearing thick black gloves over his hands that kept the metal from cutting him. "I won't be letting that happen."

I didn't know how, but I felt the truth in those words. "I didn't *what*, by the way?"

"Hmm?" He tore his eyes from the corpse, but his gaze was distant as it landed on me.

"Before, when you said I was *just lying there,* you were about to say something else."

His jaw clenched as he stood and faced me. "I was going to say that you weren't sufficiently protecting yourself."

Heat crawled up my spine. "I swear," I hissed, stepping toward him. "You men are all the same. *I was reaching for my weapon.* After wasting seven second-lives with it, I might add—"

"Six."

"What?"

"You didn't waste seven." His eyes lit with arrogance. "The one you straddled like a rabid dog didn't die until *I* showed up."

"Whatever. I would have been fine without your shining-knight-savior complex barreling in to take over. I don't need saving, and I certainly don't need you."

He recoiled. "I suppose I'll have to take your word on that."

I chuckled at his reaction, rolling my eyes. "I know it goes against every male instinct you have but try not to feel too emasculated."

"I don't feel emasculated at all. Quite the opposite, actually."

"The opposite?" I repeated with a furrowed brow.

"You've aroused my curiosity, as well as a few...*other* parts."

I stiffened. His eyes chilled me with crystal blue honesty as his gloved hands slipped into his trouser pockets. My fingers twitched toward my daggers.

For a moment, I wondered if he would attack me, if he would force me to draw my blades on him. Then he grimaced and shook his head. "Forgive me; I know that's probably not appropriate. We haven't even been properly introduced yet."

"That wouldn't be appropriate to say *ever,*" I returned.

He frowned. "Yes, well, in my defense, you suggested I have a problem with your strength, and I don't, not in the slightest. I didn't know how else to put it. I realize that might have been just about the worst way possible to convey it, now that it's out, but I find it rather difficult to think clearly around you."

"So," I raised a brow, "your lewd comment is *my* fault?"

"No, of course not." He reached up, as if to rake a hand through his hair, but he dropped his hand again when his fingers bumped into his hat. "Fuck me. Can we just start over?"

"That depends." There was no restraining my smirk. "Are you asking me to fuck you now, or are you asking for a fresh start?"

His lips twitched, and I could tell my teasing put him at ease. "I think you've whipped my ego enough for one day." He held out a hand. "My name is Lee."

I stared at the veins chiseled into his skin, the long digits and dirty nails, the blood speckling his knuckles. My gaze slid up to mark his expression, apologetic. I took his hand. "I'm Sia."

"It's nice to meet you, Sia." His hand lingered around mine, his thumb brushing my knuckles so gently, I couldn't pull away with quite the viciousness I wanted.

"If you say so."

From an adjacent alley, shouting and stampeding boots echoed toward us. *The authorities.* I nodded at the sound. "Looks like your buddies have finally deigned to show up. I should probably go."

I glanced longingly at the dead seraph.

"Don't worry, I'll take care of them," Lee swore quietly. "I'll make sure they make it where they need to go."

Coming from a detective, that destination was likely the city's morgue. I didn't fool myself into thinking the city would make any effort to send the seraph back to where it truly belonged, wasting their time and money and compassion. The morgue was the best this seraph's corpse could hope for.

If it had any chance of making it home, the responsibility would fall on my shoulders.

Not now, but soon. I didn't sense any malice in Lee's voice, no untruth. After I saw him in that mask back in the market, I was certain he would be like the rest of the humans who lived here, those who hated seraphim without ever meeting one. Seeing the way he looked at the Stymphalian now, though, I wanted to believe I was wrong. He didn't seem to hate them at all.

"I should go," I repeated, because I didn't know what else to say.

"Right. And get back to your—" Lee paused, his eyes narrowing, the muscle in his jaw working as he chewed his words. "Who *was* that little girl to you?"

I don't know why I responded, why I bothered to trust him with anything at all, but I said honestly, "She's my responsibility."

He nodded. "Go, then. Before they try to detain you."

A laugh rattled up my throat as I turned to leave. "They could certainly try."

I was nearly around the first curve of the street when shouting made me glance back. City detectives had gathered around the Stymphalian. A man with a mustache and a bowl-like cap focused what seemed to be a decade's worth of anger at Lee. His face was nearly purple as he lumbered toward my flower-market stranger, a pudgy finger raised between them. Lee just reached out, lightly tapping the man's wrist.

The older detective shut his mouth and blinked. His large body swayed backward, and Lee steadied him with a firm hand on his shoulder.

It was unsettling, the sudden shift.

Portals of blue slashed across the cobblestone in my direction, and surprise danced across Lee's features when he saw me looking back at the corner. My chest filled with warmth. I spun away, but Lee's smile flashed like the bulb of a camera, cementing in my mind. The whole way back to Gwaith, I thought of it.

CHAPTER 14

I walked the perimeter of Erlene's room, ensuring every window was sealed and locked. As the sun set, the House surrendered to a lightless haze as factories hit their evening rush. I could no longer see past the fenced grounds, and, despite being sure we hadn't been followed out of the city, the blindness bothered me.

Erlene sat on the stool in front of her mother's old vanity, waiting for me to brush her hair. She'd been quiet since we returned from the city, even when we delivered the pansies to Tova's grave.

I picked up her brush, running the stiff bristles over my palm. "What's the matter?"

Her eyes met mine through the reflection of the mirror, weighed with a seriousness I didn't know she was capable of. "That man in the market said I was strong for thinking about Mommy, but I'm sad. Sad doesn't feel strong."

I started brushing through the knots in her hair. It glistened like spun gold.

I might not have been dragged back to my childhood home today, but what I faced in the city sent my heart there. My chest ached with the memories – snippets of whispered conversation, the solitary confinement my dark flames so often earned me, the blurred recollection of a little boy with white hair. He haunted me, that child and the promise between us I couldn't keep.

"That's exactly what makes you strong," I said. "Remembering your mother and being able to embrace sadness at your age is a special gift. When you are older, you will thank the girl you are now for keeping her memory safe. Not many people who lose someone can do that."

"Why?" she asked, like it was the silliest thing she'd ever heard. Maybe it was.

"Sometimes," I replied softly. "People grow angry in their loss."

Erlene dropped her gaze, fiddling with the blue pansy, one she hadn't let go of at Tova's grave. The petals on it were wilting, the stem battered and limp. I wondered what she was thinking of in that moment, what she was hoping the pansy would take from her.

I heard a whisper, that buried memory climbing out of the rubble like a second-life emerging from death, gripping my heart like a vice. *Let your thoughts bleed out, let yourself bleed out. It's you and me.* I shook the voice and the memory away.

Forcing myself to remember could kill me. It would, someday. The frequent aches ensured I never forgot that, never forgot how close I was to ruin every moment of every day.

As I set the brush back on the vanity, Erlene whispered, "Why would he want to be like me?"

That man in the flower market. I had tried to put him out of my mind.

"Why wouldn't he?" I finally managed. "There's an entire life left ahead of you."

Erlene clutched the pansy to her chest as I tucked her into

bed. Before I could pull away, she caught the sleeve of my dress. "Can you tell me about the fire-bird again?"

"I told you that story last night." And the night before that. "Aren't you sick of it yet?"

Smiling, she shook her head.

A lump formed in my throat. I sat on the edge of her bed and leaned against the headboard beside her. "Alright," I muttered. "But close your eyes."

Erlene obeyed my request and snuggled her pillow, depositing the pansy beneath it.

I wasn't surprised by her fascination with the story, with this piece of history. Of all the extraordinary beings in our world, winged spirits were closest to divine. They were once considered gods before humans grew to despise them. They weren't gods, of course – just old, wise beings who had joined us from their own extinct worlds, only remnants of what had been beyond our universe.

I studied Erlene's sweet face until I was sure she wouldn't crack her lids open. Then, tilting my head to the ceiling, I let my own eyes flutter shut.

"Once upon a time," I started, keeping my voice barely louder than the purifier in the corner of the room, "oceans away, an island existed made of earth and ash. A people lived there, and at the center of that island, there sat a fiery cavern. The citizens of the island often heard the rumbling and call of a great bird echo from that place, but for many years, no one saw it.

"It wasn't until the island was mourning the loss of their first queen that a peasant woman received a dream. She went to the king and told him what she had seen and heard, of her dream of a bird living under their island, how it told her to come to its nest. It promised the young girl the empty throne and the king's unending love, and beyond that, immortality for their people.

"The king didn't believe her at first. He told the woman to stay far away from the depths of the island, for he knew the lava stirring in its center would only offer her death. But the woman would not be dissuaded. She asked a few of her friends to walk with her to the volcano, to witness the miracle she had been promised."

A rustle in the hallway outside Erlene's room distracted me. I glanced at the cracked door, at the shadows stretching across the threshold from the hallway.

As I fell silent, the house did, too.

Erlene tugged impatiently on my wrist.

I slouched against the headboard and dropped my voice to a whisper. "When they arrived at the cavern, the friends watched as she walked into the watery orange light at the end of the tunnel. They watched as a large spirit rose from the depths, watched as it enveloped the woman with wings of golden fire and dragged her into the heart of the mountain. They heard the woman's screams and the fiery spirit's call, a screech that echoed out into the entire island. Even the king in his palace heard it."

I swallowed the words trembling in my throat, words that I had carefully censored from the story for Erlene's sake.

It had been a mating call that razed the island that day, a spiritual consummation.

"The witnesses ran back to the village to tell the king what they saw. They told him the woman had died, because no one expected her to survive that embrace of fire. No one expected her to show up the next day, dusted with a golden sheen from head-to-toe and visibly pregnant, but she did."

The door to Erlene's room creaked slightly, and I clamped my mouth shut. Destin stood in the doorway, peering at the two of us. When our eyes met, he lifted one finger to his lips – a plea for me not to alert Erlene to his presence. I sat up, preparing to leave the story there.

Erlene held onto my arm like an anchor, her bleary eyes fluttering open to glare at me. "You can't leave yet," she whined. "I kept my eyes closed like you told me to."

I grimaced, trying to ignore Destin's imposing form in the doorway behind her, but that was impossible. "It's getting late, sweetheart."

"How can I sleep without the story being finished?"

I sighed, closing my eyes briefly as I settled back against the mattress. Turning to face her, I said, "Okay. Sleeping eyes."

As she squeezed her eyes shut, her nose furrowing in concentration, I glanced up at Destin. He was leaning in the doorway now. The bronze gun on his hip gleamed at me, and it was a chilling reminder of what I risked by living in this manor, by telling bedtime stories that weren't stories at all.

I spoke softly, willing my words to fade before they crossed the room and fell on the wrong ears. "The woman received what was promised to her, starting with the throne. When the king saw her again, he finally believed the miracle, because it was evident in her swollen belly. He took her as his wife, and after four months, the miraculous child was born, seemingly human in all ways except one: on his back, he carried a set of three-tiered, golden wings."

Erlene's sweet voice garbled, "The first angel." A weak smile spread over her face.

My lips trembled as I tried to reflect that happiness, but I knew all the parts of the story she didn't. The bloody, devastating bits. Real miracles came at a cost, and this one was life for a life. Human women weren't built to survive birth to a winged child. Perhaps they were already a little bit dead by the time they were pregnant, walking and breathing corpses, little better than the needy beings they usually became in death.

She had been a living sacrifice.

Feathering a hair from Erlene's temple, I mouthed the word "seraph" in gentle correction. I know she didn't mean the word derogatorily, but it was thrown around so carelessly in the manor – by staff and rebel guards alike – that it was impossible to shield her from it.

When Erlene said it this way, with awe and love in her voice, I didn't mind it so much.

Her breathing slowly slipped into a steady pattern, and my gaze slid up to survey the man lingering in the doorway. It was impossible to tell how much he heard, but judging from the lack of killing rage in his eyes, I assumed not enough to expose me. He raised two fingers in front of him and beckoned me from the room.

After removing myself from the bed and carefully shutting Erlene's door, I turned and nearly slammed right into Destin. He was standing close – *too close*.

"You tell the strangest stories to my daughter," he observed, his voice terse.

He'd heard some of it, then, enough to upset him.

I fought the urge to touch my necklace and ensure its placement around my neck. "I share stories that are fascinating to me," I returned. "Do you have an issue with that?"

"You're a *sympathizer*." Destin let pure disgust fester in those words.

What he believed was better than the truth. Safer. I studied his curled lip, the way it almost looked like a smile if I tilted my head just right. "When exactly did sympathy become a crime, Lord Gwaith?"

He scoffed. "You shouldn't fill my daughter's head with pretty stories about monsters in the sky. It's dangerous."

"How are you so sure they're monsters? Have you ever met one? Spoken with one?"

"I don't need to go that far," he snarled. "However, if you

must know, yes, I've had the displeasure of encountering one recently, and they're foul. They deserve to be wiped off our continent. It would be a better place without them."

His response only confirmed my suspicions about what was in the black box, and what I needed to do about it. There was a seraph in there, and who knew what they'd done to it.

I crossed my arms and shrugged. "We'll let Erlene come to her own conclusions about the world, as her mother would want her to."

His narrowed eyes followed me as I walked across the hall to my room. Before I hit the threshold, he said to my back, "Felicity and I are taking Erlene out of town this weekend."

I spun to face him. "My bleed started. I won't be going anywhere."

Destin's eyes flicked over my body, his viciousness abating for a breath. When his gaze returned to my face, he said evenly, "I didn't ask you to come, Sia. I simply told you where Erlene would be."

"And what makes you think I would place her in your care?" I countered.

"You didn't have an issue placing my daughter in a stranger's hands when you abandoned her in the city. Oh, yes, Brimley told me what happened." Destin's eyes burned. I welcomed that look, because it meant he cared. He cared for Erlene.

I smirked. "Am I to interpret that as you *didn't* assign the best guard at your disposal to accompany us in the city?"

A vein in Destin's temple jumped. "Don't be ridiculous. Of course I did."

"See? Then she was safer with him."

He crossed his arms. "And why is that, Sia? Where did you run off to?"

I met his unwavering stare, his eyes a smoky gray in the

low light. He wanted to know, was dying to know, I could tell. He had no right to that knowledge, and I was relishing in the opportunity to drive him a little bit crazy, to make him *feel* something.

I did reconsider, though.

I'd been waiting for the perfect time to get into the stables, and this was too perfect a chance to pass up. Besides, it was probably best if Erlene and Destin were far, far away when I opened that box. "Where are you going this weekend?" I asked.

Destin's eyes narrowed, as if he were debating whether to pick a fight with me. After a moment, he gave in and muttered, "To Ebonmore. The Baron invited every noble in the area to his home. Family participation was highly encouraged."

There was a layer of falsity in his answer, so faint I might not have recognized it if I weren't experienced in dealing with liars. Maybe he didn't have a choice when it came to the Baron. Maybe he was scared to refuse these orders for whatever reason.

"Fine," I said. "I would like Brimley by Erlene's side at all times. I don't want her left alone with Felicity or anyone else on the Baron's property."

Destin, surprisingly, didn't argue with that. He nodded once and then turned to descend the staircase, presumably heading back to his den for the night.

I looked away and discovered candlelight pouring into the hall from the master bedroom.

Felicity stood in front of the door, watching Destin disappear. Her hair was a cascade of careful coils. The nightdress she wore was sheer. The kohl around her eyes was smudged and running in streaks down her cheeks. Her reddened eyes met mine, narrowing in a venomous glare. She returned to the master bedroom and slammed the iron door hard behind her, waking Erlene.

Her wail pierced the night and every darkened ember of my heart. Without a thought, I crossed the hall to soothe her.

CHAPTER 15

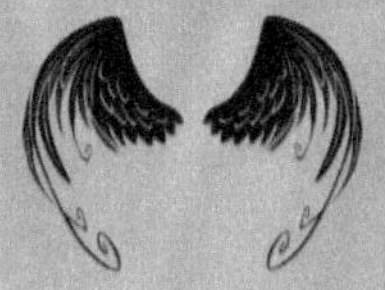

"**M**other*fucker*." I jerked my hand back from the open oven and the cookie tray now teetering on its rack.

The left side of my palm had touched the edge of the oven. Shock gave way to a biting sting, my skin blooming with a red mark as I staggered to the bucket of water on the counter. I plunged my hand under the surface, wiping my brow with a shuddering sigh. Wayward flour from my arm stuck in clumps to the sweat on my face.

Common sense kept me from screaming in frustration, kept me from setting the oven aflame and melting the iron down. In the forest, there was no one around to protect from myself.

I wished I was there again now, surrounded by dripping moss, in a place wet enough to snuff out my black fire once I was finished unleashing it. To my chagrin, I wasn't out there. I was here, and Erlene was playing with her toys in the room above me. I was...*trapped*.

I willed the pressure in my chest to defuse and spat

another curse in an effort to ease the tension. My hands shook in the water.

"You've got quite the mouth today."

I jumped, twisting to face Brimley and the butler as they entered the room together.

Brimley fought a smile as he assessed the room. His appearance sent a warmth surging under my skin. I'd walked out of my room this morning to discover a bundle of items sitting right outside my door: a metal bottle filled with boiling water and wrapped in a silken blanket, a bottle of whiskey, and best of all, a small box of chocolates. It was a care package intended to ease the pain of my menses. I'd known instantly that Brimley was behind it. He had to be.

I wish I'd been able to put them all to good use. The chocolate and whiskey, I would, of course, but the metal bottle was useless to me, because I had yet to even have my first cycle. Humans started their breeding cycles far earlier than my kind. The excuse had simply been too convenient not to use.

Still, the gesture made my heart soften toward the old guard.

The butler leaned his forearms on the counter and chuckled to himself as his eyes slid over my situation. All the surfaces were dusted in sweet, white powder. Dirty dishes were scattered around the room. It was a wreck.

The butler and I had quickly moved past the events of my arrival. He knew I was different, but he'd kept that revelation from the other staff, as Lila did.

Instead, he spent his free time experimenting with just how far he could push me before my eyes started to glow. It was a game, one that helped me stay sane in this domestic hell. He reminded me of the creature I'd been in the wild, one who forgot the pleasantries of civilization. He felt confident I wouldn't hurt him, so much so that he indulged my moods and provoked the flames lurking under my skin. His eyes silently taunted me as I turned to reply to Brimley.

"My mouth is the same today as it was yesterday," I retorted. "What do you two want?"

"There's a visitor." Brimley smiled tightly.

"So?"

"He's asking for you," the butler interjected. "I thought I'd offer to take over for you so you can deal with them."

"Destin is agitated," Brimley added.

I rolled my eyes and withdrew my hand from the bucket, my fingers dripping water onto the floor as I approached the kitchen island. "When is he not? Who's here?"

"I don't know, but he has a package with him."

My brow furrowed. I wasn't expecting any deliveries for at least another week. Turning back to the oven, I used a cloth to shove the rack back inside and shut the cast-iron door.

I turned to the butler and jerked a thumb toward the oven. "Watch the cookies. If they burn, I'll hold you responsible."

He smirked.

"I mean it," I growled. "Take them out in ten minutes and not a moment later. If as much as one piece of chocolate goes missing, I'll expose all the secrets I found out about you in that journal under your mattress." I wiggled my eyebrows in a way that said, *yes, I'll even tell the staff about the stable hand down the road.*

The skin of his bald skull turned crimson.

Brimley laughed at us. "Oh, she's got your balls in hand now."

As I sauntered past the two of them, I tossed the flour-coated towel at the butler's chest and poked my finger into Brimley's face. "The same warning applies to you, sir. Don't think I won't dig for dirt on you if I need to."

"Careful," he called after me as he opened the back door.

"The maids might keel over from shock if you spill *my* secrets."

The back door clattered shut behind him, and I bit back a smile as I made my way to the foyer. Before I even caught sight of the entryway, I heard a familiar rumbling voice, controlled and quiet, every consonant a stone dropping in my gut.

Lee stood in front of the open door, smog and muted light sifting into the house around his frame. He held a large, flat box in one hand, pressing his hat to his chest in the other, his dark blond hair tumbling in waves over his forehead. He fell silent as I came into view, his eyes sliding over my body, pressing in like a physical touch.

Destin stood beside him, long hands braced on his hips, close enough to his pistol to send unease scattering under my skin. Felicity was there too, watching from the staircase, her dainty fingers white from how tightly she clutched the banister.

"What are you doing here?" I demanded.

Lee smirked. "Gwaith is a hospitable house, indeed. Exactly how many times will I be asked the same question?"

"That's what happens when you arrive somewhere unannounced," Destin growled.

Lee didn't take his eyes off me as he stepped forward, extending the box. "I've brought you a gift."

"I don't want anything from you." The words echoed through me. Those hateful words had spun a home in my head like cobwebs, and I couldn't bring myself to swipe them away.

Lee's eyes shuttered. "Would you want it if I said it wasn't from me?"

"I wouldn't believe you."

"Don't you trust me?"

"No." I crossed my arms, studying the package more

closely. It was wrapped in newspaper and a fine cloth bow. "Why? Who are you alleging it's from, if not yourself?"

"Well...I stopped in to ask your seamstress a few questions, and she—"

"Why were you talking to my seamstress?"

"Isn't that what one does during an active investigation?"

"Investigation?" Felicity squeaked.

"He's a detective working on the dismemberments," I said flatly, and I crossed the foyer until the minty, earthen fragrance of my flower-market stranger surrounded me. "And he seems to think my seamstress is a person of interest."

He chuckled softly. "The seamstress is not of interest to me."

The air drifting in through the front door was strangely cold, far too cold for early fall. I grimaced, wishing Destin would close it and spare us the chill. He didn't, of course, and I knew why...

That black box in the stables wasn't the least bit legal. The rebels just didn't care. Whoever they hurt and how many mortals suffered the collateral damage of their cause, they didn't *care*. The open door was Destin's way of making his displeasure known to the detective. It was a silent, hovering dismissal.

"She could have sent that package with my other items," I muttered.

Lee shrugged. "It wasn't an inconvenience. I was coming here anyway."

"Because *I'm* of interest to you?" I guessed.

"Oh, yes," he breathed. "But my questions can wait." His eyes glittered as he shoved the box into my hands. "Here – I've been lugging this around for an hour, and I'm eager to see you open it."

The smog curled around our feet. I didn't like the idea of doing this in front of Destin, in front of Felicity. I almost said no, but then I looked at Lee, and we might as well have been alone with the way he watched me. Maybe, for a moment, it was only him and I.

His pale, hypnotic eyes seemed to say, *don't leave me in the dark, darling. Open the box.*

I tore my gaze from his. The sooner I appeased him, the sooner he would go. I tugged on the purple bow and let it ripple to the floor. Then, I slid the lid open.

My heart leapt into my throat. I couldn't swallow.

That dress from the shop window, the one sewn with threads of magic, was waiting inside. The seamstress must have seen me admiring it. I lifted the blue fabric, rubbing it gently between my fingers. The material glistened, and it stirred up that person inside of me who longed for weight-lessness and magic...who wanted to fly. *Loved* to fly.

Tingles of heat spread toward my fingers, and I dropped the material before I could accidentally scorch it. With my next breath, I pushed the sensation away. *All* sensation. Extreme fear and anger were triggers for the power I possessed. They were emotions so sharp, I could lash out with rare precision. Mortal kindness like this, what it made me feel, was worse. It had an unpredictable effect on me.

I didn't realize I'd lost grip on reality until Felicity's voice brought me back, her every word lined with a haughty venom. "This is clearly a mistake. What use does a woman like her have for a dress like that?" Her eyes were glazed with envy as she stared at the box.

Lee chuckled, but I couldn't sense humor in it.

A fresh gale battered the front of the house, carrying smog and the scent of burning poppy fields with it. I'd grown accus-tomed to that smell back home. That was all I did there: indulged in burning pipes and drowsy sex, parties that never ended. How Lee might have come into possession of this particular substance, I didn't want to know, but it was wafting off him in visceral waves.

Felicity swayed suddenly, gripping the banister to keep herself from falling down the stairs. Destin moved in immediately, reaching for her. "Are you all right?"

Felicity rubbed at her temples, squeezing her eyes shut as she replied, "I'm fine. I'm just feeling dizzy all of a sudden. I think I should lay down for a while before we set out on the road." She turned and started to climb the staircase. Destin followed her, his hands hovering to ensure she wouldn't collapse.

Lee watched them disappear to the second floor before his eyes met mine, a smile teasing the corner of his mouth. He looked like he was chewing on a secret. "How on our Goddess' green earth do you tolerate that woman?"

"I don't," I scoffed.

He freed his hidden smile, and it was scarier than I expected. "Good."

Before I could decide how to respond, the stairs creaked again, announcing Destin's return. As he came back into view, he said gruffly, "You still haven't explained why you're here, Detective. What is there to investigate at Gwaith House?" He paused on the second to last stair. "What you and your colleagues should be doing is casting fish nets in the bay to capture the serpents responsible, not harassing my governess."

The implication prickled over my skin. I wasn't *his* anything. The only mortal I'd ever surrendered anything to was dead and buried, but I felt her possession lingering in my bones. I didn't know how I could belong to anyone else ever again.

"Serpents never let anything shore up on the beach," I interjected. "When they kill, they do it quietly. I don't think this is them."

"There's no way to know that for certain," Destin countered with a bitter laugh. "No one knows the mind of a snake. Just look at what they devolved from."

The prickle under my skin became an itch. I should have known he would come back around to this hatred, this belief that seraphim were his ultimate enemy.

When seraphim lost their wings, scales grew over their backs to seal the wounds. Their legs drew together to form a tail, preventing them from further reproduction. Those souls were discarded to the sea, and whatever humanity a seraph carried in immortality was ripped away when they devolved. At least, that was the accepted belief, the one proven time and again by the evil deep and all that slithered within it.

When seraphim lost their wings, they became serpents.

Wings were a blessing, but every blessing from the ancient spirits came with consequences for rejecting it. That fate was used as a weapon nowadays. Losing that blessing scared all seraphim, whether they carried one set of wings or three.

"She's right," Lee said. "The barriers are intact, and there haven't been any sightings yet in the bay."

Destin scoffed. "What else could possibly be behind it?"

The detective's eyes flickered. "That's what I'm trying to determine."

"And you think I'm involved?" I demanded, setting my package on the entryway table and crossing my arms. "How?"

"I think you might point me in the right direction."

"I can guarantee you I won't."

"I'll be the judge of that." Lee returned his hat to his crown and gestured to the door. "Do you have time for a brisk walk?"

I didn't need any attention drawn to me, human law enforcement or otherwise. It was best to cooperate and show the detective he had nothing to suspect. "If you insist," I said with a smile.

Destin stepped between us, turning his back to me.

"Detective, you don't have the right to appear on my doorstep and demand things of my staff."

I elbowed past him. "Back off, Destin. You don't speak for me. Your staff? *Please.*"

He watched me step forward with wide eyes. "Sia."

I knew he was trying to help, but he was also an idiot. "It's fine. I have nothing to hide," I lied, and then I walked out the door.

CHAPTER 16

Lee and I rounded the first corner of the house, falling easily into step together. I expected him to launch into the reason he was here, and when he didn't, an uncomfortable heaviness filled my stomach. I found myself watching him silently observe the property instead. His gaze left nothing untouched.

"Would you like to see the garden?" I offered.

He scanned the hedges to our left, his eyes lingering on the stone statues guarding the arches. Shaking his head, he replied, "Just a lap around the manor should suffice."

"If you have so little to say to me, then why did you come all this way?"

Lee stretched his neck to one side and then the other, his spine clicking faintly. His blue eyes swirled, and yet he did not look at me, did not respond.

Halfway to the servant's entrance, I stopped expecting an answer. Maybe this was some sort of strategy to unnerve me, but it wouldn't work. I wouldn't let it. I folded my arms behind my back and lifted my face, letting the cool fog caress my cheeks.

If he wanted to waste his time, fine.

His tone was so sharp when he finally spoke that I tripped. "Why are you here, Sia?"

My head swiveled to study him. Back straight as a rod, the muscles in his jaw were fluttering as he stared at me from the corner of his eye. "I know you aren't from the city," Lee said in my silence, folding his hands behind his back to match me. His eyes slid over the clothesline whipping in the breeze above us, rusty pulleys attached to the second-floor windows. "I know you aren't related in any way to Gwaith House or its bloodline. So, what brought you here?"

I grimaced.

He had access to city files, had built a career on profiling and tracking people, so it shouldn't surprise me that he'd determined those details. My motive for being here seemed like such an odd thing to focus on. The answer wasn't condemning, wouldn't give too much away, aside from the hurt I harbored in my heart. Maybe that was the sort of vulnerability he needed to hear before he'd leave me alone.

"My mother was born near here," I admitted. "Initially, I started visiting the city to try and understand her, and then, I met someone. They're the reason I'm here now."

"The Lord of Gwaith?"

"No. The friend I had is no longer here."

His voice softened to a whisper. "Ah. Erlene's mother, then?"

"Her name was Tova." I stared at the smog curling around my feet, kissing the hem of my dress. It was different today; cooler, wetter, tender in my lungs, almost comforting.

"You said your mother was born nearby?" he asked. "What was her name?"

The question sent a jolt of lightning up my spine. "I don't recall."

He chuckled, and when I returned his stare, I saw the challenge in it. "You don't recall your mother's name? Pardon me, darling, but I think you're full of shit."

Ire prickled through my chest. "Why do you want it?"

"Because you've given me a reason for your presence in this House, but I'd like to verify its authenticity."

"Since when is it illegal for a woman to roam wherever she pleases? Why do I need any reason at all?" Hopefully, it wasn't illegal. Up to this point, I had refused to linger in any of the human lands long enough to know that for certain.

"It's not," he acquiesced. "But it's odd for a woman like you to wander, to linger in a place that can't be good for her."

A woman like me. He had no idea. "Who says I'm wandering?"

"We all belong somewhere."

I scoffed. "That's a pretty lie happy people say to those who don't fit in. There's no truth to it. There isn't anywhere I belong."

Lee stared at me for a long moment, his eyes widening. "Wow." He took a deep breath. "What made you so bitter with the world, Sia?"

"Life," I replied. "The pain of living on when others don't."

Lee's throat bobbed, but his gaze remained on me, expectant.

As we neared the front of the House, I decided I didn't have the energy to dodge his curiosity. After all, what could he really do with my mother's name? He was only a mortal. "My mother's name was Cinna, but you aren't going to find her in any public records. She grew flowers and herbs beyond the smog to earn coin, and from the moment she was born until the moment she met my father, she lived on the streets."

I'd been searching for the truth about my mother my whole life, and I'd found little. All I had were the rare stories my father extended to me, the journal she'd left behind, and the magic in my veins that I didn't fully understand. It wasn't enough, but I knew nothing short of my mother in the flesh would ever be enough to satisfy me.

Lee fell silent, absorbing that information. Then, he cleared his throat and said, "She must have been brave, to grow a garden in the gnashing forest."

"She was desperate," I amended. "As many others are forced to be."

"I'm sorry for your loss."

My heart stuttered. No one had ever said that to me before. My mother's death had been inevitable. From the very first moment of their marriage, my father knew she would die. I never forgave him, not just for letting her die, but also for never letting me grieve her. *He* had grieved her, extensively. Sometimes, I could tell he still mourned her memory, all that they had become to each other in so short a time. I was not given that opportunity. I was sure my family thought I could not mourn what I never had. How wrong they were.

And Tova's death…well, that grief had never been mine to claim.

I blinked the sting in my eyes away. "I'm afraid that mourning isn't meant for me."

"Well, that's simply not true. Whatever you feel is yours."

My body tensed under the weight of those words, of his compassion. There was no rhyme or reason to his questions now, no purpose in him asking about my family or my reason for living in Gwaith House. He'd unearthed feelings he had no right to.

"What does any of this have to do with your investigation?" I demanded.

"I'm just trying to get the full picture."

"Right now," I countered, "the picture is a detective asking all the wrong questions, searching in the wrong places, as innocents get torn apart on his watch."

"You're so quick to lay blame on others," Lee mused.

"Answer me this: what are *you* doing to stop them? What happened to the woman who ran headlong into a horde of second-lives? You're simply sitting around here on this property, *playing house.*"

I rocked to a halt, and he faced me fully, his smirk daring me to react. I took one fluid step to close the distance between us, the top of my head barely level with his chin.

"Respectfully, Detective," I snarled. "*Kiss my ass.*"

Lee's mouth twitched. "Unfortunately, I have a few more questions, and only then can we proceed to ass kissing. When exactly did you arrive at Gwaith, Sia? Was it before or after the newest surge of bodies started beaching?"

I narrowed my eyes at him. "Are you accusing me of something?"

"Should I be?" he shot back. "After speaking with the seamstress, and then the herbalist, I'm wondering what you're *really* doing here. Honestly, I'm a little concerned for the people who live in this House with you."

If he'd spoken with the herbalist, he could know about the tears. They were a banned substance. Terrible things happened to mortals who tried to sell it, because usually they were harvested without permission, from seraphim who were abducted and tortured. That would explain why he was here, but then, why hadn't he done it already?

I wrapped my arms around myself and murmured, "You really think I'm to blame for these dismemberments? What is my motive? Why would *I* hurt *anyone*?"

His leather-bound palms gripped either side of his midnight blue blazer. We were close enough that I felt his sigh against my face, his breath both warm and cool at once, like peppermint. "Why would you buy enough belladonna to kill a small fleet of soldiers? Are you using it here? Are you using it on the child? Just tell me."

My veins froze. That was the last straw. He could jump to

any conclusion about what kind of person I was, what kind of *monster* I was, but not that one. Not Erlene.

I poked him in the chest with enough force to bruise, but I knew bruises were better than burns. His chest was rock hard, so I poked him again as I hissed, "I would *never* harm Erlene. How dare you? What have I ever done to make you think I'm capable of that?"

When Lee replied, it was barely above a whisper. "Tell me I'm wrong for thinking the worst," he pleaded. "Make me believe the best in you."

He wanted me to convince him of my innocence, and I didn't know how. How could I reason away suspicions like that?

I swallowed tightly. "Did you ever consider that the belladonna was for *me*?"

"You?" That word took me right back to the flower market, to the moment I ran into him, and he looked at me like I was the moon and the stars. How fleeting that was.

"I have trouble sleeping." Not a lie.

His brows lifted nearly to his hairline. "You're claiming to be an insomniac with a penchant for depressants in bulk?"

I shrugged. "That sounds better than 'raging psychopath,' which you seem to think is the only other option."

Lee sighed.

In another world, another day, that exhale might have been a laugh. He might have been beautiful. My heart might have sped as he looked at me, and I would have mistaken the electricity scattering under my skin as attraction. Instead, we were here, I was me, and he'd just accused me of murder. And I already promised myself I wouldn't get hooked. Not again.

His eyes searched mine, and his hands fisted to either side of him. I wondered if that meant he was tempted to run his fingers through his hair.

His dark blond waves were designed for that kind of

disarray. I could imagine how delicious it might be to run my own fingers through it, to see it in my bed under warm candlelight. It would look like a wheat field under the harvest moon.

"I want to believe your charming lies," he said softly. "But I need more than that before I can leave you here, alone."

My palms were burning. I wondered if my eyes had started to glow, wondered if he would notice he'd completely unsettled me. I shook my head slowly. "These murders have been happening for half a decade, and this is the first time I've lingered near this city in over five years. It isn't me."

"Where *have* you been?"

"I've been—" I swallowed, my mind reeling with blurry memories. The endless cycle of day and night under the forest canopy. Featureless faces and a meaningless string of months that amounted to nothing at all. "I've been away."

"That's vague."

"Yes."

"So do better," he purred.

"You won't believe it."

"Try me."

My hands were beginning to burn holes into the folds of my dress. "I've been in the gnashing forest."

His eyebrows lifted again.

You see? You don't believe me.

"For years? *Alone?*" His hand drifted to his chest, rubbing the heel of his palm against his chest, as if to chase away some ache. Maybe I'd get lucky, and he'd have a heart attack and drop dead right here.

"Not always alone," I muttered, avoiding the real question – whether there would be anyone to vouch for my whereabouts. "There are those who pass through, thieves and shifters and friendly cryptids willing to offer company for a night or two."

None of them would remember me. Why would they? I rambled on anyway. "Besides, the dangers of the wild are better than the smog. It's better than—"

"Your father?" The air around us turned so frighteningly cold, even the warmth in my hands snuffed out.

I shivered as my eyes met Lee's. "What do you mean?"

"I can make assumptions based on what you've told me." His head tilted, leaning in, as if protecting a secret. "You sought out your mother's presence, ran from your father, even hid yourself away in a forest for years to avoid him. What could make you do that if not mistreatment?"

The detective was assuming too much. I hadn't experienced blatant abuse. My father had been ashamed of me in many ways, but he'd never punished me for my faults. He'd tried to change me, hide me. He'd loved me the best he could.

I grimaced. "No, my father's home felt like a cage. I ran from all the things he *didn't* allow, all the things he *wouldn't* do. I decided I'd rather be alone and free than contained by him."

"Alone, surrounded by death," Lee added, glancing at the rose bushes beside us.

My throat swelled. "Is that what I am to you, then? Your prime suspect?"

Lee's eyes flicked over every crease of tension in my face. "I don't know what you are to me." I heard what he did not say: *but I intend to find out.* He backed away, turning to the nearest rose bush. "For such an immaculate House, I'm alarmed by the state of these bushes."

I watched him slide a hand inside his blazer and withdraw a silver dagger – the same one he'd used in the bay to cut down those walkers. A finger of unease traced my spine.

My eyes locked on the weapon, and I shifted on the balls of my feet.

"Why?" That question was more for the dagger than

anything else, but his fingers grazed the rose bush, cradling one of the dead bulbs weighing heavily on a branch.

"The first frost is coming, and these haven't been dead-headed. They hold on, you know…the bulbs." He glanced back at me, and I was tempted to pull my own blades, but I didn't. I waited to see what he would do. With a flick of his wrist, he cut off the bulb, and the branch it had been on flew upwards. He moved on to another branch, then another, working through the heaviest stems.

"You don't have to do that," I said stiffly.

"It's fine. I want to." He shrugged with one shoulder and kept hacking. "If the old isn't trimmed, there will be fewer roses next year. The roots won't know how to stop putting energy into them, how to cast off the used and empty so they can grow past the last season."

I couldn't help but feel as though we were talking about something that went beyond the rose bushes. I couldn't help but feel exposed. Maybe that weight was something sitting inside of me, and my attention had only just now been drawn to it. The realization rattled me to my core.

I burst into motion before I could stop myself.

"Stop it," I snarled, attempting to rip the newest branch out of his hand.

That was a mistake, one I recognized immediately as a prickle caught on my skin and tore me open. I gasped, jerking away from the bush. The thorn had caught on my middle finger, opening a long gash up the length of it. Blood was just beginning to well.

"You're hurt," he muttered, his tone low and reproachful.

"I'm fine," I murmured, pressing against the cut. "It's nothing."

He stowed his dagger, the blade dripping with white sap, and in the same breath, swept forward and took my injured hand in his, pulling me toward him sharply. By the time I realized what he was doing, he already had my bleeding finger pinned between his. He leaned in to study the cut. His gaze was so serious, so intense.

I tried to pull away, but his grip only tightened.

Fear and anger filled my chest. The firmness of his hand was practically a threat, but before I could lash out, he brought my hand to his mouth and kissed it, and light exploded under my skin at the touch.

He lifted his head and smiled at me, a trace of my blood glistening on his lips.

I stared at him in shock, my hand frozen in place between us as he finally pulled away, my arm tingling. *Why...why had he done that?*

His smile turned a bit shy, and he took a step back as he said, "My mum always swore there was no greater magic in all the world than healing kisses." I blinked, and the tension in my chest eased as he looked away from me.

The blood seeping up from my cut slowed, the wound starting to close, so I quickly hid my hands in the folds of my dress. "She sounds like a suffocatingly affectionate woman," I said curtly.

My blood was still on his mouth. If he noticed, he certainly didn't show it, didn't seem to care. But what could I do, try to wipe it away myself? That would require getting closer to him again. *No way.*

"She was," he replied quietly. His eyes darkened, and I bit the inside of my cheek. That had been the wrong thing to say. I'd forgotten for a moment that his mother was gone too. I never would have guessed that I'd just insulted his dead mother from the way he looked at me then. He smiled gently, sweetly. "It's okay. I remember about as much as you do, and that's to say, practically nothing. Nothing except for the healing kisses. Do not feel sorry for me, Sia."

I didn't feel sorry for him. I *did* feel rather irritated that I no longer wanted him to leave, that I no longer felt the urge to push him away. I wanted to drift back into his orbit, feel his breath on my skin again.

With a little effort, I managed to remain where I was.

I turned to the roses. "Tova liked to care for them herself," I explained. "Because of that, she never hired a gardener, and I don't think his Lordship would be willing to spare the coin on one now. The new Lady is just about the last person I would expect to get her hands soiled."

"And you?" he prompted.

"I don't waste my time on delicate, breakable things." A lie, the biggest one I'd ever told.

He bit his lip, and I cringed as the action brought attention to the blood on his mouth. Without hesitation, he licked his lower lip like he was gathering a spill of red wine, and my heart thundered. Waves of warmth spread throughout my abdomen as he smirked.

"May they evolve quickly, then," Lee murmured. He glanced at the saddled horse grazing near the stables, whistling to it as the black horse lifted his head.

His whistle echoed in my head as the horse broke into a sprint towards us. It dredged up the memory of pale trees and pale hair, of a song bouncing under a forest canopy and warmth in my chest. A game of hide and seek. Pale wood painted with blood. The muscles in my neck tightened. Pain radiated along my spine, shocking me into the present, warning me to stop the memory in its tracks.

I didn't want to know. I didn't want to see. My body knew what my mind could not: that remembering would only bring me suffering.

I distracted myself with the horse as it reached us, surveying the beast's heaving chest and the steam billowing from its ebony snout. Tentatively, I stretched out a hand and stroked its velvety nose. The creature took a step into me, leaning into the affection. It calmed me.

"Are you all right?" I glanced over and met Lee's worried eyes. He'd noticed the shift in my demeanor, the scowl on my face.

I shook my head. "Nothing. You just – your whistle reminded me of somebody."

"Oh? And who might that be?"

"Nobody important."

He frowned. "I see. Well, I suppose this is farewell again, at least for now." He held out his hand and I fought the urge to roll my eyes.

Play nice.

I placed my hand in his, the one that hadn't been pricked, and he bent to kiss the back of it. When his lips came within an inch of my skin, he stopped as his nose wrinkled. I might have been offended if he didn't instantly flip my hand over and scan the rest of my arm.

Lee's eyes locked on the dusting of flour near my elbow. He chuckled, low and rough. "Have you been baking, Sia?"

I ripped my hand back. "Maybe."

He straightened and swiftly tugged on a lock of my hair, his hand falling away again before I could swat it. "I hope you tied this pretty red hair back. I don't believe henna dye is a key ingredient in any cookie recipe, unless your intention is to poison."

I took a step back. He knew about the dye. He'd talked to the herbalist, so of course he did. I flicked my hair behind my shoulder, out of his reach and scrutiny.

I wanted to say, *If I needed to poison someone, I wouldn't use henna to do it.*

Lee's head tilted, a sparkle in his eye. He gave me a smile, one that transformed the hard lines of his face into a pool of heat. "Interesting."

A reckless idea occurred to me, and I smiled back, inching closer to him again.

"Would you like to come inside for some tea and cookies?" I asked sweetly. "They should be done by now."

Lee clicked his tongue, tilting his head to stare at me under lowered brows. "I'm alright. Enjoy giving them to their intended targets, though." He winked, and all coherent thought flew right out of my head.

By the time his words fully registered, he had already mounted his beast and was speeding toward the gates. I watched, frozen, as he disappeared down the road.

How had he known about the cookies?

A creak tore my attention to the porch. Destin stood on the threshold of the front door, his arms crossed and eyes burning. "What have you done to bring that man here?"

"That's none of your concern." I vaulted myself up onto the porch, passed by him, and entered the house, picking up the box in the entryway before sauntering down the hallway.

He was right behind me.

"Your whereabouts and activities do concern me, because they concern Erlene."

I spun in place. "I've done nothing to endanger your daughter, Destin, and I never will. Can you say the same? Why are there so many damn guards around the stables? What are you hiding here that requires such security? Have you even thought of your daughter beyond treating her like some item to be kept polished and pretty? Do you think of her beyond what she does for you?" I'd said too much, and suddenly, it wasn't about Erlene anymore.

He clenched his jaw. "I have everything under control."

"You can't control everything. It's not possible."

"I'm not trying to control *everything*, just the things that matter."

I saw red. "The only thing that should matter to you is

your daughter. Your wife should have mattered. You couldn't control life and death, so you ran away. You can't control me, so you're scared and angry. Get over it."

I returned to the kitchen, breathing a sigh of relief when I realized Destin wasn't going to follow me. It was especially fortunate, considering I walked in and discovered that the butler had eaten one of my cookies.

The tray was resting on the counter. A glass of milk sat beside it, and the butler was snoring on the floor, the half-devoured cookie still clutched in one hand.

I swiftly transferred the baked cookies to a tin and hid it in the dress box, then heaved the butler's limp body into one of the chairs arranged around the servant's eatery table. I replaced his milk with a cup of whiskey and patted his hand in farewell. *Poor bastard.*

I stole his journal on the way back to my room. I'd return it in a few days, once he worried about it enough, and once I was sure he wouldn't share what had happened with the others.

CHAPTER 17

Destin, Felicity, and Erlene left that evening, and I caught Brimley just before they set off, making it clear that if anything happened to Erlene while they were away, I would ruin his life. He seemed to believe me.

Still, I couldn't sleep. I tossed and turned in the tiny bed, trying not to worry about Erlene and failing miserably.

The second dawn broke, and I got up and opened the dress box Lee had delivered.

As I pulled the dress over my head and the bodice slid into place, the material tightened around my ribs, the magic formed perfectly to me. I spun in a circle in front of the mirror, and particles of blue light fell down the length of the dress as the hem adjusted to my height, kissing the ground with glimmering remnants of magic.

I loved magic when it worked like this, imbued to a certain measure and not beyond. Why couldn't my power be like that?

I'd given up hope of understanding my gifts, the same way my father and brother and Spiro had. Still, sometimes, I dreamed of a different Sia, one who could face her inner darkness without fear.

Tova's blue ribbon was twined into the curls I'd formed in coils overnight. After running my hands through it, my hair was just wild enough to be beautiful. The kohl around my eyes and the dark pink paste on my lips completed the disguise: a harmless, beautiful girl. I smiled at myself in the mirror. Frowned. Simpered. Smiled again.

After ensuring my iron-plate necklace laid flat on my collarbone, I left the house with the tin of belladonna-laced cookies in hand.

Since Destin found me snooping around the back of the stables, he'd assigned additional guards to the back entrance and windows. Considering what he kept inside, I wasn't surprised, but it would require me to break in with more grace than I was used to.

I let the more feminine bits of me shine as I approached the stables, lifting my chest to the sky and smiling with my teeth. I'd guessed from Destin's reproach when he caught me the first day that the guards were susceptible to my charm. He wouldn't have tried to steer me away from them if they weren't. He was a fool for presenting the weakness so openly.

A young guard lounging at the front entrance, one I'd noticed ogling me from afar, spoke to me first. "Oy, love. You know you shouldn't be lurking 'round here."

I held my smile steady, even as my cheeks began to ache with the falsity of it. "I'm just saying hello. I thought you fellas might be getting hungry." I looked between him and the rebel stationed on the other side of the entrance.

The second was older, a little weary in the face. He'd always been kind to Erlene and me whenever we crossed paths in the gardens. I gave him an especially tender smile.

"Is that so?" the younger one purred, running a hand through his greasy hair.

I'd been watching their rounds, cataloging every break and behaviorism. These two were the most trusted soldiers, from what I could tell; they worked long hours, sometimes days at a time, napping in intervals through the night. This was the second day of their current shift, and I was willing to bet they would stay on it at least until Destin returned.

The younger had boasted of his conquests at a local brothel before, as if that was a thing to brag about. The older wore a wedding band, but he rarely left the estate. He was lonely. They both were.

The men shared a confused glance.

"I brought cookies, enough for all of you," I murmured.

I lifted the lid to the tin and showed them. Their faces reddened. Maybe it was embarrassment or a desire to please me, but they each took one and ate.

"I'll be back to keep you two company after I share with the others," I said softly.

The older man waved me on. I went on like that for each of the guards, drawing them in with flirtation, waiting with each one until I was sure they'd all taken a bite. The smog thickened, shrouding my actions from the House as I played my part well, even when the drunk of the lot slapped my ass. It took every ounce of self-control to keep a smile on my face and walk away as he washed his cookie down with the gin he stored behind a loose slat in the wall.

I promised myself retribution, in time.

When I made it back to the front, the two main guards were already passed out. In the distance, I heard a grumble of confusion and heavy bodies slamming into the earth as sleep came for the rest. I waited a few more minutes until the snoring began, and then I stepped over the guards into the stable.

The box was being kept at the end of the long hall between the stalls. Hay crunched under my feet as I approached, and the air grew eerily still, as though the cage and everything within held its breath at my presence. Light filtered in between the slats of the stable walls, just enough to study what lay before me.

Ebony marble, solid and sleek, with a subtle seam rimming the top edge.

I'd seen these cages before, but on a smaller scale. They were often placed in the forest by forest-dwellers to catch sprites, wanting to harvest strength from them either through sacrifice or extortion. They could contain anything, mute any kind of magic, except, perhaps, my flame.

They were cruel traps.

On my second circle of the box, I glimpsed a rectangular seam on the front wall, small enough to be an envelope slot. A keyhole had been hewn into the marble beside it.

This opening must be intended for food.

Seraphim lasted longer without sustenance than humans did but were still vulnerable to starvation. If Destin's intention was to keep what he'd captured alive, they had to feed it regularly, which also meant there was a key here somewhere. I skimmed my fingers along the rim of the lid, searching by touch, until I came to a divot along the back. Another keyhole.

Returning to the entrance of the stables, I pilfered the younger guard first, turning out his pockets only to find loose coin and a cigarette tin. I pocketed the coin and turned to the other guard.

As I rifled through the older man's trousers, I withdrew a photo – a *wedding* photo, on yellowed and grainy paper. It had to be at least a decade old. The photo was worn over the woman's face, as if he'd rubbed her features clean away. I carefully slipped the photo back into his pocket before continuing my search.

The key was tucked into a pocket on the side of the old man's tunic, a *very* small one. I would have missed it entirely if the rise and fall of his chest hadn't drawn attention to a lump beneath the leather. I returned to the stable hall with the key and knelt in front of the box. It slid like silk into the lock, and when I turned the tumbler, the food slot fell open to reveal a deeper blackness.

An acidic stench seeped out, and my stomach turned. They were letting it sit in its own filth. "Hello?" I whispered into the darkness.

Nothing responded.

I leaned in, holding my breath, and detected its faint, ragged inhales.

"Are you injured?" I asked. When only the silence answered again, I said, "I know you're in there. I hear you breathing."

The creature gasped slightly, then slowed its breath, as if to defy me. I waited several moments. This would be easier if it would just talk with me, but seraphim were not known for easy conversation, especially not the ones who flew low enough to be caught.

I sighed, standing. "I'm going to open the cage now," I told it. "It's in your best interest not to attack me. We aren't enemies."

A quiet huff filtered through the opening, a scoff, maybe.

I unsheathed a dagger from my thigh, then ripped the key out of the tumbler and rounded the box. I slid the key into the second lock and slowly turned it until I heard it click. The box made a low hum, and the stable floor vibrated under my feet as the seam popped free.

I lifted my dagger, expecting for the lid to fly open…but it didn't. Nothing emerged. Not so much as a feather fluttered.

The world was so quiet, I could hear the thundering of my heart in my ears. I gripped the lid and flung it open myself. It lifted a foot or so, hovering by a mechanical rotary that prevented it from sinking back down. The hall was too dark to see into the box from this angle. Perhaps the seraph really had been injured.

I took a step forward, peering over the edge of the ebony stone. "Do you need—"

The seraph struck swiftly, but I was faster.

A mass erupted from the darkness, a bronze hand curling in the air where my throat had just been. Brown speckled wings spread out over me, and I slashed with my dagger. Blood sprayed as I sliced into that reaching hand, not deep enough to amputate, but definitely to maim.

Those speckled wings shuddered in pain. The seraph growled, recoiling in a flurry of air and shadow. I held my ground, watching as he retreated a few feet then turned to face me. A break in the panels of the stable let in a stream of light, illuminating one side of his body. The hand I'd sliced into was fisted against his stomach, his brutally beautiful face twisted in anger. He shifted on his feet, his muscles coiled for another pounce.

I said softly, "I explicitly told you not to do that. What part of 'we aren't enemies' did you not understand?"

"Any human in this place is my enemy," he snarled. His teeth flashed, bared like a starving hound. That's when I knew. He had no intention of leaving any human within a mile radius of this box alive. He would slaughter them all in his fury. In his eyes, that was what he was owed – their blood spilled at his feet.

"It's a good thing I'm not human, then."

Shoving my necklace aside, I arched my neck to expose it further. The seraph's eyes widened as they locked onto my skin. Widened, because he saw the whorls of black staining my neck. His hand rose, bloody and dripping, to pull his own shirt down, revealing the crescent mark around the base of his throat.

Our mark of the winged spirits.

I forced my necklace back into place, hoping beyond reason that he didn't see too much of the pattern or the vividness of my markings. His marks had been diluted, faded from generations of messy breeding. The single set of wings trembling over his shoulders affirmed his status: a citizen of the city in the sky, but no one of importance. My marking, on the other hand, was as dark as the box beside us, starless night.

I should have known better than to hope it would go unnoticed.

"It's you," he said in a mighty exhale. "You really are hiding down here in the smog, fraternizing with humans."

My heart bottomed out. "Where I go and what I do is none of your business."

His lips curled in wry amusement. "Isn't it?"

Everything inside me went cold. He knew who I was. Reluctantly, I asked, "What exactly were you doing down here when you were captured?"

The seraph's head tilted, the slow consideration of a predator.

"What do you think, Princess?" He rolled his shoulders and flashed his teeth, a lazy show of aggression. "I was collecting a bounty."

I put the box between us as he prowled forward, raising my dagger in warning.

"Where do you think you're going?" His eyes followed my every step. "You know you can't outrun me, not with your pretty golden wings put away."

Without another word, my father's vulture pounced.

CHAPTER 18

I knew I couldn't run. There was no point when one flap of his wings sent him careening over the box toward me. I brought my dagger up as he fell over me, but he easily caught my wrist, using his momentum to knock me to the floor with him. I put my other arm between us as we collided with the ground.

He reeked.

His feathers had absorbed all the feces, the sulfur and acid and grime that filled the interior of the box. He was impossibly large. His clothes were torn and soggy, and he was right. His wings gave him an advantage.

But he didn't realize that I was no longer hindered by the weight and size of them.

Wrapping my legs around his waist, I bucked, flipping us so that he was pinned beneath me as I braced my forearm over his throat. His hands came up to push me away, but I twisted my wrist with the blade free and brought the dagger's tip to his ribs.

In the same breath, I released the reins on my power.

Black flames roared to life around us, licking hungrily at

the hay. The world became a crackle of darkness. What little light was in the hall evaporated, and the air thinned as I let myself burn and burn and burn, closing us into a tent of obsidian.

The seraph stopped breathing. His eyes scanned the enclosure, a ghost of terror flickering there, the blaze of my fire reflected in his stare.

I couldn't go back. *I wouldn't.* I'd only barely begun to live.

Years, I'd spent loving Tova, mourning us before she ever died. I refused to go back to my father now, when true freedom was so palpable, when I hadn't yet figured out how to love and live beyond her, when I *wanted* to move on.

I wasn't going to spend one more day loving anything that couldn't love me back.

The bounty hunter's hands fell away, landing on either side of his head in surrender as the fire encroached on his wings. His speckled feathers pulled in tight, contracting beneath him, shying away from the flames as much as his bone and tendons would allow. Wings were flexible like that, sheets of cartilage and skin, but I knew, and he knew, that it wouldn't be enough. Not with how fast the fire was moving.

"Please," he whispered. Sweat beaded on his brow and upper lip.

Still, the fire raged, eating up strands of straw like wicks on dynamite. My muscles were iron, my mind frozen. I burned. I couldn't stop. I needed to stop, needed to control it, but I didn't know how to make the fire listen to me. It had never listened before. I tried to swallow it, but it rolled up my throat and over my tongue in a thick film. The skin of my back prickled, tremors radiating along either side of my spine. I felt the push and pull of my bones, the knuckles of fire stretching beneath my shoulder blades, pressing almost to the point of breaking through.

My wings, wishing to be set free.

"Stop," the seraph cried. He gritted his teeth against a scream as the flames finally touched the peak of his wings and caught a few feathers on fire.

I bit my tongue. The taste of blood spread through my mouth, the pain a necessity, the pain a *gift* as it pierced the dark hold this power had on my body. My muscles unraveled. I let the iron tang cleanse my mouth, let it chase the power down, down, back to where it belonged.

My back vibrated with phantom knuckles once more, but then they slowly retracted beneath my ribs.

The only thing my past and title had ever been good for was placing me on a pedestal while I quietly sank inside, knowing I wasn't any better than the mortals, knowing that the hovering city and all it stood for was wrong. Knowing I didn't belong.

Still, I could play into expectations. I could be the spoiled princess for a moment or two.

I drew my flames back an inch and hissed, "I return home when I choose to. I don't give a shit about your bounty, about *any* of you half-winged assholes who continue to come after me. I will kill anyone who tries to take my freedom from me."

"I am under orders from our King," he whispered, his voice both a plea and threat. "You kill me, and you've committed treason."

"Who do you think they'll believe?" I sneered. "Their princess, or some back-alley mongrel looking for an easy fortune? Do not look at me with anything less than the respect I demand. Do you understand?"

His eyes shuttered, and I let my flames flare. He quickly nodded.

I leaned in and added, "And if you come back around here, looking for vengeance through the spilling of mortal blood, I will react as if these humans were an extension of my body. Got it?"

He nodded again.

"Be vocal, half-wing prick, or I might not trust that you heard me. *Promise me.*"

His eyes narrowed, his lungs rattling against my chest. "I…promise."

"Promise *what?*"

"I promise not to come back." The words were choked, but he said them, so I knew I could trust him enough to let go. Seraphim couldn't break promises.

Our word was soul-binding. Breaking a promise caused our bodies to wither, our wings to disease, our minds to shatter. Oaths were for forever or until death set us free. If he came back here after promising not to, he would forfeit any life worth living.

I rapped my knuckles on his cheek. "Good boy."

Peeling back, I suffocated my power, shoving it back into my gut. It felt like a bag being stuffed too full, but I managed it, just barely. My flames snuffed out, leaving nothing more than ash and the scent of burnt flesh behind. The seraph stretched his wings with a low groan. He still had full range of motion, so I didn't let myself pity him.

Even though I hadn't been sure I was going to stop. Even though I'd nearly killed him.

I ripped a feather from the underside of his wing, and he yelped, rolling away with a lethal growl. "Oh, calm down," I said over my shoulder. I waved the gray feather at him, its fleshy end bloody and broken. "It's just one little feather to seal the box."

The box needed a touch of magic to seal again, and the bounty hunter's feathers were far easier to access right now than mine.

I knew he didn't understand why I put them away, knew it would disgust and confuse my people if they saw the way I treated them with shame. It was unheard of among nobility.

Only spies could hide their wings and retain even a modicum of pride.

I dropped the feather into the box, and a whirring started up. The ground shook, and the lid slid shut like a snapping jaw.

"Now, get the hell out of here," I said. "Before I change my mind and pluck you bare for attacking me."

He rose slowly. "You can't keep running. You're wasting your life down here."

I glanced at the wondrous fear in his face. It was an expression I'd grown accustomed to, that I saw whenever my secret was divulged to someone new. I wasn't like my father or brother. There were no answers, no explanation. After seeing my flames, he had to know that.

"I can live my life however I want," I stated, my voice and heart void of emotion.

The male shook his head, then turned and exited the stables.

I waited, listening to the flap of his wings as he leapt into the sky. My iron necklace grew heavy and tight. Was my life really wasted down here?

Back home, my potential was ignored. I was set aside like a priceless heirloom rather than a daughter. I remembered my father's disappointment, my room in the castle, with its peeling wallpaper, burnt walls, and empty corners. I was equally wasted there, on liquor and drugs, anything to numb me to the darkness within. What sort of princess did that make me?

There was no strength in going home, no honor. At least here, my life was mine, and I was doing something that made a difference to someone, *anyone*.

I fisted my burning hands and emerged from the stables, but those thoughts followed me like shadows. I hoped that if I pretended a little while longer, I'd finally be free of them.

Withdrawing the belladonna from a pouch on my hip, I tapped some crystals into the gin bottle the guards had been sharing on the back wall. I slid the vial into the tunic of the man who had touched me earlier and carried the bottle with me around the front of the stables, gathering the left-over cookies along the way.

I returned the key to the older guard's pocket, wrapped his limp hand around the neck of the bottle, and laid down. With my head resting on his thigh, I closed my eyes…and waited.

For long minutes, I let myself doze until they finally woke.

The guard groaned, his body stiffening beneath my temple. He gasped when he realized I was laying on him, his hand touching me lightly on the arm as if to shove me off, but he hesitated. There was a sudden jostle instead, as his hand left my arm and collided with something.

The younger man woke up with a whine. "Oy, what was that for?"

"Shh, *look.*"

A moment of silence. Then the younger said, "What happened?"

I felt movement above me. They must be speaking with their hands. The older guard eventually growled, "Go check."

Air swirled beside me, alerting me to the younger guard's departure. As soon as his footsteps retreated into the stables, the older guard shook my shoulder. "Miss, wake up."

I let my eyes open slowly, blinking up at the guard's face. His gaze was wary.

"Oh, was I asleep?" I slurred, turning my body in his lap. I rubbed my eyes, shaking my head drowsily. He gasped at the pressure on his lap and brought his hands under my shoulders to lift me. I swayed, gripping his arm to steady myself. "I'm sorry. I didn't mean to pass out on you. How long was I out?"

His brow furrowed. "I don't know. I suppose all three of us fell asleep."

My jaw dropped open. "What?"

The younger guard reappeared in the doorway to the stable and nodded once, likely confirming that the box was indeed as I left it: deceivingly intact. All tension faded from the older guard's face, and when he turned to me, he smiled tightly. Then, his gaze fell on the bottle beside him. He picked it up, swirling the contents before lifting it to his nose. His eyes darkened.

"What's wrong?" I ventured.

He gestured to me with the bottle in hand. "Did you bring this liquor around?"

"I got it from the guard on the back wall. Don't you two remember sharing it with me?"

His eyes flicked to the younger guard standing behind me.

"Oh, dear." I rubbed my temples, pausing as if to think. "The last thing I remember is passing the bottle between us." I blinked a few times, tilting my head to study the older guard with a pout. "You were telling me about your wife who died. I'm *so* sorry."

His head bobbed back as if I'd physically hit him, but the suspicion slipped from his face.

"And then things get so fuzzy," I moaned, squeezing my eyes shut. I let them flash open again as I leaned in to whisper, "Do you think it might have something to do with the salt that one guard added to the bottle?"

"Salt?" the younger guard echoed, his brow stitching.

"Which guard?" the older one demanded, reaching out to stroke my arm comfortingly.

I frowned. "I don't know. It was this purple stuff he pulled from his tunic. He said it would make the ale taste better. He told me to bring it back to him when I was finished...but I guess I fell asleep. You don't think he'll be mad at me, do you? He scares me a little."

The guards exchanged another look and every softness evaporated from the air. They'd caught on. *Delightful.*

"It does look like Jeffrey's bottle," the younger guard murmured.

The older man nodded, gripping my arm firmly to pull me upright. "You should head back to the house now, miss."

"Are you sure?" I asked, pressing a hand over the steady beat of my heart. "Will everything be okay?"

The younger one smirked. "We'll be fine, honey. We have somethin' to take care of, and it's best you aren't 'round for it."

I paused a moment longer. "Okay. If you're sure you don't need me?"

The older one nudged me toward the house. "Very sure," he muttered. "Thank you for the company, and for, uh, listening."

I nodded, retrieving my discarded cookie tin, then weaving between the hedges until they couldn't see me anymore. I halted just out of sight as I heard the shouting start up, and a bottle shattered against the stable wall. The man who had touched me protested when they found the belladonna in his tunic, but naturally, no one believed him. No one listened to him as a whip was fetched from the stables, the drunk guard stripped of his tunic, and the smog reached down to choke them all.

CHAPTER 19

The gnashing forest was deceptively quiet. Of course, the world around the staircases-to-nowhere always appeared a little too welcoming to visitors, too lovely. That was how they coaxed us up the steps.

I was about to break the only rule the forest-dwellers gave me when I first entered their home: never use the portals.

Not only were they dangerous for any who dared to use them, but once activated, they were also dangerous to everything and everyone within throwing distance. Whatever was opened had to be closed again quickly. Otherwise, the touching realms would begin to contaminate each other. Unfortunately, this was my only way to reach Ehlark Qinan.

He was hiding in an elvish realm. He could travel back and forth between this realm and those without the use of a portal, thanks to his elvish blood.

I'd come here directly from Gwaith House, refusing to linger there long enough to tempt any of the guards to come searching for me. If I was lucky, my deception would remain above suspicion. If it didn't, I would deal with the repercussions upon my return. On the way out of the house, I had seen the newspaper sitting on the entryway table, saw that there had been another outbreak in the city. No mention of angels this time, and no mention of the one that had been murdered earlier in the week, so it seemed Lee had kept his word and taken the corpse straight to the morgue. I still had to figure out the best way to retrieve it...

Right now, though, I had the time and freedom to glean information from the alchemist, so I was taking it.

I tore my gaze from the grainy, silver stone staircase in front of me and looked at the items in my hand. A bundle of colorful dried herbs wrapped in twine. A page torn from an old spell book, the incantation on it circled with dark chalk. A note that said,

Tread carefully, darling, and don't forget to burn.

On the page from the spell book, a disjointed translation from ancient elvish, were instructions on how to use a staircase portal. I had to burn Blessed Fluxroot as I ascended and spoke the incantation. I'd generously been provided a bundle of it. There was a warning beneath the incantation that my mystery note-sender had also circled, detailing what kind of terrors could snatch a traveler off the staircase without the protective smoke, and while some of the translation was a little muddy and confusing, I got the gist that the results would be very, very bad.

I wasn't surprised. The elvish lands – it didn't matter which one, they were all the same – were called the realm of nightmares.

Cupping my hand in front of me, I let the heat in my palm spark into a dark flame. I'd released a fair amount of tension back in the stables, but my flame still danced wildly, pushing the limits of my control as I lit the end of the Fluxroot. Embers licked at the purple-ish dried root. I blew on it, and viscous white clouds of smoke began spewing from the bundle, falling over my legs and feet.

I walked up to the foot of the staircase and turned to the incantation. I would have to recite it in elvish. I'd been practicing the words on the way out here, but I was still feeling a little nervous about my pronunciation. Goddess forbid I say something wrong and wind up somewhere I don't want to be. I cleared my throat and began.

As my lips and tongue formed around the unfamiliar language, I let the translation of the elvish words resonate in my mind. It didn't sound as musical and fluid in the common tongue of this realm, but the meaning remained the same.

Open, open, portal mine,
With power, I do bind thee.
Wake thy steps and light my path.
Fill this empty space.

Beyond the piece of parchment in my hand, I saw the steps begin to glow green along the rises, where runes had been hewn into the silver stone. I lifted a foot to the first step and started my ascent. The light sputtered at first, as if in response to my presence, as if confused, but it grew stronger as I continued the chant.

I brought Ehlark Qinan's name to the forefront of my mind to lend purpose to the spell, as the page had instructed.

Open, open, portal mine.
I stand here at thy doorstep.
Dreams and nightmares, stand aside,
Endless, work thy magic.

I felt the staircase shudder under my toes. I felt the magic as it reached up with invisible tendrils, tickling my mind, grasping at Ehlark Qinan's name. It had full access to my thoughts, and that scared me, how easily it could take from me, how easily it could ruin me if it wished. I steeled my nerves and kept rising, kept reciting.

Air and spirit, lend me strength.
Shifting, touching, path be here.
Portal mine, open, open.

As the last consonant rolled off my tongue, I reached the top step, and I watched as the atmosphere ripped open before me, as if someone had taken a knife and tore into it. The top of the stone landing stretched magically in front of me. Transparent energy rippled like a thin veil over the portal until it was just large enough for my body to pass through.

Beyond the veil, the world spun with bright, multi-colored lights. It almost looked like fairy lights twinkling in the distance, but I knew elves had no need for them. Smoke continued to spool around me; I let it billow for a moment longer, allowing the scent of the Fluxroot to cling to my skin before taking those final steps into the elvish realm.

As I passed through the veil, my vision blurred. A rush of cold air kissed my skin, but less than a heartbeat later, I was on the other side, looking at the flourishing elven land with my own eyes.

Old trees towered all around me, the cracks in the bark giving way to glowing, sappy, green flesh. The dead bark was dark, nearly black. I quickly stamped out the bundle of Fluxroot and tucked it and the spell away in my coin purse.

Luminous flies rushed in to greet me, snagging my full attention. As they drew close enough to touch, I saw that they had bodies like the sprites of the forest back home, only their skin shone in vibrant colors rather than tan flesh. Glancing around, I saw that the little beings echoed the colors of the world around them. Multi-colored flowers sprouted from the long grass. Massive otherworldly mushrooms grew between the trees too, so much vibrant light spilling out from beneath the bulbs that I decided they must be used by these creatures as tiny houses.

There was no road.

I looked back and saw that the portal endured behind me, the silver stone landing blending in with this strange earth, the dreary world on the other side waiting patiently for my return. The portal brought me to the right place, I was sure of it. I could still feel the phantom of that magic in my head, rummaging, pulling my intention out. It knew what I wanted.

Scanning the forest spread before me, my eyes caught on a stretch of trampled earth to my right. It was glaring, the only hint of another human-like presence surrounded by the otherwise untouched nature of this world. *A footpath.* I made my way onto it and let the flattened grass guide me until I saw a brilliant light peek through the trees up ahead.

Confident I now knew where I was going, I slipped off the path and approached the beacon from another angle.

It was a tree. Well, tree-*ish*. It was a little more than that.

The rest of the forest cleared out around it, making room for the massive black trunk and its limp, drooping branches. Thousands of small green flowers smoldered on the tree, falling in lines all the way to the ground. Where the path led in, the branches had been pulled away like curtains. The roots of the tree stretched like pedestals, leaving a cavern beneath the trunk, and warm light flickered from within.

That was where I would find Ehlark.

I strode up to the entrance of the tree, not bothering to hide myself any longer. I figured it was best not to surprise him, considering everything the lycanthropes had told me.

Three grand steps had been formed in the earth, leading down into the living space.

Descending, I looked around the room. There was a large bed made from twisted wooden columns on the far end, seemingly created from wayward roots of the tree, gossamer fabric that matched the sprightly green glow weeping from the ceiling. There was a variety of wooden furniture; chairs and bookshelves and a lovely little dining table in front of a cold iron stove. On the other side of the immense space, there was what looked like a labyrinth of glass on top of a table, vibrant liquids bubbling in their containers. An alchemy table.

Ehlark wasn't anywhere I could see him, but he was close. He was in the middle of brewing something.

Behind me, I heard a familiar creaking.

I barely managed to dive out of the way as an arrow flew at me.

My shoulder popped as I hit the ground. I didn't have a chance to see the person who had done it; I only knew that I could hear their light footsteps approaching, and their bow creaked again as they notched another arrow. I rolled myself behind a large sitting chair, one with delicately hewn legs and black satin upholstery. Gripping the sides of it, I realized it was attached to the floor. It had been *carved* up and out from the tree roots. I shifted more fully behind the stationary shield and withdrew my hands just in time to avoid an arrow that struck the chair's frame.

"Ehlark Qinan, child of elf," I spoke evenly, projecting my voice. I noticed how much it sounded like my father's as the words left my mouth. "I urge you to remember the treaty your people made with mine before you unwittingly break it."

A pause. There was no tell-tale whistle of an arrow.

"And exactly what kind of creature are you?" The deep voice was cold but curious.

I took a deep breath and slowly rose from my crouch behind the chair. "I was hoping you might help me figure that out."

Ehlark Qinan stood at the entrance of his home. He held his bow at attention, his eyes glaring down at me over the arrow's shaft. He looked like he was made for this place, or maybe, it was made for him. His skin was a gorgeous almost-black brown, exactly like the trees. His eyes were a luminous green. The only thing that stood out about him in this place were the long silver locs cascading around his shoulders.

He considered me as I considered him. His mouth tightened almost imperceptibly. "No."

"I'm afraid I need to insist."

His eyes narrowed. "Who are *you* to demand anything of *me*?"

I swallowed, even though my mouth was alarmingly dry. "My father is the King of the Fenix, and my name is Sab-"

"Sabrina," he finished, his eyes softening, "the missing princess of flame and ember. Yes, I've heard of you."

I grimaced. "I'm not missing."

"Apparently not." After a moment's hesitation, he lowered his bow. He didn't put it away, but that was enough to make my mouth well in relief. A smirk played on his full lips as he descended the steps into his home. "And you, *Princess*, have quite a way with introductions."

"I could say the same about you."

He chuckled lowly, pausing a few feet away from me. "Go on, then. To what do I owe the delight of being ambushed in my own home?"

"I heard that you know all manner of magic."

His grin turned wicked. "When you're as old as I, it's hard not to."

Without another word, I lifted a hand. I willed a small flame into my palm. It crackled and spat wayward ebony sparks despite my efforts, and I saw the composure drain from Ehlark's face. His eyes widened as he staggered forward a step, his fingers tightening around his bow. It wasn't a threat, but I was still frightened.

I'd hoped he would have answers, but he looked just as bewildered as everyone else.

"Well." He licked his lips and finally returned his arrow to the bag on his back. "That *is* unexpected." His brows stitched together. "How do I know you are who you say you are?"

I smiled. "Can't elven sense untruths? You tell me."

"Do not antagonize me, Princess. I'll have you know that my sense of truth is only a mere tickle compared to my full-elven kin. Be glad for that, and that I had the humanity not to rip you to pieces the instant I found you infringing on my home."

I knew that was true. He probably could have worked a lot harder to hurt me but had held back. He could call it humanity if he wanted, but I knew it was at least a little bit of curiosity and boredom. No one who lived alone could be content all the time.

"Still..." he added after a moment. "I happen to believe you. I always thought the way your father treated you was rather strange, deplorable even. He liked to hide you away."

A sinking discomfort filled my stomach.

I didn't know why it upset me so much when strangers spoke ill of my father, but it did. He did try his best with me. His best just wasn't good enough.

I sighed. "I'm not here to spill my soul to you, elf. Only my blood."

"Oh?" He piqued a brow.

"I want you to take my blood and use it to figure out what I am, where I come from."

He tilted his head. "What makes you think I could even do something like that?"

"Anyone who has experience curing the Valgenvirus is bound to be an experimental fool worthy of this endeavor. Wouldn't you agree?"

Surprise flashed across his face before he shook his head and laughed. "It figures *they* would be the ones to send you here. Those canines are too kind for their own good, and mine."

My body was thrumming. "So, are you going to help me?"

Ehlark gave me a knowing smile. "You're not going to leave until I do. Isn't that right?" Without waiting for a response, he waved me over to a long couch farther into the room.

I sat on the edge and watched as the elf gathered a few items from his table. Because I knew better than to trust a good thing, I asked, "What are you going to ask for in return?"

"I don't know yet," he replied simply.

On his way back to me, he waved his long fingers, urging me into the center of the couch. "I'll need to take quite a bit from you. Lie down."

Frowning, I acquiesced, propping my head up on one of the pillows crowding the cushions. He sat beside me, and a ribbon of dread curled in my gut as I waited for him to arrange tools on the cushion between us: several narrow glass tubes, a tin of medicinal balm that smelled of pine when he opened it, and a long needle.

Owing an elf anything they wanted with no deadline for repayment wasn't ideal, but I had no room to negotiate. Besides, I already knew I would have given him anything he asked for.

His eyes met mine when he was finished preparing. "Ready?" he asked. I could see how old he was in that moment. Thousands of years, I'd be willing to bet. That gaze held an understanding beyond my wildest imagination, such intelligence and compassion that I struggled to breathe around the attention.

I nodded.

As he lowered the needle to my arm, he murmured, "Just a small prick."

"I doubt that," I muttered through my teeth.

He paused, his ancient eyes flashing to mine in faint

amusement. Then, the silent laughter shaking his shoulders evaporated as he focused on tapping a vein.

I watched, because I knew it would hurt less that way.

This needle was larger than those used for sewing, as large as Ehlark's slender hand. The needle flared slightly from the middle, and I could see then that it was hollow in the center. He aligned the needle with a green vein in my forearm and pushed.

At the same time, his other fingertips pressed gently against the inside of my elbow and slid down the inside of my forearm, toward the needle.

I wondered for a moment if he had done it to distract me. Then, tingles spread up my arm. I could *feel* as my blood responded to him, as it chased his fingertips and started trickling through the needle's center into the first tube.

I felt my eyes widen. "How are you doing that?"

"I have an affinity for the natural elements," he explained quietly. "Blood, earth, chemicals, and metals. I can move and shape them at will, if I'm familiar enough with the molecular structure. It just takes a bit of bending."

"That would explain your furniture."

"Yes, it's certainly convenient for home renovations." A small smile flitted across his face, and I returned it.

He worked through the tubes on the cushion, using his magic to halt the flow every time he needed to stop up a vial. By the time we were halfway through the tubes, I felt my eyes begin to droop. I tried to peel myself up into a sitting position. I couldn't fall asleep here.

He pushed me back down, shaking his head. "Almost there. Relax. Don't move, or I'll lose the vein."

Another tube filled. I blinked, and I couldn't pry my eyes back open.

My head swirled with darkness and vibrant flashes of green that played just beyond my reach. I drifted too far. I was only vaguely aware of where I was and what was happening, the blood and energy seeping away from me.

Then, I heard a voice, faint at first but quickly growing stronger. *What happened?*

I tried to reply, but my mind was so heavy.

Where have you gone?

I reached again for that light in the distance, that eerie green glow. It was so far away.

You need to wake up now, Sia. Wake up!

My eyes flashed open, my body jerking violently as if I'd been dropped back into my body from some great height. I was still on Ehlark's couch. From what I could tell, I hadn't moved an inch. I pushed myself up and saw Ehlark stepping out from behind his alchemist table.

"You're finally awake," he said with a smile.

Oh no. "How long have I been unconscious?" I demanded.

"An hour or so."

I staggered to my feet, using the frame of another chair to help me towards the entrance to Ehlark's home.

"Hold on a minute," he protested, reaching for me. "You shouldn't get up just yet. Let me get you something to eat and drink."

Maybe he was right, but I waved him away and forced myself to stand up straight. My ears were ringing and my veins were pumping sluggishly. It didn't matter, though, because I had to go. "No time." I walked briskly toward the earthen steps.

"Princess," he called. Reluctantly, I turned to him. There was concern in his eyes, but he simply crossed his arms over his chest and said, "Return in two weeks. I should have something for you by then, if there's anything to be found."

I knew better than to thank an elf, but I said it anyway. "Thank you, Ehlark."

He nodded, smiling, and I swiftly saw myself the rest of

the way out. I slogged through the trees, following the foot-path until it brought me back to the portal. My world was already creeping into this one. The grass was darker around the portal, the trees lighter, and they didn't glow. Without waiting another moment, I launched myself into the rippling cleft in the atmosphere. It was only as the darkness took me that I realized my mistake.

I forgot to light the Fluxroot.

CHAPTER 20

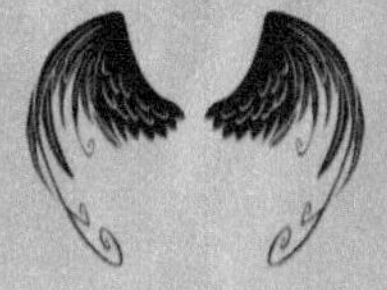

The halls were so empty.

Father had dragged me to this strange city, and that was the first thing I noticed about it, beyond how pretty the land was: how empty the walls and people seemed. I skipped down the blue hall, twirling the sticky stem of a flower I'd picked outside between my fingers. Father told me to stay out of the way today. He'd shooed me from the big room he was in and shut the door in my face. That was perfectly fine with me. The adults in that room were tense and mean, and I didn't want to be around them anyway.

Unfortunately, there weren't many kids here to play with. Not many *my* age, at least.

I'd seen a painting earlier, though, when we first arrived, of a little boy. I searched the halls for him, hoping the painting had been made recently. I flitted down several halls, looking in open rooms and jiggling doorknobs with a scowl. By the time I made it to the other side of the palace, I was trudging, my feet dragging on the lapis lazuli marble.

Then, I heard the voice of a child. It echoed from an adjacent hall, and I followed the noise to an open door.

There he was, a white-haired little boy with white wings, hunched over a set of wooden figurines. They kind of looked like pieces I'd seen on my father's war table. What a strange thing to play with.

"Hi," I exclaimed, startling him. He spun and looked at me with the widest, bluest eyes I've ever seen, backing up a step as if on instinct. Before he could think too much and decide not to like me, I smiled brightly and asked, "Do you want to play?"

He shifted on his feet. "You want to play with *me*?"

I rolled my eyes and walked into the room. Even this bedroom was bland: pale blue walls and boring bedsheets. Barely any toys at all. The boy looked like he was going to shed his skin, he seemed so frightened. Indignation filled my chest. I was *not* going to let him be afraid of me. "Of course, silly. I've decided we have to be best friends until I leave. You can't say no."

"Oh," he breathed, a small light flickering to life behind his eyes. "Okay."

Relief swept through me.

I rocked up on my toes, my wings ruffling in excitement. Clasping my hands together in front of me, I said, "I'm bored. Let's play tag."

The boy's lips quirked to the side. "Tag?"

"Yes. You run, and I'll chase you."

"For what purpose?" He tilted his head. It was obvious in that moment that he'd never played tag before, which I thought was ridiculous. *Who doesn't know how to play tag?*

I sighed in exasperation. "To tag you, silly. Now, run! If I catch you, I get to eat you up like a serpent would." I made some exaggerated slurping sounds and began lumbering toward him with crazed eyes.

He staggered back, his eyes flashing. "Wait."

"No waiting. Go, go, go!" I started running at him, and he

turned on his heel and took off into the hallway outside his room.

Giggling, I chased him. I ran on foot until I was short of breath and the hallways started to blur. He was fast. Way faster than me, I begrudgingly admitted to myself. So, when we turned down the next hallway and he veered into a large, abandoned room, I took to the sky.

I catapulted myself in front of him into the room and landed, quickly spinning on my toes to grab him by the shoulders. "*Gotcha.*"

His body crumpled. He recoiled from my hands and collapsed onto the floor at my feet, juicy tears welling in his eyes. I realized too late that he had not been running for the game but because he really didn't want me to catch him. He didn't want me to *touch* him.

I frowned, blinking away the sting in my own eyes. I didn't want him to be upset or scared, not from me touching him. That made me sad.

I kneeled, placing my hands flat on the floor between us. "What's wrong?"

He stared at me warily. "I don't like this game," he grumbled after a moment, after he'd forced his tears back down. "I don't want you to eat me up like a serpent."

I folded my arms across my chest with a huff. "The serpent was just *pretend*. I'm not gonna eat you."

He blinked a couple times. "Oh."

"Do you not like being touched?" I asked, even though I kind of already knew the answer.

He slowly shook his head.

I pursed my lips, then shrugged. "That's okay, there are other games we can play. How about hide and seek?"

"I guess," he murmured.

"Okay, I'll hide first." Looking around the room, I saw it was as vacant as the rest of the palace. It would be difficult to find any good spots, *but* I *had* seen a huge cluster of trees outside that would be perfect. "Let's do it outside."

I got to my feet.

The boy seemed hesitant, but he silently followed me anyway as I made my way down and out. I led us confidently into the sea of white trees. I felt so safe amidst them, *powerful*, like a captain or a chief or something else equally strong and special. We walked until we could no longer see the palace, and then I spun around to face him.

"This should be good. Now, close your eyes and count to one hundred while I hide somewhere. No peeking – that is *cheating*."

Worry seeped into his eyes. "But how will I know where you go?"

"That's the whole point, silly swan." I laughed, and he frowned at the nickname. I thought it suited him just fine. "I hide and you find me."

"What if you get lost?"

My eyes rolled again. "I'm not going to get lost. Come on, cover your eyes and start counting." I was excited to show him just how good of a hider I was.

Father said I needed to be.

He sighed. His shoulders slumped in surrender as he dropped his head into his hands and started grumbling numbers. I tip-toed away from him, holding my giggle in with my hand until I was sure he wouldn't hear it. Then, I climbed the thickest tree I could find, up and up until I was surrounded by red and gold foliage. The leaves were wet from a recent drizzle, but I knew the shifting fall colors would hide me nicely.

I waited a long time.

I was very sure he'd searched in the wrong direction for me first, because by the time I saw him, I had counted to one hundred three times in my head.

He was weeping.

As he walked, he wiped stream after stream of sparkling, translucent tears from his face. His eyes and nose were red. His lower lip trembled. He walked in aimless circles, searching behind every tree along the way, whispering to himself as he did it. Only when he passed by beneath my tree did I hear what he said. *"Where are you? Where are you? Please come back."*

He couldn't yell very well. His voice was cracking, so he started whistling instead. The sound was piercing; I had to muffle my ears.

His sobbing grew louder, and he left my tree behind without even looking up into it, missing me entirely. He was getting more hysterical by the second. Silly, silly swan. I was right here.

My heart couldn't bear his crying any longer.

I flung myself out of the tree and landed lightly on the ground, my large wings displacing the fallen leaves all around us and catching his attention.

A huge smile broke across his face when he saw me. He ran to me, halting inches away, and I don't know why, but it almost felt like he had wanted to hug me.

"Are you okay?" I asked him.

Wiping his cheeks one last time, he said, "I'm sorry. I don't think I like that game either."

I frowned at him.

He dropped his gaze to the ground and kicked leaves. "My mom got lost. Really lost."

"Oh." Now I wanted to hug him, to make him feel better, but I didn't, because I knew he wouldn't like it. "I'm sorry."

He looked up with a sad smile. "Me too."

Then his face fell as he focused on something behind me. Tears still filling his eyes, he reached over my shoulder and brushed his fingertips against my wing. I fluttered my feathers, feeling a little uncomfortable but unwilling to push him away. I didn't want to upset him. His hand came away covered in runny gold paint. My eyes bulged. *Oh no.* The wet leaves in the tree must have brushed up all over my wings, dampening them.

His white eyebrows furrowed. "Why are your wings painted gold?"

I shrugged, unable to tell the truth, knowing Father wouldn't want me to. "Why were you crying so much?"

He brushed the paint off on his pants and gave me another sad smile, so sad I could feel it in my heart. "I was afraid you had disappeared forever too."

"Don't worry, silly, I won't disappear," I reassured him, making a patting motion in the air beside his arm. "We can be best friends forever if you want, even after I leave."

I'd never had a best friend before. I thought he would make a good one, as long as we could find some games he didn't cry about.

Everything about him seemed to lighten at the offer. His smile grew warm and hopeful. He looked into my eyes, but it felt like he was seeing a lot deeper. "Do you *promise*?" The words reverberated in my skull and stretched my vision in a thousand different directions. His voice distorted, becoming both young and old, child and man.

The man he had to be by now.

It didn't matter. I knew I was going to say yes.

Consciousness came back to me all at once. The scent of damp earth surrounded me, and I felt that same wetness soaking into my clothes and skin. I creaked an eye open and groaned.

Multi-colored lights spun around me. It took a long moment to realize what they were.

Those little beings from the elvish realm were crowded around me, tugging on my hair, poking my face, trying to revive me. I looked up and saw a low, ribbed ceiling hovering above my face. I blinked languidly, studying it. It would seem I was lying beneath a mushroom top.

But I had walked back through the portal. I'd left the elvish realm…hadn't I?

Turning my head to the side, I peered at the sliver of the world visible to me beneath the mushroom cap. It didn't look like the elvish realm out there. I must be home.

The Fluxroot.

I groaned again, slapping a hand over my face hard enough for it to hurt. "You idiot," I grumbled. I felt the sensation of parchment against my skin and realized there was something tucked into my hand. I'd been messed with by some night-mare, or maybe an elvish trickster. They'd intercepted me before I could reach the other side and managed to knock me out cold.

Not that it would have been difficult to do that – I was in a terrible condition. I was actually shocked I made it out alive. My head pounded in agreement.

I slowly crawled my way out from under the mushroom.

Yes, I was definitely home. The staircase was there, the runes dark and magic-less beside me. The portal was gone, but the evidence was all around me. In a large circle around the staircase, the forest had sprouted mushrooms and grass and flowers. The trees had turned black. It was more than it should be, which meant I'd been trapped in the portal for some time.

I looked down at the folded parchment in my palm. As I opened it, I realized it was the page from the spell book. Written in the corner was a note that said,

My head jerked up. *They'd* been here. I was willing to bet they'd even braved entering that portal to get me out themselves, then deposited me under that mushroom to shield me from the gnashing forest. I turned in a circle, scouring every inch of the forest, searching for the eyes that I knew must be watching me.

I saw no one.

CHAPTER 21

I quickly learned that I'd lost so many hours in the portal, between worlds, that it was dusk when I woke. I spent the night sleeping in a tree on the outskirts of the city, gathering strength and regenerating the blood I'd lost, and when the sun rose, I prowled the grimy paved streets for Lee.

There was something off about him; I just couldn't put my finger on what.

He acted so at odds with how I expected a human detective to behave. I was starting to worry he was simply better at hiding his feelings, that perhaps he buried his deep-rooted hatred for the seraphim under a pleasant facade. That was dangerous. It made me want to trust him, seek help from him. At least with Destin, I always knew where we stood. He despised me in a vicious way, at a base, existential level. I knew exactly what to hide from him. The fact that Lee had decided to look closer, was asking questions of and about me, made me nervous. If he dug deeper, he would inevitably discover more questions I couldn't even begin to answer. If he kept digging, he might figure out everything.

It was imperative I knew how badly that would turn out, if Lee discovered the truth.

The Gwaith name couldn't afford the slander that would come from harboring seraphim on their property, imprisoned or not, and I couldn't allow that. Erlene deserved to inherit a pristine reputation. I had to do everything in my power to ensure her future happiness, because I wouldn't be there to protect her when that future came.

If I was being totally honest with myself, I also desperately wanted to talk to Lee. I needed to feel him out, to see if he knew exactly where the seraph's body was being kept in that beast of a morgue. It would take me too long to search the place myself, without any direction or guidance, and I had no desire to force my way through the human employees working there night and day. I hoped to be able to persuade the detective to help me get the seraph home. If I could keep him from suspecting too much of me, of course.

I would allow him to believe I was a sympathizer, as Destin did.

Maybe I was a fool for thinking Lee might be so reasonable, but I had to try, for the Stymphalian's sake.

I finally found Lee in a pub nestled into an especially soot-coated street that afternoon. His fine suit stood out amidst the workers of the city, but he drank and talked easily with the patrons filtering through. I kept a healthy distance, watching from a dark corner with my hood hanging low over my face. I was fairly confident he hadn't seen me slip in. He'd been deep in conversation with the young woman manning the bar, his head tilted back in raucous laughter and his hand reaching over the counter to brush hers.

He was too beautiful not to stare, I'd give him that.

Only snippets of his conversations drifted back to me; discussions about the city, about the factories and the state of the ports, about what came in and what went out. Nothing even remotely connected to the murders. I wasn't sure whether to be irritated that this detective seemed as useless as the rest of his colleagues, or relieved that he never uttered my name.

As evening fell over the city, the pub turned several shades rowdier. Men and women crowded the bar and the small, rickety tables placed throughout the room.

Lee weaved between them with an artful grin.

He was handsome when the lines of his face softened like that. His eyes turned to liquid crystal, and they seemed to steam up as they landed on men and women alike. They fell for his charm instantly, trusting him, speaking openly about themselves and their jobs and families. Those he touched seemed to swoon under the weight of his fingertips.

Somewhere in the depths of the crowd, I caught the scent of a poppy pipe, and I frowned at the sweet, resiny allure of it.

The longer I watched Lee, the more I wanted to drown myself in ale. No one had the right to look like he did, to talk and move like that. He was obviously clever and strong, and he cared for the city, this city that secretly meant so much to me. Too bad all his potential was being wasted on inane, worthless questions that would never lead to a suspect or justice. It was maddening.

I stuck my tongue out at Lee's back and drained the rest of my third glass.

A group of men settled in at the table closest to my corner, and I slouched further. My hands idly shuffled a deck of playing cards I'd swiped from behind the barkeep's counter on my way in. Usually, patrons had to pay to use them, but that was what she got for being so distracted.

One man said to the others settling in around him, "I heard the visitors are Halcyon."

My fingers fumbled, nearly spilling the deck of cards all over the table.

Halcyon were another race of seraphim, their own subset of people, like the Fenix and Stymphalian. I was surprised the humans bothered with the proper term for them around here, especially when there were ten groups to keep track of: Fenix, Halcyon, Stymphalian, Sphinx, Harpies, Impundulu, Cocaktriz, Malforian, Quintessentials, and The Great Ravens.

Halcyon were born to a winged spirit of winter. They lived on the opposite side of the continent, on the northern edge of the coast, where their sacrifices drifted on the surface of the sea until they froze to death. A particularly brutal genesis, if you asked me.

Back home, we referred to them as "frosty bastards."

It was rumored that Halcyon hearts had been turned to ice by their patron, and the nature of their spirit made them incapable of any real emotion. I couldn't speak to the truth of that. All I knew was what I'd absorbed from my father's teachings. My father and brother belonged to the Fenix, a spirit of flame and ash, the ones who had honored peasant women on an island far, far away from here. Based on spirits alone, Halcyon were our natural adversaries.

Then there was the matter of alliances, *affiliations*.

The Halcyon were the only seraphim who held a treaty with the serpents, either because they felt a connection to the monsters due to their patron's favor for the sea, or they didn't mind offering up the humans of their land to feed them. It was easy to assume the implications of their treaty. That was why they'd stopped allowing travel over their borders, and why they did not welcome visitors. Everyone knew they were farming mortals like cattle.

Unfortunately, the humans speaking beside me were correct. The visiting seraphim to that city in the sky had to be Halcyon...because I was betrothed to one of them.

I huffed a laugh, bitterness seeping through the tang of ale on my tongue. My father couldn't understand why I refused to come home, but it wasn't so difficult. Who would want to marry someone with a heart of ice? Maybe if I'd been promised to anything else – an ugly Harpy, a blinding Sphinx, even one of those blood-sucking males of the Impundulu – I wouldn't have run. *Maybe.*

Tilting an ear toward the men, I resumed shuffling the deck.

Another male voice, gravely from smog damage, replied, "Good. I hope they kill each other and spare the rebels all this trouble."

"We wouldn't be that fortunate," the first voice returned.

A third man sighed, slamming his cowl down on the table. "Yeah, well, I don't know how much longer I can deal with rebels in our factory."

I perked up. The rebels were visiting the factories? For what?

"We just have to hold out a little longer," the second murmured.

The third scoffed. "You can't really believe that. It's always 'almost' and 'a little longer'. They have no idea what they're doing. They never have. Look at how many workers we lost in this last quarter alone." I inched to the edge of my chair, leaning on my elbow to listen closer. "Think of the friends we've lost. How could this possibly, *logically* end? When we're all dead? When no one is left to keep the machines running, to keep up this ruse?"

I leaned a little too far. The table tilted, giving under my weight and its uneven legs. I fell off the edge of my stool, stumbling a couple steps toward the table of men, the cards flying everywhere. They turned to stare at me.

I chuckled at myself. "Whoopsie," I mumbled, raising my head enough for the men to see a lopsided grin peeking out from under the hem of my hood. I wasn't anywhere close to being inebriated, but I swayed as if I might be. I didn't want to draw any more attention to myself. It was best if they thought I was a simple drunk.

The third man at the table rolled his eyes and left the table, waving down the barkeep.

As I stooped to gather up the cards from the ground, the second man craned his neck to watch me. I felt his eyes on me, taking, claiming. I tried to ignore him, wondering if I had made a mistake, if I had made myself seem *too* innocuous. I focused on putting the deck back together as quickly as possible.

Then, his voice crooned from right behind me. "Need help with that, sweet cheeks?"

The warmth of his body encroached on my back, and I shot up, forgetting the scattered cards in order to put some space between us. He braced a dirty hand on my table.

A thick beard covered most of his face, the hairs gnarled and coated with what could only be machinery exhaust.

I grimaced, clutching the cards in my hand a little tighter as he stepped toward me.

The other male who had still been sitting at the table was nowhere to be seen. We were alone. I scanned the crowd, pinpointing Lee and his golden hair, heading in my general direction. I wasn't sure I wanted Lee to know I was here yet, watching him, and what I wanted to do to this stranger as he reached up and caressed his dirty knuckles against my cloak would certainly draw attention.

"I don't need your help," I said evenly, abandoning any facade of drunkenness. "I would appreciate it if you would return to your table and leave me alone."

His hand curled around my upper arm. "But you look so damn lonely, sweet cheeks. Is that why you were eavesdropping on us? You wanted one of us to notice you?"

"No."

He leaned in, and it was an effort not to gag at the

blooming death in his breath, the sickness festering in the crevices of his mouth. His hand pulled me toward him.

"Let go of me," I growled, attempting to wrench my arm free. The cards exploded from my hands, scattering once again as I tried to shove him away. His eyes flashed black, his pupils dilated with a poison worse than the smog outside.

He opened his mouth to speak, his rancid breath curling in my nostrils, but then a shadow moved over us. My cheeks chilled.

"She told you to leave her alone."

A gloved hand appeared on his shoulder. He was ripped off me, and then flew sideways into his table as Lee's fist swung up and slammed square into his face.

Wood snapped and splintered beneath his body. The tables close enough to hear the scuffle barely acknowledged us, to my surprise, but I had *seen* it. Lee stood over him, eyes stormy and narrowed, jawline taut and sharp as a scythe. The force in that single punch... I'd never seen a mortal do that much damage without even breaking a sweat.

The man rolled over the remnants of the table, cradling his face, blood seeping up between his fingers. His two friends returned from the bar at that moment with a pitcher of ale. They paused a few feet away, the crowd parting just enough for them to see what had happened.

"You made a big mistake," the male on the floor groaned. He looked to his friends. "Did you see that? He fucking attacked me."

They must have recognized the danger in Lee's eyes as clearly as I did, because neither of them so much as breathed in his direction.

"What the fuck are you waiting for? Go—" The man's voice cut off in another groan. In the next breath, he passed out. Only the rattling but steady rise and fall of his chest assured me he was still alive.

Lee turned to his friends and growled, "Get him the fuck out of here. Don't come back."

They discarded the ale on my table and dragged their friend out without so much as a whisper. I ducked my head as Lee turned to me, hiding my face. It was pitch black outside, and the pub was dim, so I was hoping he might not recognize me right away. It was supposed to be *me* in control of our next meeting. *I* was supposed to approach *him*.

I should've simply walked away, but the words burst from me before I could swallow them. "You shouldn't have hit him like that." Breathlessness contorted my voice, and hopefully, that was enough to keep him from guessing who I was. It wouldn't look good for me if he knew I was here, if he thought I was following him around. Which I was. He was too suspicious of me as it was.

Lee blew out a sharp breath. "Yeah? Well, he should've listened to you when you said no. He didn't, and then you weren't taking care of him yourself, so I stepped in."

I frowned. I had allowed more than I usually would, but only because I didn't want to make a scene. A useless effort, clearly. Still, it really wasn't his business how I responded to an assault, and it certainly didn't seem fair that he was angry with me. I fought the urge to show him exactly how capable I was of incapacitating someone who bothered me.

His eyes softened with a few more heartbeats. He cupped my elbow and asked, "Are you okay?"

I shook him off. When I tried to side-step him, he did the same, irritating bit he'd done in the flower market and moved with me. Wisely, he kept his hands to himself.

Lee looked at the table beside us and crossed his arms. "Cards for one? How boring."

"It's relaxing," I said tersely, keeping up the wispy breathlessness in my voice.

He feigned a yawn, lifting a hand to pat his open mouth. "Sure."

Now he was irritating me. "Go away," I snarled.

"Tell you what," he drawled, leaning forward to rest an arm on my table. "Play a card game with me. If you win, I'll leave you alone."

I expected his sentence to continue. When it didn't, I prompted, "And if you win?"

His teeth flashed, clacking together as if he were holding back a laugh. "Hmm. Well, let's see. What do I want?" He stroked his shadowed jaw. The slow smirk he gave sent a chill up my spine. "You could let me walk you home?"

"What makes you think I need or want that?" I grumbled.

"I don't know." His eyes turned a deeper shade of blue. "I just get the feeling you're looking for a friend."

It wasn't a terrible idea, to let him think I was just another miserable mortal, playing cards in a tavern because she was lonely. I mean, I *was* lonely, but I didn't expect anyone to come along and fix it. I'd stopped expecting that a long time ago.

He grinned fiercely. "Besides, I'm not the one who's been sulking in this corner all evening. If you want to spend time with me, you don't need to be shy, Sia." He winked.

Fuck. I ripped my hood back. "How long have you known?"

"I knew it was you from the moment you entered the tavern. The red hair gave you away. Try tucking the ends away in your cloak next time."

"Thanks for the scintillating advice," I said through my teeth.

"Easy now, darling." Lee laughed, his eyes gleaming with suffocated amusement. "Come on, what do you say? Up for a challenge?"

You aren't a challenge, I wanted to snipe, but I clamped my teeth down on the words and nodded, crawling under the table to collect the cards.

He took a seat, not even bothering to help me. *Asshole.*

As I drew back from under the table, my eyes traveled up his long legs, the dark trousers stretched out to either side of me. Lee lounged in the rickety chair, one hand resting beneath the table. His fingertips thrummed his inner thigh, against the solid, straining muscles there.

Almost like he was nervous.

The smirk on his face suggested otherwise. Maybe the tapping was a lure...maybe he expected me to respond to it and crawl right into his lap.

I silently begged the splintered wood of his chair to give out and send him sprawling. His eyes followed me as I stood and perched on my stool, shuffling the sticky cards. He was staring at me like a crazy person again. Every inch of my skin was being filleted by his prying eyes, every movement and breath. I shifted in my seat, trying to shake away the tingles spreading through my limbs.

My foot slipped on the chair, and I accidentally kicked Lee's leg. I quickly wiggled back on my chair, my face and neck flushing.

Lee smiled and said, "Are we playing footsie now, too?"

He'd like that, wouldn't he? Before I could stop myself, I muttered, "Sorry."

He leaned over the table. "What was that, darling?" I wondered if he called the barkeep darling too. I wondered if that was what made her blush every time he talked to her. He certainly liked to say it. I glared at him from under my lashes. This close, I saw the faint freckles across his nose and cheeks, barely visible beneath his tan. He must spend a lot of time outside.

"Nothing," I grumbled.

Lee whistled softly. "It was your manners. Incredible. I

wasn't sure you had them." His foot found my stool, the rail between my heels. I wondered what he'd do if I drove my heel into his shin so hard, it broke bone.

You'd be surprised what I'm capable of, I hissed in my head, shuffling the cards with more ferocity.

He hummed. "Why so skittish?"

"I'm not."

"It's okay if you are."

I sighed, flinging two cards over to his side of the table. "Is there a reason I should be?"

"Not at all, darling." He picked up the cards.

Tension filled the air as I stared at him, his nonchalance rendering me speechless. After a long moment, I finally asked, "Why do you call me that?"

He shrugged. "Don't you like it?"

Endearments were weapons. I didn't understand why he wasted them on me. I didn't understand why I felt the warmth of it like a bleed in my chest. "No."

His eyes narrowed in on me as I flipped several cards over in the center of the table. "Tell me something, Sia. Do you believe the falsities you give to others, or do you just expect everyone to believe them because you're pretty?"

I huff a laugh. "You think I'm a liar? You're the one speaking in riddles here."

Lee folded his hands on the table. "Fine, I'll be blunt then. I think there's something going on in this city, beyond these dismemberments, and I think you sense that. I'm wondering what you plan to do about it."

"I thought taking care of this city was *your* job." I surveyed my cards with disinterest.

He poured the free ale into my discarded stein, guzzled a long sip, and smacked his lips. "My responsibilities are...complicated."

"I can imagine," I agreed. "Drinking stolen ale and flirting with barkeeps. It must be so hard for you."

He met my gaze with a smirk, and it was such a knowing look that I practically heard the words in his head. *Jealous, are you?*

I tore my eyes from his and glared at my cards. "Do you have responsibilities with the morgue as well?"

He hummed, tilting his head toward me thoughtfully. "Not really, but I hear the factory workers are quite involved in burning bodies as of late. Maybe you should ask one of them. You might learn a thing or two about the current state of your mother's birthplace."

My eyes snapped back to his, and I leaned back in my chair.

His expression had suddenly fallen into something more somber. What was he implying? That *I* was responsible for the city's state? There was no way he could have meant it that way, but it was so alarmingly close to the guilty thoughts that so often assailed me when I walked these streets and observed the suffering here that I suddenly wanted to cry. In a way, I felt connected to this city. It had been my mother's, and I never forgot that.

I said through gritted teeth, "The seraph's resting place is the only thing that matters to me right now, and it should matter to you too, oh officer of the *law*. The strangers around us, these very *alive* strangers who still have access to their homes and families and aren't currently wrapped in a black bag being turned to ash, are *not* my priority." That might have been too honest of me, might have revealed too much.

Thankfully, Lee's smile didn't falter.

"And yet, here you are, sitting in a pub alongside them." He gestured to the tavern around us, wielding a sly grin. "Unless it's *me* you just can't stay away from, darling?"

Fuck it. I would find a way to the dead seraph myself. I

threw my cards face-down and kicked his shin away from my chair so I could get up. Sadly, his leg shifted at the last second, and he missed the brunt of the blow. I stalked around the table.

"*Wait.*" His hand shot out to hover in front of my torso, and I jumped back to evade his touch. "Please, I didn't mean to upset you. Let's just finish our game."

"I don't want to."

"Why not?"

"Because I don't *like* you."

Lee's eyes flickered. "That's a shame. I've given you plenty of reason to like me."

"Oh," I scoffed. "You think so?"

"Well, I have helped you twice now."

"You're an overbearing, obtrusive jackass," I hissed, leaning over him.

His humor reignited, rushing over his features like water as he grinned. The scar beneath his ear tightened. "You know you want to beat me."

I hesitated, his voice swirling in my head and twining with my pride, tickling my sense of competition, which felt so small and weak right now that it was more of a flicker instead of the flame it used to be. I used to care so much, about everything. Slowly, I backed away and returned to my stool. I slid my cards off the table and into my lap. "What I want," I muttered, "is to know why you're wasting your afternoon in a tavern."

He rolled his lower lip between his teeth, then shrugged again. "I'm perplexed by this city. This is the only place on the whole continent covered in smog, and I'd like to understand why. From what I can tell, it makes life here untenable."

"So?" I countered.

"So, it's insane to tolerate what slowly kills you."

I shrugged. "What do you expect them to do? They can't just shut down the factories."

"Why not? What's made in the factories that's so essential to this city? Do you know?"

I held his gaze as I slipped the stiff parchment from my sleeve, the card I'd hidden there to replace one in my hand. I shrugged again. "No. Does it matter?"

"None of the citizens I've talked to seem to know either. Don't you think that's odd?"

I blinked, considering his words as he reached forward and flipped the final card laid out in the center of the table. He's right. It *was* odd. Had anyone asked questions about the factories before? Was there more to them than the fumes they produced?

It intrigued me, but I wasn't going to share my thoughts with *him*.

"I think," I sneered, splaying my twin queens in front of me. "That you should see yourself out."

The other two were already displayed in the center of the table, and I smiled, knowing that nothing beat queens all around. *Nothing.*

Lee set his cards down. "All right, I'm a man of my word." He stood and leaned over the table, and maybe I was too distracted by his intense pale gaze again, but I didn't register his hand until his knuckles were brushing my cheek. I suddenly couldn't *breathe.* "I won't even complain about the way you won, you lovely cheat."

His fingers trailed my jaw, skimming almost to my neck before suddenly falling away. He turned on his heel and left the tavern. I watched in a state of shock as my heart slowly quieted, and when his broad frame finally reappeared, sliding past the windows outside, I followed him.

Darkness wasn't a sufficient descriptor for what happened to the city at night. The streetlamps alleviated the haze just enough for mortals to get back to their homes, between the factories and pubs, but otherwise, it was a black hole. I could barely see through it. Lee walked into the utter darkness and turned onto the dirt road leading out of the city.

I followed him into the forest, on and on, mile after mile, until we arrived at a familiar crossroads.

Lee halted between two of the roads. I knew one led deeper into the wilderness, the other in the direction of Gwaith. He deliberated for a long minute before his head swiveled to my position in the trees along the road. His blue eyes pierced through me, all the humor evaporated from them and alarm crystallizing in the hollow left behind.

Could he see me?

Before I could determine that, a stampede of hooves and creaking wheels drew my attention down the road that we took here. The smog swirled, and as it parted, a carriage appeared. Backing away between the trees, I let darkness camouflage me as it passed. When I turned back to the cross-roads, Lee was gone. All four roads were empty. He must have fled into the forest.

I walked to the place where Lee had been. There was no trace of him, though I didn't expect there to be. I did discover something else instead. *Wolves.*

Dozens and dozens of mutilated carcasses were strewn like ribbons between the trees, their fur bloody and meat carved. It was a fucking massacre. I tried to make sense of what stretched out before me, but I couldn't look past the wolves torn apart closest to the road, their yellow eyes staring into nothing. Every single long jaw was parted in a death-howl.

Why had these wolves roamed into the smog? Beyond that, what could have possibly taken on an entire pack of wild animals and survived?

Recognition scraped down my spine as I spotted a pair of

dull red irises a few feet away, and I realized these weren't wolves at all. A full moon was peeking through the canopy. These were lycanthropes, drawn here while trapped in their most uncontrollable form and slaughtered by someone, or something. I entered the carnage to get a closer look, and immediately recognized the fully healed scar on the red-eyed Alpha's hind leg.

"Oh, my Goddess," I choked out, even though I knew there was no one left to hear me.

Hot, painful tears sprung to my eyes. Kneeling beside the Alpha, I realized something else. They hadn't died howling, as I first thought. No, their jaws had been forcefully wrenched open until the bone and joints snapped. And their teeth...all of them were missing.

CHAPTER 22

By the time I arrived at the Baron's manor, the moon was high, and the horse I'd borrowed from Gwaith was drenched in sweat. I hadn't bothered saddling the creature, preferring to travel light, so the scent of hay and iron and earth clung to me as I dismounted, handed off the reins, and waited for the guard who had accompanied me here to do the same.

I couldn't wait for them to come home tomorrow. I had to talk to Destin *now*.

Once I saw the dead lycanthropes and knew for certain the killer was closer now to Gwaith House than they'd ever been, I decided I would tell his Lordship everything. I needed his help, and I refused to let Erlene travel the roads home without me.

Thanks to the rebel guard I brought along, we made it past the Baron's security without issue, and damn, there was a lot of it.

We entered the manor – mansion, really – through the servants' entrance. The kitchen was bustling with food preparations, droves of servants filtering in and out, holding platters and drink trays. My guard gave me directions to the guest quarters where I would find Erlene – I'd used her as an excuse for the late-night trip – before slinking away after a young maid who'd recognized him and beckoned him into a dark corridor.

I'd chosen my companion well.

As I walked out of the kitchen and down the hall towards the front of the house, I saw that the party was in full swing.

The commotion was spread out between two neighboring ballrooms and the main foyer. My stomach growled as I caught a whiff of the tray a maid carried in beside me, some kind of sweet bread with corn filling. *Delicious.* I couldn't quite care about the blood on my shoes or my disheveled hair as I followed her. The effects of the ale had long faded, and I was *starving*.

I should probably grab a bite to eat first; Destin was bound to be furious and would send me away from the party once we discussed the reason I was here, and I doubted Erlene would have anything in her room when I left to watch over her.

Slipping through the grand, pointed-peak archway, I approached the food table nestled into the far corner of the room.

No one gave me a second glance as I picked up a napkin and filled it with cheese and fruit. Those who lingered by the food were already too drunk to realize I didn't fit in with the room; this corner was surrounded by laughing and frightfully shallow conversation, women decked in ribbons and men in fine suits. Add a few feathers and a hell of a lot more space, and it might have felt like home.

Tucking the stuffed napkin between my breasts and popping a cube of cheese into my mouth, I scanned the floor for Destin. I was sure he knew how to dance. There was no way he would have won Tova's heart if he didn't.

I couldn't find his mop of dark hair out there on the floor. The dance swelled with dozens of pastel colors, but I didn't see his signature black uniform anywhere. I didn't see Felicity's light blonde head weaving through the dancers, either. *Odd.* She seemed like the kind of young woman who would live on the dance floor at a party like this.

I did spot one familiar face: Felicity's friend, Kim.

She was dancing with an elderly gentleman, her expression warm, but I could tell it was false. Her body was tense beneath his possessive touch.

It seemed she'd gotten sick of being alone. He looked closer to death than life, so at least there was that. When the gentleman turned to speak to a couple dancing beside them, her facade fractured a bit. She glanced at the array of tables arranged at the back of the room.

Where Destin and Felicity were sitting.

Felicity was a vision in gold and peach satin. Gems glittered in rivulets from her ears and neck. She played with them as she stared longingly at the floor. Her dress shimmered with iridescent orange layers, the tones complementing her creamy skin and the neatly pinned curls around her head. She looked like a blonde flame.

It made bile creep up my throat, threatening my composure. I wanted to *set* her on fire. I wasn't proud of the thought, because she really didn't deserve it, but she looked so much like Tova in that grotesque orange dress.

Felicity's eyes flicked to Destin, jealous desire burning in them. He wasn't looking at her, wasn't looking at the party or the dancers. No, he wasn't looking up at all. He rolled a glass of liquor on the table, watching the ice slosh from one side to the other with a furrowed brow.

Talk about a downer.

Yet, I couldn't take my eyes off him as I leaned against a wall and stuffed another morsel of cheese into my mouth. I watched him sip at his drink. I watched Felicity teeter on the brink of tears. She made him uncomfortable, that was obvious, but I noticed too, the way his eyes would flit up to her when she looked away.

He felt guilty for ignoring her. He felt guilty for not asking her to dance when she so badly wanted to. His mood was a cloud. The rain fell out of him, whether he wanted it to or not. I felt the storm within me reflected in him. I felt seen, even without his mournful eyes on me.

Grief was a wearisome creature. That truth was still as true for him as it was for the lycanthropes, as true as it was for me. He just carried it differently.

Sharing this grief with him, for Tova, made me feel not so alone.

That tender thought, perhaps the first one I'd ever had toward him, was interrupted as a group of men approached Destin's table. He shot up from his seat, feigning a polite smile. An older man with a thick build and slick brown hair spoke to him, and Destin nodded. He even forced a convincing laugh.

Felicity sat up straighter but kept her eyes locked on the table, her countenance filled with respect and fear.

The man beckoned Destin away, leading him and the group already with him around the dance floor and past me to the exit. That must be the Baron, which meant wherever those men were going, I wanted to go, too.

With slow steps, I approached the open double doors and peered out of the room, noting the direction they turned outside in the foyer. It was easy to mark their route, with their drunken, lumbering feet. It was easy to follow them up the stairs without being noticed.

On the second floor, they squeezed into a room, and the door slammed behind them.

The door was narrow, tall, and darkly stained. The brass

handle gleamed beneath the flickering light sconce. The door-knob panel teased me with its delicate etchings, luring me even closer. I knelt before the door, and my lungs filled with the scent of wood polish and musky parchment as I peered through the lock.

"—can't keep housing your men, Baron. Our Houses are bleeding money as it is." The man who was speaking seemed hesitant to say that, almost *fearful*.

Another man laughed. The bodies in the room shifted enough to see the Baron sitting on the edge of his desk, his eyes narrowed at the man who'd just spoken. "It's better than bleeding life. You feel safer with them there, don't you?"

"Of course, sir."

"And this is what you demanded a meeting for? To complain about my leadership?"

"No. It's just that you are already asking a lot of us. With these new troops—"

"Are the factories in good shape?"

"Yes, but—"

"What about the iron wall in the bay? Is it intact? Is it manned?" The Baron's smile became a sharp, angry thing.

A pause. "Yes."

"Then I am taking care of your city. Your Houses can endure a little hospitality for my sake, and for yours. I could bring one of my men in here to show you how capable they are of killing those who make enemies of us. Would *that* convince you?" There was violence in his eyes.

The man who had been complaining quickly shook his head and backed away, tripping over his own feet as he hid himself amidst the others.

The Baron continued in a harsh voice, "Does anyone else have something to say to me tonight, before you return home to your Houses that have been generously safeguarded by me? Any other *concerns*?"

The room was deafeningly silent in return.

"That's what I thought." The tension eased from his body as he rolled his neck. Then, his eyes swept across the room and locked onto someone else. "Destin, how is our leverage?"

Destin replied instantly, his voice soft. "Doing well, sir."

The Baron nodded. "Good. We'll make our move soon. I have it all arranged. Prepare for transport later this week."

"I will, sir."

The Baron vaulted off his desk and surveyed the rest of the room. "I should have more news in a few weeks. Keep on with business as usual and don't talk about what we discussed here with anyone, not even your wives. We can't afford their gossip getting out of hand. I'm looking at you, newlywed." The Baron winked at Destin.

Destin grimaced. "Not an issue, sir."

"Let's get back to the booze then." The Baron spread his arms out, a fierce grin lighting his face. "Shall we?"

I scrambled to my feet and ran on my toes to the other end of the hall, where the corridor continued to the left. It was dark here, the sconces all burnt out. The hall only continued a couple feet, marked by a single door. This section of the wall was just long enough for me to hide my body.

The door to the office opened, and I heard the men file out. I knew it was stupid to do it, but I carefully peeked around the corner. They were all headed back the way they'd come, back to the party. Destin was one of the last ones out, engaged in conversation with the Baron as they emerged side-by-side, and the back of the Baron's head bobbed as they spoke.

Destin forced another laugh, and then his eyes slipped past the Baron and landed on me.

I threw myself back behind the corner. My heart thundered as the sounds of the group grew fainter and fainter. Had

Destin seen me? I looked down. My hair wasn't tucked away, so chances were not in my favor.

Eventually, the hall fell silent.

Maybe he had drunk so much that his eyes skipped right over me. It was possible. Whether he saw me or not, I couldn't just stand here all night. The party would end eventually, and then I would be more likely to get caught walking out of this area of the manor.

I swung around the corner and ran right into a black-clad torso. My heart jumped, enlarging painfully in my throat. Thank the Goddess, it was only Destin. A very glassy-eyed version of him, anyway. He glared down at me, his forearm braced against the wall beside him, as if it were the only thing holding him up. He'd been waiting for me, the pretty bastard.

"What are you doing here?" he growled.

I crossed my arms. "I was worried about Erlene."

"So worried that you traveled here in secret, snuck into the Baron's house during a party, and then eavesdropped on a private meeting?"

"I was looking for Erlene's room."

"You're lying." Destin's eyes narrowed, the anger in his voice somehow muted by the liquor. I found it strange. For most drunks, I'd noticed that liquor had the opposite effect. "You don't trust *anyone*, do you?"

"I have my reasons." I lifted my chin.

"We all have wounds," he slurred, his eyes sweeping over every inch of me before he added, "I'll show you mine if you show me yours."

Liquor might not have made him violent, but that didn't mean he wasn't dangerous right now. Sharing wounds with him wasn't part of the plan. I couldn't afford to understand him, or worse, *like* him. My heart barely had enough room for hate. Despite my resistance, I felt myself softening towards him.

Could grief be shared? Could it draw a line from one person to another, like ink on paper, connecting them through nothing but the loss they felt? I suddenly felt like it was possible.

Yes, he was more dangerous than I ever anticipated.

"That's a terrible idea," I told him.

"Maybe, but it's tempting, isn't it?"

I grimaced. "Not exactly."

"I thought you were suffering from your bleed too much to come here."

Shrugging, I said, "I recovered quickly."

"I'm glad. I hope the items I left at your door helped ease a fraction of your discomfort."

I blinked as his words hit me. *He* had been the one to leave that care package? *Why?*

Destin suddenly twisted to look over his shoulder, and then his arm hooked around my waist as he whipped us into that short hallway I'd hidden in moments before.

I started shoving at his chest. "What are you—"

His hand clamped down over my mouth. That was when I saw the alarm in his eyes, the fear. My hearing picked up on a scuffle down the hall, the belligerent voices drawing closer, passing the office door. We were about to be seen.

"Sell this," Destin rasped, "or we're both dead." He gripped the front of my dress and ripped it off my shoulder, and then he crushed his lips to mine.

I froze. My head spun, cataloging the moment in sensation. There was no other way to endure it. The buttons that had been freed from my bodice hit the floor and scattered. Destin slid his hands around to my back. He fisted the material of my dress so roughly that I was certain he'd leave permanent creases. As he pulled me against him, I felt every inch of him.

He moaned into my mouth, the sound filthy and delicious.

His inhale dragged on mine as he pulled the air from my lungs, sucking my breath into him like I was clean air, and he was suffocating. I let him. *Goddess Divine, why was I letting him?*

My heart was a traitorous whore.

Someone cleared their throat beside us, and Destin abruptly jerked away from me. I was left alone against the wall, still reeling. Destin's emotions were carefully curated, the way they always were. Shock, embarrassment, and thinly veiled detachment. He looked at the Baron and the gaggle of young men following behind him and adjusted his pants. The bulge in it, at least, wasn't at all feigned.

"Destin?" The Baron's voice was threateningly calm.

These were different men from the ones I saw standing in the office earlier with Destin. Younger. Drunker. The door across from us must lead into the Baron's bedroom.

"Sorry, sir." Destin chuckled. He rubbed a hand over his mouth, then through his hair, as if to get rid of the feel of me, which I found incredibly rude. *He* was the one with brandy breath. I also knew he was playing a role, like I often did. He was protecting us both.

I glanced down at my ruined dress. *Damn.* This was one of the few dresses I had that reasonably fit me.

"Who is this?" The Baron turned his glare on me.

Destin cleared his throat, smoothing the front of his tunic with trembling hands. "My new governess, sir."

"I thought Gwaith had already employed a much older woman for that purpose."

"I let her go. She no longer suited my family's needs."

The Baron smirked. "Yes, I can see that." After another moment of charged scrutiny, his suspicion slipped, and he continued with more levity. "Very good. Well, you should get back to the party before that wife of yours notices your distraction."

Destin bowed his head. "Yes, sir."

The Baron gestured to the men behind him and led the way across the short hall.

I turned and walked swiftly down the corridor. I might have tried to push my luck and check out the Baron's office for myself now that no one was in it, but Tova's widower was right on my heels. As we turned down the last hall on the second level, he finally caught up with me.

"What were you thinking, following me into that hall?" he hissed as he grabbed my arm, keeping his voice low. "Do you have any clue what the Baron would have done to you if he caught you alone? If he caught you snooping?"

"He wouldn't have succeeded in doing *anything* to me."

"Sure, because you're such a tough little girl, right? This may come as a shock to you, but whatever you faced in the forest is nothing compared to the Baron. You couldn't have taken on all the guards in this house and survived. You're just a girl with a talent in blade work. Two blades against a hundred; those aren't great odds."

I faced him, forcing the heat in my body to remain safely beneath the surface. "I guess I should be glad *you* were with me then. I didn't have to fight anything but your tongue."

A smile teased at the corner of his mouth. "You're welcome."

I stepped back before the temptation to smack the smile off his face grew too strong to resist. He followed me, step for step. His hand grabbed a fistful of my skirt and drew me closer. I allowed it, the same way I'd allowed my body and mind to do so many other things tonight.

"Come back to the party with me."

I scoffed, slapping at his hand. "I need to go be with Erlene. Besides, I'm not dressed for a party, especially now that you've had your wicked way with me."

Destin's eyes widened slightly, and then he huffed a laugh.

"Did I just hear you spout a joke, Sia?" I didn't entertain his question, the bait that it was. He tugged me even closer, until I could smell the alcohol on his breath again. I wondered if I could get drunk off his lips. "If it helps, *I* think you look perfect."

"Your senses are severely hindered right now," I said flatly. "I'm sure my face is nothing more than a blob to you."

"It's much more than that...but I suppose you're right." He sighed.

"I know I am." I slapped his hands again, hard enough that they fell limp at his sides.

"I'll see you in the morning, then." The way he said it sounded almost like a question. More bait, more temptation, but he wasn't the only one who wanted something.

According to Lee, employees from the factories were getting involved with the morgue, which was a government building. How likely was it that the Baron was behind that, too? How likely was it that the rebels were now infiltrating the rest of the city? He already clearly controlled the Lords of the Houses, which meant the city's funds were firmly under his command.

I took a leap.

Stopping in the center of the empty hall, I crossed my arms and asked, "What do you know about the seraph that died in the city?"

Destin's eyes flashed and his nostrils flared, his gaze quickly flicking around the hall before he stepped closer and growled, "This is not the time or the place to talk about this."

"Why not?"

The vein in his temple pulsed. After a moment, he blew out a sharp breath and shook his head. His voice was as soft as a caress as he said, "I had guessed you were the one to find it. Anyone else, and it wouldn't have made it to the morgue."

"You know where it is in the morgue, don't you? The corpse."

His jaw clenched. "I might."

I moved in then, obliterating the space between us until I was consuming his air. "Tell me." He didn't respond, didn't blink. I reached up and clutched at his lapels. "Help me with this, Destin," I whispered, "or I'll make you wish you had."

Destin said through gritted teeth, "I can't. The Baron has his own plans to retrieve it."

"To use it. To violate it. Please, you can't help him do that. I won't let you do that."

"What do you plan to do to stop me, Sia?" Destin sneered.

My hands were trembling around the material of his jacket, so I let go of him before he went up in flames. I let a predatory smile surface. "Perhaps I *will* come down to the party with you, Destin. Perhaps I'll share my situation with these *honorable* strangers and find someone who *is* willing to help me. I'm sure the Baron won't find it concerning at all that the woman he caught you with is a sympathizer. After all, we can't help but fall into lust with despicable people now and again." Destin eyes hardened, and I smiled wider as I leaned in to add, "But then, he knows I'm also your House's governess now, so maybe it *will* worry him a bit."

I was bluffing. I couldn't do any of that, because it would endanger Erlene's life too, but Destin didn't know that. This was another test. I was dangling his daughter, just waiting for him to choose her, waiting for him to realize that the solution was to take her hand and walk away instead of diving in before her. I wanted him to realize that sacrificing himself would kill her.

Destin curled his hands into fists and took a step back. "Fine. I'll help you."

"Tomorrow," I pressed.

"Just this once."

My heart swelled. He started to walk around me, his eyes on the stairs, but I caught his elbow.

"And just so you know," I said softly. "If you ever force yourself on me again without permission, I *promise* I'll make you regret it. I don't care what the circumstances are."

CHAPTER 23

I found Brimley sitting in the hall outside Erlene's guest room.

"You came," he said as I approached. "I thought you were indisposed."

I halted beside him, waiting as he dragged himself upright. "I guess I just couldn't stay away," I mumbled to the wall.

"Well, you'll be pleased to know she's still in one piece, and that she spent the entire journey here criticizing my nose hairs." He brushed a palm over his face. "She called them whiskers."

Some of the tension in my chest eased. "That's my girl," I said under my breath.

He surveyed my dirty cloak and torn dress, frowning. "What have you been doing?"

I unclasped the cloak from around my neck. "Dealing with morons. What else?"

Brimley's nose wrinkled as I passed by him and leaned against the opposite side of the doorway. "You smell like you've been rolling in manure."

"I can't smell that bad."

"You can, and you do." When I glared at him, he straightened and asked, "So, does your being here mean I'm relieved from my post and your ire?"

"Why?" I smirked. "Do you have somewhere else to be?"

"Not tonight, but I won't be traveling back to Gwaith in the morning." He smiled. "The Baron wants me to stay here and train some new recruits." *Interesting.*

"You seem happy about that."

Brimley shrugged. "This is my home," he replied. "Plus, when I'm here, I don't have to fear being threatened within an inch of my life by a difficult woman who is *not* my boss."

So, the Baron was training rebels on his property, and apparently housing them here, too. I wondered if they understood how foolish it was, to gather in one place like this.

"Don't worry, Brimley," I said with a smirk. "I'm sure you'll find another woman to put you in your place."

"It was both a terror and pleasure to know you, Ms. Sia." He bowed his head and retreated down the hall, leaving Erlene in my hands.

I entered the room. It was small, but clean. Smog kissed the windows, lit up silver by the moonlight. I spotted her small body in the bed and watched for a few long minutes, her chest rising and falling in a peaceful cadence. Safe. She was safe.

I perched on the edge of her bed and pressed a kiss to Erlene's blonde hair, frowning as she turned away with a grunt. Maybe I smelled worse than I thought. Taking a pillow and a small blanket from the end of the bed, I laid on the floor and dozed to the sound of her breathing. I didn't lay there for long, though, before footsteps echoed down the hall, followed by voices seeping through the door I'd left cracked open.

I sat up in the darkness, watching the sliver of corridor still visible to me.

A woman's voice came into focus, and it took me a

moment to realize it was Felicity speaking. "Why did you even bother to bring me here this weekend? What purpose did I serve you by sitting alone every night, watching everyone else have a nice time?"

Destin came into view first, but only for a moment as he passed by the cracked door. I heard his shoes squeak as he turned on his heel. Then, Felicity appeared in her bright orange ensemble. She halted right in my line of sight, crossing her arms over her chest as she frowned at her husband. They must have been placed in the room across the hall.

Destin's voice was tired. "You served to maintain the image of Gwaith House, and I appreciate it, Felicity. Truly. But I couldn't stay down there any longer."

"What image?" Felicity scoffed, her voice edged. "You were brooding all night, and then you pulled us away from the party hours too soon. For what? No one else has gone to bed early. Gwaith House appears only as strong as our marriage. *You* were the one who told me that. You could have given me just one dance, one kiss, even the *slightest* bit of affection, and you didn't."

After a long moment, he whispered, "I'm sorry I'm not an affectionate man. You knew what this was going to be like."

"That's not what I heard."

"What?"

"You say you aren't affectionate, but people have told me how odd it is, the way you act towards me. That's right. They've *all* noticed. They tell me you were affectionate to *her*. Disgustingly so, in fact."

He stepped forward, back into my line of sight, one of his long fingers extending toward her in accusation. The vein in his temple looked large enough that I half-expected it to burst all over her face. "Don't you ever bring up Tova, to me or to anyone else. *Don't you dare.*"

I watched Felicity's back bend, her arms wrapping tighter

around her body as she leaned away from him. Her eyes welled with tears. I knew the sorrow written across her face was real. I could taste it, like a mountain stream running across my tongue.

"Why are you treating me this way? I've given up *everything* for you. I've lost proximity to my family and my—" she choked, her voice cutting out. I knew she was thinking of Kim, and a well of guilt stirred in my belly. Felicity swallowed her emotion and continued, "I had *options* back home, men who actually wanted me, even if they were a little below your station. I also understood that you *needed* me. I understood what was expected of me, and that you would need time and patience, and I still chose you. Why can't *you* choose *me*? Why can't you *try*?"

Destin dropped his hand. His eyes shuttered, and the hardness in them faded until he was finally looking at her the way he did earlier, like he desperately wished things could be different.

Slowly, he lifted his hands to her upper arms, gripping them gently as he looked into her eyes. They were already so close, it wouldn't take much more for him to kiss her. I could tell he was considering it. I could see the warring emotions plain on his face, guilt and compassion.

She melted in his hands, her eyes fluttering, a flush filling her cheeks with color.

The battle was lost before it began. He quickly let her go and retreated a step. "You should get some sleep," he said coldly. "We'll be heading home earlier than we'd planned."

Felicity was transparently, and understandably, upset.

I knew the way he kissed now. I knew what she was missing.

"And you won't be joining me," she said tightly, a question and a statement.

Destin didn't respond. He only stood there, staring blankly at her.

She huffed a short, bitter laugh and walked away. As soon as the door on the other side of the hallway clicked shut, Destin released a heavy breath, bending at the waist and bracing his hands on his knees. He looked like he was ready to vomit.

I continued to watch him from my seat on the floor.

Eventually, he straightened himself out and lifted his gaze to the door between us. He pushed it open, and when our eyes met, he didn't seem surprised to see me listening in. He was too exhausted for that. Silently, he closed the door behind him, ambled across the room, and sat down next to me. We stared into nothing for a long while.

"I feel cruel," he whispered. "Am I?"

It was painful, how deeply I felt that confession. I didn't want to tell him that he was or that he wasn't. No one else had ever been able to say anything that changed the way I saw myself. I knew what I was. He knew what he was. So, I settled for, "Sometimes, we must be."

He looked at me with those dull gray eyes. "I don't *want* to be cruel."

"Then you are a better man than I thought." Once the words were out, I bit the inside of my cheek hard enough to draw blood. I'd said it without thinking.

Destin's brow furrowed, and his eyes slid past me to Erlene. "She really is the spitting image of her mother."

Without a word, I draped half of my blanket over his legs. I felt his eyes drilling into me as I relaxed against the hard floor and turned my back on him, lifting the blanket over my shoulders, just in case my necklace shifted during the night. I wouldn't give him anything more. The blanket was enough. My thoughts were enough, even if he couldn't hear them.

I waited quietly, allowing Destin to believe I had drifted off, both of us listening to the silence. That is, until I heard him whisper over my head, to the little girl on the other side, "Please, forgive me."

I knew then that the widower was not as lost as I'd feared.

CHAPTER 24

We left the Baron's manor a couple of hours before daybreak. Apparently, that was the best time for me to break into the morgue. Destin was adamant about hitting the place between shifts.

I imagined it was quite the scene in that carriage – me and Erlene on one bench, Felicity and Destin on the other. Destin had left Erlene's room shortly after his plea for forgiveness. Where he went, I wasn't sure, but I was fairly certain it hadn't been to Felicity's bed. She was glaring at me. She'd been utterly *fuming* from the instant she watched the three of us – Destin, Erlene and I – exit Erlene's room and walk down to the carriage together.

Destin obviously hadn't made her aware of my presence, and I could only imagine what she thought of me being here when I should've been at Gwaith. Maybe she suspected he'd been with me last night. I couldn't even tell her she was wrong, couldn't fault her. I knew the only place he'd wanted to be last night was in that room next to me and Erlene. After he left, I realized I'd have liked him there, too.

It was nice, not being alone.

Our carriage rolled to a stop in front of two, towering buildings and the narrow alley running between them. The bricks were blackened with exhaust, and the sidewalks were, too. It was closer to the factories than I'd ever been before, but luckily, we'd arrived when the smog was at its lightest, which meant I could see to either end of the empty street and each flickering lamppost that fought against the night sky.

Felicity frowned out her window, her eyes puffy and bloodshot from either lack of sleep or the early hour, or both. "What are we doing here?"

"That's none of your business, dear. Just stay here with Erlene and we'll be back in a moment." Destin moved toward the door, but I stopped him with a sharp look.

"I don't need your help. You told me what I needed to know, so I'll take it from here."

All I needed to do was get in, grab the body, and haul it out. The luggage carrier on the back of the cab had been left available to me. Destin informed me of the morgue's layout early this morning while he watched me brush Erlene's hair into curly pigtails.

She was fast asleep again, tucked against the carriage wall and wrapped up in my cloak. Luckily, I wouldn't need it here. No one was on the streets right now.

Destin scowled, but surprisingly allowed me to exit the carriage by myself without protesting. The air was dry and rough in my lungs, and I bit back the instinct to cough as I entered the narrow alley, following it toward the frontside of the buildings.

Halfway down, the passage opened, allowing room for wagons to be parked and for the bodies they carried to be unloaded into the morgue. I hesitated when I saw there was one here. The back door to the morgue was open as well, but there was no sign of movement, in the alley or beyond the morgue's door. The atmosphere was too still.

I slid along the alley wall until I reached the door, and then slowly peeked inside.

It was empty.

I felt my brow furrow as I scanned the room again, not quite believing my eyes. Candles flickered inside, though they were burned down nearly to the nubs. The aluminum of several rolling autopsy tables gleamed in the low light. Most were vacant, but it looked like there were a few black bags occupying tables on the far end.

Did these morticians often leave bodies alone like this? Leave the door to the streets open? I knew the poor didn't have the privilege of being delivered to morgues like this, not with how many died here daily. They were simply buried or burned in piles outside of the city. Any corpse here was one that had wealth or value to the city.

It felt wrong that no one was here, watching over the room.

Slipping inside, I cataloged the dark corners to either side of me. I made out the cracked door to my left that would lead into the rest of the building, where the morticians ate and slept, where they held the farewell ceremonies for the deceased. On the other side of the room, there was a small worktable, the walls covered in steel draining tubes, glass jars, pumps, and other unsettling human contraptions I knew served to embalm corpses. The entire room smelled faintly of garlic and iron, and beneath that, a bitter odor I couldn't quite place.

Chemicals.

Stepping lightly, I walked across the tile floor deeper into the darkness, letting my eyes adjust. There was another door just past the worktable. I approached it, ignoring the black bags looming like spectral visitors up ahead, and the air around me grew cooler. This must be the ice box. The Stymphalian had to be inside somewhere, kept preserved until the Baron decided exactly what to do with it.

I heard the door to the street clasp shut and I whirled, my hands flying to my thighs.

Destin stalked toward me with a frown. When he reached me, he growled lowly, "Really? You didn't even bother to close the door behind you? Are you insane?"

Before he could say another word, I grabbed his hand and dragged us both into the box. The chill swept us up. I stifled a gasp as the metal door clicked shut behind us, sealing us in, and my eyes were drawn up to the shifting gray ceiling. A snow charm had been cast over the room. Delicate flakes were falling all around, dissipating before they could touch the floor. The clouds radiated a soft blue glow, too. Another charm. It was just bright enough to see the contents of the room and Destin's grimace.

"Fucking magic," he muttered at the ceiling, then turned to me, his lips parting in what I was sure would be another reprimand.

"Shut up," I snapped. "Just shut up and listen to me for a moment, you utter buffoon."

His head bobbed back in surprise.

"There's something wrong here," I said quickly. "I don't know what it is, and I don't really feel like finding out. So, since you went against my wishes and followed me, the least you could do is be quiet and help me find what I came here for before we get caught."

Destin's jaw clenched. "Fine."

"You take that side of the room, and I'll take this one."

I spun without waiting for a response and walked to where the massive steel shelves were built into my side of the room. Sheets covered the bodies, but luckily, they were arranged with their heads toward the center of the room, so I only needed to lift each cover a few inches to get a glimpse of their faces. There were so many of them, nameless and lifeless beings, lying here alone, waiting for the fire or the grave dirt.

"Shit," I heard Destin hiss. "I think I found it, or what's left of it."

My heart stuttered as I turned to him. He was standing in front of an empty steel bed. It was the only bed vacant on the bottom row, and there were scratches on the surface of the metal plate, the kind of scratches metal feathers would make. Some of the fringe had broken off and was now scattered across the bed. This had definitely been where the Stymphalian was kept.

It just wasn't here anymore.

"It looks like you weren't the only sympathizer looking out for that thing," Destin grumbled. "I'm guessing someone here cremated it without permission. The Baron is going to be furious."

My eyes started stinging as I stared at the remnants left behind. I was too late. They'd been taken. It took every ounce of my will to keep the tears at bay. My heart was pounding, and yet it felt like my whole chest might collapse.

"They'll never make it back home now," I croaked.

They had a home, a place where they belonged, and they would never see it again. That triggered an ache buried deep inside me. I tried to imagine never again seeing the place I grew up in, the place I was born, and I realized I was mourning that loss alongside the Stymphalian.

Destin scoffed, shaking his head. "You should be relieved. Cremation is better than what the Baron would have done to it, and now you don't have to bother hauling the thing somewhere else. This is *good*."

I swayed back a step, then another, and then I swiftly exited the room. I gasped for fresh air, gagging as the putrid scent of lukewarm death filled my senses instead. My body trembling, I lurched forward and shoved the closest autopsy table, delighting in the crash and clatter as it tumbled over itself across the room. I did it to another, letting a vicious growl loose.

Arms wrapped around my chest, trying to pin my arms. "Sia, stop," Destin growled in my ear. "Someone's going to hear you."

"*I don't care,*" I cried.

Because I didn't. I *refused* to care. My body was thrumming, near-bursting with the realization that I was too late, and that, for some reason, I missed my childhood home. If I didn't do something to ease the anger and grief I felt, black flames would come pouring out instead. Destin would see it. He would see them, and he would hate me for it, the way they all did.

I lashed out with my body because I didn't want to give my power an opportunity to surface. If that meant we were going to get caught down here, so be it.

I shook off his arms and toppled another table before he grabbed me again, squeezing me so tightly, I could barely breathe. His breath was hot against my neck. "Please, Sia," he pleaded. "Listen to me. I know I can't fully understand what's going on in your head and heart right now, but I am sorry for how deeply you're hurting, for whatever reason."

I jerked in his arms, but the fight left me. I didn't want him to let go.

"*I hate you,*" I whispered, but I had really meant to say I hated *them*, everyone and everything who had played a part in the Stymphalian's ugly fate. Destin was just the only one here to bear that burden with me.

His face turned into my overheated skin, his soft lips caressing the column of my neck. "I know. I hate me, too."

My entire body seemed to come alive. The thrumming in my body shifted lower, and I found myself wanting him to do more than hold me. I wanted his lips on more than my neck. I wanted to lose myself in this carnal attraction, even if it was a little broken and fucked up. I let my head loll to the side, arching my neck, hoping it might encourage him to continue touching me, might encourage him to take things further.

Then my eyes landed on the tiled floor, and what I'd revealed in my outburst.

Blood.

Which might not have meant anything, if that crimson trail didn't lead to the door into the rest of the building. The door that, at that very moment, swung open to reveal a very bloody, *very dead* mortician, drawn to us on his mission to find another soul to take into the afterlife.

"Goddess beside us," Destin breathed as he saw it, his arms loosening around me.

I tore free from Destin's embrace as the mortician charged us. Pulling my daggers, I dodged the mortician's arms and slashed at his stomach, tearing through his apron into his distended gut.

Blood and fat oozed out of the gash I made, but he kept coming. His guts were spilling over. His foamy spit was hitting my face. I hadn't struck deep enough to pierce the life chakra, but I wouldn't make that mistake a second time. I thrust my dagger into his stomach, allowing his innards to swallow the blade and the hilt and my whole hand. As I tore through nearly to his spine, he froze. His eyes went dark as I wrenched my dagger out and stepped back, and his corpse collapsed in a twisted pile at my feet.

I looked up and found Destin standing exactly where I left him, his eyes wide and his face pale. He pulled his gun and I laughed at his woefully delayed reaction.

His throat bobbed and he nodded at the back door. "Let's get the fuck out of here. There might be others. I can inform the authorities of an outbreak once we leave."

I did hear some faint shuffling in the hall, so chances were, there were more undead coming for us. It was best for us to leave and let the authorities deal with this. Unfortunately, I only made it two steps toward the exit when I heard something else. A garbled voice.

"Wait," I paused, turning back to the open door. "Did you hear that?"

"Hear what?" Destin demanded in an irritated tone.

It came again, a little clearer. *Help.* There was still a human in the building, *alive.*

Before Destin could stop me, I ran into the hall, blades at the ready. Destin was right: there were more walkers in the halls. They were as bloody as the mortician, because they had been cut up the same as the ones I saw the last time I was in the city.

The killer had been here. They had taken their limbs and organs and flesh, and I was once again the one to put them out of their misery.

The trail of undead led to a brutalized door. It looked like it might be a closet. The human voice cried for help from beyond it as one last walker slammed its body against the door. The undead was so preoccupied, it didn't even notice me before I slid my ichor-slick dagger into its back. It collapsed and slid heavily to the floor.

"Hello? Is someone out there?" a shaky voice asked.

I saw movement in the room, through the strange slashes that had been made in the door. With the hallway clear and Destin slowly approaching, I stowed my daggers and replied, "Yes. You can come out now, you're safe."

The door opened, and a small man rushed out and wrapped his arms around my waist, starting to sob hysterically. I froze, my hands flailing as I tried to figure out what to do. He gasped out, "Thank you so much. Thank the Goddess you came. I was so worried I was going to die here."

I glanced over at Destin for some assistance, but the

bastard was snickering and not doing a damn thing to try and hide it.

Shoving this human off me seemed a tad severe given the circumstances, especially in his current mental state, so I patted his head a couple times before disentangling myself and guiding him gently to the wall. He sat down and I knelt in front of him, waiting patiently as his hysterics passed. He was wearing a nice suit, though the jacket was missing, and his linen shirt was now wrinkled and spattered with black blood.

Destin asked the question before I could. "What happened?"

The man sighed shakily and scrubbed at his bald head, his eyes flicking up and down the hall. "Fuck, I-I don't even know. Honest. It was just work as usual. Corpses were being delivered; there was a ceremony earlier in the evening. Someone came in to take a look at a body, a detective, and Martie, you know, the boss – or, I guess he *was* the boss...*fuck*, he's dead now, isn't he? Anyway, the next thing I know, I'm waking up from a stone-cold sleep at my desk. I don't even remember falling asleep." He shut his eyes tightly, his lips trembling. "And then the screaming started up from the back room. I got so scared, I ran in here and hid. I'm a coward, I know, but I'm telling you, whatever that thing was tonight, it was like nothing I'd ever seen before. It was making this crazy sound that made the hair all over my body stand up. It tried to break into the room to get me! You see those holes?" He pointed at the door. "It stabbed at it over and over, until the dead finally started waking up. Then it just...left. I don't know, I thought I was going to die. I can't believe I didn't. *Thank you.*"

I glanced up and Destin was already watching me, the concern I felt etched into his face.

Was it a coincidence that some detective showed up to the morgue the same day this killer did? The same day the Stymphalian was removed from the ice box? Were those two things connected somehow? If they were, I couldn't see how, but I didn't have to speculate about which detective had been here. I already knew.

Was my flower market stranger the one killing all these people?

CHAPTER 25

I sat at my desk at Gwaith house, staring at the note in my hand.

The day had passed in a blur of travel and play. While it soothed the tension of the morning to know that Erlene had missed me as much as I missed her, I was restless.

When I'd finally put Erlene down to bed, I retrieved the note and my quill. I tried to think of what to say, how to explain to them that I *did* want to meet them, but that I was so afraid. Because once they truly knew me, I would drive them away.

Real connection was a fantasy. It only worked at a distance, far enough away that they couldn't feel or see me, far enough away that I couldn't burn them. Yet, I was starting to think maybe I was wrong about the person on the other side of this parchment. They'd come for me. They'd saved me.

Warmth bloomed over the nape of my neck. "Hello, my exquisite misery."

I slammed the book of psalms closed over the note and turned to find Destin leaning over the back of my chair. He was swaying, and dusty barrel drifted from his mouth.

There was a softness, an openness, in his eyes that sobriety didn't allow. That slant of his lips was almost a smile as he leaned in closer and whispered, "This is when you say 'hello, hateful Lord.'"

I sighed. "Exactly how drunk are you right now?"

"Drunker than I was last night. Enough to torture myself by seeking you out."

I stood up and pushed him away from the desk with the heel of my hand. He was so soft, so warm beneath his tunic.

He squinted at me through the haze of liquor. "I need to discuss something with you. In the den." He staggered back and tripped over the rug, and I caught him before he fell on his ass.

"Are you sure you can manage the stairs?" I didn't need to deal with his injury or death right now, as frustrating as he was.

His hands found my waist. "No, but you have a lovely, solid body that can assist me."

My hands dropped to cover his, but I didn't remove them. I was half-afraid he would fall over if I did, and the other half of me thought...well, I didn't leave much space for that voice. "I think you overestimate my capacity for kindness."

"Do I?" He leaned forward, his fingers digging into the curve of my waist. "I think you can be incredibly sweet when you want, like the way you are with Erlene."

I squeezed his fingers so hard, I knew I had to be crushing them, but he didn't react. He was so far gone that his body was numb. "I'm not going to be that way with you," I said.

"Why?" His lower lip pushed out. "I'm drunk enough to consider tolerating you for a while. It could be nice."

I sighed and led him to the stairs. "There isn't enough alcohol in the world to warm me up to that idea."

He snorted. "After what you did to the bottle on my desk, I'm convinced you *can't* get drunk."

"Just shut up and focus on getting downstairs without tripping us."

When we reached the den, Destin grappled for his key, but I quickly plucked it from his fingers and let us both inside. He staggered in, collapsing against the nearest wall.

I tossed the key onto the smooth surface of the piano and turned to leave.

"Ah, ah." Destin fell forward, blocking my escape. "I told you we need to discuss something."

"I honestly didn't expect you to remember long enough to follow through."

"This happens to be of the *utmost* importance," he slurred.

"You finally figured out how to please your wife?" I tilted my head, absorbing the moment my barb sunk in. It was belated, naturally, and when he glared at me, I laughed loudly and said, "No, wait – you want to ask *me* for pointers?"

His eyes flashed.

"Well, Destin," I continued. "There happens to be a special little bud, right—"

He moved, propelled by gravity and liquor, and suddenly, I was pressed up against the door. His arm was braced above my head as he returned my snide smile. "I'm well acquainted with the clitoris, Sia."

I tried to catch my breath. "You'd be the first man I ever met who was."

"Is that a challenge?" His gaze dropped to my lips, the venom missing from his words. Was that...*want* in his voice? Had there been want in mine?

I shoved the heat out of my veins and pushed at Destin's chest. "It's a statement. Now, what do you want?"

His smile slipped away. "I heard about what happened while I was gone." I didn't have to worry about heat then, because my blood turned to ice. Destin straightened and braced his hands on his hips. He was still wearing his gun, and a tingle spread along my spine.

Was that why he brought me into the den? Did he know what I'd done?

"I know about the guard attempting to drug you." Destin's eyes met mine, and I saw his worry. Perhaps a bit of anger, too. "I wanted to make it clear that if you're *ever* harassed again, if any of the men on this property try to hurt you again—"

A laugh bubbled out of me.

He paused. "Is something funny?"

It was more relief than anything. "Yes. You, attempting to console me."

"This isn't a joke," he growled.

A smile remained on my face, despite my best efforts. "No. Of course not."

"You're impossible," he muttered.

"Thank you." I reached for the doorknob again and he lifted a finger.

"There's one more thing." His other hand curled around my upper arm, and he guided me back into the room, toward the couch. I perched on the edge, next to his pile of blankets. I had to make a genuine effort not to want to wrap them around me. "I saw something in the Ebonmore market, and it reminded me of you."

"Was it a scythe?" I asked sweetly.

He reached behind his desk and pulled out a large, square briefcase. The cover was dark leather, with bronze straps locking the two sides together.

I frowned. "What is that?"

When Destin looked up at me, there was mischief in his eyes. He unclasped the buckles and opened the case, and my mind went quiet. It was a miniature phonograph, with a bronze trumpet and a black record already set in place.

My eyes stung as I stood up and drifted over to the desk.

Music boxes were common back home, treasured even. Here, in the human lands, they'd only just started gaining popularity; it took decades for mortals to realize the boxes could be made without charm or enchantment. This tiny player must have cost him a small fortune.

My fingers skimmed over the cool metal.

Destin folded his arms, giving me space to admire the novelty. "I remembered what you said the other night, about the quiet. I thought this might help you."

I lifted my gaze to his. "You're *giving* this to me?"

He held my stare, the silence affirmation enough.

"Why would you do this?" Why had he provided me with comforts for my cycle? Why did he do *anything* for me?

The answer was so absurdly obvious to me in that moment.

It was because Destin loved to care for others; he was simply afraid of failing at it. That was why he left Tova...and why he hesitated to get close to his daughter now. If they died, he would feel it was his fault. He withdrew because he believed the isolation was what he deserved.

Goddess, I thought. *I hate him because he is so like me.*

He looked away, to the bundle of blankets on the couch. A small smile danced over his face as he shrugged. "It's a selfish purchase. You pace for hours at night directly above my head. When you can't sleep, neither can I."

My thoughts started racing. I couldn't stop touching the bronze gilding, the silky edges of the record. I said the first thing that came to mind. "You could always sleep in your bedroom, you know. Next to your wife."

Destin's upper lip curled, and as he turned away, he muttered, "You hate it."

My stomach turned. Maybe I didn't want to feel sick anymore. Maybe I was tired of holding onto this hatred that poisoned every muscle and made me ache, because I said, "No, I don't hate it."

He turned and studied me sidelong, his body swaying.

"I don't hate it," I repeated, smiling. "This will help me. Thank you."

I reached for the case to close it, but Destin's hands closed over mine.

"I only have one request," he murmured. I searched his face, my curiosity piqued despite the voice in my head screaming at me to push him away. "I'd like the first dance."

My lungs burned, begging me to breathe, but I wasn't sure I could.

I shouldn't allow this. It was too familiar; he was the lure reeling me in. His humanness. This gift. I hadn't guarded against him, didn't think I would need to, but here I was, officially hooked.

"I wasn't planning on dancing at all," I replied, the objection soft and malleable.

Destin clicked his tongue. He drew my hands away from the case and pulled me toward him. "Ah, but you see...*I* was."

Without breaking eye contact, he reached over and flicked the phonograph on. He lowered the needle to the record, and a sweeping instrumental guttered to life.

"One dance," I grumbled through a smile. "And then we forget this ever happened."

"Fine." He tugged me into the empty space behind the piano. I allowed him to place a hand on my waist and draw me closer. I wanted it, this warmth and proximity, this sense of companionship, even if it was only to dance. Only now, after being disregarded so long, did I realize how much I *wanted* partnership. I leaned against Destin's chest, aligning my body with his so nothing stood between us except a few layers of cloth.

His eyes widened at the proximity, and I realized my mistake.

"Sorry. Where I'm from, dances aren't so formal." I tried to separate myself, to put that space between us he expected, but his hand slid lower on my back and stopped me.

"That's all right," he whispered, his words stirring the hair around my temple. "I think I like this better."

My body rolled under his touch, curling around him like mist. For one dance, I could let my anger go. For one dance, I could love his humanity and forget he was a less than wonderful father and an even shittier husband. I could forget he was the reason Tova wasn't here anymore.

"What was Tova like with you?" he whispered.

Of course, he would ruin it. My fingers dug into his shoulder. He seemed to think it was an invitation, because his arm tightened around my back. I said tightly, "Conversation wasn't part of the deal."

"It wasn't," he conceded. "But now I'm sweetening the pot."

"I already told you, I'm not going to be sweet with you."

"Then be bitter." His fingers rapped against my lower ribs. "But I'd like to know. Please?"

His face turned into my hair. For a moment, I thought of Lee's concern about the henna, and I hoped Destin would swallow some of it and get out of my head. Then I sighed and continued to give myself up. "Single-minded. Tova cared for Gwaith House more than anything. I think I made her feel wild and free for a time, like she was something more than the woman destined for Gwaith's fortune, but her loyalties were surrendered before I ever met her."

He nodded slowly, thoughtfully.

I blamed it on my own morbid curiosity as I asked, "What was she like with you?"

The music filled out around us, lulling my muscles into a

false sense of safety. Eventually, he said, "Tova was…a bright spot in my darkness."

"I was never a good match for her," he muttered. "I didn't deserve her or this place, or the title it offered, but life-long poverty is an exceptional motivator. Before Tova, it was just my father and me, and he did what he could to keep us from starving. He was remorseless, clever. When he set his sights on Tova's parents, he was sure we'd found our final scheme. The one that would make us rich."

I peeled away from him, my eyes wide. "You're a con artist?"

"I *was*." He grimaced. "It wasn't my choice. If you saw the way I grew up, you'd understand." I didn't know what to say, how to respond. So, I waited.

"But then I met Tova. She ruined every plan, every expectation, all the contentment in my heart. She seduced me so thoroughly that I couldn't imagine my future without her. Even after I told her the truth, about my father and how we had planned to swindle her out of the House's fortune, she still chose me. She *wanted* me." A small smile danced across his lips, as if he still couldn't believe his luck.

I looked away.

My thoughts spun like threads being weaved, around, in and out, forming a tapestry. I'd stowed them for so long, but now they were unraveling, spilling out in spools of luminous grief. "I think about her," I admitted quietly, "and I try to remember what she loved aside from this House. I wonder if she could have truly loved me the way I loved her, the way she told me she loved me."

Destin's jaw feathered against my temple.

There was something so incredibly special about opening up to Destin, because I knew he understood what I was going through better than anyone. He knew how easily Tova stole hearts and consumed minds. I let out the brokenness she left behind, and I didn't fear that he would judge me for it.

"She didn't value falling in love like I did, wasn't the sort to allow herself to *keep* falling once she'd started, if she knew it wouldn't line up with her future." I paused, swallowing against the burn in my throat. "I loved her more and more as she learned to stop, as she learned to love me less."

The music was the only sound for a few long moments, but then Destin squeezed my waist and murmured, "I don't think that's true. She spoke of you all the time. It drove me mad."

I shook my head. "I *fascinated* her. Yes, maybe she adored me for who I was and what we shared." I pulled back enough to look him in the eye. "But I wasn't *home* to her. I couldn't fill the space in her soul that needed someone like you. I never could have given her Erlene, but *you did*."

A shadow crossed Destin's face. "Are you suggesting she loved me for my cock?"

"No, no," I said quickly. "She loved you because she saw the future of her family in you. You can *choose* to love as much as you can fall into it."

His eyes narrowed to slits. "Really? How do you imagine that?"

That hurt him. It hurt me, too.

I spoke as gently as I could manage. "The existence of thought requires us to accept that anything is possible, that we are capable of *anything* if we have the bravery to think it, and that includes creating love where we need it to be. Making a conscious decision to love someone doesn't make the feeling any less authentic. The moment we stop choosing, we stop feeling."

Destin's steps were stilted as the words sunk in, and I didn't shield the emotion on my face. I'd tried hating him, tried intimidation and insults and brutal honesty. None of that had worked. He was no closer to seeing reason. He was more human than I wanted to admit. Desperate for tenderness. Overwhelmed by life. Beautifully mortal.

I cradled Destin's face in my hands, ensuring I had his full attention as I said, "I'm not what Erlene needs, either. She needs *you*. She deserves her flesh and blood, her bone and sinew. She needs her family. You can't change the past, you can't control what's to come, but you can make the decision to love her when it feels easier to run."

Destin's eyes misted over.

I caressed his hollow cheeks, his temples, marveling at all the chiseled lines. "Love," I breathed, "is a reckoning magic."

A heartbeat later, his hands found mine, his thumbs brushing against the inside of my wrists. "I don't know anything about magic, but maybe we could find a way forward…together."

I choked on the hot relief in my throat. This was progress. He was still afraid to do it alone, but this was a great place to start healing, for both of us. As his thumbs continued to brush over my skin, I felt a cool strand of metal trace my skin, and when I glanced down, I saw the golden band there on his left hand. Tova's wedding band.

He'd resized it for himself.

My eyes slid back to his. "I thought you were going to give her ring to Felicity," I admitted.

He blinked, his brows pulling together as he shook his head. "I could never do that. It wasn't just Tova's, it was *ours*. I'm never letting it go."

I brought his hand back to my cheek and covered his fingers with mine. His thumb brushed downward, grazing the corner of my mouth, and I instinctively turned my head toward it, parting my lips so that the pad of his finger slipped into my mouth. I sucked it deeper, until Tova's ring was between my teeth.

This felt as close to her as I would ever get again.

Destin inhaled sharply. "What are you doing to me, my nasty little angel?"

He said it, and my body tensed. Judging from the wicked humor in his voice, I knew he had said it without realizing the truth in it, said it teasingly to spur a reaction. He was using my love of seraphim against me, but even so, my mouth salivated. I sucked on his flesh. I wanted more of him inside of me. I wanted *everything*.

The door to the den flew open.

Felicity was there, seething on the threshold.

I jerked my hands away from Destin's face and stepped back, as if that would help anything. I knew she'd already seen everything. She took one step into the room, then paused. Her eyes flicked to the disheveled couch, the music box on the desk, and the negligible space between Destin and me.

When her gaze returned to her husband, she hissed, "You won't dance with me, but you'll dance with her?" Her face was flushed crimson. She didn't look at me directly, but I felt murderous rage rolling off her in waves. I smelled it, the sulfur boiling through her blood.

Destin didn't say anything. He only ambled across the room and shut the phonograph case, cutting the music off. Then, he tightened the straps and extended the box to me. He didn't meet my gaze as I took it from him, and for that, I was grateful.

As I approached the door, Felicity moved farther into the room to let me exit, but she cursed at me under her breath, and I laughed at her. Her eyes sparkled with ire.

The sulfur lacing with her blood intensified, rotten to the core.

I said loud enough for both of them to hear, "He's all yours, *trust me*."

Back in my room, I settled the phonograph on my bed and

restarted the record, letting it drown out the argument drifting up from the den. The edge of parchment peeking out from the book of psalms taunted me. All the tension of the day returned to my body, filling me with so much pressure, I wasn't sure how to relieve it without exploding.

I took the note from the book and wrote, *how do you make someone care?*

A long silence stretched, and the record moved on to the next song. I was undressed and walking to the bed when the parchment reappeared.

You can't.

I snarled softly. *So helpful. Thanks.*

Would you rather I lie and pretend to know?

For once, I just want an easy answer. I don't know why I keep indulging these stupid notes. You and I both know this isn't real. We aren't real. Nothing in my life ever has been.

There was another long wait, and then, it came.

I care.

I didn't fool myself into thinking that admission mattered. They were just a voice screaming to me from the ink, with words that could curve into lies the moment I believed in them, nooses rising from the parchment and tightening around my neck. They were a voice that might say it cared, but I couldn't trust it.

I returned the note to the space under my pillow, cradled the music box in bed, and fell asleep before the needle ran off the record. For the first time in months, I slept through the night.

CHAPTER 26

Apparently, during the argument last night, Felicity convinced Destin she needed more *quality* time with Erlene. So, I was currently watching Felicity teeter on the cusp of losing her mind as she managed Erlene's every move in the sitting room. *Sit straighter, don't slump. Cross your ankles. Hold your embroidery needle like so.*

Erlene had lost her patience after half an hour, and I was relishing in her ability to frustrate Felicity with ill-timed giggles and stamping feet.

I sat in my chair, searching for any important detail I might have missed in the newspaper clippings I'd collected over the last few weeks. It had been a week since the incident with Spiro, and the clock in my chest ticked louder with each passing hour. I felt it, like one might sense the sun setting before looking outside. I saw the color of my life here draining away, the color of my freedom. Night was coming. My *father* was coming. He was looking for me, and now that he knew I was close, he wasn't going to stop until he'd found me.

As if punctuating my worry, a low sound reverberated

through the window to my left, gently shaking the pane. I looked over and scanned the garden, immediately noticing when one of the statues guarding an archway moved.

The moss-covered satyr tilted its head toward the window. Black eyes pierced through the fog, and the statue leapt from its perch, fog swirling as its hooves sank into the dewy ground.

I shot up from the chair, nearly toppling my cluttered workstation.

"Clumsy much?" Felicity sneered.

I was already gone, bursting into the hallway and out the servants' door into the yard. I found the empty perch of the statue, the disturbed smog…but no satyr. I passed under one of the boxwood arches and into the small courtyard, spinning in a tight circle.

"I know you're here," I growled into the shuddering fog.

"That was the intention."

I faced the gravelly voice. The pillar of porous, carved stone emerged from the hedges. Moss hung in a heavy curtain down the right side of the satyr's body, a lyre in its left hand. Its jaw worked, stone whining with the movement.

"How did you find me, Spiro?"

He smiled, stone fissuring. "You made that poor male promise not to return for revenge, but you did nothing to prevent him from reporting your whereabouts to us." The statue clicked its tongue in mock disappointment, and it spit out a mouthful of rubble. "It was an amateur mistake, Sia. Your father was worried you'd suffered brain damage somehow."

My chest tightened. I had made a mistake – a huge one, forgetting where that bounty hunter would be returning I sent him away from Gwaith. I feigned a careless grin. "Well, he'll be relieved to know I'm still capable of telling him to fuck off. He's with you right now, isn't he? Pass the message along."

Spiro was a Great Raven, a seraph of thought and memory, blessed with the ability to travel by spirit alone, inhabiting inanimate objects where necessary in order to interact with the physical world around them. Great Ravens were messengers, so rare a species that they couldn't sustain a community on their own. Those who had their gifts wandered, pledging loyalty and ruling alongside whatever family they believed would best benefit them.

Spiro's loyalty to the Fenix ran deep, *unbreakable* really, with all the centuries of trust built between them.

The satyr's head swiveled back and forth, the moss swinging with the motion. "Why do you insist on provoking your father? One of these days, you're going to wish you had respected his long-suffering patience."

I chuckled. "His patience? You call him constantly hunting me down a show of his *patience?*"

"Are you so blind?" Spiro huffed. "These last few years have been nothing. Do you think the King has somehow exhausted his resources? These bounty hunters have been child's play, a mere *reminder* that he has not forgotten about you. He lets you wander as a courtesy, giving you the time and space you need to come to terms with your future, but he's done now, Sia."

Maybe I should have known. I had let myself hope for freedom, but that was turning out to be the biggest mistake of all. "I can't go back."

"You must."

"No," I snapped. "You don't understand. I *can't.*"

The satyr's onyx eyes drilled into mine.

"I've made promises," I whispered.

Spiro's beady eyes flattened, undulating with gray rock for a moment before a disembodied voice roared, *"You've done what?*" It was the same gravelly tone, but with a vastly different inflection. A father's wrath. The statue gleamed a faint gold.

I stumbled back a step, recognizing the presence.

The Great Raven must have pulled back into his body to update my father, and now he was touching Spiro's body back home, projecting words through his spirit. Stony debris showered the grass as the statue undulated a second time, and my father's influence faded.

"Why?" Spiro's voice was back. "Why would you give anyone a promise down here?"

"Our kind begin and end with promises. Why shouldn't we live by them, too?"

He lifted a hand, pressing it to the stone of the satyr's stomach. "Because at any moment, you could make a promise you cannot keep, and then what will we do?"

My whole life, I'd been asking myself that question. What was going to happen to me? What could I do? Promises were binding, but like truth, promises could be manipulated, twisted into enough knots that a loophole usually formed. Seraphim learned to be flexible. *I* learned to be flexible. It was the first and only *meaningful* lesson of my youth: How to Bend Promises.

Death was the most common remedy. If there was no one to be bound to, the promise fell away. The second remedy was easier and one I most favored: to use the constructs of time to my advantage.

That promise I had made to the white-haired boy didn't hurt me because I hadn't broken it, not yet. I'd been running, telling my soul I had an eternity to make it right, an eternity to return to him. It was a decent enough loophole. I only hoped that wouldn't change as time went on and circumstances wore thin.

Sometimes, I let myself wonder what would rot away first,

if things changed and my soul finally decided to punish me: my wings or my mind?

My father had allowed me to make that promise so long ago. How ironic that he now forsook my use of them. Promises with mortals were so fleeting, so small, in comparison.

I scoffed, looking away. "Who cares what happens to me?"

Stone groaned as the satyr crossed its arms. "We all care, Sia. Deeply."

Oh yes, they care. They cared about my return because they cared about my betrothal, because they cared about my role in the alliance they'd made. Did any of them care about *me*? I've never been convinced. "If you care about me," I said quietly, "then just give me a little more time. If Father agrees to wait a few more days, I'll return home on my birthday. I *promise.*"

Warmth rippled down my spine, the promise fluttering into place, laying claim on my bones. Spiro frowned, his dark eyes swirling with disapproval.

"*Please,*" I begged him. "I'm almost finished here."

His gaze wavered, hardening as Spiro pulled back home. My ears rang in the silence. After what felt like an eternity, the satyr blinked and said, "Your father accepts these terms. He says he loves you, and he'll see you soon."

The fluidity slipped from the satyr limbs at once. All I could think as the stone burst into a million pieces was: *No, Father, you won't.*

I'd promised I would return home on my birthday, but I didn't clarify which one.

Staring at the scattered rubble, I forced my racing heart to calm. Spiro was being genuine when he said all that. I knew they loved me, every one of them, in their own way. It was never that I felt *unloved* by my family. It was that I came to realize it was possible to be both loved and injured, and that those two truths could exist independent of one another.

Love did not cover the hurt, did not make it better.

Now they knew about Gwaith, about the family housing me. I rubbed my forehead with the heel of my hand. *What the fuck am I going to do?*

Slowly, I walked around the house to the front.

There had to be another way to protect the property when I left. They would need it. Considering I'd wasted that charm in the city, the solution wasn't going to be a magic I could perform myself. I needed a powerful witch who could create a ward.

It was just a hunch, but that herbalist in the city—

As I ascended the stairs to the front door, shouting drew my attention to the property gates. Guards surged from their posts, a few pulling pistols, others lifting crossbows from their backs and aiming them between the slats of the iron fence.

One word echoed across the property. *"Incoming."*

Emerging from the surrounding forest, dozens of second-lives appeared, their souls set on Gwaith House.

CHAPTER 27

My blades were unsheathed in an instant. I leapt off the staircase and ran to the gates, ignoring the slam of the front door as Destin emerged from the house, the sound of his voice as he called my name. The thundering steps behind me were my only hint to his pursuit.

The guards stumbled over each other as they shot at the horde.

Arrows showered the dead, but rarely hit the mark – the spirit contained in their sacral chakra. Bullets struck wide, hitting their shoulders and arms and legs, and rotting fluids sprayed the road, filling the air with such a brutal stench that one guard paused to empty his stomach.

Two of the guards struggled to shut the gate, battling second-lives as they attempted to push their way into the property. Blood and pus coated the iron, the swollen limbs reaching between slats in the fence. They were gaining entry, inch by inch.

I sprinted through the rebel guards, dodging their arms as Destin shouted frantic orders for them to grab me. The guards holding the gate glanced back and saw me, and they shook their heads, telling me to stay back.

"Let me through," I roared, waving my arms.

I didn't give them a chance to argue. I sent thrumming heat spiraling down into my legs as I jumped, and the guards opened the gate in time for me to hurtle through.

I collided with the second-lives, my momentum knocking a walker right off his feet. I landed on his chest, his ribs crunching and guts squelching as my boots sank through brittle skeleton. I slashed at the next two, sticking both in the stomach.

Shouting echoed from behind me, but I didn't have time to understand who or what was being said.

Creaking iron sang in my head as I kicked a fourth walker back. Three more replaced it. They surrounded me. My daggers danced across my knuckles, a nervous tic I'd developed over the years. Spin and grip. Assessing. Waiting.

All three surged for me at once.

I dispatched the first easily, ducking between the second and third to gain a breath as I drove my blades into another. The horde encroached on my back as I lashed out with my daggers again and again. My eyes swam with blood and amber, spinning with all the power I couldn't use with all these rebels watching. I would have to rely on my blades alone.

Before I could fully face the rest of the horde breathing down my spine, a crack split the air. The nearest walker's skull exploded, and the corpse slumped. I drove a blade into its stomach as it fell, to prevent it from rising again. Another crack, and a walker dropped a foot away from me, a bullet embedded in its stomach.

Breathless, I glanced back.

The gates were open, and guards were pouring out of it, forming a wall of defense to either side of the entrance.

Archers kneeled to take aim. Their hesitation was a distant memory as commands were barked from the man standing in the center of it all.

Destin.

Veins bulged in his temple as he roared his orders, and the barrel of his pistol was still smoking from the bullets he'd shot. He stalked toward me. "Get back to the House, Sia," he ordered. "You shouldn't be out here."

I turned away before he could grab me.

Destin said my name, but it was little more than a sigh of exasperation as he followed me into the fray. We slaughtered the rest, their bodies slipping off the edge of my blades, their stomachs turned inside out from bullets, spirit after lonesome spirit, until it was finally done. The pistol's last cry lingered in my ears as the final walker fell.

The world went quiet.

I flipped the daggers over my slick knuckles and slid them into their sheathes, spreading my fingers to keep from feeling too much of the sticky decay on them.

Destin's limbs shook with adrenaline as he holstered his gun.

For a long minute, there was nothing to say, nothing that wouldn't desecrate the sudden peace around us. These bodies had been in water for a long time, and not water from the ocean. Even with all the evil in the deep, the ocean still managed to feel and smell *clean*. This water smelled like a chamber pot, stale and murky and tinged with sulfur.

Bits and pieces of the corpses strewn around us were missing, which meant the dismemberment killer had struck again.

Destin said softly, "I knew them." He frowned at the road, his gaze sweeping over each body. "They're our neighbors. The Davies family from down the road. Their entire staff, the nobles..." He gestured to the road, then swiped an errant tear from his cheek, gunpowder streaking there from his fingers. "They're all dead."

I touched his shoulder.

His brow suddenly furrowed, his eyes flicking over the gore as he stepped out from under my touch and between the bodies, as if looking for something.

"What is it?" I demanded.

"I don't see the youngest of the House. The daughter."

I scanned the forest, but all was calm. Maybe she'd escaped. Maybe she had seen who did this. "How old is she? Would she have wandered into the woods on her own?"

"I don't know." Destin ran a hand through his hair. "She isn't much older than Erlene."

My heart stuttered, because there was another possibility. When given a choice, second-lives chose to gravitate toward the souls most like them. A child would be less drawn to adults if they sensed another child nearby, and that meant her absence from the slaughter could mean...

"Destin, would she have been small enough to slip through the fence?"

His eyes widened, slashing toward the house. The front door was open. "Erlene," he breathed. Then, he was sprinting. I followed, but there was no catching up to him. He ran with the delirium of a man chased by fear, by death, by his own breaking heart.

He ran even faster as a scream echoed from the House.

The widowed guard I'd dozed on a few days ago suddenly turned the corner of the house. He must have been patrolling the rest of the fence.

Destin waved his arms, catching the guard's attention. "Valo! *Check inside!*"

Another scream came, and Valo spun toward the door. He leapt over the railing and into the house. Destin made it there in the next heartbeat.

As I crossed the threshold, Valo's voice echoed into the entryway from the sitting room. "*Stop*. Here, look at me, sweetie. It's okay."

Destin stood at the opening of the room, holding his pistol. The faint sound of weeping caressed my ears. He thumbed the hammer, aimed the barrel into the room, and pulled the trigger, but it only clicked. His gun was out of bullets.

As he scrambled to dig more ammunition out of his vest, I shoved past him into the room, palms on my daggers.

Felicity and Erlene cowered in one corner, the chairs and tables overturned and piled in front of them in a makeshift barrier. My newspaper clippings were all over the floor.

Valo threw his hand toward me, trying to keep me at bay. "I've got it under control."

The little girl was here indeed, a vision of blue skin and soaked white silk, her bloodshot, cloudy brown eyes locked on Valo as he approached her in the center of the room. Her chest had been cracked open, her heart ripped out. The girl's head tilted toward Valo in interest, her dark ringlets following the movement. Her eyes flicked to Erlene for a moment, a growl pealing in her throat as Valo drew close enough to grab her.

"It'll be okay," he murmured. "Keep your eyes on me, sweetie."

The Davies child turned her attention back to the guard and took a slow, dragging step toward him. Her growl shifted, and the sound became a whimper. A plea.

"That's it. I've got you." Valo started lifting his arms to her and knelt. In one hand, he had the photo of his wife, the yellowed parchment crumpled in his fist. His knife, a serrated blade, was clutched in the other.

The girl took another step, nearly into the circle of the

guard's arms. He tightened his grip on the knife and I let the air out of my lungs.

Valo was going to put her out of her misery.

I inched to the side, to walk along the wall to where Erlene was, but I realized Destin was already doing the same. He was reaching for the corner, his eyes glued to the living corpse as he neared his daughter.

And Erlene...

Destin was so distracted that he didn't see the way his daughter reached for him, the way she leaned over the wooden legs of a table, mouthing one word. *Daddy.*

That was when Valo dropped his knife and embraced the child.

I realized too late what the guard's intentions were. The photo should have been my first indication. He couldn't kill the child for whatever reason, so he had decided to grant mercy to it in another way: by giving her soul a companion. I cried out, lurching for them, but the gift had already been given.

Valo gasped as the little girl's fingers dug into his back. Their eyes locked and her mouth creaked open – open and open, wider and wider, until her tiny jaw popped out of place.

A low hum rattled the room as Valo's soul rose from his stomach like a mist, hurtling up his throat, into his mouth and out, shooting towards the little girl. Her soul mirrored his, and the air between them shimmered with silver as his soul twined with hers.

It was done in a heartbeat.

I slid across the room on my knees, catching Valo's empty body as it slumped back, and the girl fell with him.

The photo of Valo's wife tumbled to the floor. It fell in a small puddle of acrid water, and the ink of the photo started swimming, fading. I could only hope Valo's death meant they were together now, beyond the veil. All three of them. Brushing a hand down his face to close his eyes, I pushed away the emotion swelling in my eyes. My heart ached. This man had sacrificed himself for a little girl he didn't even know.

Such was the way of human bravery, of compassion. Wonderful creatures, indeed.

Destin had already turned away, running to Erlene. Her little arms continued to reach for him as he tossed back the tables in his way.

Felicity threw herself toward him, positioning herself between Destin and Erlene. She started blubbering, gripping the front of Destin's jacket, but he quietly and firmly pushed her aside. He knelt in front of Erlene and took her small hands in his.

"Are you okay?" he demanded.

Erlene sobbed harder, nodding. She didn't hug him, wasn't sure enough of him to do that, but she gripped his fingers tightly and brought them to her face. She let him wipe away her tears before he tenderly smoothed the blonde hair flying wildly around her face.

This was *progress*. Finally.

Then, my eyes shifted to Felicity, and I saw the shock and irritation register on her face before she composed herself. The sulfur and death in her blood became too much to bear, so I quietly stood and grimaced at my stained dress and sticky skin.

No one paid any attention to me as I left the room.

CHAPTER 28

By the time I returned to the foyer, the scent of death had faded enough that I knew Valo and the little girl had been carried out.

Through the open front door, I watched guards flit around the property. Linen wrapped bodies were lined up along the fence, holes being dug. I fidgeted with the collar of my tunic, pressing the high hem flat against my neck. I forwent the necklace when I changed, and the leather was black and soft. *Perfect*.

I had found it collecting dust in the very back of Destin's wardrobe, so I doubted he'd notice its disappearance, especially since the state of their rooms suggested he hardly spent any time in there at all. I was beginning to think he hadn't touched his wife since they arrived here, but I couldn't understand why. I also couldn't understand why it bothered me so much to think about it, *him* with *her*.

"Are—are those my pants?"

I whirled to find Destin walking down the hallway toward me, gawking. *So much for slipping away unnoticed.*

"Yes." I crossed my arms, shifting my weight from foot to

foot until he met my stare. "I've decided it's best for me to get off the property for a while, take a hike. I need to think. I hope you don't mind me borrowing these old leathers for it."

His eyes fell again to trace the length of my body. "When your legs look like that, it's hard to be upset about anything."

Surprise warmed my blood, followed by the cold ache of guilt. He was Tova's. *Had been.* She was dead because of him. None of that had changed. I couldn't let him look at me like that. I shouldn't *like* it.

I cleared my throat. "I spoke with the butler, and he's agreed to look after Erlene while I'm gone, but I'm going to try to be back before nightfall so I can put her to bed. If not, the butler agreed to do that, too." All it took was returning his precious journal.

Destin nodded. "I'll pull a guard from the burials to accompany you."

"No."

"It's dangerous outside the gates." He narrowed his eyes at me. "Look at what happened to the Davies. We have no way of knowing whether this has happened to others, or whether there are other walkers roaming the forest. You should take someone to protect you." He hesitated. "Take *me.*"

My ribs tightened, and I forced a breath through my teeth. "You should be here for Erlene. Like you said, we don't know what else might be coming."

His eyes darkened; he knew I was right.

I shrugged. "Besides, I'm safer by myself. Let's not forget how useless you were at the morgue."

He glared at me. "I was surprised."

"Most danger comes as a surprise." I chuckled darkly. "Thank you for worrying about me, but I don't need you to. I don't *want* you to, and I wasn't asking for your permission."

"I see," he said tightly. "Well, good luck with your *enlightening hike.*"

He slipped around me, his arm knocking into mine before he stalked through the door and slammed it behind him.

I sighed.

After what happened at the Baron's house and the morgue and in his office last night, the pull between us had become impossible to ignore. Whenever he looked at me, I felt it. I wanted to indulge it. I certainly thought about it, about pushing him into the cushions of that couch and riding him until we'd both gotten rid of this tension.

But he couldn't treat me like I was one of his servants. Like I was his property. Like I was his wife, something to carefully arrange and keep in this House for all eternity. If I were to fuck him, he'd definitely get the wrong idea about me, about us.

Approaching the sitting room, I lingered in front of the door as I brought my emotions under control.

Then something thumped beyond the door. A giggle. Someone hissed, and then there was a cry, a distinctly *Erlene* cry. The sound unnerved me so thoroughly that I burst through the door with a hand on my dagger. Felicity and Erlene were standing just inside, but Erlene was cowering where she stood. Felicity had one hand wrapped around Erlene's wrist, twisting her little body around as her other hand raised as if to spank her.

I was on Felicity in an instant.

She yelped as I wrenched her by the hair and threw her into the wall. She tried to push me away, but I was already in her face, pinning her. If we were alone, I would have ripped her apart. She'd already be dead. But Erlene was watching us, so I used words when I desperately wanted to take action.

I knew action would keep for a night, and the terror I could instill in her tomorrow... Oh, how delicious justice would taste when I finally took it in full.

"You want to tangle with death, my dear Lady?" I bared my teeth in a vicious smile. "Well, look no further. I'm right here."

Felicity panted, glancing up at her arms pinned to the wall on either side of her head. "You're hurting me," she whimpered.

"You hurt Erlene first."

"I was *disciplining* her."

"The moment you raised a hand against Erlene," I snarled, "you lost any right you had to life, to this title, and to this House. If I ever see you alone with Erlene again, I will make you suffer in ways you could not comprehend." Her face paled as those words sunk in. I smiled, leaning in to whisper, "Pray to the Goddess that you never trip up around me. You may discover you have a long way to fall."

Felicity's eyes flashed with fear and *understanding*, a hatred beyond her years. "You *savage*." She spat on my face, and I had to admit, it was a very brave, very reckless thing for her to do.

"That's where you're wrong." I laughed. "Foolish woman, I am a *god*."

Or, at least, the closest anyone in this world got to one.

My fingers tightened around her wrists, and she cried out as my skin branded hers, as the heat of my palms sizzled into her flesh. It only took a moment to mark her. As I shoved back, she caught herself on the walls before collapsing totally, tears spilling over her cheeks as she examined her melted skin. She sprinted for the door, and I laughed as her fingers met metal and she hissed, jerking back from the heat I'd instilled there in the doorknob.

I ambled toward her, and she retreated as far as she could into the corner beside the door. I slid my hand over the doorknob. The heat didn't sting me, because the flame was my own.

Felicity's eyes bulged.

I nodded at the wrists she cradled against her chest. "Let

those marks remind you that someday soon, you're going to *burn*."

My eyes flared with amber as I opened the door and gave her room to pass.

Felicity ran, and as she did, I grazed her skirt with my fingertips to catch it on fire, just enough to ruin her pretty dress. When she saw the black flame, she screamed and dropped to the floor, snuffing out the fire before it could consume her.

I shut the door and leaned against it. I listened to the scrambling of Felicity's slippers as she retreated up the stairs. Only when I was sure she was in her room did I finally turn around. Erlene stood where I'd last seen her; she hadn't moved an inch. I'd expected fear and disgust, but that wasn't what she offered me.

In her eyes, there was only childlike wonder.

I sank to my knees, hoping I would seem less imposing, less intimidating that way. "Erlene, I'm so sorry—"

My voice cut off in a sob as she ran to me. Erlene wrapped her arms around me and buried her little face in my neck. "Is okay, Sees." The silly nickname she'd coined for me.

I wept in her arms, my inky tears clinging to her hair. I knew I had to go, but I didn't want to. She'd run to me, embraced me even after seeing the worst parts of who I could be. It was cathartic, her love. It could heal anything, anyone, better than holy tears, I was sure of it.

CHAPTER 29

The Davies House had a pond.

Drag marks had been made in the mud around the water, and blood darkened the dirt. I knew right then, as I gazed into it, that the bodies were disposed of here.

I just didn't know why.

The house didn't have a fence or gates; it was clearly a family whose fortune had been dwindling. The gnashing forest bordered the backside of the Davies' property, the smog temptingly thin in more than a few areas. There was also a road to the beach bordering one side of the property, with the road to the city on the opposite. They had no barrier against any of the evils in this area. They never stood a chance.

I climbed the hill leading to the manor, the unkempt grass brushing against my legs as I surveyed the property. There weren't any other bodies lingering here or movement beyond the breeze, nothing to suggest anyone had ever been alive. The murders happened on land, and so I was thoroughly convinced now that serpents had nothing to do with this. Even the most powerful of serpents couldn't survive long beyond the wet shore.

Who else would have a use for their limbs and organs?

Certain witchcrafts came to mind, since some rituals required organs. Witches could be found anywhere on this continent, but they were rarely cruel. They were selfish, sometimes unpleasant, using every earthen practice to further their own wealth. There were kitchen witches who took a particular interest in tonics, and other witches who let their fingers guide magic into the seams of a dress. They ran the best shops in any city. Still, the magic attained through study and dedication like that usually made the seeker *more* compassionate, not less.

It was a far different power than the one I carried. The cognizant magic roaming our world only chose mortals it trusted.

Starved shifters were known to tear out a heart now and again, but not arms and legs, not eyes. The fact an entire pack of lycanthropes were massacred by it ruled out any sort of rogue among their race. The cuts made on the bodies didn't match up to teeth, either; they'd been made with something sharp, every cut clean and precise. This was something new, greater and darker than anything I'd ever seen before.

The Davies House was in grave disrepair.

Their roof dipped in the center, and several bevels were missing. There were no roses, no bushes, nothing to suggest that those who had lived here cared about the appearance of the grounds. Shriveled wildflowers swayed amongst the grass. In the spring, this meadow might have been a haven. Now, with blood smeared up the hill to the home, large clumps ripped out as if the victims had grappled with it as they were dragged down, and the front door splintered in half...it was a travesty.

My footsteps echoed as I entered the house, too loud for the silence I found within.

The walls were a dirty cream, and the wooden stairs were

worn but polished. Paintings hung on the wall, passion radiating from every brushstroke. There was no avoiding the blood; every inch, every corner was covered. I passed through the foyer, my boots sticking with every step, the loss wrapping itself around me. It was as if the dead could still be here, mourning the lives they'd had, standing in the rooms where death came for them, watching as I trespassed over their dried blood and tears.

The rest of the main floor was more of the same, crimson streaks marking the route to and from the servants' quarters.

In the main hallway, a massive portrait hung on the wall. I halted in front of it, studying the family, blood flecking the ornate gold frame. It was a few years old, at least. That little girl who had passed at Gwaith was a bundle of draping blanket in the mother's arms. The young woman was seated, staring up at her husband, a look of pure love on her face. He looked down at her with the same, his hand resting affectionately on her shoulder.

At least it was a happy marriage before it ended so horrifically.

There was no warning before the pain hit. I doubled over as a fierce ache stabbed into my heart, my scar. Drawing a fist up to my chest, I massaged the tingling skin until the ache at last, *slowly* faded. I don't know how long it took. Time ceased to exist in the face of such overwhelming agony. As my heart slowed, I straightened again. *Fucking ouch.*

I waited there for another long minute to make sure the pain was truly gone.

A cold sphere spun in my gut. If the attacks continued on like that, I didn't know if I'd be able to bear it. I knew why it was intensifying. It had to be because of my birthday – my 25th, just mere days away. Maybe my body was finally turning on me due to that suspended promise, now that I was nearing total maturity. If that was true, I may not have a choice. I may have to return home after all, at least until I figure out a way to free myself from this promise.

I didn't dare glance at the painting again before I moved on.

Coming back to the foyer, I turn up the stairs, bloody pools dried in clumps from one step to the next. A few wooden slats along the banister were broken, scratches burrowed into the mahogany. The blood led me to the little girl's room. Furniture had been overturned in it, her toys scattered, a rifle with a bent barrel discarded near the entrance. Across the room, her window was shattered, a tree filling out the pane just beyond. One branch grew right up to the bedroom: a perfect entryway. That girl, and her perfect little heart, had been the true target.

It looked like she'd tried to hide in the closet at some point. One of the folding doors was smashed in, clothing ripped from the hangers and strewn about the room. Judging from the tiny nail marks, she'd been drug from the room *alive*. Perhaps she had been alive all the way to the pond. In the window, hanging on a jagged piece of glass, was seaweed.

Head spinning and stomach rolling, I took a step toward it.

Then I heard footsteps behind me, rising on the stairs. I twisted toward a shadow as it appeared down the hallway, and a sinister trail of ice bled down my spine.

Black fire tumbled between my fingers as I backed into the closet, sliding behind the side with a folding door still intact. I couldn't see into the hall through the thin slats. I could only wait, biting down on the heat in my mouth as those footsteps grew louder, before the man finally appeared on the threshold of the room.

The detective, Lee.

He strolled into the room and turned to survey it, his leather gloves whispering as he clenched his fists. His dark coat was parted slightly to reveal a crisp white shirt and the silver dagger on his hip.

I wiggled my fingers, relishing in the heat swirling through my arms, the control that this anger gave me. Of course, it was *him*. Who else would be here, studying this room without a speck of emotion? The fact he was here quicker than any mortal could travel in from the city solidified the suspicion in my gut. He was involved somehow. Maybe he was even the one responsible.

Why was he here now? Did he forget something?

Lee saw the seaweed, as I had, and frowned. He approached the window and ran the green tissues between his fingers. After a moment of staring down at it, the hold on his emotions suddenly dropped away. His upper lip curled as he turned in place.

With a guttural roar, Lee grasped the edge of a broken shelf beside him and threw it across the room. The wood cracked apart and tore the floral wallpaper. The room dropped in temperature. It became so cold, even my black flames guttered. Lee's face twisted in pain and outrage as he shattered a mirror with his fist. The force of it radiated into the walls, and it shook around my hiding place.

I stumbled backwards into the silk and satin, lifting a hand to clamp over my mouth, to keep me from gasping.

There it was again, that shocking expulsion of power and strength. My stomach turned. The arteries in my chest burned so hot, I couldn't believe the clothes around me didn't catch fire.

Lee turned away from the mirror, growling as he kicked toys and clothing out of the way, sifting through the mess. He was *searching* for something. I could attack him now if I wanted. He hadn't seen me yet, and considering how preoccupied he was, he probably wouldn't notice until I'd already struck. Still, I waited, breathing through my fingers. I wanted to know what he was looking for.

He worked his way around the room, his body flexing powerfully through his suit. As Lee flung the torn goose-down mattress aside, he froze.

There was a moment of silence.

I heard the blood rushing in my ears, the breeze blowing through the broken window, the faint twang of something being wrenched from the floorboards in front of Lee as he crouched. "Fuck," he whispered. Then, he stood and turned for the door.

Before he could cross the threshold, he staggered to a stop. Seething a breath, he spun in place, his pale eyes sweeping the room as a hand rose to rub against his chest, the same way he'd done it at Gwaith House, right over his heart.

His gaze locked on the closet door, and he squinted, as if he were attempting to see through it. I bumped into the wall at the back of the closet. I don't know how he'd done it, how he'd known I was here, but I would be prepared when he came to investigate. I would burn him alive if he tried to pull me out of here and down to the pond like he did the others.

He didn't come.

Lee turned with a frown and left the room. As his footsteps hit the staircase, I quickly emerged from the closet, approaching the spot where he'd crouched. In the sea of dried blood, a divot had been left behind in the floor, just the right size for a blade.

Hearing Lee whistle for his horse outside, I took off after him. By the time I'd descended the stairs to the front door, he and his beast were flying across the meadow.

And then…they were *truly* flying.

Ebony wings burst from the horse's back as the beast leapt into the air, disappearing through the smog in the direction of the city. That explained how he'd made it across the forest. He must have flown right over it. I didn't have many answers, but I knew one thing for sure in that moment: Lee wasn't mortal.

I didn't know what options that left me, why he was here, or what villain or monster he might reveal himself to be, but I needed to figure it out. For Erlene and the city. For myself.

CHAPTER 30

When I finally reached the outskirts of the city, I pulled my cowl up to cover my hair and tucked the ends beneath the collar of the tunic.

I had followed the instinct of my body here, guided like the pendulum of a compass by my supernatural senses. I'd emptied my mind of everything but the direction I was headed, relying on pure adrenaline and the power coursing through my body to weave through the forest faster than I'd let myself move in a long time.

I was skilled at tracking. I had to be in order to survive in the gnashing forest.

Lee wouldn't walk into city limits with the beast's black wings out. It would draw too much attention. I knew they were going to have to pause just outside for Lee to bind them.

Binding was the process of charming winged appendages to retract into the body, and it was a fairly complicated endeavor. The smaller the body, the more delicate the containment. One bend or fold in the wrong direction caused excruciating pain. Where it took countless hours, and several failed attempts over the years, to learn how to successfully bind my own, an experienced rider could bind their pegasi in less than an hour. Pegasi, unlike seraphim, had plenty of room in their back, between and under their ribs, and I had to assume Lee was experienced in working with his beast. I only had so long to catch up with them.

I found the stallion farther from the city than I expected, and alone.

The pegasus was left untied about a mile north of the city gates, his saddle removed and perched on a branch. Its dark wings were free and flared, and it danced sprightly between the trees.

It had to be difficult for the animal, being contained like that, especially one with his coloring. Black and white pegasi were often left wild, untamed and unwanted by breeders. They had no color, no novelty in their coats. A small twinge vibrated in my chest, knowing that Lee had kept it, seemed to cherish and care for it.

That warmth in my chest quickly faded when I saw black sand dunes peeking through the trees. He'd gone straight to the ocean. *Why?*

It had to have something to do with that seaweed.

I climbed the dunes, following Lee's footprints up. Near the crest of the hill, a second set of tracks joined Lee's. They were similar, large, and I dropped to my hands and knees when I saw them, nearly kissing the dunes as I continued my ascension. The black sand was silk between my fingers. Conquering the climb, I peered down at the black expanse. Through the thinning haze, I saw a speck of white against the sand. *Two* specks. They were *wings*.

A seraph walked beside Lee down on the beach, heading toward a formation of boulders in the distance. Once they passed through, I'd lose sight of them.

I hauled myself up and crossed what was left of the dunes, leaping down into the main stretch of sand. Crystal crunched under my feet as I flew across the beach after them. The ocean, though swarmed with serpents, also carried a high vibration of magic. It kissed the shores, leaving fingerprints in the shape of jewels, crystals, and otherwise precious materials that tempted even the greediest or most desperate of mortals. It happened on every shoreline, every coast. I sometimes wondered where it came from, what the source of that magic was, whether it be the deep unknown itself or some creature slinking through the waters. There was no way to know for sure, not without going under, and absolutely no one with a will to live did that.

Here, that magical vibration manifested in chunks of silver and transparent stone, most of it crushing easily or burrowing into the sand beneath my feet, while others were solid enough to withstand my weight, dribbles of diamond hidden in the darkness. In the winter, there was ice along this shore too.

The treasure was also evidence of the shifting seasons. It was well-known in these parts that the ebb and flow of the ocean's magic came in seasons, like everything else. Winter was a season of beach-combing, for those brave and well-armed enough to try. Serpents ate exceptionally well in those months.

The two males in the distance slipped between the rocks, disappearing into what I knew was a maze of jagged edges and tidal pools. I'd explored enough of this coast on my own when I was younger.

The tide was low now, as the sun eased toward the horizon. Dark gray clouds churned past the smog, signaling a storm headed this way. As if reading my mind, the atmosphere dropped all manner of pretense, and the sky began to weep. Within a few minutes, the rain had soaked me through.

As I passed between the boulders, my world whittled down to the sound of rushing water, echoing off the imposing porous stone. The nearby tidal pools masked my gasps for air as my hands found the salt-crusted rock.

A roar ripped through the rain and tide, bouncing off the walls of stone. The rain turned to hail, and a frisson of terror raked across my back as that cry continued, deep and rough, *agonized*. I started running again.

The maze of stone led me down to the ocean, and when I turned the last corner, my feet sank into the oddly wet sand. I looked down to find the black sand gleaming with blood. Blood and...*feathers*. Beautiful, flawless white tufts trailed towards the water, toward a blond seraph clawing at the beach as a serpent pulled it into the steadily-rising tide.

One of the seraph's wings was missing. His face was screwed in panic, blood pouring across his back and trickling down his arms beneath his shredded navy tunic.

I ran to him, gripping his arms and dragging him back up the shore toward the boulders. My face drew close enough to his to mark the pain in his light blue eyes. Long, golden hair clung to his cheeks. Muscles shifted under my touch, his limbs straining as hope filled his face.

The serpent snarled at me, her claws latched onto the seraphim's legs. "*Let go.* This one is *ours.*" I'd never seen one so close before. She was fearsomely beautiful, her body glittering with a silver sheen all over, covered in scales from the waist down. Her full figure and bare breasts were gleaming with saltwater, her silver hair sticking like a sheer curtain over her shoulders and arms. Her eyes – they were dark like coal, the only remnant of her life above the surface.

She hissed as I studied her, baring her teeth, which were sharpened into several tiny points. Her words suddenly hit me, and I looked again at the male in my hands.

Already, scales were forming over the wound on his left shoulder blade, sealing the shattered joint to his severed wing. The scales were spreading toward the other wing, which was barely hanging on, and I knew from my studies that there wasn't enough attached to his shoulder blade to save him, that the scales developing would eventually sever the rest of it.

Total devolvement was only a matter of a time now.

The serpent was staking her claim on him, on the new addition to their population, but he wasn't one of them yet. He didn't want to go. If I were him, I'd be crawling my way up the sand too, if only to cherish the last few moments with my wings.

My hands tightened on the male, and I pulled with all my might, my boots digging into the dark beach.

The serpent began to crawl up the male's body. Her scales rippled, the razor-sharp edges slicing into the male's legs as they flared. He cried out, his eyes locking with mine. He nodded slightly, telling me that he wasn't going to go, telling me not to let go. I didn't. I wouldn't.

"I've got you," I whispered to him. I pulled even harder, and we left the waves behind.

The serpent reached up and gripped the male's other wing, her pointed black nails curling over a blood-soaked peak. I went for the dagger at my thigh, but before I could draw the blade, a blisteringly-cold wind blew around me, freezing me in place as Lee appeared next to me. He sank a dagger into the serpent's shoulder, knocking her off the seraph.

Metallic silver blood sprayed the black sand.

Lee grabbed her by the hair and dragged her into the ocean. The serpent writhed, scratching at the iron blade sizzling through the tissues of her shoulder. She barked at Lee to remove it, but he ignored her as he pulled her into waves and crouched to whisper something into her ear.

My gaze scoured his broad frame, marking every movement. The tension in my body eased when I saw he was untouched, unharmed. I wasn't sure why that mattered to me.

A groan drew my attention back to the male beneath me.

He stared up at the stormy sky. He'd wrapped his arms around his torso, his body trembling violently, either from the cold or the immense pain he must be feeling. When I placed a hand on his, his gaze cut to mine. A single tear slid over his temple, glittering like a star.

"Who did this to you?" I demanded.

I only needed him to tell me it was Lee, and I could make it right for him. I *would* make it right.

He shook his head, another tear rolling free. He shouted incoherently and curled up on his wingless side. The scales were now encroaching on his second wing, starting to cut into the final, delicate sinews at the base. Then, the scales would come for his mostly-intact secondary tier. This male was a noble, and judging from the color of his wings, he hailed from far, far away.

White wings, this pure and pristine, belonged on the east coast. *Halcyon.*

I scrutinized him, scanning his every feature for a speck of recognition beyond those blue eyes. Certainly, I would know if this was *him*? My betrothed? This male was dying, so if it was that boy from so long ago, I should know. I would feel this through my promise, wouldn't I?

The thought made my chest tighten – I didn't know, and I probably never would.

Fresh blood spurted from his wound, soaking his tunic. I bowed over his body as I brushed his wet hair out of his face. "It's going to be okay."

He choked out a laugh, crimson spattering his lips. "Liar."

I held him tighter, offering him what little comfort I could. I didn't know if he appreciated the affection, if his icy heart could even feel it, but that didn't matter to me, not right now. His large fingers wrapped around my forearm as another cry ripped from his lungs.

A breeze caressed my cheek, dipping under my chin as if

to lift my head. I looked up to see Lee stalking out of the ocean, the blade in his hand dripping with silver ichor. His eyes were locked on the male in my arms.

He hadn't been here when I first turned the corner. A quick scan of the cove we were in brought my attention to another opening in the rocks. The seraph's missing wing laid in the mouth, bloodied and mangled. Had Lee been the one to sever it? None of this made sense.

Lee knelt in front of us, his face cool and drawn. He didn't even glance at me. The seraph reached out and took Lee's free hand in both of his.

He nodded. "Do it." Gills were already forming in his neck.

Lee threaded his hand through the male's thick blond hair, lifting his head from the black sand. The male winced, and then Lee's other hand snapped forward, the blade sinking through the male's chest, between his ribs and straight into his heart.

I gasped, a moment too late as the seraph's eyes went dull and dark.

Seraphim only had one life, one death. It was a gift of our evolved nature, that we no longer had to fear the afterlife. We were strong enough to face it on our own, but I found myself feeling as though this whole thing was so incredibly unfair.

Lee withdrew the dagger, his expression stoic.

"Why?" I demanded, my throat tight with restrained tears. "*Why* would you do that?"

Lee stood, fluidly sheathing his dagger. As he did, his blazer parted enough for me to see another Halcyon feather hanging off his weapon's belt, old and yellowed. This wasn't the first time he'd killed a seraph, apparently. Before I could examine the feather further, his blazer fell back into place and obscured my view.

"Why wouldn't I?" he countered silkily, walking to the discarded wing on the other side of the cove and lifting it off the sand. "He didn't seem particularly eager to become a serpent, did he? I gave him mercy."

"Death isn't mercy," I snarled.

"If you truly believe that," Lee said quietly, carrying the wing back to the dead Halcyon, "then you do not know suffering." He laid the wing over the seraphim's face and hefted the body into his arms, pivoting toward the rocks to leave.

I staggered up and forward, cutting off his escape. "His body needs a proper burial. He needs to be returned to his people."

Lee clenched his jaw. "I'm aware of that, trust me."

"*Trust you?*" A wild laugh erupted from me. "You're the reason he was here in the first place. What are you doing out here? *What are you doing in this city?*"

Lee's eyes flashed, the anger in them suddenly as bright and vivid as the sun. "Get out of my way, Sia. I'm not in the mood."

"Pardon me for not *trusting* the man with a dead seraph in his arms," I sneered. "Would you like to tell me when you *can* explain yourself? When you can explain *all of this?*"

His nostrils flared.

A breeze whipped around me, chilly and intoxicating. The scent of poppies filled my senses, burning through my thoughts and muscles, turning me pliable as a ribbon. I blinked, trying to shake the exhaustion as I collapsed against the rock wall. My vision swam with dark spots, and it took every last ounce of the strength I had left not to fall to my knees.

"I'm sorry, darling," Lee whispered. "Just…not today."

By the time the heaviness in my body finally faded, Lee was gone. I didn't know what he'd done to me, what sort of witchcraft he'd wielded, but it left a foul film on my tongue, like burnt flowers and scorched earth. He'd stolen my strength, every ounce of it.

I braced my hands on the rock wall and tested my legs, making sure they were firm now. The rain at last stopped, and moonlight glimmered through the smog, dancing across the ocean. The tide had risen nearly to my feet by the time I was able to leave the beach.

Just beyond the shallows, I saw them: several serpents floating with their eyes above the surface, watching me.

CHAPTER 31

The Gwaith grounds were empty, all the usual guards gone from their posts. I figured they were letting the new graves settle in peace.

As I slipped in through the back door, everything was so silent, I was sure the Goddess Herself could hear my footsteps through the main floor to the stairs. Passing by the den, I found it unusually dark, no scent of liquor. Maybe that was a sign Destin had decided to stop drinking himself to death. A sign that when he'd seen his daughter today, he *really* saw her.

All I wanted right now was to collapse into my bed and let that record player lull me to sleep. I was exhausted. In fact, I was surprised I'd made it all the way back home without passing out.

My thoughts spun with what I saw at the beach, of the dead seraph and that feather I'd seen on Lee's belt. It was forbidden to keep feathers from dead or devolved seraphim. Severed wings were burned, *always*. Not even underground markets dared to trade them, because my kind had made examples of too many mortals who'd attempted it.

I tried to ignore the phantom flame burning on my hip, the outline of the feather I'd snatched from the beach.

Under different circumstances, I would have done what was right and turned them all to ash before they were caught up in the tide, but if I wanted to pinpoint where Lee took the seraph body, I needed to keep at least one.

I released a sigh as I entered my room, and my gaze fell on the packages stacked in the middle of the room. My new dresses had arrived, and someone had rifled through my delivery. Felicity, more than likely. I doubted she had found anything to suit her tastes.

My cloak and cowl fell to the floor as I crossed to the dresser in the corner of the room. I lit a candle and began removing my weapons.

As I unclasped the belts around my shoulders, the door opened.

Destin stood on the other side, his body swathed in shadows. I paused long enough to meet his gaze, his blue-gray eyes heavier than the weight currently crawling along my bones.

I slid the weapons belt from my waist as I said, "My walk took me farther than I expected, and I'm tired. If you're looking for conversation, I suggest you search elsewhere for it."

He didn't reply, only stood there as I set my belt aside and moved on to the sheathes on my thighs. A ripple of warmth coated my back. He wouldn't stop staring, and I wondered if he'd been drinking after all.

I didn't have the patience or the energy to deal with it tonight.

Discarding my daggers, I stalked across the room to shut the door. "Go ogle at your wife instead of at m—"

As he crossed the threshold into my room, the candlelight illuminated a swollen eye and several cuts that hadn't been on his face earlier that day. It took me a moment too long to remember what I'd done right before I left, to realize that Destin wasn't staring at me with anything more than predatory intent.

A growl ripped through the air between us before Destin slammed into me, and I was thrown backward into the wall.

Destin drove a curved ebony fork up against my neck, pinning me with it as the edges imbedded into the wall behind me. It was the same stone material that had been used to construct that black box in the stables, crafted in an attempt to nullify the magic in my blood, dulling it like ice would numb nerve endings in the skin.

I felt my power react, crawling just below the surface, writhing for release. Even the knuckles along my spine shuddered. Wrong. It felt so wrong. The barrel of Destin's bronze pistol pressed under my chin, lifting my face toward his.

"Move an inch," he spat, "and I'll shoot you right here."

I went still at the threat. Death by bullet was the worst way to die. Human hands could make brutal things, more brutal than winged spirits, more brutal than me. I could choose to fight back, but if I did, it would only end with one of us dying; he was too focused, too swallowed by hatred to settle for anything less.

If he died, what would happen to Erlene? Force wasn't the answer. I had to get him talking or, at the very least, distracted.

"Well," I drawled, lifting an eyebrow. "I wouldn't say this is my *ideal* foreplay, but I'm game to try almost anything once."

His eyes flashed in surprise.

Abruptly, he reached up and tore the front of my tunic open, earning a genuine gasp from me as the brass buttons scattered around our feet. Pulling the material off my shoulder, he exposed my collarbone and half of my chest. He glared at my markings.

My arms twitched, yearning to cover the swell of my

breast and the long, white scar over my heart, but his pistol kept me in place.

I composed myself, recovering my smug smile. "You like it rough, huh?"

"It was you," he spat. "*You* snuck into my stables and released the angel from its cage."

"*Seraph*," I corrected him.

Destin pushed the mouth of the gun into the underside of my chin so hard it hurt. He leaned in, as if he wasn't already so close that I could count the golden flecks in his eyes. "You made a mistake today, attacking Felicity. She came to me the instant you left."

"Is that what she told you?" Bitterness bubbled up in my voice. "That I attacked her? Aren't you curious as to what provoked me?"

"You're a monster," he hissed, his pelvis twitching against mine. "You don't need to be provoked."

"That narrative helps you sleep at night, doesn't it? You don't even care if it's not true."

His lips curled. "You won't trick me with your words, angelic bitch."

"No," I agreed, responding to the language of his hips with a sonnet of my own. "We both know my body is far more effective."

Destin's next inhale was ragged. "I'd rather be dragged across a field of nails."

I chuckled. "Is that why your fingers haven't left my skin?" I challenged. His hand lingered beneath the material bunched on my shoulder. "You could have shot me the moment you opened the door, and yet, you're sharing breath with me, pinning me to this wall with your body. Does the onyx collar not hold me in place well enough?"

His eyes shuttered, but he didn't disagree.

To my delight, the barrel of his pistol gentled against my

skin, and a thrill speared through my spine. He really was a beautiful man.

Since the night he gave me that record player, I wondered what Destin might be like in bed. Would he be as rough and angry as he was on the outside, or would that inner generosity of his reappear? I was willing to indulge that curiosity, was willing to do *anything* that could get me out of this mess. I leaned forward as far as the onyx collar would allow and asked, "Do you want to fuck me here, like this? I might let you."

"You are vile," he snarled.

But his breathing had already shifted, and my core ached so fiercely, I could hardly think around it. The heat in his eyes gave way to something else, something I understood.

Deep, soul-twisting lust.

"And you want me anyway," I whispered. "Admit it."

I just needed him to give in long enough to lower the gun, maybe long enough to feel him thrust inside of me, and then I'd strike fast enough that neither of us would end up hurt. I could tie him up, make him listen, make a promise to get him to trust me – *something.*

"Fuck me as hard as you want to, as hard as you can," I urged him. "I can take it. I'll probably even enjoy it."

His eyes softened slightly with a wanton haze. He rasped a curse, his face drifting closer to mine as his gun slid down the length of my body. My fingertips dropped too, grazing the waistband of his trousers, slipping inside.

A wail tore through the night, startling both of us.

Destin peeled back immediately, glancing toward the door and the cry of his daughter, and I quickly grasped the collar with both hands. Destin's attention snapped back to me, and his pistol drove back up into the hollow of my neck before I could free myself. "Don't even think about going to her." He thumbed the hammer of his gun.

All these weeks I spent caring for Erlene, all the days he left her in my care, the trust I'd earned, somehow meant nothing to him now. He'd replaced it with fear. I was nothing more than an *angel*, a monster who would...what, hurt an innocent child?

That made me angrier than anything, made me reckless.

"Go ahead," I sneered. "Pull the trigger. I hope you're prepared to comfort your daughter afterwards, to shield her from my lifeless body. *Me*, the only person who has bothered to care for her the way she deserves in Tova's absence. Tova was right not to trust you. You have no idea what you've done, involving yourself with the rebels, endangering this House by imprisoning a seraph on your property, but I made it right. *I* did."

Erlene's crying continued, ringing behind my voice like a drum.

Part of me expected Destin to interrupt me, to silence me, but instead, he listened. I might have admired that he let me speak my piece if the pistol wasn't such a heavy presence, a death sentence where I did not yet deserve one.

"You kept it here," I continued, letting the words rush out. "As if the male wouldn't have eventually gotten free and brutalized everything you hold dear. My kind are trained from infancy for situations like these. I *saved* you, but you didn't think of that, did you? You see me as an enemy for being born. Well, Destin, if you're still so sure I need to die because of what I am, if you refuse to remember that Tova placed your daughter's life in *my* hands despite that fact – because yes, she did know – you'd better be prepared to put Erlene first, as I have. Especially now that she'll need protected from your own fucking wife."

He started, the barrel trembling against my marked collar. "What do you mean by that?"

Erlene's bedroom door creaked open across the hallway.

"Oh, nothing," I said sweetly. "After all, when the bruises appear on your daughter, Felicity will reason it away, and you'll believe her, won't you?"

The pistol fell from my neck, his eyes suddenly wild with concern. "Did Felicity—"

"I caught them in the sitting room after the walker attack. Your wife is jealous of her, can you believe that?" I chuckled, my hands tightening on the collar as I braced my back against the wall. "Felicity has quite the temper, but, thank the Goddess, it does not compare to mine. I don't regret what I did to her. I'd punish her again. I'd burn anyone who touched Erlene or, Goddess spare me for saying it, *you*."

Destin staggered back a step.

In one, smooth motion, I wrenched the onyx fork out of the wall and flung it across the room. "Call me what you will," I muttered as Erlene's footsteps closed in on my door. "But I would *never* raise my hand to a child."

The bedroom door swung open, and Erlene rubbed her bleary eyes as she stepped over the threshold. "Sees?"

Erlene's presence seemed to anchor Destin. He quickly turned away, hiding the pistol from view as he holstered it.

I surged forward and took Erlene in my arms. "What's the matter, sweetheart?"

"I had a nightmare."

"Oh, it's all right. I'm here." I smoothed her knotted hair. The butler hadn't brushed it before tucking her in, damn him. "Would some warm milk make you feel better?"

She nodded.

I glanced back at Destin, who raked a hand through his hair as he watched us. "Do you want to take her?" I asked.

He looked over at the hallway, his thoughts a thousand miles away. "You go. There's something I need to take care of."

I didn't think twice as I lifted Erlene and carried her out of the room, down the stairs and into the kitchen. As I lit a fire on the stove, the shouting started. Felicity's voice was frantic, while Destin's calm tone rumbled through the house, pervading every room with a honey-thick coating of sovereignty. The calmness of his tone didn't fool me. Even when he'd pinned me to the wall, he didn't speak like that, like he might detonate at a moment's notice.

Erlene fell asleep in my lap despite the disruptions, halfway through her mug of milk. I cradled her against my chest to carry her back to bed, pausing in the hallway leading to the foyer when I realized the front door was wide open.

The butler had been summoned to carry suitcases down the stairs, and I held Erlene a little tighter. We waited in the shadows as Felicity stomped down the stairs, her face red and puffy. She didn't notice us standing there, but that was probably for the best. Destin padded down after her, stopping in the middle of the staircase.

Felicity glanced back from the threshold of the front door, a wad of crumpled papers clutched in one hand. Whatever she searched for in Destin's face, she didn't find it. She said not a word as she turned and walked the rest of the way out the door.

As the butler followed her, Destin said to him, "No stops, no detours. Take her straight home."

The butler nodded, pulling his cowl up over his scalp as the front door closed behind them. Destin released a heavy breath and leaned heavily against the banister. He scrubbed a hand over his face as I emerged from the shadows, my boots echoing into the foyer. His eyes shot open, landing on me.

I focused on the staircase, taking each step carefully as I edged toward the side he wasn't obstructing. My efforts to avoid him went unrewarded. He stepped into my path; I glared up at him but found he wasn't staring at me at all. He was looking at Erlene.

Destin reached up and brushed back the bangs that fell

across her eyes. His lips twitched, the very beginnings of a smile that he didn't allow to come to fruition.

"She's only sleeping," I murmured dryly. "I haven't poisoned her or anything."

His hand dropped back to his side. "I didn't think that. I'm sorry."

I was silent for a long moment, but then I couldn't help myself. "For what?"

Destin sighed, the sound trailing into a soft growl. "All of it." He remained in my way, and I didn't barrel past. I wanted to know what was going on in his head, what he thought of me. He hadn't followed through with killing me, so that was something.

In his hesitation, I murmured, "You sent Felicity away."

"No one touches my daughter in anger and remains in my good graces," he explained quietly. He met my gaze, searched it as he said, "Besides, I have the feeling you would have killed her the next chance you got if I didn't send her away."

I smiled fiendishly. "You're not wrong."

His throat bobbed. "You're terrifying, you know that? And nothing like I expected."

My grin softened as I brushed past him. "I would imagine not." I made it nearly to the landing when he called my name, and I peeked over my shoulder.

His hands squeezed the railing so hard, his knuckles were white. "I'm not finished with our conversation. We have much to discuss."

"I know," I whispered. "But we still have tomorrow."

He didn't try to stop me again as I turned my back on him and walked down the hall to Erlene's room.

THE SUN ROSE, its gray light seeping through the curtains and over my bed. I watched the record player as it spun lazily beside me.

I had to leave. I should have left last night or this morning, before anyone rubbed the sleep from their eyes. I should have scoured the city for Lee and put this whole situation to rest. Alas, I stayed.

Lying in this bed, I felt the loss of Tova all over again.

Not the pain of her death, but rather the loss of who I had wanted her to be. She hadn't longed for adventure, hadn't desired her freedom. She didn't grapple for those far-off stars in the night, angry they were out of reach. She was not wild like me. I had laid myself at her feet, searching for a way out of who I had been, searching for something different. I was told that who I was didn't matter, wasn't right. I tried to become something new, thinking she would love me more that way if I did.

She hadn't been the answer; she was the question.

I had needed to choose myself, because no one else would. That was why I had run away from the only home I'd ever known, why I kept running to this day. Maybe it was time to stop feeling scared, particularly of myself.

The floor nipped at my toes as I stood and walked to the stacks of clothing in the corner of the room. I donned a silken blue dress that matched Tova's ribbon. I knew eventually, I would need to say goodbye to it. The ribbon was already falling apart.

And Erlene...I would need to say goodbye to her too. She deserved that.

I couldn't take her with me. There was no place for her in the city above the smog. There was no place for her in the gnashing forest. I wished it didn't have to be that way, but wishes couldn't change anything, wouldn't change my people or what I was, what I needed to do. Wishes were only dreams I did not have the power to make come true.

I stepped out into the hall and noticed the breeze blowing up the stairs.

The front door was open. Erlene's door was open, too. Peering into her room, I found it empty. I'd never felt such terror, such worry, as I did flying down the staircase, calling Erlene's name, leaping over the final flight of steps and out into the chilly morning. Her name was forming again on the tip of my tongue, but it died in my throat when I saw her.

Padding across the front lawn.

A silhouette stood in the distance, in front of a grave, the one whose dirt had already settled, one that concealed only ash. Destin was standing in front of Tova's headstone.

Erlene's blonde head bobbed, tall and sure, leaving behind the darkness of the House. When she arrived at her father's side, she reached up and took his hand. He jumped slightly, then turned toward her. I didn't have to be close to them to know what she held up: that last pansy, the one she kept under her pillow. It might have been shriveled now, void of color and life, but she had kept it *for him*.

Destin took it.

Her little mouth moved, no doubt informing him of what it meant, and I heard a faint, broken sob as his legs gave out. He brought the pansy to his chest, clutching it to his heart, and then, as if he'd decided it wasn't enough, he took Erlene in his arms, holding her as delicately as he did the flower. As if she were precious to him, as if she were cherished.

She hesitated a moment, but then slipped her little arms around his neck.

I backed away, into the house, and reached for the front door to close it. This moment was more than progress. It was everything. I could not share it with them, because they did not belong to me. *I did not belong anywhere.*

CHAPTER 32

"The cut on your brow opened up again," I said from my perch on the kitchen counter.

Destin looked up from his oatmeal, touching the weeping slice above his right eye with a wince. I leapt down, drawing close beside him to study the wound. I turned to Erlene, who had just finished her own breakfast and was now smearing it across the counter to draw her name.

"Would you fetch the healing kit from the linen closet, sweetheart?"

She was all too happy to be given permission to scale the shelves. When she returned with the bag, I handed her a tin of sweets and sent her to the sitting room to work on her needlework. Destin watched her skip away with a faint smile on his lips.

"She listens so well to you," he commented, facing me as I opened the bag and unloaded the tools. "Adores you, as Tova did."

I chuckled. "I bribe her with sweets and bedtime stories."

Maybe I'd spoiled both of them.

"Love can't be bought from a child. Not truly."

My chest tightened. "No, I suppose it can't. Take a swig of this." I offered him a vial from the kit.

"Why? What are you doing with all that?" He nodded at the splayed kit.

"You need stitches. The cut will keep opening because of where it is, and it might get infected if we don't help it."

I could have healed him with my tears, but he'd already learned enough about me today. He didn't need to see exactly how different I was. Being a seraph was despicable enough. Destin eyed the needle as I brandished it, grimacing.

"Oh, give me a little credit. If I wanted to stab you to death, I would use something bigger."

He bit back a smile and accepted the vial, coughing when the alcohol hit his throat.

"Careful," I smirked as I tilted his face up. "Potent stuff."

I poured another vial of alcohol across the tools and over his gaping cut. He hissed, flinching, but I kept him from slipping off the stool by tucking my pelvis between his legs and pressing his back firmly against the counter. I leaned around him to access the items I'd prepped: the needle, thread, and tweezers.

Destin squeezed his eyes shut as I pressed down on either side of the wound, lining up the skin. As the needle slid in, his hands found my waist. His fingers squeezed hard as I pulled the thread through to the other side.

I murmured, "Are you going to explain to me how this happened?"

"That depends," he said roughly, his fingertips sliding back to press into the divot along my lower spine. "Do you really care?"

"I wouldn't have asked if I didn't, Destin."

He inhaled sharply as I sank the needle through his flesh again. "The Baron came by to check on his prize," he muttered.

I paused, swallowing the anger that rose from my chest. *Prize.*

"When he saw the box was empty, he punished me for losing it. He took the guards back and told me I had a week to capture another angel on my own, or he'd collect on my debt from Gwaith House's coffers."

I secured the newest stitch, absorbing what he'd just admitted. "Why tell me?" I wondered aloud. "You could have offered *me* as the replacement."

He would have failed if he tried, but still.

Destin nodded, and my fingers caught his chin.

"Don't move your head right now," I scolded him. His hands on my back shifted, slid an inch lower, and I tried to ignore the warmth of him seeping into the small of my back.

While I made the third stitch, he whispered, "That was my plan last night, to capture you, but I should have known better. Nothing readied me for you, Sia. I have no schemes, no defense. Even if you hadn't told me about Felicity, I'm not sure I could have gone through with it. Knowing you has destroyed everything I thought I believed."

"You would have killed me," I disagreed softly. "You hated me enough in the moment."

He clenched his jaw. "I have *never* hated you. I hated the truths you made me see. I hated that I could not lie to you as I have lied to myself."

I took an unreasonable amount of time tying the next knot, and Destin's hands slid even lower, grazing the swell of my ass. I couldn't ignore it anymore. His eyes met mine, and I knew he knew I'd noticed. Something flickered between us, feverishly hot and salty.

I couldn't get the temptation out of my veins.

I'd slept with plenty of people since Tova, but it hadn't felt like this, like I wanted to move on. Like I needed that passion to help me close this chapter and burn her out of my body. Everyone before now had only been distractions.

This thing between us meant something, even if I wasn't quite sure what it was.

He was the widower. He'd fucked and bred and hurt her, and I hated myself for wanting him. I knew I didn't love him, and I knew I would never be able to, but there was more to sex than love and desire. It was freedom. It was the only thing that had always been my choice.

"What are you going to do about the Baron?" I asked. I stepped even closer, and his hands moved to the curve of my thighs.

His fingers molded to me, squeezed and then stilled, as if he were testing the waters. "The only thing I can do. I'm going to appeal to leave the cause."

"I didn't realize that was an option."

"It's not, as far as I know," he smiled bitterly. "But I have no choice. I can't support the cause if it means hurting you. If I run, I know the Baron will find me. He might even come after Erlene for it. So, I'll gladly face him and the consequences of my own cowardice."

"You aren't a coward for wanting to leave the cause."

"I'm a coward for going to them in the first place. I'm a coward for leaving *her* to do it." The agony in his voice was crushing. When we met, I'd told him he was just an ugly soul with a pretty face, but the truth was that he wore his greatest flaws on his sleeve. His fear of loss. His isolation. Destin didn't hide his ugly from the world; he simply hid himself, buried himself under the ugly like it was a disguise. Goddess knew I'd done my fair share of that.

I was finishing another stitch when his touch brought me out of my thoughts. One of his hands shifted to graze across my ass, and his other hand slid around to explore the top of my thigh through my skirt. "You're distracting me," I said through my teeth.

"I have a hard time believing that." He smirked, his eyes heating beneath his dark lashes. "You don't seem like the type to be distracted by anything, especially not a worthless mortal like me." His fingertips inched upward, crawling along the sensitive skin of my inner thigh.

I focused on the needle, on the stitches; it was all I *could* do to keep from groaning.

He drew me closer until our bodies touched all over, until his chin rested against the skin beneath my breasts. I'd never been so grateful for a plunging neckline. His venturing fingers moved in circles, drifting closer and closer to my center, always pulling back at the last moment.

He refused to touch the place that was aching, pounding for him. I couldn't think straight.

It took what felt like ages to complete the next two stitches, but Destin didn't even flinch. His eyes were alight with heat and darkness, edged with an intention beyond pleasure. He wanted something else out of this; I just wasn't sure what.

"You aren't worthless," I whispered.

One of his brows rose. Goosebumps sprouted over my chest, and his eyes caught on my nipples straining against my silk bodice. He said a bit absently, leaning in to flick my clothed nipple with his tongue, "Aren't I?"

I gasped and clamped my legs together, waiting for him to stop. He smiled knowingly and forcefully pulled my thighs back apart.

"If you were worthless," I said. "I wouldn't bother stitching you up. I wouldn't still be here."

Destin stilled, his enjoyment faltering. "You say that as if you plan to leave."

"I do," I said simply.

He blinked a couple times. "Why?"

"This House is not my life, and it will not be my future."

He heard what I'd left unsaid: *he* wasn't my future. I didn't let myself feel bad for telling the truth. He needed to hear it, and so did I.

"There. All fixed." I snipped the thread and placed the tools back on the counter.

I made all of one step away before Destin slipped his hands through the slits of my skirt, wrapped his hands around my legs, and wrenched me back into his arms. One hand moved up, damning the inch of skin he'd left unscathed before his fingertips finally met the apex of my thighs. He paused there, his hand light as air against me.

"What are you doing?" Even to my own ears, my voice was like a fly caught in a web.

"Getting your attention," he replied. "Because I have a question."

His fingers pressed down with the softest pressure. It was enough for me to grip his arms, to arch into him. "Are you listening?" His fingers moved again with a friction that stole the breath from me. "Will you be honest with me?"

I wondered if he felt how deeply my body pulsed for him, for this connection, for this moment. "Ask it," I gasped.

He tilted his head in scrutiny. "Why are you here?"

"You already know why. I told you that Tova—"

"No," he growled. His fingers dug into my backside, and he scraped his thumbnail against the side of my clitoris, just far enough from pleasure that it was pain. "I mean your *kind*. I saw the burns on Felicity. You're a Fenix." I grimaced. *If only he knew a fraction of the truth.* "Why did your race come to the mainland?"

"You really want to discuss *this*? Now? What does it matter to you?"

"I want an answer to the rebels' question, the one they've

rallied a small army for. Why didn't you stay on your own damn island and leave our coast alone?"

I could see him wrestling with his allegiances. When we were raised to hate so fiercely, that sickness clung beyond reason, I knew. "You speak with such pointed blame, Destin. Do you even realize I wasn't *alive* when the events you speak of occurred?"

He thought a moment, then shrugged. "How was I to know? You might live for generations and look the same as this. You could lie about your age, as many women do. In fact," he squinted, "is that a gray hair I see?"

"What? Where?" I ran my fingers through my hair, pulling the dyed tresses forward to study the strands for myself. Had the henna bled out that quickly?

Destin laughed. "My mistake. It must have been a trick of the light."

I glared at him. "For your *information*, asshole, I'm twenty-four. I'm younger than you."

He nodded and pressed more firmly against the bundle of nerves between my thighs, laughing as I moaned. The mirth left his eyes as he said, "Whether it was you or your ancestors who came here, blame is assigned the same way. You allow the oppression to continue." I had nothing to say to that, no objection. "Now, give me the answer I seek."

The truth about our island was knowledge that every Fenix carried. It haunted us and our fathers and our fathers' fathers. Not only us, but every group of seraphim that had lived in that cluster of islands and no longer could.

I removed Destin's hands from my body and staggered back, letting the space between us steady my thoughts. I gripped the edge of the counter. "We didn't have a choice," I whispered. "We never would have left if it wasn't for the—"

My gaze caught on the discarded thread on the counter. *Stitches.*

Everything clicked into place at once. The world paused around me as my head spun with the sudden revelation, the clarity Destin's question had given me.

"Oh, my Goddess," I breathed. "That's it."

"What?"

Releasing the counter, I spun in a tight circle in an effort to gather my wits, then rushed out of the kitchen and into the hallway. Destin followed closely, so I said over my shoulder, "The dismemberments. I think I know why they're happening."

As we entered Destin's office, I closed the door pointedly behind us. "Erlene doesn't need to see this."

"See *what?*"

I went to his desk, rifling through papers until I finally found a map of the area. Unfolding the parchment, I ordered my thoughts, forcing words from my lips instead of letting them ricochet off the walls of my mind. "I can't believe I didn't guess it sooner. He's a sutilis."

Destin approached the desk. "Who is *what?*"

"The detective. The one who came to the House – he's a sutilis." When Destin's brow remained furrowed, I remembered that this might be the only secret the seraphim have succeeded in keeping. I took a deep breath and said, "They're the evil that drove our seraphim off the islands."

Destin paled. "Your people were overcome? How?"

My fingers grazed the lines of the map between us. "Sutilis…are not of this world. They're masters of a magic similar to alchemy and healing, but it's nothing we're familiar with." I reached for the sheath on my thigh and withdrew the feather I'd tucked beneath it.

I placed it in the center of the map and drew my blade.

Destin shifted on his feet but remained beside me, quietly listening…watching. I held the dagger against my chest in an attempt to warm the metal.

"Their practice grants immortality, and they pay that cost with others' lives. They harvest organs to replace what is failing in their own bodies. That's why the wounds were so clean, why the cuts were so precise. Everything they take is used to heal themselves, held together by stitches and magic."

Stretching a hand out over the map, I sliced my palm. I pressed my fingertips into the cut and let my blood dribble in a large circle, encompassing the city and the surrounding forest.

Destin's jaw dropped as I muttered the spell, unfurling my palm toward the ceiling. My other hand transferred the feather directly to the wound. As the incantation fell from my lips, black sparks erupted and ate the white tuft.

My hands fell away as the magic took effect, the cut on my palm already healing.

The blood on the map quivered, spidering inward like a fisherman's net. A mass rose up, a bloody outline of the feather I'd burnt. As it lifted in the air, drawn up by an invisible gust, the blood sloughed away and left behind a cloudy, transparent semblance of what had once been solid, been real.

I smiled. Leaning over the desk, I watched as the phantom feather whirled, whipping toward its target.

I'd seen a witch perform a similar spell to track an enemy once, with nothing more than a strand of hair he'd left behind in her home. Curiosity and desperate circumstances led me to try it for myself. It didn't work the same way her spell did; her item didn't burn. It didn't turn to a phantom, but rather slithered over the map in its solid form. The spell worked for me, though, so I wouldn't complain, even if I wasn't sure how it did.

"Neat party trick," Destin grumbled. "Creepy, but neat."

I smiled at him, then returned my gaze to the map. "From what I've learned, sutilis bodies are constantly falling apart. They can never stop hunting, killing, stitching, or else they'll wither." I pointed at the area on the map where the phantom feather hovered, slowly following the path of who was walking beneath it. The fact that the feather was moving told me Lee had likely already sewn the wings onto his back. "There. That's where he is."

"Hold on." Destin grimaced. "Why did no one think to warn the human lands of this threat?"

"Because this shouldn't have been *possible*." I was unable to tear my eyes from the floating feather. "The sutilis drove us from our home, but we retaliated. We ensured the sutilis would never step foot off those islands. They should all be dead."

"Apparently, your ancestors didn't succeed."

"Apparently not," I echoed, my eyes burning as I glared at the bloody map. "The knowledge we have is minimal, only what we managed to glean from our short battle against them. They could be capable of anything."

Destin didn't respond.

After a moment, I met his terrified gaze. "Don't worry, I'll take care of it."

"I'm coming with you."

"Over my dead body," I snapped, gesturing toward the sitting room. "You're staying here with Erlene, where you'll both be safe."

He rounded the desk. "This is more my fight than yours. This creature killed my people, my friends. He nearly caused Erlene's death, too. I'm not letting you go after him without me, and you should not ask me to." He took another step, drawing close enough to touch.

I understood the need in him, that desire to prove himself, to be seen for what he wanted to be rather than what he'd been dealt.

"Fine." I reached for the map, but Destin grabbed it first, folding it up, feather and all.

"I'll hold onto this," he said with a smirk, tucking it into the pocket on his chest. "Insurance to keep you from running off without me."

"Fine," I repeated. I kept my eyes forward as I walked to the door. "I'll send for Lila, so she can care for Erlene while we're gone."

"Sia."

I halted, my hand lingering on the door as I glanced back at him. *Only one more time*, I told myself.

With an unexpected light in his eyes, Destin said, "Tell Lila to come home for good."

CHAPTER 33

The butler returned around mid-afternoon, only to be sent off again to fetch Lila from the city. I sent him with a letter instructing the governess to arrive at Gwaith House before nightfall.

A heaviness settled over me as I prepared Erlene for bed, knowing this would be the last time I brushed her hair, the last time I washed her feet, the last time I sat beside her and lulled her to sleep with my stories.

Destin remained beside Erlene and me, a warm presence she delighted in hour after hour. He sat beside the bed now, his head resting on the mattress as we watched her drift off.

Erlene's hand gripped mine abnormally tight, loosening only as sleep finally claimed her. She'd lasted a long time, an hour longer than usual. It was as if she sensed the goodbye I didn't know how to make. Destin blew out the candle on her nightstand before I could tell him not to, before I remembered that it was Tova who had been afraid of the dark. Perhaps Erlene didn't ever need to share that fear.

It was cowardly to say it when she could not hear me, but I'd never been brave when it came to endings.

"Dream of this," I said to her sleeping face. "Of a girl who took a lost seraphim by the hand and taught her how to love again. Who taught her that there is always more life to live, always choices when it feels like there are none." I tucked her hair back and kissed her temple. I whispered against her golden hair, "I will never forget you. Even as the years pass and your memories of me fade, when the pansies sprout every spring, I will remember."

I left the room, following Destin out, and faced the door as I closed it for the last time. I sensed Destin watching as I rested my forehead there, praying the Goddess would wrap her grace and protection around the little girl inside.

His hand hovered over my back.

"I can't stop thinking about what you said this morning," I said to the wooden panel.

Destin chuckled. "Something I said actually made it through your thick, beautiful skull?"

I lifted my head and looked at him. "You weren't what I expected either. I hated you before we ever met, before I knew you. I thought you were the worst human to ever exist."

He blew out a heavy breath, his eyes slanting with hurt. "Fuck, that's honest."

"But I was wrong," I said quickly. "The soul has facets that are not always beautiful or kind. You came out the other side of grief intact, and that gives me...indescribable hope."

Destin's jaw tightened, the lines of his face sharper than ever.

I took his hand. "Thank you."

He shook his head. "I do not deserve your gratitude, or your kindness." He tried to pull away, but I held on, wrapping my other hand around his.

"Perhaps the man you were didn't," I said. "I choose to believe the man you are becoming does." He lifted pieces of me from the dead, from where I'd sealed them away in the casket of my soul. Tova had been nothing like me, but Destin…

We both ran from what we couldn't change, ran instead of trying. What if our running was the problem, not the loss? Maybe facing our fears was the only way to change.

"When you are born as obsidian amidst magma, strong and stubborn and *different*," I whispered, "change hurts. We must break before we become something new. For Erlene's sake, don't give up on yourself."

His eyes filled with tears. With an encouraging smile, I turned away from him, but before I could leave, Destin caught me around the waist. He pulled me into him, his hand plunging into my hair and guiding my face to his. His lips crushed mine, trembling as he coaxed me open. It wasn't a kiss. It was despair and heat, wet and sloppy and filled with need. His body enveloped me, not smelling of liquor or gunmetal, but something more familiar.

My fist connected with his jaw before I'd even realized I pulled away to throw a punch.

Destin stumbled back, slamming into the wall. He blinked the haze in his eyes away as his fingers touched the fresh cut on his lip. He looked down at the blood on his hand with a frown. "I'm sorry. I shouldn't have done that."

I hadn't meant to do it, but I'd made a promise to him back at the Baron's manor, about how I'd make him regret it if he ever forced himself on me again. My body took that literally.

The aroma that had assaulted my senses…

He was wearing Tova's perfume.

I stepped forward, not a thought in all the world except for feeling that again, that anger and passion, that closure.

Destin gave me a panicked look. "I said I was sorry, Sia. Please."

He stiffened as I wrapped my arms around his neck. This time, I closed my eyes as our mouths met, and he melted in an instant, a curve forming across my lips as he brought me closer. My tongue swept across his bottom lip, and I tasted agony. His blood, tangy sweet. I welcomed his sadness and desperation and returned my own to him. Pain to pain, our hurts tangled until one could not be separated from the other.

Destin turned abruptly and pinned me against the wall. His hands grappled with my skirt, searching for the slits.

"You know, I recall you asking me to fuck you like this." He gripped my legs and lifted me so that I could wrap myself around him, thrusting his hips between my thighs so roughly that I gasped. He whispered, "Do you still want me to fuck you as hard as I can? Are you going to come for me, dirty little angel?"

My nails dug into his shoulders. "Make me."

"You've...have you been with a male before?"

"What makes you think I would let you be my first anything?" I laughed. "You should worry about being my *best*."

Destin's eyes darkened as his hands slid up my thighs, but a thud down the hall interrupted him.

Lila stood at the top of the stairs, her arms crossed, those beaded braids sliding over her shoulder as she considered our situation. "I'll admit, when I'd heard you annulled your marriage, I wasn't sure what to expect, but it certainly wasn't *this*."

Destin placed me back on the ground and straightened the sleeves on his shirt, opening his mouth to reply.

The old woman lifted a hand. "I don't want to know." She picked up her bag and aimed for the room she'd let me borrow.

"Annulled?" I repeated to myself as Lila disappeared over the threshold.

Destin nodded.

"On what grounds?" I demanded. "You were married for weeks."

He looked away, his cheeks flushing. "I never touched her."

I should have guessed it. All the evidence was there. I knew it was a mistake to pry, but... "Why not?"

"How could I? When she looked like—" His hands curled into fists, a deep breath sawing through his chest. "I loved Tova with my entire heart. Despite the law concerning our House and fortune, she couldn't be replaced there."

I didn't know what to say, so I muttered, "That law is barbaric."

Destin walked past me to the master bedroom. "Yes. Perhaps it's time for someone on this coast to go about abolishing it." He paused on the threshold to wink over his shoulder, patting the map in his pocket. "I'm going to change into something better suited for our *enlightening walk*, and then we can leave."

CHAPTER 34

The first frost of the season was finally here.

Dry leaves crunched beneath our feet, and the bare trees groaned as we weaved through the forest. The metal necklace covering my collarbone had absorbed the chill and was slowly burning its way into my bones, but I refused to go without it. Destin had strapped so many weapons to himself that every step he took clinked a little.

The idiot clearly didn't understand the element of surprise.

"Let me see it again." I paused between two trees, hoping it would shield me from the breeze as I reached for the map in his hand.

He rolled his eyes. "It hasn't changed since you last checked, which was only a few minutes ago, in case you were wondering."

A cold gust blew under my skirt, but thankfully, I was also wearing Destin's old leather trousers. Tilting the map and phantom feather towards the stream of moonlight sifting through the trees, I said, "It's better to be sure than sorry." My teeth were chattering.

"You should have worn something warmer."

I glared at him over the map. "If you hadn't ripped the tunic I wore yesterday, I *could* have." As it was, I'd settled for the thickest dress I had: a navy velveteen. This bodice wasn't suited for northern winters. Despite the long sleeves, it was cut low, and my cloak didn't help much. I'd planned to travel south before the weather turned, but it seemed I was a day late.

Destin was right. The feather hadn't budged from the area it was hovering in when we left the House: just beyond the smog, where the gnashing forest started. We were less than a mile away now, and the air around us was cleaner than any I'd breathed in days.

"Lucky for us," I muttered. "I think he's sleeping, but we'll take this last stretch slow, just in case."

As we continued forward, Destin cleared his throat. I tried to ignore him, but then he did it again and I asked, "Is something the matter?"

"Not exactly." He tripped over a fallen tree limb, his blades clattering loudly, causing a physical ache in my muscles as paranoia swarmed me. I shot him a glare over my shoulder. Once he'd found his balance, he said, "I just realized you never really told me what happened on the islands, how the sutilis drove your people out."

"I don't think the details matter."

"I think they do," he argued. "We're headed towards one of these sutilis. Shouldn't I be aware of what they're capable of?"

I couldn't find a decent enough reason to refuse him, so I slowed a bit, watching my feet traverse the uneven ground. "A rift opened on the island," I said, "allowing travel between this world and another. By the time the island even realized what had happened, sutilis were pouring in. They overwhelmed our people, wielding strange blades that could cut through bone and steel. They beheaded the Fenix king and stitched his face onto their leader. It was a week-long massacre, which ended with our people barely holding them back. The sutilis coming through the rift never slowed, not for a second."

Destin's eyes burned a hole into my back.

"The Fenix king who died had five children: four daughters and one infant son. When our people were pushed to the cape of the island, those daughters made the decision to put an end to the suffering with the last weapon they had. They ordered the island to evacuate, utilizing every ship in their arsenal. It wasn't enough to carry everyone, but if the population took turns flying the ships to the mainland, most would make it. The princesses sent their brother off to safety, and they stayed behind. They died for their people."

"I don't understand," he said quietly.

I grimaced. "In sacrifice, the flame of a Fenix comes to life. They tap into the full power of the winged spirit who first gave them breath. When the four sisters surrendered to its presence, they summoned a burst of magic large enough to cover the island, to burn everything, the sutilis included. Flames were the one thing we found that worked well against them. The rift was a separate issue, one the princesses had begged the seraphim on the other islands and on the mainland to help remedy. Most ignored the letters, some openly forsaking our people and blaming us for the invasion." I paused, swallowing hard. "But the Halcyon responded. *They came.*"

"That was noble of them."

"It wasn't," I replied, my voice as sharp as the fear in my heart. "They don't fear death. They don't fear or feel anything."

Destin fell silent.

"The King of Halcyon brought a small troop of soldiers to the isles," I continued. "They surrendered their lives to the cause as well, encasing the islands in an eternal storm that covered the rift in solid ice."

We finally left the smog behind, and the pines had never looked so green to me, the night sky peering through so black and alight with twinkling stars. I smiled weakly at them, breathing in the scent of fresh air. "I don't know how any creature could make its way out of that. We should be grateful we're only dealing with one sutilis here, instead of an entire army." We could hope this was an anomaly rather than an omen. I peeked at the map. "We're getting close."

A glimmer of light appeared first, and as we drew closer, I saw it was the dwindling embers of a fire. A large tent had been pitched beside it.

There was no sign of movement except for Lee's winged beast, which ambled between the trees with its feathers tucked in tight. Clothing hung from a branch near the fire pit, and a skewer remained hoisted above the embers, remnants of burnt meat clinging to the metal.

In the distance, hanging in the sky like its own miniature galaxy, was my people's city.

From here, I could see the red and burnt orange glow of the castle. It was too dark to see the water mills turning, the water cascading off the edges of our magic-formed island. I was too far to sense the altitude in my stomach or feel the breeze on my cheeks, too far to see the paved streets and brick buildings, but I remembered. I wondered if my brother was there tonight, entertaining a lady in his wing of the castle or training in the armory, his auburn hair drenched in sweat and his blades singing with bright flames. I wondered if he was standing on his balcony, looking down at me as I looked up at him.

Yearning tugged at my chest. For all that I had been denied there, I knew I had been loved. *I only wish things could be different.*

I folded the map and tucked it back into Destin's breast pocket. "We found him. That's his horse."

Destin stared at the creature with wonderstruck eyes. "It's incredible."

"Maybe I'll teach you how to care for it," I said in a small, taunting voice. "Erlene can keep the beautiful beast."

His eyes grew even larger.

"What?" I giggled. "We have to do *something* with it once we're done here."

"Let's just get on with it," he rumbled with a smile as he made to step forward.

In the same heartbeat, I saw the meadow floor in front of us, saw the untouched circle of flowers that should have died months ago but instead were thriving through the mulch of pine needles and leaves, kissed with the beginnings of frost.

I grabbed Destin by the collar and yanked him back from the clearing before his foot could touch down.

"What the hell?" he growled.

I pressed him up against a tree trunk with a finger to my lips. *Be quiet.* I pointed to the clearing and whispered, "Don't speak too loudly. Look at the ground. That's an elven ring you were about to step into, and it would have called forth evil even *I* do not deign to face."

He muttered, "Elves? Wouldn't we be safe if I were with you? I've been told they're just another twisted sort of angel."

"Not even close." I shuddered. "Elves pass into this realm through dreams. They're dark beings made flesh from our worst nightmares."

"What does a thing of nightmares care if I walk through a ring of flowers?"

"You'd be surprised what they care about. Do you wish for your soul to be captured, for your body to be sent back to Erlene as a changeling? Elves love to play that way. If you trespass on their homes, they'll trespass on yours."

Destin swallowed, glancing at the flowers with a touch more reverence. "Goddess."

"Who knows..." I whispered, leaning in with a smile. "Maybe you would have summoned a female who fancies you instead, and you'd have a new wife."

"No, thank you."

I turned back to the clearing. "It's a clever trap. He placed his tent here strategically, so that any lurker from the smog would take care of itself."

"So, we go around it." Destin attempted to brush past me, but I stopped him.

"*I* will go around it. You stay here." He shook his head, but I cut him off before he could argue. "We don't know what other traps he has. Considering the elven ring, it seems as if he's using the forest to his advantage. You are not prepared for those dangers, but I'm used to them."

"I can help you."

"You'll endanger us both," I retorted. "You're louder than a damn church bell with the way you've strapped all these weapons to yourself. I'll sneak in without alerting him, burn his tent down, and then the whole thing will be over with."

He glared at me. "Be reasonable, Sia."

I wouldn't gamble with his life, not when he meant so much to Erlene, and now, to me too. "If I'm not back in half an hour, you can come after me. It's better for you to wait here in case something goes awry anyway. Keep an eye on the camp and the forest around you."

Destin snarled, a hand tightening on the sword at his hip. He turned and stalked to a bald spot amidst the trees, where unfiltered moonlight hit the forest floor. After unsheathing and spearing his sword into the ground, he slumped against the nearest trunk.

"Half an hour. Not a minute more."

CHAPTER 35

Slowly, I lifted the leather canopy, and the scent of wet earth filled my nostrils as I ducked under it. Through the darkness, I saw the silhouette of a table crowded with books and weapons, as well as two chairs. Across the room, against the opposite wall, was a cot.

The mountain of furs rose and fell in an even cadence. The monster, sleeping.

I straightened, keeping one eye on the slumbering form as I approached and cataloged the table. There were several maps of the area, marked with charcoal at different points in the city, a collection of especially worn volumes, and a familiar weapons belt with Lee's iron dagger and a new white feather hanging beside the yellowed one.

I reached out to touch them, intending to make them the first items I set alight, but my gaze drifted to what sat beneath.

It was a scythe-like blade the size of my forearm, engraved with strange characters down the vicious curve. The metal seemed to shimmer, glowing a deep, eerie blue. The surface reflected darkness the way glass reflected light, and the edge was near white with how sharply it had been filed. Was this the blade that had torn through the door at the morgue? That had been carving people up? I'd never seen a sutilis blade before, but I was willing to bet this was one.

I turned my attention to the cot, every step I took forward offering more clarity as to the body within it.

Lee's dark blond hair peeked between the blankets, the strong slant of his temple and jaw. He seemed so harmless like this. The sweep of thick pale lashes kissed his cheeks, and that pucker of his lips almost made him look like a child. Squeezing my dagger's hilt, I wrestled with the sudden doubt wriggling in my stomach. I *had* to kill him. I'd dealt with plenty of monsters like him before, so why did the thought of raking my blade across Lee's neck build bile in my throat? Maybe all this time with Erlene had softened me in dangerous ways, but then, the heart beating in his chest was a child's. It was no wonder I saw innocence – none of this was really his.

Swallowing my hesitation, I leaned over the cot and raised my dagger.

Lee's brilliant blue eyes flashed open. He lurched forward, snagged me around the waist, and pulled me down, rolling me over his body to lay me down beneath him. "Hello, darling." His head tilted to survey me, a dimply grin etched into his cheeks. "To what do I owe this midnight visit?"

I slashed at him. He saw it coming from the corner of his eye and jerked back as my blade came within nicking distance of his neck.

"*What the fuck?*" Lee collapsed on top of me, one hand seizing the wrist of my armed hand and pinning it across my chest, the other tangling in the tendrils of hair that had escaped my cloak to keep me from lashing out with my head or teeth. A smart move.

He twisted my wrist, forcing me to release the dagger, and it slid off the bed and clattered to the ground. I bucked under him, but he was ready for that, his full weight pressing me down into the pile of furs. He was wearing a turtleneck sweater and thin, cotton trousers that left absolutely nothing to the imagination.

"A dagger, Sia?" He seemed genuinely offended. "Are you totally nuts?"

I drove my knee up between his legs.

Lee grunted, his face twisting in pain. I freed my hands with a circular sweep between our bodies, knocking his arm out from under him and shoving as hard as I could. He hit the ground beside the cot with another grunt.

I scrambled off the bed, black flames flickering between my fingers as I leapt over Lee.

He caught my ankle and I careened into the ground, my teeth singing upon impact with the packed earth. An ache spread through my temple and my vision swam, the flames on my hands snuffed out. I tried to push myself up, tried to kick my leg free, but a heaviness seeped into every inch of my body. The scent of burning poppy seeds filled the tent, filled my head.

My arms trembled and gave out.

Lee said from behind me, "Would you listen for one moment, you impossible female?"

He flipped me over sharply, his hands wrapping around my calves to drag me toward him. I tried to shake my head, but it rolled lazily against the ground. I couldn't lift a finger.

"What are you doing to me?" The words came out slurred.

Lee crawled over me, his knees framing my hips, his hands enclosing my shoulders. "Don't worry, I won't knock you out completely." His lips twitched. "Unless you target my malehood again, in which case, all bets are off." He shook his finger at me, smiling sadistically. "You've been warned."

My mouth dried up as I waited for him to do something to me, but he just kneeled there, his bright eyes flicking over my face.

"You really are the prettiest female I've ever seen," he murmured, shaking his head. "It knocks the air out of my lungs every time I look at you."

"That was my knee," I hissed.

He laughed. "And you're cold-blooded, too. That's good. You'll need that."

"How are you doing this?" I tried to glance around the room, but my eyes ached from the effort. "Where are those poppies coming from?"

"Is that what you smell?" He frowned. "Interesting."

What the fuck does that mean?

When he saw the question in my eyes, he explained. "The scent of my magic changes depending on the person I choose to affect. You sense whatever soothes you most. I'm like a walking belladonna cookie, only better, because I intoxicate by presence alone." He smirked at me, his voice thick with arrogance. "How long have you been a poppy user?"

Gritting my teeth, I managed a weak undulation of my body. "*Was* a user, not that it's any of your business. Now get off me."

He raised a golden brow. "So you can attack me with the blade in your boot?"

I huffed a sharp breath. "Yes."

"Then no. You're being rude and I think you've earned yourself a lesson."

"I'm going to rip you apart," I hissed.

"Boo. How very dull of you. Where's your creativity?"

"Fine." Every move I made, every effort to sit up or lift my hands, had me gasping for air. "I'll skin you alive."

He smiled with one side of his mouth. "Better."

"And when I'm done, I'll throw your skull into the ocean."

His eyes darkened, his mouth flattening to a grim line. "And we've arrived back at rude."

I spat in his face, and he blinked, his cheeks flecked with

blood from a cut on the inside of my lip. He didn't wipe it away.

"Am I that repulsive to you?" he asked quietly. When I snarled in response, he leaned in and pleaded, "Can't you *feel* me?"

"If I feel *any* piece of you, I will cut that piece off."

"So vicious, so closed-off. What happened to you, darling?"

I'd been so distracted, I didn't notice Destin until he appeared directly behind Lee, his pistol raised and aimed at Lee's head. Lee hadn't sensed him yet. I quickly looked away, not wanting to give away Destin's position. "You should be more concerned about what's going to happen to you if you don't let me go."

Lee sighed, a chill breaching the hood of my cloak. "I calmed you down before either one of us ended up hurt. We need to talk, Sabrina."

His use of my full name clicked in my head at the same time Destin's pistol hammer did. Lee started, turning toward the noise. Destin pulled the trigger again, but nothing happened as the gun jammed. Destin's eyes bulged as he realized what was happening. Before Lee could get to his feet, he threw his arm out, pummeling the side of Lee's face with the butt of his pistol.

A searing pain ripped across my chest and vision, sinking through vessel and bone into my heart. I screamed. The pain tore through Lee's magic – or maybe he'd pulled it back, I didn't know. Dread prickled in my stomach. It filleted me open. I was exploding from the inside out.

Faintly, I registered Lee's voice. "Stop! Can't you see you're hurting her? Listen! *Ah, holy hell.*"

There was a clash of steel, and my awareness came back, inch by inch. The pain made its way out of my body, tingling into the tips of my fingers and toes.

Lee's voice anchored me further, "Stand down, mortal. I'd prefer not to have to kill you."

Fuck. Destin. I opened my eyes and found my limbs were no longer weighed down, my sight had cleared. I turned onto my side. Destin swayed on the other side of the room, his eyes drooping as he tried with all his might to remain upright. The sword in his hand vibrated. Lee stood opposite him, his jeweled dagger extended, his presence taking up all the air in the room.

"Wait," I said weakly.

Destin didn't hear me, or maybe he simply ignored me as he swung his sword again. As the blade came down, Lee caught the blade on the hilt of his dagger and disarmed Destin with one, swift motion. Destin reached for the extra rapier on his back.

"*Stop fighting.*" I staggered into the space between them. "You," I pointed at Destin, "sit down. Your nose is bleeding."

He did, begrudgingly.

Then, I faced Lee. "And you. You called me Sabrina."

He pressed a hand to the side of his head, where his blond hair was matted with blood. "Isn't that your name?" His voice was different from how it was before, when we were all alone. Now, it was turning bitter around the edges, like rotting fruit. He walked to his bed and ripped a piece of cotton away from his bedsheet to press against the wound.

"Yes," I conceded. "But how—"

The quiet outside snapped, broken by the faint blare of an alarm. We turned toward the sound, toward the city alarm being carried across the forest. Beneath the horn, bells echoed, repeating in a sequence of…of *five*.

"Five," Destin whispered.

I turned to him. "What does it mean?"

"It means," Lee interjected, "the city is being massacred."

"But I don't understand," I muttered. "You were…I thought the sutilis was—"

"I'm glad you solved it, darling." There was no kindness in Lee's voice. "But, honestly, it's a little disappointing how long it took you to figure it all out. I expected more from you."

My chest prickled with anger. "Don't act so proud. What does your cleverness and deceit matter now that I have you cornered?"

I reached for my dagger, realizing too late that it was still on the floor next to his feet.

He lowered the bloody material from his head, his eyes narrowing. "Hold on. You think *I'm* one of those things?" When I didn't say anything, he tossed the rag on the cot with a rasping laugh. "I've never been so insulted in my life."

Destin and I exchanged a brief, bewildered look as Lee paced his side of the tent, his laugh turning maniacal. He turned to me. "Have you ever even *seen* a sutilis, Sia? Come, I'll show you." He waved me toward a second set of flaps cut into the wall of the tent, leading to a second room.

"I'm not leaving you alone with her." Destin fought to stand up.

Lee smiled, crossing his arms, and the tent dropped a few degrees. Destin moaned as his knees buckled again.

I swiped the sutilis blade from the table and pointed it at Lee. "Stop casting spells," I demanded. "Let him go right now or I'll slit your throat, sutilis or not."

"Spells, huh?" Lee scoffed, then wiggled his fingers in Destin's direction. "Oogie boogie."

Destin finally managed to get to his feet, his eyes clearing. Then, he drew the rapier from his back and gestured at the second room with it. "Go on, then. You first."

Lee rolled his eyes and led us in. A long table dominated the space, covered by a stained canvas. He stalked forward and ripped the material away, revealing a burnt body. At least, I thought it was burnt at first. Upon closer inspection, I realized it was only flesh covered in spores and rot. The skin might have once been alabaster or tan, but now it curled back in several spots to reveal sludge-filled veins and mold between tissues.

Death filled my nostrils, the kind of stench that developed over several decades, the scent of ancient crypts.

There were pieces of creature I recognized: a fully intact leg; two bloodshot, black eyes staring at the ceiling; a full set of sharp, wolfish teeth. Every limb was attached to the torso by shimmering black thread, and there was a cross threaded into its chest. Even with the newer features, there was no mistaking the decay.

"I've been studying the body since I caught it in the city," Lee explained. "They've been traveling in from the ocean. Gills were stitched into its neck, harvested from a serpent by the looks of it. I suspect they've been living underwater for a long time. They have to, because their bodies degrade at a rapid pace once exposed to sunlight."

The pond at the Davies House...

It must have run out of time and drug the corpses there to hide from the sun. If that was the case, then they were still in the pond when I arrived. My skin prickled with disgust.

"Satisfied? Are you going to call off," Lee shot a look of annoyance at Destin, "well, whatever he is?"

I raked another cursory glance over the corpse, then shrugged. "I don't see all that many differences between you and him, if I'm being honest."

Destin choked on a laugh.

Lee pressed a hand against his sternum, pouting. "You wound my sensitive feelings, word after word. Won't you take pity on me? I was ambushed tonight, bludgeoned in the fucking skull."

"Not hard enough," I retorted. "You're still talking."

Lee flashed a bright, brief smile. "That tongue of yours is ruthless."

Destin's laughter cut off cold. He looked between the two of us, and I don't think he liked what he saw.

I ignored Destin's glare and tucked the sutilis blade into my belt. "If you're not human or sutilis, what are you?" I crossed my arms, waiting. I wanted to leave the room, to get this corpse away from me, but I refused to show any discomfort.

Lee watched the blade glow at my side with a frown, then lifted his gaze to my face. His eyes were burning ice. "You really have no idea?"

He said it as though I should.

Did I?

There was certainly something...familiar about him. Something had drawn me toward him since the day we met. Several moments rushed into my head at once, moments with him. His voice speaking to me over a sticky table in a tavern. Pale blue eyes following me through the smog. His words, mismatched edges in a pile. *Darling, you're ruthless. You love it when I bother you.* How had I not seen it earlier?

My mouth turned down in understanding. "I know who you are."

"You do?"

His eyes glittered in a way that said, *It's about time.*

I crossed my arms, fending off any lingering affection in my heart. "You're the one who's been stalking me over the last year."

"Stalking you?" He smiled. "I thought we had a rather sweet back and forth."

"Do you work for my father?" I demanded.

"Hardly."

My nails dug into my arms. It was worse than I thought. "The Halcyon, then. You're one of their spies." That was why he'd been talking to a Halcyon noble. He was an informant. He worked for my betrothed, I was sure of it.

Lee's eyes cut to Destin, then back to me. He didn't respond, but that admitted enough: he was a seraph, a lesser Halcyon. A *spy*. That was why his wings were put away.

I swept toward him, my breath coming faster, my head pounding in my ears. I felt as though my chest was going to cleave open. "I should have known they'd do something like this, let me get attached to a spy for the sake of keeping a thumb on my life. Are you here to retrieve me?"

His smile grew. "You've grown attached to me?"

"It doesn't matter," I spat. "It's not like your frozen heart can reciprocate anyway."

Lee's eyes shuttered, every trace of his happiness dissipating. I could almost see the words fall from his lips. *Don't be mad at me.* I hated that I could see it. I hated that I felt every message we'd ever exchanged flutter into place between us. Every joke. Every estranged comfort. "I know trust must be earned." He stretched a hand toward me, and I pointedly dodged it. "Let me start tonight. I'll fly us into the city, and we can take care of what's happening there."

"We don't need you," Destin cut in.

Lee turned a glare on him. "Do you really have the gall to refuse me in this? Do you think your city has time? How much are you willing to sacrifice for your pride?"

"He's right," I interjected, trying to appease them with a calmer tone. "We'll go together."

What else could I do? What other option did I have? I certainly wasn't going to hurt him now and force the Halcyon to retaliate on the Fenix. I had my family to think about.

A small part of me wanted this person behind the notes to be okay. He had given me something in the wilderness. For a moment, he'd been a friend, even if it wasn't because he wanted to be, even if that was only his job. We all had our responsibilities, and right now, the city was mine.

Lee stalked out of the second room to his table of weapons. "Just give me a moment to load up." He reached for a pair of leather pants, and I knew I had to get the hell out of here before I saw more than I'd already felt.

Destin marched across the tent, using his rapier to cut through the flap's ties, and I followed him. As I passed Lee, I paused to whisper, "After this is over, I expect an explanation. About all of it."

He barely glanced at me. "I'll explain, Sabrina. I promise." The words sent a prickle across my neck.

Lee emerged a few minutes later wearing a set of navy-blue leathers. His weapons belt hung low on his hips, the twin feathers fluttering as he walked across the grounds and whistled for his pegasus. I wanted to ask why a spy was breaking the law and carrying around feathers that didn't belong to him, but I didn't. I told myself I didn't care.

As the pegasus approached us and nuzzled into my side, I asked, "What's its name?"

Lee scratched the horse's chin. Without looking at me, he ducked under the beast's wing and hefted himself onto its back. "Legend."

I raised an eyebrow as Legend turned its head, nudging me with his snout toward its back.

"I have a seat for you here." Lee patted the space between his legs. "Front and center."

"So you can fling Destin off the beast mid-flight? No way. Scoot forward."

Lee shrugged, but I could tell from the set of his mouth that the idea had indeed crossed his mind. "Have it your way."

I swung up onto the pegasus myself, leaving plenty of space between us, and Destin swung up behind me, grabbing my waist. Lee tapped the beast's sides with his heels, and we took off into a run.

"Unless you want a mouthful of dirt," Lee shouted over his shoulder. "I'd hold onto me."

As much as I hated the idea, he was right. I wrapped my arms around him, my hands spreading over his beveled chest plate. When Lee whistled, his beast leapt, and its massive wings lifted us into the air. We slid at gravity's mercy. My chest lined up with Lee's back, and sparks danced across my veins.

I peeked past the wings, watching as we left the earth, and a slow smile spread across my face. I'd missed flying. I glanced up at the moon starting its descent towards a new horizon, a new day.

Happy birthday to me.

CHAPTER 36

Before we hit the city, the alarm cut off cold. The smog was dissipating.

I'd never seen the city so clearly before: all the soot-coated brick and the crowded streets, every alley and mismatched roof. The constant hum of the factories had disappeared entirely, instead replaced by screams and thunder.

On the horizon, red lightning crackled through the sky. It was touching down along the walls and gates out in the bay.

I glanced back and saw that Destin's shock matched mine.

Legend dove, our trajectory aligning with the town square. As we landed, I noticed the bell tower had been abandoned too. Bodies were scattered across the cobblestone, most dead, though some only severely injured. The sounds of battle roared nearby, all the way down into the narrow streets leading to the ports.

A faint cacophony of clicking hit me, raising the hair on my arms.

The rebels had taken to the streets to fight. In fact, it looked like every well-abled citizen had, but the bodies strewn about told me they were dying as quickly as they jumped in.

The moment we were on solid ground, Destin slid off Legend, his body shaking. He closed his eyes and bent at the waist, his fingers digging into his knees. Lee chuckled at him. I was tempted to shove him off the horse, but I settled for flicking his ear as I slid down. He laughed even harder.

Destin straightened, his eyes traveling across the gore. "Goddess have mercy on us all."

"I don't see Her fighting for us today," I said. "And neither will you."

His eyes flashed, mirroring the storm clouds above us. "You can't keep doing this to me, Sia. I want to fight with you."

If he fought, he would die. I'd never been so instinctually sure of anything before.

"Someone needs to stay and help the injured," I said. "Carry as many as you can to the herbalist shop across from the flower market. Tell the woman there I sent you. She'll know what to do."

"Legend can help transport," Lee added, clapping his horse on the neck before heading off toward the echoes of battle up ahead.

Legend huffed, turning to stare at Destin with one black eye. Destin grimaced at it. "You'd think the magical flying creature could transport them itself. I should be with you, fighting. *On the ground.*"

"Think of Erlene," I whispered.

He was seething at the reminder but nodded all the same. When I turned to join Lee at the mouth of the nearest bloodied intersection, he caught my wrist and pulled me close enough that I felt his exhale on my lips. "Come back to me."

Maybe, if I were a mortal, the words would have endeared him to me, but I knew what I was. Spirit made flesh. An immortal with rage and teeth. Human in all the ways that hurt myself, divine in all the ways that hurt others. I also knew what I wasn't. I wasn't a possession to be returned to him. I would never be his wife.

I'd never felt like I belonged to anyone, and this moment wasn't any different. I didn't know how this day was going to end. I didn't know if this was my last chance at goodbye. If it was, I wanted it to mean something…if only to him.

I pressed my mouth to his, a kiss too broken and false to last.

Then, I followed Lee down the street, between the sidewalks covered in death and the dying, and I didn't look back.

WE JOINED the mortals already fighting in the streets. The night grew even colder, the blood of the city freezing under my feet as we pushed to the front lines.

Where the serpents went silver and flawless in the ocean, the sutilis had festered. Or maybe they'd always looked like this: imbalanced and spoiling and utterly bizarre. I saw stitches more than the limbs, individual pieces more than the whole. They wore smiles and advanced with jerky movements, their glowing blades spinning wildly in their hands.

An inhuman clicking invaded the air, the sound surging and crashing upon us with each new wave of sutilis that poured into the street.

Lee's eyes scanned the swarm, steam puffing from his mouth.

The humans were doing their best to push the sutilis back to the bay, working in millimeters and inches. I was impressed they managed even that much. It was thirteen blocks to the ocean, but at this rate, the sutilis would exhaust the city before morning.

This was a futile war. Even if we pushed them back into the ocean, they'd come back the next night, and the next, and the next. We needed a more permanent solution, one I would have to think of later.

I jumped in and swiped at a sutilis, lopping off its head. A low creak replaced the clicking, and then it fell apart. After the first couple, I realized that these creatures were like the seraph and didn't need to be pierced through the sacral chakra. Another sutilis suddenly appeared on my right when I was engaged with another, bringing its blade down to sever my extended arm. Lee was there in an instant. He intercepted, driving his sword into the creature's stomach, ripping upward until the sutilis split in half. I didn't have time to thank him, though I felt the words raze through my body. From that point on, he settled permanently at my side.

We became a driving force.

Inches turned to feet, turned to yards, turned to blocks. Decrepit limbs scattered around us. My cloak was lost in a flurry of steel and claws as black blood soaked my dress. Several humans, rebels and citizens, died; we were unable to save them. At the end of the street we were on, the path opened up to three more. Guided by rebels, mortal troops split to either side of the perpendicular street as Lee and I continued forward.

Five blocks remained.

With just the two of us, it took ages to eat up the next two blocks. They were rushing us, overwhelming us. Lee roared in frustration and upped his pace, hurrying his movements. Each slice was unbearably perfect, like silken death. "What are you waiting for?" Lee screamed at me. "Let go, Sabrina."

My brow furrowed. I spun, driving my dagger into a sutilis's heart and kicking it backward as I wrenched the blade out. "Let go of what?"

"Your flame."

I ducked under another sutilis blade, processing his words as I swept the monster's feet and ripped its throat open. I didn't understand how he knew, my flower market stranger, this man with the ability to soothe anything in his path. Maybe he'd assumed, as most did, that my magic stemmed from the Fenix.

He knew who I was, after all. Princess of the floating city. A Princess of the Fenix spirit.

I wished it was that simple. I wished that I carried flames of warmth and light, to a certain measure and not beyond. My life would have been easier if I inherited that flame. Instead, I was the flint rather than the spark, free and sharp and flammable, as dark and unknowable as the night. I shook my head. "I can't."

"What do you mean you *can't?*" His eyes sliced into me. I couldn't bear it, his judgment, his irritation. It didn't make sense to him, but how could I explain?

We cleared another block before I finally admitted, "I'll burn everything. I-I can't control it. I'll ruin the entire city if I let it out." *The way I ruin everything.*

His returning growl bounced off the alley walls as Lee decapitated a sutilis and faced me long enough to say, "Then let it burn. That little girl at Gwaith needs you. *I* need you."

All the homes, all these people. The clang of steel twined with our gasping breaths. The sea water dripping off the sutilis froze as they approached, their bodies moving with less precision as the chill deepened. My lungs burned in the sharp air. Some of the sutilis were freezing solid, and Lee's longsword promptly shattered their limbs. My body started pulsing. As we cleared another block, I yearned for more. Darkness radiated around the hilts of my daggers, and I felt the metal soften under my touch. There was blood pooling on my tongue from how hard I tried to swallow the magic down.

Away, away, it begged. *Let me become you.*

Lee's voice returned to me through the black blood and violence. "I promise you, Sia, everything will be fine. Trust yourself. Trust *me*." There were those words again, spreading like nails across my neck.

My dark heat rose to the surface. I sheathed my daggers before they melted in my palms. When the next wave of sutilis arrived, I met them with a burst of black fire. It radiated through the decaying flesh, debilitating a dozen in the blink of an eye. Lee fell back, blinking through the wave of warmth that washed over him. He didn't react to my strange flame; he only nodded and said, "Good. Keep going."

I took the lead. My fire razed the cobblestone, hitting and skittering over the brick walls. Lee learned the rhythm of my violent dance, bursting forward to join the bloodshed with his sword and slipping back as I sent my flames out.

As we neared the bay, my flames whipped even more wildly. There was so much more inside me, just waiting to be set free.

There were more obstacles here, crates stamped *hazardous materials*. It was just my luck, or perhaps the Goddess's cruel humor, to ensure gunpowder had arrived yesterday. At that moment, an especially dense troop of sutilis poured in from the opening of the ports, and I flung my power at them. One of my flames spun wide, landing on a crate. I tried to reel it back in, but my body was vibrating – I couldn't close the lid on my magic. We were about to be blown away, and it would be my fault.

I opened my mouth to warn Lee, but as quickly as the flame caught, it snuffed out again. I watched as blue-tinted frost spread over the scorch marks.

Lee sidled closer to me. Without tearing his eyes from the fray, without skipping a beat, he said, "Focus on where you want the power to go and keep your eyes forward. Sight serves as your guide. Don't let the fear distract you."

I listened to his instruction, willing my eyes to focus on the incoming wave. I blocked out the crates, pretended they didn't exist. My next slash of magic hit true, and I could hardly believe how *good* it felt.

"Yes, that's better." Lee surged forward to cut down a flaming sutilis. Then, he looked over his shoulder and nodded. "Again."

I did. Again and again, I threw my flames until the sutilis thinned enough that we could see the ports beyond them. The streets merged, and we caught up with the humans as we entered the ports as one. I quickly swallowed my flames, not wanting to alert the rebels to them.

Lee abruptly grabbed me by the arm and dragged us behind a wall of crates. There was barely enough room to stand chest-to-chest back here, but he shoved us farther between them.

"What are you doing?" I protested.

Lee's hand tightened on my elbow as he finally paused, his eyes scouring my face. "Just take a moment. Are you feeling sick at all?"

I shook my head, alarmed by the gentleness in his voice.

"Tired?"

I considered the heat rolling through my body, the ache of my limbs and the lightness of my head. Sweat coated me everywhere, but I'd never felt so exhilarated in my life.

When I didn't reply right away, Lee smiled, "There's so much more in you, isn't there? I can practically taste it."

All I could see in my head was the fire, the ashes of this city underneath my feet. "Please, I—" *Can't.*

Before the word even left my mouth, Lee gripped my shoulders. "Don't be afraid," he said fiercely. "You can do anything."

I took a ragged breath.

"And if by some fluke you can't," he added, "we'll find another way."

There was something about him, something about his presence, that gave me peace and strength like I'd never felt before. Was that his magic, or was it him? Was it what he was to me, the friendship we'd created out of thin air? I didn't know, but right now, I was feeling incredibly grateful for it.

"Okay," I breathed.

Lee nodded at the other end of the narrow space between the crates and the brick wall, grimacing as the scar on his neck pulled taut. I felt a twinge echo deep in my spine. "Let's burn through the other side of the port. That way, you don't have to dodge citizens."

I was hardly aware of myself as my hand raised, my fingers brushing against the mangled tissues of his neck. He flinched and snatched my hand up immediately, his blue eyes wide.

"Where did you get that?" I whispered. "It still hurts you, doesn't it?"

He smiled grimly. "That's a question you can ask me when we're done with this bloodshed."

Lee dropped my hand and shuffled away, and I followed him, wrinkling my nose at the sulfur wafting off the crates. He peeked around the corner and held up a finger, as if that would be enough to keep me behind him. I pushed my way in front of him to look for myself.

The bay was lit up from the endless red lightning. It swirled above the port, above the piers, rattling the earth with its accompanying thunder.

Lee's breath audibly caught. "*What the fuck?*"

I followed his gaze, squinting at the figure standing atop a stack of crates near the water's edge, its copper wings and brown hair whipping back in the ocean breeze. "Is that—"

"An Impundulu," he confirmed. "What's it doing so far from the mountains?"

Impundulu was a lesser-seen group of seraphim, sustained on blood and the energy they drew from the earth. Statues often depicted them as being struck by lightning, because their relationship with the world empowered them to manipulate electrical charges. On the flip side, they were susceptible to all forms of power, spells and charms included. That was why they lived in the mountains, surrounded by nature and isolated from magic unlike their own. It was too dangerous for them to integrate with society.

I was reminded of the massacred wolves, the way they'd been led into the smog. The sutilis must have a way to draw in the supernatural.

"Look at her eyes," I muttered.

The Impundulu's eyes flashed with a crimson glow, in tune with the flashes of lightning across the sky. "I think she's tampering with the water gate, letting more of them in. Look at the sutilis."

He hummed. "They're guarding her. Her wings are drooping. She's likely not in control of her body." It was rare, but not unheard of. That was why witches were barred from the mountains. Impundulu feared their influence.

I nodded. "But if we get close enough …"

"We could try to snap her out of it," Lee finished with a smirk. "Let's go."

We launched away from the crates, paving a path straight to the Impundulu. What felt like a hundred sutilis died between us and the Impundulu, and blood made its way into my mouth, my nose, my eyes. The rot of the sutilis covered me.

When we finally reached the tower of crates bolstering the seraphim, Lee started climbing. "Hold them back," he yelled over his shoulder. "I only need a minute."

I put my back to the crates, my head spinning as I scanned the cobblestone to either side of me, my dark fire licking everything in my line of sight. Then, they came. Each wave of sutilis that appeared fell swiftly at my feet. The more power I expended, the more I felt simmering beneath the surface.

The knuckles along my spine strained against my skin, scraping tissues and grinding bone. Pain rippled up my neck and I groaned softly, darkness spewing out of my very pores.

My wings wanted out.

I knew, if I let them, my real power would be released, and it terrified me. I wasn't prepared for that.

I glanced back to mark Lee's progress: he was hefting himself onto the crate below the Impundulu. A clicking echoed to my left, and I turned to scorch another swathe of sutilis rounding the pyramid of crates.

"Look at me," I heard Lee say. "Push them out of your head."

When I looked up again, I saw the Impundulu pivot. Her eyes burned with electric light. That light flared as she lifted a hand, and the red lightning above us slivered toward her... toward *Lee*. She was going to electrocute him.

Lee turned his face to the sky, seeing the same thing I did, and he shook his head. He snapped his fingers, and the sky went dark.

A storm cloud billowed above us. The lightning endured there, retreating through the darkness as the Impundulu sagged forward. In one, smooth motion, Lee crouched so her body collapsed over his shoulder. Another wave of sutilis turned the corner, and as Lee leapt off the crates and landed beside me, I set fire to a stamped crate.

"Back to the alley," I shouted.

I shoved Lee and the Impundulu in front of me, and we ran for it.

The crate exploded behind us, triggering several more explosions. Heat kissed my back, hotter than I expected. Okay, so maybe I'd underestimated the flammability of the shipments. I bit my cheek, hoping the pain would offer some clarity, some control over the flames, but when I glanced back, I realized they'd moved beyond my power.

The fire wasn't black anymore. It wasn't *mine*.

"Goddess protect us," I whispered.

Lee threw an arm toward the red flames.

Before my eyes, the fire guttered and dwindled to nothing as blue frost smothered the remaining crates. As I returned my attention to Lee and the road looming before us, it hit me: Lee had been blessed with the Halcyon's most treasured magic. *Hoarfrost*. I couldn't believe it. Why would someone who inherited magic like that choose to be a spy, choose to put away his wings and knee-cap his power? I added it to my list of questions to ask him when this was over.

"We'll take her to the herbalist," I said breathlessly. "She should know of something to ward off the sutilis' influence."

Lee nodded as we entered the alleyway. I glanced back one last time to survey the ports, the explosions no more than a blackened memory, when I heard Lee roar, *"On your left!"*

I spun.

A massive sutilis lumbered toward us, close enough to smell the sea water and chemical compounds oozing out of its skin. It was not humanoid like the others; it was barely a creature at all, hundreds of limbs stitched onto a mass of fat and excess skin. It turned a dozen seeping, deflated eyes on Lee and the Impundulu. The signature clicking started up, a disembodied chant that echoed off the alley from a handful of directions.

It surged for us, the body stretching and slithering like a centipede. I reacted out of instinct, raising both hands to the street as power ripped from my veins.

My vision shook with amber light.

A snap split through my ribs, my wings straining for freedom. I felt the edge of them break skin, felt the blood drip down my back, but I managed to keep them contained as I funneled the pain into my flame and screamed.

I went blind for half a second, seeing into a place of light and stars and music. I blinked, pushing the flames away, and returned to the city.

I returned to a street full of ash.

"Utterly beautiful," Lee said, and his knuckles brushed mine as he led the way into the smoldering street. "Who the hell made you think you could ruin anything?"

CHAPTER 37

I held the shop door open for Lee, helping him maneuver the Impundulu's wings through the door frame.

The shop had tripled in size since the last time I was here. Several cots were set up along the walls, and a fire pit roared in the center of the room with a cauldron simmering above it. Logically, it shouldn't be possible. The building itself took up less than a yard of sidewalk and was crowded on either side by other shops, but I knew as well as anyone that magic worked beyond the scope of probability. Time and space could be manipulated, and they often were.

I smiled to myself. *I knew it.* She *was* a witch.

If the room surprised Lee, he didn't show it. "We can't leave her in this room," he muttered under his breath. "With these people."

I followed his gaze. The injured were taking notice of us and the winged creature we carried, the rebels especially. "No, we can't," I agreed.

Footsteps echoed from the back of the shop, above the crackling flames and pained moans. The herbalist burst through the curtain behind the counter, strung crystals chiming to announce her presence. She wasn't nearly as old as she had appeared to be when we first met. Her hair had lightened, turned from dark gray to a muddy blonde, all her wrinkles gone.

Her eyes locked with mine as she rounded the counter. "I have a bone to pick with you, missy. Would you like to explain why you've turned my shop into a—" Her green eyes drifted to Lee and the Impundulu over his shoulder, and she halted. "Oh, gods."

I cleared my throat. "A more private room, perhaps?"

She scanned the room behind me with flighty eyes and quickly waved us through the curtain. Even this area had expanded. She led us down a long hallway to a door at the end, ushering us into an immaculately decorated bedroom, complete with finely-woven rugs and a four-poster bed. "There." She gestured toward the bed before turning and locking the door.

Lee deposited the Impundulu on the silk bedspread, and I came behind him to tuck the bronze wings beneath the woman for her own comfort. She didn't need to wake up in any more pain than she already would. As I did that, I informed the witch of what we'd seen, what we suspected, and what we needed from her.

Quietly, she listened. Then, she said, "I'll do what I can. There are no guarantees with otherworldly magic, but I know how to contain her if it doesn't work. All spells have an expiration, so she should come to eventually."

"At least there's that." I blew out a low breath.

Lee leaned toward me and said, "We should get back to the ports. The sun isn't rising anytime soon, and who knows how many more made it through the gates."

I nodded, aiming for the door.

The witch stopped me with a firm hand. "I expect a handsome payment for my trouble."

"You'll have it," I assured her. I covered her thin fingers with mine and squeezed. "Thank you for all of this. Truly."

She blinked a few times, her eyes studying me intensely before she said, "My name is Peppi." Rare. It was so very rare for a witch to gift their name.

I smiled. "It's a pleasure to meet you."

Peppi straightened to her full height and released me like one might toss away a viper, though a small curve teased her lips as she pushed us out of the door.

We emerged in the same hallway, but now it was lined on both sides with doors identical to the one we just exited. A safety measure. If anyone from the front room came snooping, there was no telling what they'd find in the doors leading up to the right one. It was possible that the room might even move as well, never to be discovered, like a game of switching cups.

As we walked down the hall, my thoughts churned. I searched my mind for a solution. After tonight, the sutilis would no longer have the advantage of surprise, but judging from the death they'd caused so far, they didn't exactly need it.

The human lands were not equipped for war. They were not ready for this, and the only beings with experience in dealing with the sutilis did not care to defend those below them.

I wondered if my father knew of any of this, if he'd even bothered to look past his desire to bring me home to see what was happening to my mother's city. If he knew, would he have done something about it? Or would he simply allow this place to die like she had?

Lee's arm brushed mine.

I peered up at the Halcyon beside me, the one I'd gotten to know and who had drawn out a control of my magic I didn't know existed within myself. I had been furious when I realized who he was. It had felt like a betrayal. My feelings were shifting now, as easily as the moon changed shape from one night to the next. Who he was felt less like a betrayal, and more like a gift.

This relationship could change things.

My life back home and my engagement to the Halcyon prince might not be so insufferable if I had someone like him. Someone to talk to, who would listen to me. Someone who could make me laugh, the way Lee had all these months with his notes. Would he stay beside me, if I asked? Would he stay?

Lee caught my gaze before I could look away. "What are you thinking?"

We passed through the curtain to the front room, and I said, "When the sun rises, the sutilis will still be in the bay. Sooner or later, they're going to take the city."

"They'll try." He touched my arm. "But we can—" For whatever reason, he trailed off, his expression torn.

"What? Do you have an idea?" I urged.

"Promise me something first," he murmured.

I recoiled from those words. It was one thing to make a promise on my own, and another thing entirely to be coaxed into one.

Lee slid a hand around my back, holding me loosely. "Promise that you won't hate me. Promise that we'll be friends after this, no matter what."

I wanted to know what he knew, and all the answers that seemed to fill him up like air filled my lungs. A spy's secrets. The way he helped me tonight…no one had ever done that for me before. He'd known exactly what I needed. Unfortunately, the fact of the matter was that I didn't understand him well enough to surrender anything of myself.

"Let me go." I pushed out of his arms.

I burst out of the shop's front door, hesitating on the threshold when I heard wings descending. Legend landed in the middle of the street, dancing across the cobblestone with Destin and another human slung across his back.

Before I could even blink, a massive lump of flesh plowed into them.

My body shut down. I couldn't process it. I watched, frozen to the step beneath my feet, as the pegasus attempted to take to the sky, and the sutilis reached out with several hands and broke one of the beast's wings. Then, Legend was thrown, flipping over and over down the cobblestone street.

Lee was already pushing past me, rushing at it, his sword driving into the monster's body. I didn't know what to do. I couldn't breathe. *Destin* had been on Legend's back.

A chill razed my spine. *Move.*

I burst into motion, running to where Legend had been thrown. One black eye looked up at the moon, unblinking. A sob of both relief and despair escaped my mouth when I realized the body Legend was lying on was the injured human they'd been transporting.

Cries drew my attention to the sidewalk a few feet away. Destin was lying there, miraculously alive, his body intact but writhing in pain. I ran to him, ignoring his protests as I gathered him into my arms. His blood coursed over my arms as we stood.

Lee suddenly appeared in my peripheral, sinking to his knees. "Legend," he breathed.

The beast was already gone, but Lee pressed a kiss to its cheek anyway. He swept long strokes over Legend's neck and mane. With a swift motion, he plucked a feather from the pegasus' wing and tucked it behind his tunic's chest plate.

That was when it hit me. *The feathers.* Like the pansies, they were keepers of memory. He kept them close because they once belonged to those he cared about.

Lee stood, turned on his heel, and stalked back into the on-going battle.

I looked back down at the man in my arms. Destin's eyes were glazed, the cut on his brow ripped open again and another wound gushing from the opposite side of his head. I screamed for Peppi as I lugged him toward her door. She was waiting for us, the way she always seemed to be waiting.

All I said to her was, "Give him my tears," before returning to the street. I found Lee winding his way through the street, away from the crowd of sutilis bearing down on the mortals. I followed, dodging steel, and caught his arm at the mouth of an alley.

"Where are you going?"

He wrenched his arm out of my grip. "I can't let it get away."

Then, he took off. As I ran after him, I realized our footsteps weren't the only ones echoing off the brick walls. Past Lee, I glimpsed a shadow turning the corner up ahead. A sutilis. Lee was leaving me behind. Every muscle in his back flexed and coiled, driving him forward with a stamina I could only dream of.

"Why are we chasing one sutilis when there's a dozen behind us?" I demanded.

His growl drifted back to me. "This is the one from the beach."

"What?" I gasped out. My lungs tightened, burning as I flung myself around the corner and realized he was now yards ahead of me.

The alley opened to the ports, and as we emerged, we were swallowed instantly by a chorus of clicking and human cries. I swam through the warfare, fighting against the current of bodies, leaping over corpses, tracking Lee through it all. There seemed to be as many deaths as there were stars in the sky. Too many.

Lightning had overtaken the sky.

Gray clouds flashed red, and all sense of order to the

storm was gone. The electric currents cut into the ocean, stirring up massive blasts that burrowed through the bay like worms displacing dirt. The lightning struck hard and loud, and thunder rumbled under my feet as I chased Lee into enemy lines.

I unsheathed my daggers and sliced through their ranks. The battle blurred around me, all rot and blood and stolen teeth.

Until lightning struck at my feet.

I jumped back in time to avoid it, but the charge echoed over my skin. Continuing forward, I realized the red light was brighter here, as if coagulating above the sutilis. Another strike touched down on my right, the electricity skittering over the ground and rattling up a nearby sutilis. The light burned through the monster's body, and as it fell, the lightning latched onto the blade it held, turning the blue glow red.

Lightning struck on my other side, sending shocks toward me, tickling my ankles. Again, it happened, and again.

The hair all over my body stood on end as lightning ripped through the soldier in front of me, his blade transferring the shock into my dagger and into my hand. I dropped my blade with a cry, shaking out my wrist as I spun and leapt over the burned corpse. His blade was still glowing on the cobblestone. It was then I realized what was happening.

The lightning was targeting sutilis blades. Either nature was drawn to it, or the magic in the sky was acting on its own, fighting back against what had tried to manipulate it.

I glanced at my hip, where I stowed the sutilis blade from Lee's tent. The sky must sense the magic in their weapons. Right now, it saw me as a threat.

I pulled the blade from my belt and the rumble of thunder instantly intensified beneath me. Static fizzled through my hair as I slammed the blade into a sutilis and spun away in time to evade the crack of lightning that cleaved the air and siphoned into the other-worldly metal. Burning flesh filled my nostrils as I left the blade behind.

The lightning ignored me after that, hitting troops of sutilis around me as I searched for Lee. My bones cried out from the pressure building inside me, but I held back my flames, my wings. *I can't do this without him.*

His words echoed in my head. *You can do anything.*

So maybe I didn't *want* to do it without him. A loss settled in my bones the farther he ran from me, hollowing my limbs and raking poison through my veins. I needed to be beside him, needed to know he was safe.

I finally caught a glimpse of him at the edge of the port.

The sutilis Lee was in pursuit of jumped onto the building, digging its claws in to scale the brick. Lee swerved, pulling himself onto a ladder leading to the roof.

For whatever reason, Lee had to chase this particular sutilis, had to capture it. This was important to him. I guess I did want to be his friend, because that was enough for me to sheathe my dagger and leap for the ladder. Pulling myself into the metal chute, I climbed the rungs as fast as I could.

Lee and the sutilis made it onto the roof within seconds.

Maybe it had been a mistake to chase after him, to follow when he didn't ask me to, but all I could think about was the way he'd looked at Legend in the street, the white feathers hanging from his hip, the truth that felt so close, I could taste it.

Promise we'll be friends, no matter what.

What kind of lonely soul would ask for that? I imagined only one like me.

Halfway up the ladder, I heard a woman scream, and I glanced back to scan the ports. From this angle, I saw everything: the legions of sutilis rising from the bay, the maze of the crates, and every human in it fighting for their city. I saw the sutilis who had cornered a woman wielding a meat cleaver. I could almost hear their synchronized clicking from up here, a dozen rotting reapers closing in for the kill. Someone had to do something. *I* had to do something.

A shimmering blanket coated my mind, cool and bright as drifting snow. *Then do it.*

Black sparks rolled between my fingertips. My focus locked onto the sutilis directly in front of the woman, a blade spinning in its hand.

I let the sparks go.

A ball of darkness erupted from my hand and speared through the air. No wayward sparks. No mistakes. It razed through the swarm gathered in front of the woman, setting fire to all of them at once. She sank her meat cleaver into the ring leader's neck, and death sprayed.

I could hear Lee's voice in my head. *Magnificent. Do it again.*

I swallowed the thrill in my throat and continued climbing, blasting the largest troops I could pinpoint. The ladder grew hot beneath my palms, and I climbed even faster. Too soon, the sutilis realized where the aerial flames were coming from, and dozens ran for the ladder. Then, I was hurtling wave after wave of flame down the chute beneath me. The ladder started melting, but they didn't stop, even as the skin and tissue of their hands and faces burnt away from the molten metal. I wondered if they would keep coming even as skeletons, if their magic was that powerful.

A ripple of blinding light passed through my mind. *They may be powerful, but so are you.*

The bottom half of the ladder finally snapped away, the loss vibrating up the chute. Most of the swarm dropped with it. Only a few sutilis held on to the building itself, and I sent flames skittering down after them. I didn't wait to see if they met their targets before ascending the final rungs, finding the roof stretching out before me empty.

Several rooftops away, I spotted him.

Lee swung his sword against the sutilis, keeping the creature from escaping off the edge of the rooftop bordering the bay. If the monster made it into the water, there would be no tracking it.

I leapt from rooftop to rooftop as it began to snow, thick flakes clinging to the blood on my dress. I slipped once on a slanted roof, on the clay shingles coated in frost, but I caught myself and kept running. Lee ducked under a swipe to his head before he shoved the sutilis back with a powerful kick to its chest. The creature slid across the flat roof, over the ice forming on the stone, and rolled to stand upright again, moving as if it had no spine.

My flower market stranger sauntered forward, his sword raised to deliver a final blow.

The sutilis shuddered, whatever bones it had under the surface beginning to shift. The monster's back opened up from behind, and bones jutted out and around, coated in blood and greenish mucus, curling forward to block Lee's sword. Then, the sutilis snapped forward and sliced Lee's stomach open.

My knees buckled as the echo of pain shot through my stomach, laying waste to my thoughts and nerves. I could barely see through the pain-induced haze. *What the fuck is happening to me?*

Lee heard me cry out and turned to look at me.

I crawled across the beveled roof. Trying to reach him. Trying to keep him. His hand clutched at the gouge in his tunic, the blood seeping past his fingers. I cast my flames out, trying to touch him, but I knew there would be no stopping this.

The sutilis drove its blade into his shoulder, and they tumbled over the edge of the roof. I felt all of it, the pain searing through my spine like the hottest brand. It shook me free. It ripped me open. His promise repeated in my head like the cruelest symphony, his voice so clear, it could have been whispered in my ear: *Everything will be fine. Trust me.*

I couldn't trust anyone; my life alone was evidence of that. I screamed loud enough to shatter the clay under my hands.

The material of my dress tore as my wings burst free.

I lifted my face, rising from my knees as the muscles of my back worked in unison to pull my wings inward. Twin peaks of ebony stretched on either side of me, the feathers ruffled and slick with my blood. I jumped and landed on the rooftop, perching on the edge to look down at the bay below.

A white feather drifted on the water. The new one from Lee's belt...

I flew down, staggering to a stop on the pier as my eyes scanned the waves. There was no sign he'd survived the fall, no air bubbles to suggest he might ever resurface. It wasn't fair – he shouldn't have died this way. He shouldn't have died *at all.*

I leaned down to retrieve the feather but pulled back as a sutilis suddenly broke the surface and grabbed at me. I palmed my daggers, backing up into the center of the pier.

Clicking sounded from behind me, and I spun to find three more sutilis rising out of the ocean, their frozen smiles trained on me. All the way down the length of the pier, they emerged. I spun in a tight circle, only to find they had me surrounded. Sure, I could take to the sky. That would be easy, but I didn't want to run anymore. I wanted to fight.

Heat flooded my body. Darkness flickered, whipping around my body in a whirlwind, enclosing me in a chrysalis of power and black flame as hoops of amber flickered to life around my head. With the release of my wings, I had access to a far greater well of power. I surrendered to it and detonated.

My mouth opened, but so much more than a scream came out.

It ripped through the synchronized clicking, stretching out in every direction, traveling across the surface of the bay, from the shore to the water gates. The water boiled and bloomed several shades darker – blood was so much thicker than water. The wooden panels of the pier broke apart beneath me until I hovered above the ocean by the beating of my wings alone.

I didn't stop burning until the bay went silent, until even the faintest clicking disappeared.

CHAPTER 38

Destin found me kneeling at the edge of the destroyed pier, staring out at the bay, which was now filled with guts and bobbing limbs. I'd barely recognized him as he pulled me to my feet. He was barely whole, beaten up and slow, but alive. I knew the city would be fishing corpses out of the water for weeks, sutilis and humans and serpents alike, and that was all I thought of as Destin left me to bargain for a horse to get us home: all the terrible things I was capable of.

Still, I drew myself out of my head long enough to return to Peppi's shop.

She was waiting for me at the back door when I arrived, her arms crossed and expression set like stone. After leading me into the hallway, she craned her neck to look beyond my wings. "Where is the other one who was with you?"

My chest squeezed, an ache pulsing around my heart, the pain that hadn't gone away since the moment that blade embedded in Lee's shoulder. I fought the memory with every ounce of my being, but it rose up anyway. His death was my fault. He wouldn't have been there if it wasn't for me. In the short time I'd known who he really was, I wasted it by pushing him away. A tear slipped down my cheek. I turned away, toward the door, trying to hide the dark essence streaking down my face.

Peppi stepped toward me, producing a handkerchief and swiping the tear on my face away. She studied the stain it left on the satin.

The witch didn't show any sign of surprise, only folded the material and returned it to her pocket with a satisfied smile before turning back to the bedroom door. It hadn't been a gesture of tenderness on her part, I suddenly realized. She took the tear because she knew what it was, what *I* was, and she'd wanted it for herself.

"Life will out," she said.

I frowned at the witchy sentiment as she unlocked the door. *Life will out.* In other, less witchy words: life goes on, and what is alive will triumph over tragedy. I saw it for what it was: just another way of saying *get over it.*

The Impundulu was awake already, her bronze wings stretched out in front of the headboard. Her skin was slightly paler than mine and freckled all over. "Thank the Goddess," the seraphim sat up straighter with a wince, "A familiar form. I was starting to worry no one would come around to explain what happened."

I smiled politely and perched on the bed beside her as she launched into an introduction.

Her name was Kori, and she was a second-generation noble belonging to the mountain range directly north of here. A couple years younger than me. A quiet talker. I smiled and nodded, letting her get the words out in her own time. I didn't breach the details of my own rank, but I noticed how her eyes caught on my wings. Fascination spilled out of her stare as she cataloged the size, the sheen, the color. I decided I would let her speculate.

She had a few fuzzy memories pertaining to the last couple days, but nothing substantial. One moment, she'd been flying over her family's estate, and the next, she'd been blinded and deafened to her own senses, drawn into the city by a compelling voice in her head, by a clicking that drowned out any self-awareness. "I remember summoning lightning at one point. It was all over me. My mind was screaming at me to stop, the lightning too, but my body kept calling it forth anyway." She rubbed her forehead, her face twisting. "A different voice broke through the haze and tried to bring me to the surface. Then…there's nothing." She paused, lifting her head to look at me. "Was that you?"

"No. The male who saved you, he…" I trailed off, glancing at the tapestry hanging on the wall.

"I see," Kori whispered, regret etched into her voice. "I'm sorry."

I shook my head vehemently. "It wasn't you, none of it. What happened to this city wasn't your fault, so don't let anyone make you think otherwise, today or any day that comes after. Do you understand?"

After a moment, she nodded.

I patted her hand. "Good. When you get home, spread the news of what happened. Inform your Queen. If the attack on this city is only the beginning, then we'll all need to be ready."

"I will."

"And leave soon," I said. "There are humans here who might try to find and harm you. Are you recovered enough to fly?"

A shade of pink flushed her cheeks. "I-I can attempt it." I could tell from the paleness of her lips, the starkness of her freckles, that she still wasn't well enough. The exhaustion of her power had likely starved her.

"How long has it been since you last fed?"

Her eyes widened, and she sat back a little, as if the mere mention of feeding had triggered her thirst. "It's been a while," she muttered. "I was headed out on a hunt when the sutilis captured my mind." Only the Impundulu seraphim fed on blood, life essences. Whatever world their winged spirit came from was one of sensitivity and intimacy. They were often artists, and passionate lovers.

I considered our options; there weren't many. "Then you should eat before you go, in case you run into some mortal temptation on the way home." I rolled up my sleeve.

"What are you doing?" Her voice trembled.

"I'm letting you feed from me. It's the best solution."

Kori shook her head. "You don't understand."

"I do," I countered. Impundulu fed on beasts of the forest and other members of their race. Feeding on anything or anyone else was considered a predatory act, and it was against our law. "You won't find any animals in this city, and I'm strong enough to stop you before you drain me. A human won't be so lucky."

She didn't seem comfortable with my offer, but she didn't reject it. She was too hungry to argue. I drew a dagger from my thigh to slice into my forearm but hesitated when I saw the rot and blood still coating it.

"It's okay," Kori murmured, scooting closer. "My teeth will do the work."

Her lips curled back, revealing a set of pointed teeth descending from her gums to cover the regular ones. The skin around her eyes thinned, and the blue veins bulged as she settled in beside me. Her wing brushed mine, in comfort and gratitude.

She gingerly took the wrist I offered her and lifted it to her mouth.

There was a sharp prickle where her teeth sank into my

inner arm, and then her soft lips suctioned to my skin. I hissed as she drew blood from my veins. It was a faint sensation, easy to ignore as I looked around the room for a distraction.

Only a few moments more, and her thirst should be satisfied.

I wondered if this pocket of space had always been here, or if Peppi was its creator. How much of this room, these priceless antiques, could have been inherited from the previous owner?

An ache pierced the back of my skull.

Glancing down at the Impundulu, I realized she was completely absorbed in her feeding, drinking deeper now. When I tugged my arm, her teeth sank deeper into my flesh, as if trying to hold me there. Her animalistic growl radiated through the room.

"That's enough," I said, attempting to shake her off.

Her teeth burrowed further, numbing the nerves in my fingers. I gasped. I tasted my own blood in the air, crackling with fire and fear. She was stronger than I expected, hungrier. I had to get her off before I panicked and set her mouth aflame.

Reaching up, I fisted her hair and grimaced as I pulled it roughly. "Enough."

Kori pulled back, a gasp splitting her mouth and releasing me from her teeth. She bit her lip, and the vivid veins around her eyes faded as she blinked the bloodlust away. She realized how close we were, how my hand was in her hair, and quickly disentangled us, scooting to the other end of the mattress. "I'm sorry. I've just never tasted anything like that before. I could feel your blood...*open* inside of me." Her fingers pulsed, opening and closing against her chest, trying to imitate the feeling, I imagined. Whatever that meant.

"It's fine." I stood from the bed and rolled my sleeve down

over the clotting bite mark, intending to leave her scrutiny behind.

But then she screamed.

Kori scrambled back until her wings slammed into the headboard. Her eyes were glowing, not with the red light her spirit carried, but with an amber tone that I recognized. It was like looking into a mirror; that was, if that mirror had a face contorted in terror and wings that were bronze instead of black.

"Get away from me," she screamed. "What have you done to me?"

I watched her, stunned.

Her eyes scoured the room, flicking from one corner to the next, as if seeing something beyond the furniture and art. She lifted her hands to her face, covering her eyes, fingernails digging in as if she might start clawing at any second. "Get away from me. Get them all away."

I staggered back in disbelief as the door to the room burst open behind me. "What's going on?" Peppi appeared beside me.

I shook my head. I had no fucking clue.

Red light started sloughing off the Impundulu in waves as thunder crackled outside. Goddess, could she summon it in here? Could it tear through the roof and into this pocket of magical space?

My concern was echoed in Peppi's face. She lurched forward, her hands stretched in front of her. White, earthen magic radiated from her palms, caressing the Impundulu, trying to ground her.

"Get her away from me," Kori cried.

"Go. I've got her," Peppi said over her shoulder. When I didn't immediately leave, she turned to look at me with distant green eyes. *"Get out of here."*

If there was one thing I knew, it was that a witch wasn't to be trifled with, even if she did trust me enough to give me her name. As I left the room and collapsed against the hallway wall, the door behind me disappeared. I would not be welcome back.

What *exactly* had my blood opened inside of her? What had the Impundulu seen?

As the sky lightened with the impending dawn, I scrubbed all the blood and guts off my body and changed out of the ripped dress. The only items that allowed room for my wings were the dress Lee had delivered to me and my thin nightclothes. I couldn't bring myself to wear the gown, to feel anything beautiful against my skin after what I'd faced and done in the city, so I walked through Gwaith House in a silk slip.

As I entered the foyer, my gaze caught on the mirror at the foot of the stairs.

The henna had burned away from the roots of my hair, leaving behind my natural black, cascading into the remnants of red at the ends. My collarbone was obscured by the bronze necklace. I had kept it there intentionally, my last defense against the truth.

I knew where I was going once the sun dawned on the horizon.

I didn't recognize the female in the mirror, especially with my wings out. The female in the reflection missed the raw quartz tub back home that was large enough to clean her feathers in. She missed the dangling jewels and intricately beaded dresses. She missed the dark pigment she used to wear on her eyes and mouth that always annoyed her father, but that she loved because they brought out the fiery amber of her eyes. She was nothing she had once admired about herself, because she had given it away in exchange for freedom.

What was freedom if I had to be alone in it?

Hours ago, I thought things might change for the better. I thought I could have my wings and power and someone on my side. Someone I could believe in. But that hope slipped through my fingers. It tumbled over the edge of a building and fell several stories to a watery death.

Lee's death was a devastation, but it didn't change this decision.

There'd be no more running, no more hiding. There was a way to hone my magic. I knew that for certain now. Even though Lee wasn't here to show me the rest, I could continue on my own. I could find a way to be myself back home. I could show my father that he had no reason to be ashamed of me.

Besides, if the human city fell, my family would be the first seraphim in the sutilis' path.

No one was going to advocate for these human lands like I could. No one in the hovering city was going to defend them. Refusing to face my father would hurt everyone.

I let the warmth of the roaring hearth envelop me as I crossed the threshold into the den. Destin wasn't here. The bedding on the couch had disappeared. The desk was cleared and clean, so I assumed that meant he'd moved back into the bedroom. Maybe he was sleeping there right now. He'd been in bad shape when we arrived back at Gwaith, even with the healing help of my tears.

I drifted over the red rug to the piano and slid onto the stool.

The ivory teeth blurred in my vision. I let my fingers kiss the polished bone and tried to recall that song, the one I'd heard in the city with Lee at my side as I turned an alley of rot to ash. My pinky pressed down on a key, one I thought might be close, and the note spun through the room. It wasn't quite right, but I doubted there was any instrument in this world that could imitate the music I had heard.

A floorboard creaked.

I twisted to see Destin leaning in the doorway, bruised and bare-chested. He'd taken some time to wash up as well. He was wearing cotton pants, but the button was undone between his hips, a trail of dark hair peeking through the panels and leading my mind farther south.

His eyes scanned the wings tucked in behind my head, then dropped to my face. "Can't sleep?"

"Something like that," I murmured. My fingers slid across the keys, falling into an old piece – the first one I'd learned for myself, once I realized I could enjoy music without the nagging of my piano instructor.

Destin pushed off the doorway.

I kept playing, my head bowed over the teeth and my eyes tracking every stretch of my hands. If I could disappear into the music, I'd let it take me to a world beyond hatred and fear, beyond these expectations and class systems and differences. I'd fall into a bit of precious sky and never return. But that was impossible.

He walked in a wide circle, skirting the piano and the edge of my wings to stand directly behind me. The warmth of his body washed over my back. As light as a breath of air, his fingertips caressed the rise of my left wing. A tingle rolled through the cartilage and into my spine, and I gasped, my hands stilling over the keys.

"Keep playing," he rumbled.

As my fingers returned to the song, he swept my hair to

the side and pressed a soft kiss to the back of my neck. I was better prepared this time when his fingers curled around the top of my wing and traced the rounded peak.

"Now," he said against my neck. "How do I get you to make that delicious little gasp again?" His fingers trailed to my neck, and the plates of my necklace shifted as he unclasped it. The metal piece dropped heavily into my lap.

His palms flattened on my shoulders, his long hands splaying around my neck…over my markings. As his calluses scraped, I couldn't help it: my back arched a little. It was stubbornness that kept me silent as his fingers slid over my skin, exploring every slight dip and curve of my bones. My head leaned back against his bare chest as his mouth moved to a sensitive spot just beneath my ear.

Destin hooked his thumbs under the straps of my slip and slowly slid them off the slope of my shoulders until it fell in a bunch around my waist.

"Look at you," he breathed.

One of his hands moved down my front, headed straight for the scarred skin over my heart. The music cut off as I caught Destin's wandering hand and pulled it away.

"Don't," I whispered. "Not there."

Common sense pled with me to tell him to go, but my desire quickly silenced it. I wanted him to stop. I wanted him to keep going. I wanted so many things, I couldn't put any of them into words.

Destin pulled his hand out of mine and cradled my neck. With his middle finger and thumb, he squeezed the uncertainty from my mind. His knuckle nudged my chin, guiding my face up until I met his gaze. "What about *here*?" He brushed his lips against mine, a kiss so soft and taunting that I stretched for more, but every inch I reached, he pulled back. Touching, arousing, but not enough to itch the desire blooming in my stomach.

With my eyes closed, it was easy to let Tova's perfume fill my nostrils, to pretend it was her kissing me, ripping my heart to shreds with every teasing stroke. It was both her and him. She was there, and part of this feeling between us was that we both knew she always would be.

I moaned against Destin's mouth.

He chuckled. "And here?" His other hand trailed down the center of my body, sweeping to the opposite side of my chest to flick my nipple. These hands had been the last to touch Tova. I could feel the ghost of her on his skin. Her name lingered on my tongue, the goodbye I had never been able to say. It was as if we were saying it together, in the only way we had left.

I gasped. "Yes."

Destin groaned, flicking the hardened tip again before rolling it roughly between his fingers. "Dearest guardian angel, do you have any idea what I plan to do to you?"

"Show me." There was no hesitation.

My body was the bow of a ship, tense and arcing off the piano bench. My legs shook as Destin's hand tightened on my neck, his roaming hand sliding down the planes of my stomach. As he bit my lower lip, his fingers slipped through my center. A shudder rocked me, and I realized I was whimpering as his fingers, wet with my arousal, centered on the apex of my thighs. My fingers clutched at the piano, wisps of dark power skittering across the ivory keys. I lost all sense of surrounding as his tongue twined with mine, as our moans seeped into my bloodstream, as his touch seduced me into oblivion. He didn't yield, didn't falter. When I tipped over the edge, my release was borderline painful.

Destin stroked me through the end, and once I was finished, his hand slid up to rest on my lower stomach. I opened my eyes. He was watching me with a small smile, and his thumb brushed the side of my neck before he started pulling away.

I caught his arm, twisting to face him, barely avoiding slapping him in the face with my wing. "What are you doing?"

He shrugged. "This was enough. You don't need to indulge me."

"*Indulge* you?" I blinked, an iron of rage piercing my gut. "I don't do unfair exchanges. Finish what you started."

"This isn't a transaction, Sia."

"Shut up and fuck me," I snarled. "*Now.*"

Destin's lips pursed. He wasn't going to, I could see it in his eyes.

"What is it?" I demanded. "You want me to beg? You want to see an angel on its knees?"

I stood, kicking the bench out of my way. My nightgown and necklace slid to the floor, and I was left naked, vulnerable. Then again, I'd always felt that way when we were together.

Before I could kneel, Destin grabbed my waist to still me. His eyes burned into mine. "Sia, we only do this if it's what *you* want." His chest expanded in a deep breath, then caught. He was...stupidly beautiful.

Looking at him, I decided I did want this. I wanted his strength and hardness wrapped around me, wanted the dusting of hair across his torso to scratch my chest. I still had my freedom for a little while longer, and I would do with it as I wished.

My hands dropped to his pants. "You're such an idiot sometimes."

His eyes fluttered as my hand slipped beneath the leather, and he groaned, pushing into my hand as his reticence melted away. I didn't have a chance to grip him fully before he shoved me against the piano. He lifted my ass and dropped me onto the keys, a discordant tone filling my ears as he discarded his pants and spread my legs open.

I wasn't thinking of Tova or anyone else… not anymore.

Destin filled me in one swift motion. I cried out, digging my nails into his neck.

"*Fuck yes*," he moaned. "You're so fucking *warm*."

A thrill ravaged my body. I hadn't set fire to anyone mid-coitus since my first time, but just to be safe, I removed my hands from his neck and braced them on either side of the piano's keyboard. The wood groaned between my fingers as his thrusts turned rough and wild.

Chaos resonated from the belly of the piano behind me, every pull of Destin's hands on my hips striking a new cacophony of sound.

The tension built, pushed higher with each drive into my body, his cock stretching muscles I hadn't listened to in months. I forgot how delicious it could be, how freeing and necessary to the deepest depths of my soul. In these moments, I could embrace every piece of myself.

Destin whispered formless filth in my ear, removing me from my body and my endless worries as the world seemed to crash down around us. He came with a rasp, thrusting hard enough to trigger my own release. Stars spun behind my eyes, and I collapsed against the piano, my head tilting back to rest on the lid. My flames crackled on either side of me, licking at the wooden frame of the keyboard, but I couldn't find the strength to pull them back in yet.

Destin saw the black fire and jerked into motion. "Oh, shit."

I giggled as he scrambled for his pants to smother the flames. When they were snuffed out, he raked a hand through his hair and glared at me. He said with the slightest hint of humor, "If I was that bad, you could have just hit me. You didn't need to set fire to the house."

"You weren't bad," I smirked at him, "for a mortal."

Destin lifted a brow.

Before I could blink, he seized me around the waist and carried me to the couch. As he threw me onto the cushions, he said, "What makes you think I'm anywhere close to done with you?" He knelt between my legs, gripping my knees to spread them again. His gaze drifted to my wetness, still gleaming with his release and my own as he bowed to taste me.

Icy panic seized my chest.

I sat up and kissed him, looping my arms around his neck and tangling my fingers in his hair. Deepening the kiss, I guided him up the length of my body. I hooked my legs around his back. Destin followed my direction willingly, shivering as he laid on top of me, chest-to-chest, skin-to-skin. He didn't even ask why…but, of course, no one did.

I ran my hands through his hair, across his sharp features and around to his shoulders. Light, sweet caresses.

He moaned, the sound rumbling against my tongue as I swept in and stole his air. My ankles locked at the small of his back. I kept our mouths fused as he hardened, driving the warmth between us on and on, pulling him closer, letting him in. This time wasn't at all like the last. He rolled into me with smooth, gentle thrusts, letting the pressure build slowly, letting my hips rock on their own. Impatience eventually had me lifting my hips as he drove forward, helping him hit just the right angle.

I reached above me and clutched at the arm of the couch as I came apart, sparing as much attention as I could on keeping my flames contained. The smell of burning polyester filled my nose anyway.

Destin caught my slumping hips and raised them to continue slamming into my body, and a quiet whimper fell from my lips.

"My beautiful angel," he said. He shuddered and stilled, spilling himself inside me again.

All the warmth slipped from my bones as he collapsed on

top of me, sinking us into the cushions. I opened my burning eyes, staring at the ceiling as he brushed wet kisses against my collarbone, along the markings that set me apart from this land. Apart from him.

I'd gotten what I desired, but it wasn't even close to enough.

CHAPTER 40

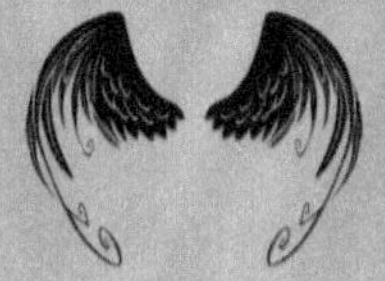

The tree branch swayed under my feet.

Pine needles prickled my wings and bare legs. I'd flown for miles in just the nightgown and my boots. At least the old cloak I found in the House offered some resistance to the bark digging into my back. I'd left Destin back in the den, sleeping on the couch. I couldn't tell him my plan. I stood near the peak of an elder tree, allowing the wind to lull me into a sense of numbness, my existence reduced to movement and instinct.

Wood groaned and shuddered, and I felt it. I was a creature of the forest again, one with the wild itself.

That was how I *had* to be to endure this.

Morning drew pastels across the sky, close enough to dawn now to see light spearing through the trees on the horizon, but my eyes were focused on the Baron's estate spread below me. I'd overheard the injured rebels talking as I left the herbalist shop. Everyone who survived the invasion were ordered to come back here, and I found the barracks easily, nestled into a corner of the Baron's property, half a mile behind the main house.

There were three sets of guards patrolling the fence, all pairs, walking fifteen minutes apart from each other.

After their second rotation, I plunged through the forest canopy and landed on a limb hanging over the fence. It was dimmer down here, where shadows merged and the sun had yet to touch the world. As the first set passed beneath my perch, I dropped down onto them. I knocked the first one out with a blow to his skull and slashed the other's throat open in one, smooth swipe.

I leapt back into the trees, traveling from branch to branch until I dropped down beside the barracks, where the second set of guards were just turning the corner of the building.

I sheathed my daggers and dispatched them both with quick, brutal blows to their skulls, dragging them around the back of the barracks.

One window of the barracks was facing the forest and had been left wide open. A fire blazed within, in the fireplace, illuminating a reading room with an elderly man snoring in a chair. I coaxed my heat to life. Inch by inch, I guided flames from the hearth onto the carpet using ebony sparks. Once the room had caught on its own, I lit the windowpane with a black flame. Then, every windowpane on the main level. I lit the single barracks door.

No way out. No mercy. Not today.

Before the last set of guards appeared in the distance, I ran up to the Baron's mansion, allowing my wings to flutter and lift me onto the roof once I was sure the flight would go undetected. I clung to a spire and looked back at the groaning elder pine hanging over the barracks, the one I'd set on fire before attacking. The bottom of the tree was fully alight now, crumbling as the bark turned to ash.

I blinked, and the trunk snapped.

The tree pitched forward and crashed into the barracks. Screaming erupted from the fire. Flames burst and spat, shifting from black to red, at last moving beyond my control.

Rebels strapped with weapons and leather erupted from the Baron's mansion – guards who'd been assigned to the house. They flagged down the remaining patrollers and chaos ensued as the rebels and several of the estate's staff worked to put out the fire.

Short of a miracle, I didn't see them succeeding.

I wound my way across the roof, peeking through windows as I passed: dim hallways and ballrooms, balconies that led to nothing and staircases embossed with iron and gold.

Reaching the front of the mansion, I peered down at the front steps.

I hadn't gone through the servants' entrance for a reason. By the time I killed my way to the staff, I knew most of them would flee.

Two rebels were stationed at the front door, both of whom I recognized: Brimley and that younger rebel who'd guarded the entrance to the stables the day I set the seraph free. They had hands on their weapons, alert. My heart skipped a beat as I imagined what I would have to do to them. I had to do this. I had to protect Destin and Erlene, because no one else was going to. I tried...I really tried not to care, but nothing was ever that simple for me.

I slammed into the earth, my wings splayed and daggers at the ready.

The rebels drew their weapons. Behind the mansion, the sun was finally cresting the horizon. Second by second, the world grew brighter. Yet, here I was, stuck in the shadow of the Baron's castle, alone in my duty and bearing their deaths on my shoulders.

Brimley's face contorted as he took in my form. "Reveal yourself, coward, and come bleed."

I tossed back my hood.

"You?" he breathed, his brown eyes bulging in recognition.

The word echoed in my body. Lee had said that to me once, too. His voice had been so gentle, filled with awe and warmth. Brimley said it so differently now. It was only a word. It shouldn't have the power to dredge up the past, to open a wound of what-ifs and should-have-beens, but I heard him again in my heart. *You.* A stranger who might have been a friend.

The young rebel laughed. "It looks like Lord Gwaith managed to deliver his replacement after all. I owe you a shiny gold piece, Brimley." He reached for an item on his hip and whipped out an extendable collar of ebony stone.

Brimley withdrew the same.

I felt for the glass ceiling of my power, the limit I'd teetered on since the pier. I had a measure of flame in my body, but the true power was in my wings. I'd kept them contained for so long because I knew it contained my magic, fettered it. In my wingless form, I'd been mustering sparks and flickering embers, and it had sufficed. My first set of wings were unleashed, and I'd been able to boil the bay, but now, that measure of power was exhausted. Embers wouldn't intimidate the men before me.

The single set of wings on my back had made them underestimate me.

I shattered through that ceiling on my power. Fresh jagged edges tore down my spine, the knuckles a little lower on my back ripping through muscle and sinew. I bit down on a cry, my blood coating my tongue as thickly as it coated the second set of wings curling into place behind me. Ash filled my mouth as I tapped into the secondary portion of power surging through my veins, enough to summon a wall of dark flame to surround the three of us.

"I'd drop your weapons if I were you," I said through gritted teeth.

The younger rebel did just that and fell back a step. Brimley's eyes flickered past me to the rest of the property.

"The guards you're looking for are already dead, as the rest will be soon enough."

Brimley held on to his weapons while the younger rebel started to tremble. I took a step toward them, raising my chin. "I will offer this mercy to you only once: drop your weapons, leave this place. Abandon the cause, and I'll let you live."

Confusion crossed the young rebel's face.

"Don't listen to her," Brimley spat.

"Why not? Would you like me to promise that no harm will come to you? Because I will, if you cease hunting my people. I'll promise to let you go, and I'll wish you a long, happy life."

He smiled grimly. "Your kind love to manipulate promises in any way that suits them."

"I'm lethal enough to kill you in a heartbeat. Why would I bother offering you a way out if I didn't mean it?"

"To toy with us," he retorted.

"Maybe," I said, looking between them. "Or maybe not."

Brimley showed no sign of relenting. The other rebel glanced at him, then at the flames surrounding them. He dropped the sword in his other hand and stepped to the side, toward the wall of darkness. I parted the flames in a section wide enough to let him through.

Brimley didn't move an inch as the young rebel leapt over the scorched earth. I let the flames close behind him. Then, there was only the old guard and I, staring at each other, the crackle of flame and hatred spilling into the air between us.

"There is a time and a place for honor, Brimley," I said softly. "Death in the Baron's service is not where you'll find it."

"I don't submit to angel scum," Brimley snarled, raising his sword.

"Then I'm sorry," I gripped my daggers a little tighter, "but you know too much."

Brimley's sword came down as I shot forward, clashing between my crossed blades. I brought my flames in to caress his back. It wasn't a fair fight, but I'd never promised one.

He let go of his sword, arcing in pain, and I sank a dagger into his gut.

"I'm sorry," I whispered. A tear slid down my cheek, fizzling to nothing under the assault of my heat before it had a chance to fall.

There was no shock in his eyes. He'd known he wouldn't stand a chance against me.

"A crying angel," Brimley mused, laughing wetly. He spat blood in my face. "Now I've truly seen it all."

I twisted the blade, slicing upward to nick an artery or two, accelerating his bleeding, beckoning a quick death.

"You can't kill all of us," he choked out, even as his eyes fluttered. "One of these days, we're going to send all your pretty cities crashing down. We will become your equals."

Another tear escaped down my face as I replied, "I hope that's true."

Doubt crossed his expression, and I ripped my dagger from his stomach. As he fell to his knees, he didn't look away from me, didn't blink. For what seemed like the thousandth time in my life, I witnessed the true treasure of humanity: their undying spirit.

The blood on my hands was wrought with their wonder. I was so sick of killing.

I almost let myself tremble with the weight of what I'd done and what I would need to do yet, but my wings twitched behind me. I reminded myself of who they were, what the rebels and the Baron would do to Gwaith if I didn't intercede, what they would do to the people I cared about. What the rebel cause would do to my mother's city.

Sacrifice a few for the hope of many.

Those words played like a psalm in my head as I walked through flickering darkness into the violence beyond...and I carried my flames with me.

CHAPTER 41

In the city, the factories had started up again. The smog wasn't as thick as usual, but there was enough of it to curl around Gwaith House by the time I returned. As I surpassed the clouds to land on the property, I saw that my time had finally run out.

Because my fucking father was here.

The landing radiated up into my legs. I stared at the front steps, where Destin had been bound and gagged in front of the main door. Four sentinels stood on the porch guarding him, their metallic gold wings tucked in tight.

Father's crown gleamed at me from the top of the stairs. In fact, everything about him defied the dreary surroundings. His short, auburn hair fluttered against the collar of his coat. An orange tunic peeked out from under his fox furs. Even his bronze skin glowed beneath the cloudy sky, one of the rare similarities between us.

He smiled and descended the stairs to meet me in the yard.

His two sets of golden wings flared out, a subtle sign of domination. They took up nearly the entire width of the staircase, and a primal part of me quivered, *thrummed*, as my own wings attempted to spread, too.

My eyes met Destin's, and he writhed in his restraints, glancing pointedly toward the left side of the House.

They'd found Erlene, too.

Spiro was coaxing small faerie statues to life in the side garden to aimlessly dance with and chase her. His four miniature black wings fluttered as he leapt into the air and cut her off before she could run too far in this direction. Erlene was wholly unaware of the danger on her doorstep, and for that – only that – I was grateful.

I turned my eyes on Father as he stepped onto even ground with me. "Let them go."

"Don't look at me like that, Sia." He brushed a bit of soot from his shoulder. "I'm simply ensuring you'll return home like you said you would."

"I already promised you I would do that."

Father gave me a knowing look. "*Today*, little love."

The name struck me in the gut, because there was affection in his voice. I knew it was the remnants of feeling he had for the only person he'd ever loved. His second wife. My mother. I was a child again, standing before the only portrait that existed of her that he'd hung in the throne room, staring at the thick sweeps of paint across the canvas. Darkest ebony for her hair, a bloom of pink for her dress, brown for her painfully ordinary eyes.

In the painting, she cradled a swollen belly.

That womb was the closest we ever came to meeting and sometimes, when I looked into her painted face, I imagined I could remember her heartbeat singing to mine. Other times, I thought I heard it when my father looked at me like this, like he truly cared.

Father added, "You've kept our guests waiting long

enough." The Halcyon. I dreaded having to face my betrothed, having to explain what happened to his spy.

I wondered if they would bother mourning him.

I shook the thought away. "Mortals aren't ammunition, Father." I glanced at Destin, who'd gone utterly still. His eyes flicked between the king and me. He was realizing who I was. This was the beginning of the end for us, I was sure of it.

"I'm aware of that." Father raised his arms to gesture at the property. "They'd be more of a problem for us if they were, wouldn't they?"

Silent tears slid down Destin's cheeks. Squeals echoed from the garden, accompanied by Spiro's gravelly laugh.

"Leave them out of this," I pleaded. "I'll go with you now, whatever you want."

Father's eyebrows shot up to his red hair. "Well, that was easier than I expected it to be, considering your recent antics."

"You know how much I love to shock you," I muttered, brushing past him to address the guards on either side of Destin. "Unbind him."

Father caught my arm. "Not so fast, little love. This man injured one of my guards when we arrived. He shot a bullet straight through Alldrich's wing." I threw a brief glance at the guard, who was staring at the back of Destin's head as if he wanted to punch it. A thin trickle of blood had dried on his gilded feathers.

"His wing looks fine to me."

Alldrich's glare shifted to me. "It *hurt*."

Father held up a hand. "We can afford a minute to teach your friend how to welcome a king into his home, and what to expect when he doesn't comply."

Orange flames sparked in Father's hand, wrapping around his fingers like swimming, molten glass. It dawned on me what he intended to do. I'd seen it happen once or twice before, whenever a mortal tried to breach the city or when a betrayal occurred among our ranks. Father was a good king, but only because he showed kindness to those who earned it and brutality to those who earned the opposite.

He was going to leave his mark on Destin, on this House, the same way I'd left my mark on Felicity. I learned it from him, after all.

Flames burst from me before I made the conscious decision to do so.

My third set of wings, small and delicate and sacred, which so often remained hidden under my last set of ribs, ripped open. Blood coursed down my lower back, soaking the nightgown. My magic flared, the final well of my power rising to meet me.

"You're not going to touch him. So help me, Father, if you do, I will return the favor." Black flames swam around the length of my forearm.

As expected, Father didn't flinch, but his eyes flicked to the guards behind me, who were now watching us closely. Warmth enveloped me as Father summoned more of his flames, his sparks caressing mine as he locked us into a room of light, where no one could watch or listen in.

"Now is not the proper time to test your limits or your self-control," he said.

"I've tested enough to know I'm stronger than you. I always have been. That's why you treat me the way you do, why you've withheld training from me. You're afraid of me."

Everyone was so fucking afraid of me. All my life. So, I learned to be afraid of myself...but no longer.

"Little love, that's simply not true," he sighed. "No one has ever known what to do with you. You're too emotional and unpredictable. Look at you. You've just openly threatened your father, your King, over a *human*."

I knew it was true, as much as it hurt. Not about Destin, but the way the staff and trainers had looked at me when I was little, the way they'd avoided me. It hadn't mattered to them that I was a child. I was different, and not in the way my brother was.

My brother had these sacred wings, too. He was born of flesh and spirit the same as me. When my father came into his power as the sole heir of the Fenix, the *only* royal who'd survived the islands, he'd been instructed by our philosophers that our people needed a revival of power. It was the only way to make up for our loss of numbers. So, Father enacted the rite of sacrifice, marrying human women who would willingly die for children born with three sets of wings.

Kahem was born first, golden and perfect. Then I came along, and I was not. Father had always been ashamed of me for it.

"Human or not," I whispered. "He doesn't deserve to be punished for protecting his home."

Father's forehead creased as he considered my argument. Finally, he said, "We disagree on this matter, but I'll let the mortal go undisciplined, if that will make our flight home more pleasant. Will that make you happy?"

I chuckled dryly. "You stopped caring about my happiness a long time ago."

His frown deepened. He reached up, as if to comfort me somehow, but his hands fell away before he made contact. "I'm sorry you feel that way."

I released the grip on my power, surrendering, and Father dropped his flames as well.

"Call for the carriage," Father shouted to the guards. Then, he looked me up and down. "Sabrina, please tell me you have something more suitable to wear home."

I nodded, not bothering to meet his eyes – *anyone's* eyes – as I climbed the stairs to the front door. "I'll be ready in a moment. If the child hasn't been returned to her father by the time I get back downstairs, I'm going to break every single one of Spiro's fingers."

Father's voice followed me into the House. "Duly noted, dear."

TEN MINUTES LATER, I stood in the center of the room Lila had let me borrow, freshly scrubbed and in Lee's dress, staring at the phonograph. The dress was a weight, despite the charmed material. My quill danced between my fingers.

Lee's last note spun on the silent record.

It took longer than I imagined to pick it up for the final time. I simply wrote, *I could never hate you.* Then, I sent the message away to the pit of the bay.

The minute the note disappeared, a raging inferno of pain erupted in my chest. It was the ache of my scar, my compromised promise. Sweat broke out over my face as I doubled over, clenching the edge of the table in front of me to steady me. I fell to my knees anyway. I curled into myself, trying anything in an attempt to alleviate this horrendous pain. It squeezed my heart so tightly, I was sure the vessels were about to pop. I was sure I was about to bleed out.

Through gritted teeth, I moaned into the floor. *Please. Make it stop. Please.*

I had to return home. I had to meet my betrothed. There was no doubt in my mind now.

After a few eternities, the pain finally passed. I rocked my forehead against the cool floor as I came back to myself and slowly rose to my feet. Then, I walked to Erlene's room and left the phonograph and Tova's blue ribbon there, hoping they would bring her a fraction of the peace they gave to me here on this coast.

Destin had been released by the time I made it back to the stairs. He held Erlene in the foyer, watching as I descended. Sentinels waited at the bottom of the staircase, likely stationed there by my father to keep Destin from coming up after me while I changed.

I brushed past the guards and approached him.

There was no telling how he felt about what he'd seen, about what he now knew, and his face gave away nothing.

Erlene twisted in Destin's arms to look at me. "Sees," she gasped, her eyes bulging as she took in my wings. "You're *beautiful.*"

I gave her a weak smile. "Not as beautiful as you." I lifted a hand and gently bopped her nose with one finger.

Destin finally looked away from the sentinels and met my gaze, and a hint of gentleness filled his face. "You can't leave us," he whispered to me. "You promised Tova you would stay, for Erlene. If you leave, you break it."

"The bonds of that promise expired the moment she died," I admitted. "I've stayed here longer than I needed to, longer than I should have. I brought you two together. I did my part."

"I'd say you did more than your part, little love," my father said from the front door. I turned to glare at him, but he continued in a mockingly jovial voice. "You protected their city and burned a local resistance to the ground. You're practically a hero at this point. I hope they carve a statue."

Destin started. "You did what?" His eyes returned to me. His eyes scanned the speckles of blood I couldn't quite scrub from my wings. "What is he talking about, Sia?"

"I took care of the Baron," I said simply.

His jaw slackened. "There were hundreds of soldiers stationed at his estate." I saw the outrage in his eyes. The question he didn't dare ask: had I killed them all?

I steeled my spine and tried not to care that he held Erlene a little tighter, a little closer. "And they fell swiftly. The nightmare is over."

"Or maybe," he retorted under his breath, "it has only begun."

He wasn't looking me in the eye anymore. It was the reaction I deserved, but my heart still broke when I reached for Erlene to say goodbye and he stepped away. She began to cry, wiggling in Destin's arms, reaching for me. He didn't allow me to have her.

I should be proud of him for protecting her, for clinging to her like she was the only anchor in all the world. I just wish it wasn't *me* he felt she needed protecting from.

But then, that was the cost, wasn't it?

I folded my hands behind my back and flared my wings, catching Erlene's attention. Fat tears continued to roll down her cheeks, but she quieted enough to hear what I had to say. "Don't be afraid," I told her. "You have your Daddy now, don't you? Your Daddy will *never* leave you on your own. If he does, you'll get a visit from Auntie Sees to make it right."

Destin nodded, almost imperceptibly, taking another pointed step away from me. Erlene's crying intensified as I stalked out the front door.

A pegasi-drawn carriage waited at the bottom of the staircase. The blue beasts in front of it huffed, impatient to get moving. Alldrich greeted me with a snide smile as he opened the cab door for me, offering his hand to help me up the steps.

I ignored him and grasped the loading grip on my own, launching myself back into a past that had suffocated me so thoroughly. I wondered if this was how Lee felt when he drowned in the bloody bay.

CHAPTER 42

"*What have you done to your hair?*"

My existence stilled at the voice that spoke in the hollow of the carriage. I looked up at the magically-extended bench running beside me, leading to the crown prince of the Fenix who sat at the end of it.

Kahem lounged against the red cushions, his legs stretched out before him and his six golden wings behind. As usual, he'd forgone his crown, but his ears were covered in several thin golden hoops. He wore a billowing cotton shirt that gaped down the front of his chest, displaying as much of his markings as possible without going shirtless. His pants were tight tan leather.

I launched across the cabin and into his arms.

He squawked as I landed on him, his wings twitching as he re-settled himself on the bench and wrapped his arms around me. "Holy divine. You smell awful." Even as he said it, his arms squeezed me in a vicious hug.

"Apologies," I muttered. He smelled like citrus and cinnamon and *home*. "It's been a really difficult couple of days."

One hug, and I felt like a little sister again.

The cab shuddered as the others climbed in, and I leaned back enough to meet Kahem's dark golden eyes. They swam with glittering warmth, but I didn't dare point it out. He was trying hard not to let the tears spill over. I almost felt bad for making him miss me.

"What's your excuse?" I sneered, pinching his side. "Your hair is longer than mine right now." His auburn hair cascaded over one side of his shoulder and down his chest, tied with a single strap of leather.

Kahem had darker skin than I, a deep, warm brown he'd inherited from his mother, Father's first wife, the first willing sacrifice to the Fenix spirit in several generations.

I tugged on a flyaway near Kahem's temple and he threw me off his lap with a growl. As I landed beside him, I laughed. The joy I felt was *effortless*. Irritating my brother had always been that way. He made it so easy. Sliding backwards, I lifted my boots onto the bench, planting them within kicking distance.

Kahem eyed them. "Don't even think about it, Sia." He smoothed the white cotton of his shirt and sat up straighter.

"Still refuse to get dirty?" I crooned. "The girls back home must miss me dearly."

He flashed a vulgar gesture at me.

"I'll take that as confirmation. How *is* Elena?" I smiled, remembering the way she'd tasted. Stolen treats always tasted sweetest.

My brother sent a stream of radiant red flames to bite at my ankles, and I tossed my feet off the bench with a hiss. He smirked and, without looking at me, gently took my hand.

I was relieved he came.

Kahem rarely left the city with Father. It wasn't smart for both the ruler and the heir-apparent to travel in the same carriage, just in case enemies found out and tried to wipe out the crown in one foul swoop. Father must have known I would need Kahem, need this sense of comfort and normalcy. Maybe he wasn't as uncaring as I'd—

Something cool and smooth suddenly slid over the wrist Kahem held.

My brow furrowed as I looked down.

I glimpsed a flash of charcoal stone before the same sensation came from my other arm. I looked up to find Father cradling my other wrist. There was a bracelet wrapped around it.

"What the hell are you doing?" I ripped my hands away from them, lifting my hands to study the things.

The stone was engraved with runes and the purest gold. It was a feeble attempt at making them appear as less than what they were: shackles. The ancient characters twined together to create a tracking spell. I pried at one of the cuffs, but the seal was solid, welded into place with magic rather than a mechanical tumbler.

I turned to my brother, who instantly shrank back from me, and then to my father. I should have known better. He had *no* intention of giving me freedoms from here on out, and he'd dragged my brother into his scheme, destroying the very last modicum of my trust. "How *could* you?" I demanded.

Father reclined into the red cushions. "Don't bother trying to break them, little love. It took a long time to find a material durable enough to withstand your flames, but we managed it."

I scoffed. "That's not possible."

"You can test my theory yourself, but I've been experimenting for over a year with great success. You have no clue what I went through to get those crafted."

"Nothing short of selling your soul, I'm sure," I spat.

"Easy," Kahem interjected. "We're just trying to keep you safe."

I pointed a finger in his face. "Silence, you snake."

It was just about the harshest thing I could have said, and it hit Kahem like a physical blow, his eyes shuttering before I turned away. I tucked myself into the corner where the bench met the carriage wall, staring out the window as we took to the skies, until Gwaith became nothing more than a speck below the smog.

WE FLEW for an hour in silence. A little while after we cleared the smog, the carriage descended toward the gnashing forest, aiming for a valley between thickets.

"Why are we stopping?" I demanded.

Kahem was pouting, fiddling with the gold chain on his chest. He didn't so much as look away from the window as we dipped below the forest canopy.

"You need to get cleaned up, little love," Father said. "I don't think you understand how impatient your betrothed is to catch up with you. He made it clear he intends to welcome you the moment you arrive home."

"Throwing me to the wolves so soon?"

Father's eyes narrowed. "Do not forget my leniency over the past few years, Sabrina. I could have done worse than send a handful of incompetent bounty hunters after you, and you know that." I rolled my eyes. "Besides, Alezandral is no wolf. He's barely older than you are."

Yes, I knew that, but age had nothing to do with it.

As it turned out, we also stopped for breakfast. For Father, that meant a hunt for sport. I spun the bracelets around and around. The stone didn't weigh much, but they made up for that with a metaphysical burden. The runes pulsed with my every movement.

Spiro produced a basket from under the carriage seats.

When I saw he'd packed the fruit of the Fenix – a hybrid citrus between orange and lemon – I quickly snatched one up before they could be divvied out. As I tore at the fragrant peel, Father produced a crossbow from the cab and ordered Spiro to sight a target for him.

The Raven complied, raking a hand through his jet-black hair before collapsing onto a log. I knew what he was doing without needing to ask – jumping from the dead bark of one tree to the next. I'd always wondered what happened the first time a Raven tried that…and who they might have dealt a heart attack in the process.

Probably some poor, unsuspecting human. They always bore the consequences of our strange and cruel jokes.

After a minute, Spiro said a bit absently, "A quarter of a mile to the west…there's a fluffle of rabbits."

I snorted, a little juice shooting up into my nose and making me cough. Kahem tried to hide his smile as Spiro opened his eyes and glared at me.

"What's so funny, Sia?" he demanded. "That's the proper term for them."

"I'm sure it is." I shoved another piece of citrus in my mouth and said, "I just never expected to hear a word like that come out of your mouth."

"I say all sorts of words. I have an excellent vocabulary."

My delight was lost on him, so I waved a hand to disperse the conversation. Spiro turned on his heel and entered the forest, presumably in the direction of said *fluffle*.

Father gestured toward a gathering of trees and brush behind me. "The river is that way. Be thorough. You look like you've got a weeks-worth of grime and death on you. I'll keep the water warm for you."

I bit my lip. I didn't want to accept anything from him. "That's not necessary. I've bathed in a lot colder conditions."

Father only shrugged and followed Spiro into the forest.

Kahem hung back with a couple of the sentinels, prepping a small fire to roast the rabbits over. He offered me a smile, but I looked away from him and slipped between the trees to search for the river. I knew he'd already forgiven what I said, even if *I* hadn't forgiven *him* yet.

He'd always been like that, the quickest to take offense, but also the quickest to forget. Sometimes, when I was younger, I wished for the same graciousness.

The river was easy to find, the burble of water leading me straight to a riverbank. Animals must use this area often, because the slope down to the water was gradual and worn, and there were plenty of shallows between this side of the river and the other. I stripped quickly and sank into the current. It was the perfect temperature, of course, a testament to my father's never-wavering control. I tried not to feel too thankful for it.

He always did that, offered a small kindness in place of a massive wrong, as if the good wouldn't immediately get swallowed up by the bad. I was sick of holding onto these kindnesses, grappling with them on the edge of a cliff until it felt like I was falling too.

My hair took the longest to rinse clean. Some of the red was still there, adhered to the ends, and I knew I would have to color over it once I got home or cut it away. I could try burning out the henna, I supposed, like I had the rest of it, but I didn't really want to take the risk. My wings were the cleanest they'd been in years. They fluttered in the water, gleaming like polished onyx under the sun.

I savored the delicious stretch of these forgotten muscles. My sacred tier of wings flexed out from the middle of my back, silky soft and edged with a translucent, blue-black sheen.

Once fully cleansed, I turned my attention to the cuffs. I tugged and smashed the metal against rock, I scratched at the runes. Other than some of the gold flaking off them, the bracelets were impenetrable. Then, I summoned my flames. The metal warmed as I pushed more of my power up and out, willing it into the bracelet, willing the metal to warp and melt.

It happened so fast.

The metal took on every ounce of the power I offered it, consuming it all, and the bracelets began to vibrate as they heated a little too much. I hissed as the metal sizzled into my skin. I dropped my flames, but the metal didn't cool off so quickly.

My wrists were *burning.* I quickly sank beneath the surface of the warm water, resting the metal on the rocks at the bottom of the river. I held my wrist precariously between the two sides of the bracelet, avoiding any direct contact with my skin.

Under the water, holding my breath, the reality of my situation sank in.

I would never be able to get out of these cuffs on my own, would never be able to use my magic without it hurting me. Not only had my Father shackled me to the floating city, he was preventing me from ever exploring my magic, keeping me from training all over again.

The anger in my chest bubbled over as I screamed into the water, my eyes stinging, my heart breaking.

I thought of everything I had done in order to find the truth over the past few years. How many people I'd helped, favors I'd earned. How thoroughly I'd scoured the gnashing forest. Just when I thought I'd found something, when there was a measure of hope on the horizon…

Even if Ehlark figured out what I was, I would never be able to return to him to find out.

I screamed until I had nothing left, until all my air was gone, and I had to break through the surface again to replenish my lungs. I gasped through the tightness of my chest. How was I supposed to live through this, love through this? How could anyone be happy when they were trapped? Perhaps this was my punishment for all the horrible things I'd done, all the mortals I'd hurt and killed. Maybe I deserved this.

A strange gurgling sound made it past my water-logged ears, and I turned toward it.

Down the river, something glowed under the surface of the water. I felt a tug towards it. I swam over, at the mercy of that pull, my brow furrowing as I saw it a little clearer.

There was a rift in the river. An actual *rift*.

A scene glittered within it, distorted under the running water, but I saw what was on the other side. It was dark, even darker than the black river rock beneath my feet. I watched a streak of silver dance beneath the surface, whipping back and forth, and it took me a long moment to understand that it was a person with silver hair I was watching.

They turned toward me, and I saw a flash of green eyes.

Something surged out of the rift toward me, bursting out of the water. Water sprayed everywhere as a massive hand erupted from the rift, long, rotten fingers stretching toward me, swollen arms oozing black ichor into the river around me as it tried to grab me.

I didn't think. I only reacted.

I slammed a deluge of black flames into the otherworldly appendage, and it retreated. I think it screamed, but the sound was muffled by the veil.

I spat fire at it until that arm at last fell back into the other world. My bracelets were burning me again, but I didn't care. After the arm disappeared, I still felt that pull, tugging me toward the veil, but I refused to succumb. I shoved my flames into the rift as well, fending off anything else that might try to tear through. The rift ate my flames. It *devoured* them. Then, suddenly, the rift began closing right before my eyes.

The rifted winked out of existence.

With a gasp, I dropped my power, wincing at the slide of the metal bracelets against my raw skin as I dropped my hands back to my sides. I wasn't sure what to make out of what just happened. Where had that rift come from, and how did I close it?

Why had the figure I'd seen inside it remind me of Ehlark?

It wasn't real, I told myself as I emerged from the river, but I feared deep in my heart that it was.

CHAPTER 43

"Your hair is still wet," Kahem muttered when we were finally back in the carriage and rising into the air. He beckoned me toward him. "Come here."

He'd been trying to start up a conversation since I got back from the river.

My anger eased a fraction when I met his eyes, squinting with concern. I sighed, turning my back to him so he could run his fingers through my hair. The dampness of my hair fizzled as his heat sparked. His heat slowly dried out the strands as he touched them. I hated that he had so much control when I didn't.

"Okay," he eventually grumbled. "Seriously, what happened to your hair?"

I winced as his fingers caught on a knot. "The henna burned away from it when I boiled the bay."

He gasped and leaned over my shoulder. "You're *joking*." There was a thread of awe in his eyes.

I waved him back. "Just hurry up and finish; you're pulling half my hair out with your stupid man rings."

"It's not my fault you're knotted to hell and back." When

he was done, he tugged the leather strap from his hair and handed it to me. "Here. You might as well tie it up until you can find a brush back home."

I gathered my hair up and hid the red ends as best I could. As I adjusted the strap, I turned to Father, prepared to have the discussion I'd been planning out in my head for hours now. "Speaking of what happened in the city—"

"It's okay," he interrupted me. "I was informed of everything that transpired in the city last night. I'm meeting with the Impundulu Queen by the end of the day to determine our best course of action. We're flying there after I've delivered you home."

From the way he glanced over at Kahem, I assumed *'we'* included him.

I slid to the edge of my seat, leaning over the aisle to catch his full attention. "That was my mother's city. Let me come with you. I've lived down there. I think I could be useful in coming up with the right measures to protect everyone."

The gold in Father's eyes darkened as he took my shackled hands between his. "Sia," he whispered. "You know I do not make promises lightly, but I *promise* I will do everything in my power to keep the sutilis off this continent. I won't spit on the sacrifice of our ancestors."

The sacrifice of his father and sisters. I knew he wouldn't. "Let me help you."

I was pleading now. *Let me in. See my worth.*

His hands slipped away from mine. He waved my request away, waved *me* away. "We'll discuss this again later, once your engagement is underway. That should be your primary focus right now."

Years had passed, and yet I received more of the same. It was always *later*, when he really meant never. *Don't make a scene. Do as you're told. Don't let anyone see how different you are. Your darkness is our weakness, little love.*

"People are dying," I countered.

"And if the threat spreads, we will need the alliance your marriage will offer."

I drew back in my seat, my soul incomprehensibly dim.

Did the sutilis feel anything beyond survival? Beyond their rot? I wondered if they felt like me, if I felt like them. I'd traveled the entire continent these past few years, searching for myself in the pieces I took from others. Each connection became a limb as I collected them, stitched them into my heart as if it could make up for the decay I felt, my power and family, my withered ability to trust.

Before I could retreat to my corner by the window, Father said, "I do need to know one thing, though…if we're being completely open and honest with each other."

I lifted a brow.

He lifted his palms between us. "Why did you run?"

"You really have to ask that question?"

"I can postulate." Both my brows were raised now. He continued, "Were you bored of us? Because if it was a matter of adventure, all you had to do was ask for a bit of leeway to explore the continent. I would have sent you anywhere you wanted to go, in a safer manner than you running off to do it on your own. It would have been more comfortable than sleeping in a tree and hunting every meal, I'm sure."

A chuckle started low in my chest, bubbling and growing until it filled the whole cab. Bitter, manic tears brimmed in my eyes. "You think I ran from my family, *my home*, because I was *bored*? Did you ever consider I was running from the life you'd laid out for me, the marriage I never asked for? For fuck's sake, I simply didn't want my future to be determined by a pair of crusty old men."

Everyone in the cab gaped at me.

Father blinked a few times, waiting patiently as my

laughter ebbed. I was wiping tears from my cheeks when he said, "Little love, *you* were the one who chose Alezandral."

Of all the excuses I'd prepared myself for over the years, I never anticipated that one. I shook my head. "*What?*"

"What do you remember from the day of your heart bond?"

As if sensing the turn in conversation, the skin over my heart began to tingle.

Heart bonds were the most sacred of promises our kind made, if we were lucky enough to find a seraph compatible with us. It was a promise of forever, a match of equals. It was a promise intended to carry the love and partnership of an entire lifetime. Here I was, barely of age, bound to a Halcyon I hadn't seen in several years.

I tried to remember the details of his face, any feature beyond the pale hair and blue eyes.

Flashes of his home flickered in my mind, the cold halls and chill. A whistle carried on the wind. My chest clenched so hard that I had to remind myself of how to breathe through it. A wall was veiling my memory of that day, a mental version of the smog we'd left behind hours ago. "No. I don't understand," I murmured. "I thought it was *you...*"

"You made the promise, not I." Father sighed. "You and Alezandral did it, without anyone knowing or approving of it in advance."

"But...how...I," I sputtered. "We were *children*."

"Exactly," he exclaimed. "Imagine the shock I experienced when Alezandral's father and I finished up a week-long negotiation and tracked our missing children down to a bloody thicket behind the Halcyon castle. There the two of you were, smiling at each other like you'd just pulled off the greatest heist of all time."

"I don't—" I couldn't find the words right away. "Why can't

I remember that? I vaguely remember him. Bits and pieces, but…"

I blinked, and the memory flashed behind my eyes in a burst of light. A promise made between two birches. Bloody hands and clumsy blades. A streak of blood smeared across his pale cheek.

I'll never leave you alone, he'd sworn. A whisper in the trees, the slice of a blade. He handed me the blood-slick knife and said, *Your turn.*

My promise echoed in reply. *I won't let anyone else hurt you again.*

The implications burned through me. I couldn't remember beginning to tremble. All I knew was that I was now shaking on the carriage bench.

Kahem's hand caressed my back, but I barely felt it.

"When Alezandral's father saw what you two had done, he reacted…harshly." Father paused, grimacing. "I'm not surprised you blocked it out. Alezandral was punished on the spot, quite brutally." *Blood. All that blood.* I stopped blinking, because every time I did, I saw it. It sent phantom twinges through my scar. "The way you screamed…Sabrina, you went half out of your mind trying to intervene. The bond was too fresh for you to control your reaction, and his father had to cover the forest in several layers of ice just to keep you at bay."

I held up a hand, squeezing my eyes shut and shaking my head against the memories. "Stop. I don't want to hear any more."

There was a moment of silence, and I opened my eyes to see my father smiling faintly. "You see? You *could* remember if you tried."

"I don't want to," I said tightly. "Whoever Alezandral is now, he is not that boy. Remembering will only make me fear what he's become, what his father has turned him into."

Father exchanged a look with Spiro. Then, quietly, he said,

"You also may find you have nothing to fear. The most beautiful bonds begin with friendship, and despite what his father has taught him, your bond would never allow him to harbor ill will toward you."

"It's not myself I'm afraid for," I whispered to the clouds kissing my window. "It's everyone around us who isn't me."

CHAPTER 44

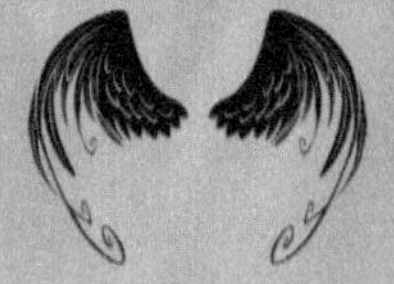

Our carriage flew in a wide circle around the hovering city as the gates were opened for us.

Through the window, I saw the whole expanse of it: the water-wheels churning, the brick homes and stores gilded around the edges, all the streets bustling and the castle towers rising from the center of the city. In the daylight, there weren't bright electric lights or magical orbs dancing in the streets. There were no revelries.

Not all winged colonies lived in the sky, but everyone knew the Fenix loved drama.

It all seemed so bland to me now. It wasn't all that different from a wealthy human city, except for the fact that it hovered high above the earth. The carriage passed through the gates, the cab bouncing as we shifted from air to solid land, and I carefully slid back in my seat, hiding from the window. I heard the citizens anyway. They cheered as we rolled through the streets, their voices growing louder block by block.

Across from me, Kahem leaned out the window, laughing and waving at the crowd, blowing kisses.

"You look like a moron," I grumbled.

Without letting his smile falter or even tearing his eyes from the crowd, Kahem shoved a vulgar gesture across the aisle and into my face. I slapped it away.

"Why do you let him act like this?" I asked Father. "It's painful to watch."

"He might as well charm the people while he's young and exciting. The newness will fade with a couple centuries," Father replied with a droll smile. "You'd best learn a thing or two about that. The people you're going to rule won't be your own; they won't trust you as easily."

Alezandral was the Halcyon king's only child, so he was the crown prince of their entire race. If we married, I would be their princess and, eventually, their queen. The reminder made me shift in my seat.

I was born into royalty, but I wasn't meant for rulership. Everyone knew that, especially me. "They shouldn't trust me at all," I muttered. "And I certainly don't trust them. What's the point in charming hearts and wings of ice?"

"The point," Father said emphatically, "is to keep yourself safe. Unloved queens run the risk of being assassinated, and your head is far too pretty to be placed on a pike in the ocean. At the very least, you'll need to win Alezandral over. Charm the hell out of him. You don't have to fall in love with him to give him an heir, and once you do, you'll have plenty of freedom and time to entertain men and women alike, to fill your time with whatever you'd like."

I turned a sharp look on him. "Why do I have to go through with this at all?"

"A promise is a promise," he said quietly.

I knew better than to argue, to instigate, but I couldn't help it. "And a trade is a trade, isn't it? What exactly does the Fenix get from the Halcyon in a union like this?"

Father's eyes softened. "We negotiated the terms for

several years, and I only ever thought of you, little love. Anything they give us, I plan to give to you."

I had nothing to say to that. There was nothing for my anger to latch onto.

Father turned to Spiro and made a motion with his hand. "You must be prepared when you step out of the carriage."

Spiro tugged his bag onto his lap and plunged an arm into its depths. His tongue peeked between his lips as he rooted around the charmed interior. He eventually withdrew a hard leather box. He unclasped the straps and presented the tiara they'd brought for me from the family jewels.

A lot of the collection had melted on the islands, but a few survived, thanks to our historians. This one had copper latticework, twined in thin braids across the front of the tiara, peaking in the center with a single, raw diamond. It was simple and old and completely Fenix.

I hated it.

Father watched me unceremoniously plop it on my head.

Spiro withdrew a pair of heels from the bag and placed them in front of me. "Shoes, Princess. Keep your chin up." As he returned to his seat, the old Raven smiled at me, and I couldn't ignore him. He'd always treated me with kindness.

I sighed. "Thank you, Spiro." I wiggled my feet into the heels.

"At least you're wearing a decent gown," Father said, more to himself than me. "There's nothing we can do about the wings." *There's no time to paint them*, he meant. "So Alezandral will be made privy to your *uniqueness* sooner than we'd hoped. Cross your fingers that it doesn't unsettle him too much."

I smiled at the challenge.

Father added in a growl, "Try to be agreeable."

I slumped back in my seat. As we drew closer to the castle, my heart ran away from me. I could barely think around the pounding. I couldn't look away from the sliver of light peeking through the curtains, the world outside passing in a blur of cobblestone and statues as we turned down the castle drive.

Father had asked why I ran, and I told him the truth...*mostly.*

It had been easier to leave, to avoid the disappointment and silence that came when there was nothing left to say. My father didn't know how to deal with me, so he pushed me aside and away, giving me so much space that it felt like my world was an ocean and my heart a wandering buoy in the center of it all. Always at sea and never home. Never at rest.

By the time I was old enough to ask questions, he treated me like a house guest he'd grown tired of. Eventually, I stopped talking. Stopped trying.

My loneliness turned into a hunger that burrowed in my stomach and made a hollow one that went on and on with no end in sight. I slowly starved, and no one noticed. No one cared. Except for Lee, this last year or so. Then I'd lost him, just as I had lost my mother.

Cinna was the only one who might have given real answers as to why I was different, why my wings were black and not gold, why I burned hotter but not brighter. I'd pieced it together on my own, as I scoured the city for any trace of her: that my mother had been mortal, but never ordinary, because she'd been a witch.

With her flowers and herbs, the shop had been shuttered for years before Peppi came and revived it. My mother's magic had something to do with my conception, with what I was, but I didn't know why or how, and no one, especially not my father, ever talked about it.

My fingers twisted together in my lap, my nails picking anxiously until the skin tore.

A warm hand brought me back to the cab. Kahem had moved to sit beside me, and his hand gently squeezed mine. I thought about fighting him, about reinforcing the space I'd held between us for most of the ride, but this was my brother, and I'd missed him fiercely.

I would forgive him.

I turned my hand over, threading our fingers together as I returned my attention to the carriage door. I didn't waste time on fear when we finally stopped. I quickly let go of Kahem's hand and stood, waiting for the door to be opened by a sentinel.

My father might have been brutally honest, but he was also right. When I emerged, I could show no weakness. I didn't know if my future would be with Alezandral or not, but every path left led me straight towards him. It was time to face it.

As the door opened, my eyes locked on the mural painted onto the staircase, the red and blue and purple blending together into a tapestry of history. The glory that led to my father.

I exited the cab, my gaze following the story of the Fenix to—

My stranger from the flower market. *Lee.*

He was *alive.* And he was here?

Lee met my gaze from the top of the staircase, three pairs of white wings spread in greeting and a bushel of colorful flowers in hand.

All the disjointed moments snapped together like bones into place. The way he'd rubbed his chest whenever he was forced to leave my side. The pain I felt when he got hurt. The feather I'd seen on the water hadn't been from the belt. It had been *his.* The pivotal moment of our heart bond fluttered in my mind's eye.

I saw it.

His hand rested on my chest and mine on his as we bled into one another, every darkness we carried being drawn out of us to make room for the binding. He had been afraid of being touched by anyone but had made an exception for me. I had been afraid of never being touched in any *meaningful* way. We'd laughed in the face of our fears by making that promise, thinking it would solve everything the way children were so easily fooled by pretty dreams.

We were ripped apart anyway.

He said he wouldn't leave me alone, and then he did. Even as we grew old enough to seek each other out, he never came, never came, *never came*. I suddenly decided it was a good thing I forgot about him, because I would have waited a long time for that boy between the birch trees. It would have been in vain.

A promise was not always a promise. Sometimes, it was a debt, a cage, a regret.

I saw the truth of it in Lee's actions, in his deceit, in the wretched compassion I remembered and still felt for him but could no longer trust. When I grew up and learned the reality of our world, I searched for connection in places I didn't belong, because that was better than what I already had: lone-liness when I was not alone. And Lee became *this*: someone I couldn't believe in, like every other person in my wretched life. I didn't know why that sliced its way into my heart so deeply, causing my arteries to burst with liquid fire.

Back in the tent, when he'd hovered above me with such beautiful treachery in his eyes and asked if I could *feel* him...I knew what he meant now.

He'd meant the binding, that connection between us.

Yes, I can feel you, I wanted to scream up the stairs, *but I wish I didn't. I hate you for making that promise with me, for making my heart long for what it couldn't have. This is your fault. You're the reason I can't trust anyone.*

Father nudged my back, jostling me from my memories, and I began climbing the stairs.

Alezandral's wings were massive, stretching at least a foot larger than mine in either direction. *What sort of crazy magic lurked in the sacrificial waters of their coast?* He wore a navy tunic, unbuttoned low enough that the full expanse of his markings was visible. They were as dark as mine, with whorls that crept down onto his chest. I'd never seen markings quite that large before.

I lifted my eyes to his as I hit the top step.

"Darling," he breathed, his mouth curling into a broad grin. Creases formed in his cheeks. "You look beautiful."

"You're a fucking liar," I spat.

Father gasped loudly behind me.

Lee had the decency to look ashamed for half a second, but then he composed himself and offered me the bouquet in his hands. "A little birdie told me tulips were your favorite. I wasn't sure which color, so there's one of each that I could find. Happy birthday."

I didn't know how he managed to find tulips at this time of year, when the earth was so cold and the bulbs were all dormant, but I didn't really care. He'd kept the truth from me. He let me believe he was *dead.*

'*The way you screamed...*'

I ground my teeth. If I was truly forced to marry him, I'd just seen how the rest of my life was going to play out. Always one step behind, always in the darkness. Right here, right now, I wasn't going to hide any piece of myself, *any* emotion when I felt so damn much. He would see exactly what I thought of his deceit.

Without blinking, I hooked my thumbs under the thin straps of the dress and shoved them off my shoulders.

All the blood drained from Lee's face as my breasts and then the rest of my body was revealed. I hoped he would see the remnants of Destin on me, the marks across my chest where he'd suckled on my skin.

"*Sabrina,*" Father said in a warning tone. "What the hell are you doing?"

"Come now, Father." Kahem's voice was exuberant, joking, but I heard the falsity to it. He was just as bewildered and uncomfortable. He turned away from me as he addressed Father. "She seems to have taken your words to heart and plans to charm him with her vulnerability."

Oh, I'd charm him alright.

The dress suddenly felt a thousand tons, weighing on my skin like a brand – *his* brand. Lee gave this to me. There was a reason for that, a meaning. I didn't know better until this moment. It was blue, the color of his family's coat of arms. In my pursuit of forsaking my family's colors, I had naturally gravitated toward it.

The realization made my stomach churn with shame.

I forced a smile, stepping out of the glittering material, stepping away from the mask I'd been so ready to don again. The obedient daughter. The dutiful princess. For what? *Him?* He was nothing to me. *Nothing.*

Father pointedly turned away from my lewd behavior, anger and age-old dismissal in his eyes. "For fuck's sake," he hissed to himself, but I wouldn't stop.

I didn't want this dress. I didn't want any of this.

My brother turned away as well, subtly spreading his wings to shield me from the guards' wandering eyes. "Hark!" Kahem shouted toward the city. "I hear the wedding bells already."

I crouched to gather the dress up into my arms.

Lee's eyes never left mine. Not once. There was plenty for him to see, and it made me wonder if it was politeness restraining him, or something more. Maybe his callous heart rejected me as much as I wanted to reject him. That would explain his absence from my life, his lies and games and everything else he'd done instead of simply telling me the truth.

He didn't care for me and, chances were, he *couldn't*.

Shoving the fabric into his chest, I whispered, "I said it once and I'll say it again: I don't want *anything* from you. All the worthless flowers in the world won't change my mind."

Lee's brow furrowed.

Before I could read the emotion in his eyes, I elbowed past him into the castle. Orbs of red and orange light enveloped me as I crossed the immaculate, gilded foyer. My heels echoed against the marble floor and up the curving staircase to the second-floor catwalk.

Only when I was on the cusp of the main corridor, where the lights dimmed to twinkling red bulbs on either side of the hall runner, did I finally glance over my shoulder.

Lee had disappeared from the top step.

His tulips were on the ground, scattered and bereft. I saw the speckles of blue in the bouquet now, the pansies he'd hidden between bursts of red and pink and yellow. The sight of them clanged in my heart. It hurt me, and I wondered if it had hurt him, too, when I walked away. If his scar had begged him to chase after me or ached when he took to the skies.

I didn't let myself wonder if *I* should ache for *him* as I turned back to the maze of halls. These dark halls that shored up the phantom scent of burning pipes, broken memories, and an inevitable, brutal loneliness.

EPILOGUE

Alezandral

Alezandral sat in one of the cramped, covered tower platforms high above the palace, watching the sun slowly dip towards the horizon. He reclined against the curved bronze metal of a broken bell, his wings spread to either side of him. The bronze was cracked, useless.

He felt like the bell.

He'd fucked up, spectacularly. His failure was a sinking, rolling emptiness in the pit of his stomach. How had he expected her to react? Had he really believed she would be *happy* to see him? Happy to learn the truth? He should have known better, but he'd been blinded by his desire to reunite with her, his scar aching for her the instant he left her behind in that human city, *alone*. She'd been alone too much of her life already, and it seemed like that was all she wanted now: for him to leave her. It didn't matter that it wasn't his choice; it hurt the same.

The fragile promise made him want to crawl right out of his skin.

He felt the tendrils of retribution tickling the back of his mind, raking sharp talons across his thoughts. The promise would take him if he didn't get back to her somehow. It would take his shame and gift him madness in return.

Alezandral wished he knew how to be someone Sia wanted at her side. Given the chance, he would become whatever was required, if only just to sit in the same room with her, to have her glare at him, snap at him. Her spite was an attention he'd cherish.

Sia was more than he'd ever hoped for, and he had hurt her. He'd seen it in her eyes. She pretended to be this person who felt nothing, but inside, she felt everything, excruciatingly deep.

A breeze slithered across the nape of his neck.

The scent of pine and salt water filled his senses, and the atmosphere shuddered beside him as a folded sheet of paper appeared, slicing through the air in front of his face. He sighed as he caught it in one hand.

He watched the sunset for another long minute, savoring his last few moments of solitude. Then, he opened the letter.

Are you ready for us?

Alezandral withdrew the pen from his tunic and wrote back, *Not yet, but soon.*

Sia needed to be ready when they came, they *both* did, and right now... they weren't. After Alezandral sent the letter away, he returned the pen to his tunic and pulled out the piece of paper he'd tucked away. Sia's last message.

I could never hate you, she'd written.

He frowned at the paper. If she didn't regret those words by now, she would soon, because he wasn't leaving. He couldn't.

Alezandral dropped his hands to his lap and fisted the soft

material there, the beads of the dress she'd given back to him digging into his palms. She'd looked beautiful in it. He smiled; she'd looked beautiful out of it. When she first shoved it into his chest, he had resolved to burn it, but… no, he wouldn't do that. He would hold onto it for her, just in case. Maybe she'd change her mind and decide she wanted it, even if she didn't want him.

A male could hope.

Destin

He stared at the liquor, and the liquor stared right back. His body was itching for a drink, trembling as he paced in front of the bed he'd once shared with his wife, his truest, deepest love. That was as true now as it had been before.

There was more, though, now that he'd met Sia.

More love, more loss, more pain. He didn't know what to do with it. He only knew that he wanted a drink, and from the moment he retrieved the bottle from the kitchen after getting Erlene back to sleep, he'd been resisting the man he used to be. The man who ran. The man who lost precious time to the bottom of a bottle and lived like his life was already over.

The liquor sat on the bed where he had once made love to his wife, where she'd given him their beautiful daughter, and it mocked him.

Destin paced the length of the mattress, back and forth, picking at his lower lip as if he were trying to tear the memory of Sia's lips from his own. How could he still feel this way for her? How could he miss her after what she'd done? She killed all those men, *good men*. He'd known several of them. They'd had families and friends, and she killed them all without entertaining one speck of remorse.

How could she be both the person who wrought such darkness and death and the person who'd brought him back from the brink of all-consuming grief?

In his head, she was both simultaneously.

Destin tripped to a stop as that revelation settled over him. She was more than one thing… and so was he. He was both the person he used to be, the loving husband and fearful father, and the person he was *trying* to be. The man who got things right. There would be no change until he accepted who he once was, and there would be no acceptance until he realized that who he used to be wasn't all bad. He didn't regret the love. He didn't regret the things that led him here, to his wife and his daughter and… Sia.

So perhaps Sia was not all bad either, for being more than a woman, more than her time here. Perhaps it simply made her more human: to hurt and be hurt.

She was gone now. Both of them.

Destin's next breath caught in his chest, and he lurched forward, snatching the bottle off the mattress. He hurled it against the wall, watching it shatter through teary eyes. The smell of whiskey permeated the room as he sank to the edge of the bed. Tears streaked down his cheeks, hot and angry. He'd pushed them both away in the end. He'd pushed them away and lost them, and now he was alone in the house that had once held so much joy.

The sudden wail of Erlene down the hall cut through his thoughts.

He swallowed his tears, wiping his face dry as he stood and walked to the hallway. Erlene wasn't taking Sia's absence well. She'd woken up a couple times that night already, calling for her. Searching for her.

He would give anything for the right words to explain it to Erlene. The right words to comfort her.

There were none, though.

Lila was already in the hall, but Destin waved her away and walked to Erlene's room himself. He could soothe his daughter at night. That was what Tova would have done. That was what Sia did. He'd already decided he wasn't going to marry again and give that job to someone else, not when his heart was in tatters and his daughter needed his undivided attention.

He didn't care what the law of the Houses said: things were going to change around here, and in all the ways that mattered, they already had.

ACKNOWLEDGMENTS

First: to my reader, if you've made it this far and care enough to look at this page, THANK YOU. My dream of writing these stories would not be possible without you.

To my husband, you are everything I never knew I needed. Whatever forces in the universe brought us together, I thank them every day. You are my partner and my friend. You are my truest family. I hope you know that every ooey gooey cinnamon roll love interest I write is inspired by you. Because you love me *well*.

To my editors, I cherish your incredible minds. Jeni Chappelle, your developmental feedback was so valuable. To my line editor, Alexa from The Fiction Fix, thank you for your sharp eyes and for polishing this story until it sparkled. You are beyond amazing. Thank you for supporting us indie authors. <3

To my sensitivity reader, Lo, thank you so much for the time you spent on my project and for being so supportive and kind while doing the emotional labor of sensitivity reading. That epilogue wouldn't have existed without you, and now I can't imagine ending the book without it.

To Shannon Bright, what can I say here that I haven't said before? You are the CP goddess of my heart. You are the magical rom-com sun to my dark fantasy moon. Thank you for being the best kind of co-worker (you know, the one you work with day after day and somehow never get sick of), but thank you even more for being my friend. I LOVE YOU!

To my beta readers and author pals who read Sia's story and gave me feedback, I cannot thank you enough: Erin, Kait, Camri, Skyler, Hannah, Jeremey, Rae, Clare, Jayné and everyone else who set eyes on this project at some point in the creative process! I hope that both sides of your pillows are cool at night and that you always find a good parking spot at the grocery store.

And to Sia. I know I put you through it in this book, and you might hate me a little bit for what's still to come, but thank you for showing me what it means to stop running.

Here's to embracing our darkness, and loving every second of it.

ABOUT THE AUTHOR

Beka Westrup is a genre-hopping author of fantasy and romance. The Seldom Wings is her second full-length novel. She lives in the PNW with her husband and two children, collecting more books than she'll ever be able to read and drinking copious amounts of iced coffee.

Stay in the know with Beka's Newsletter:
https://www.bekawestrup.com/coming-soon-03

facebook.com/bekawestrup
twitter.com/bekawestrup
instagram.com/bekaboowrites
tiktok.com/@bekabooauthor

www.ingramcontent.com/pod-product-compliance
Lightning Source LLC
Chambersburg PA
CBHW030054310726

48970CB00004B/1008